Hot for

LOVE

The Bradens & Montgomerys
(Pleasant Hill – Oak Falls)

Love in Bloom Series

Melissa Foster

ISBN-13: 9781948868549
ISBN-10: 1948868547

Cover Design: Elizabeth Mackey Designs
Cover Photography: Shelly Lange Photography

WORLD LITERARY PRESS
PRINTED IN THE UNITED STATES OF AMERICA

A Note to Readers

Nick Braden and Trixie Jericho just might be the most stubborn couple I have written to date. I had so much fun writing about this gruff, golden-hearted hero and snarky, loving heroine. Their journey to their happily ever after is funny, sinfully sexy, and as always, deeply emotional. I hope you adore them and their menagerie of animals just as much as I do. If this is your first Love in Bloom book, all of my love stories are written to stand alone, so dive right in and enjoy the fun, sexy ride!

You will find a Braden family tree included in the front matter of this book.

The best way to keep up to date with new releases, sales, and exclusive content is to sign up for my newsletter and join my fan club on Facebook, where I chat with readers daily.
www.MelissaFoster.com/news
www.facebook.com/groups/MelissaFosterFans

About the Love in Bloom Big-Family Romance Collection

The Bradens & Montgomerys is just one of the series in the Love in Bloom big-family romance collection. Each Love in Bloom book is written to be enjoyed as a stand-alone novel or as part of the larger series, and characters from each series make appearances in future books, so you never miss an engagement, wedding, or birth. A complete list of all series titles is included at the end of this book, along with previews of upcoming publications.

Download Free First-in-Series eBooks
www.MelissaFoster.com/free-ebooks

See the Entire Love in Bloom Collection
www.MelissaFoster.com/love-bloom-series

Download Series Checklists, Family Trees, and Publication Schedules
www.MelissaFoster.com/reader-goodies

BRADEN FAMILY TREE

Love in Bloom
A CONTEMPORARY ROMANCE SERIES

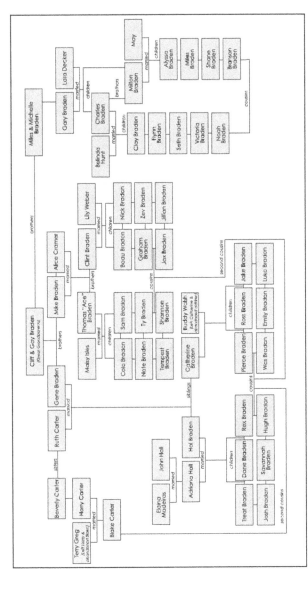

MELISSA FOSTER

Chapter One

NICK BRADEN KNEW better than to mess with trouble.

As an elite freestyle horse trainer and showman, he had buckle bunnies at his beck and call. So why the hell was he hanging out in Justus "JJ" Jericho's pub in Oak Falls, Virginia, when he could be back home in Pleasant Hill, Maryland, where one phone call could scratch that itch with no ramifications?

He took a swig of his beer, his gaze drifting to the answer, who was wiggling her fine ass on the dance floor in skimpy cutoffs and cowgirl boots. *Welcome to Oak Falls, Virginia, home to horse farms, midnight rodeos, and the hottest risk-taking, Daisy Duke–wearing cowgirl on the planet, Trixie Fucking Jericho.* The way his close friend made him feel was Trouble with a capital *T.*

"Hey, Nick, are you finally going to seal the deal or what?" Shane asked.

Nick dragged his eyes away from Trixie, and as cheers filtered in from the mechanical bull room, the crowded bar and the band came back into focus, and he realized he'd zoned out watching her again. Jeb and Shane Jericho, two of Trixie's four older brothers, flanked him at the bar. Her brother JJ was bartending, and Trace was at home with his new wife and baby girl. Nick looked at his buddies, trying to remember what they'd asked. Like him, the Jericho men were tall, dark, powerfully built, and used to working their fingers to the bone. Shane, Trace, and Trixie ran their family's cattle and horse ranch, and Jeb was a furniture maker and owned a shop in town.

"Sorry, man," Nick said. "What was the question?"

"I'm right with you, bro." Jeb lifted his chin in the direction of the band. "It's easy to get caught up in Sable strutting her stuff onstage in those tight jeans, isn't it? *Mm-mm.* She just keeps getting hotter."

Sable Montgomery was a mechanic by day and the lead guitarist and singer in the band Surge by night. The tall, stacked brunette was loaded with enough snark to bury a man. Nick liked a fine, challenging woman, but Sable did nothing for him, unlike sharp-tongued Trixie, who could drop a weaker man to his knees with a single sentence.

"Gotta love ladies' night," Shane said, making eyes at a buxom blonde a few feet away.

"Sure," Nick said halfheartedly, taking another pull of his beer. The joke around town was that the Jericho men could finesse the wildness out of a horse as well as they could charm the panties off a woman. What no one was stupid enough to say out loud was that Trixie possessed the same abilities toward men. Like metal to a magnet, his eyes found Trixie again. Her wild dark mane swung over her shoulders. Nick's fingers curled with the desire to be buried in that hair. *Fuck.* He turned around and leaned on the bar before his buddies noticed him leering at their sister.

"So, are you going to make an offer on the horse you came to check out?" Shane asked, his eyes drifting back to the blonde. "You've been here twice in the last few weeks to see it."

"Right, the horse. *Nah.* I'm not buying it." Nick *had* come to Oak Falls to check out that horse, but he had no idea why he was still there. It wasn't like he was going to seal *any* deal with Trixie, and not just because there was an unspoken rule between guys about not going after their buddies' younger sisters. He and Trixie had been friends for years. She had been taking part in the same running, biking, and swimming races as Nick's younger brother Graham and their cousin Ty since she was a teenager. But over the last few years, she and Nick had become incredibly close friends. He could be a gruff bastard, and she was one of the few women who understood his die-hard work ethic, his moods, and his connection to his animals. She was the unique combination of smart, confident cowgirl, badass thrill seeker, and sweet, caring *woman.*

It was that last part that was causing him the most trouble lately.

They'd become so close that he found himself thinking about her when she wasn't around, which was too damn often. They saw each other five or six times a year when he was down her way for work or family events, or when she'd come through Maryland to pick up horses, deliver cattle, take part in a race, or when she just needed a break from Oak Falls. As the second oldest of six siblings, Nick understood that need to get away. He loved his close-knit family and their quaint hometown, but he knew how suffocating both could be.

Trixie stayed with Nick when she was in town, though she spent time hanging out with his younger sister, Jillian. Jillian was a clothing designer and a night owl, and like any good rancher worth her salt, Trixie was up with the sun. When Trixie had first come to him four or five years ago, asking if she could stay at his place instead of Jillian's, it was a no-brainer for him to say yes, even though he liked his solitude. He was a natural protector, and Trixie was like family. It had taken some getting used to, having another person in his house, much less a beautiful woman. But Trixie wasn't like most women, fussing with their hair and makeup and talking about nonsense. She didn't mind getting her hands dirty and always pitched in to help around the ranch without being asked. Luckily, she also enjoyed giving him hell and telling him he was doing things wrong. If there was one thing Nick hated, it was being told what to do. It hadn't taken much effort in those early years to slide her into an off-limits category.

At least until a little more than a year ago, when Nick and Jillian had taken an impromptu trip to Colorado under the guise of watching Graham and Ty cross the finish line of the Children's Charity Mad Prix, a five-day race through the Colorado Mountains. They'd really gone to check up on their oldest brother, Beau, who had been having a hard time. Beau had been doing renovations at the Sterling House, where the awards banquet was taking place and the contestants were staying. Trixie had also taken part in the race, and a late-night celebration had led to too much tequila and an unforgettable evening that had haunted him ever since.

She'd looked stunning that night in a skintight minidress and sky-high heels, drawing the attention of most of the single guys in the room, including their friend Jon Butterscotch, a cocky doctor who had also competed in the Mad Prix. Jon had been all over Trixie, and like a guard dog, Nick had been on full alert well before she'd dragged him to the bar as her protector. *I need you to keep me from doing something stupid, like body shots.* That thought had seared erotic images into his mind, which should have clued him in to the switch she was flicking inside him. She and the other girls had a great time. They had all done too many shots, but they were safe in the Sterling House.

Safe was a relative term, because it turned out that he hadn't been safe from whatever spell Trixie had been casting on him that night. When he'd walked her back to her room, she'd hung all over him, rubbing her soft curves against his hard frame as she ran her fingers through his hair, down his arms, and over his chest, laughing and talking like she hadn't even realized she was doing it. Meanwhile, her every touch sent bolts of heat straight to his groin, as if she'd uncapped a reservoir of desire. Trixie kept trying to go back to the bar, and he'd had to redirect her down the hall so many times, he'd finally swept her into his arms and carried her to her suite. Their eyes had connected for a split second with the sizzling heat of the Sahara and the wickedness fantasies are made of. He'd never forget the sultry sound of her voice as she'd wrapped her arms around his neck and said, *My very own Prince Charming.* He'd laughed at that, because after having had her hands all over him, and with her gorgeous body in his arms, his thoughts made him feel more like the hungry wolf.

But there must have been something even bigger than lust at play that night.

Once he'd gotten her into her suite, she'd continued trying to coerce him into going back to the bar. *I just want to have fun. A few more minutes? Come on, Nick, don't be a party pooper. Let's go have fun together.* Her speech had slurred, and she could barely walk without stumbling. She'd had her fun. More fun than he'd approved of, but while he watched out for her, Trixie was her own woman, and she liked to be told what to do about as much as he did. But there was no way he'd let her go back to the bar and do something she might regret. Instead, he'd put her to bed, took off her heels, and since she'd continued in her sleepy, drunken state to try to get up and leave the room, he'd stayed in the chair beside her bed until morning, slipping out the door before she'd woken up.

But the damage had already been done.

Seeing his take-charge friend, who took life by the horns and was always in control, let her guard down had changed him. He'd protected family and friends for as long as he could remember. But as he'd watched over her that night, the feelings that had settled into him like fog following summer rain were unlike anything he'd ever felt. He could no longer think of Trixie Jericho without remembering the feel of her hanging on him, the eagerness of her touch, the sweetness of her breath, and the perfectness of her in his arms, or those adorable murmurs and smiles she'd made in her sleep. He'd craved the sight of her ever since, wanting to take care of her, and worse, to feel her legs wrapped around his neck as he devoured her and around his waist as he buried himself eight inches deep.

Trixie Jericho was the worst kind of trouble, and she didn't even know it.

The morning after the banquet, he realized that she hadn't known he'd stayed with her that night. She'd apologized for getting drunk and had thanked him for walking her back to her room. When she'd said, *For all your bullheaded arrogance, it's that big ol' heart that's going to get you in trouble one day*, she'd had no idea how true those words were.

But he knew better than to play with dynamite. Because underneath all her sass and snark were dreams of a white wedding. Nick wasn't in the market for a wife. Even if he was, while Trixie liked getting away from her hometown to gain a little breathing room, she was, and would always be, a daddy's girl, a Jericho rancher born and bred, and a forever Oak Falls, Virginia, resident—and Nick was never going to move away from Pleasant Hill, Maryland.

If only he could shake the need to be near her.

TRIXIE WONDERED WHAT her ridiculously hot and too bullheaded for his own good friend Nick Braden and her brothers were talking about now. She loved her brothers, but while they supported her dreams, that support came with a side of amusement, and she was sick of not being taken seriously. Had they told Nick her plans to open a miniature therapy horse business? At least she knew *he* wasn't laughing at it. Nick always took Trixie—and everything about ranching—seriously, and he wasn't a *laugher*. He was gruff, smart, and honest to a fault. He also loved his family as much as she loved hers, all of which was why she believed he was her perfect match. But since he didn't see her the way she saw him, he'd become the man she compared every other guy to.

Her friend Lindsay shimmied closer, her blond hair swinging over her shoulders. "Girl, you're going to burn a hole in that big-muscled cowboy's back."

She and Lindsay had grown up together, along with every other person around their age in Oak Falls. Their hometown was about as big as a fist. If she tripped on the sidewalk, the whole town knew it by nightfall. But Trixie had a handful of close friends she trusted to keep her secrets, like her forever crush on Nick Braden, and Lindsay was at the top of that list.

Trixie stole a glance at Nick. "I'd need laser vision to get through his armor."

"Don't pretend you don't want to straddle his hog," Lindsay teased.

"That doesn't mean he's offering." Nick wasn't just a truck-driving cowboy. He also drove an elite Silver-Stone motorcycle, which gave him an even sexier edge.

"Maybe he sucks in bed."

Trixie laughed. "There's no way that man sucks in bed. I swear he bathes in testosterone."

"Then maybe he's little-sister-zoned you," Lindsay said, and twirled around.

"He has definitely *not* little-sister-zoned me." She and Nick often tossed flirty comments around, but they were always in jest. *At least on his end.*

Trixie was bold when it came to almost everything, except her crush on Nick. She'd never been as comfortable with a man as she was with Nick. They got along in all situations, and when she was at his place, she fit in like she belonged there. They worked great together around his ranch, and his animals loved her. She didn't want to screw up their friendship, especially since the one time she'd *tried* to get him to take notice of her as a *woman* instead of just a skilled rancher he respected and liked to hang out with, it had totally backfired. It had happened in Colorado after a race Trixie had competed in. Nick had shown up in support of his brother and cousin, and she'd had too much to drink at the awards banquet. She'd thrown caution to the wind and had gotten a little handsy and flirty with him. But as in sync as Nick was with his animals—she swore he could read their minds—he was oblivious to her womanly wiles. He'd acted like the same old teeth-grinding, protective Nick. He'd carried her to bed, taken off her heels, and left her to sleep it off like a perfect gentleman. When her head had cleared the next morning, she'd been relieved that he hadn't noticed her flirting because things could have gotten weird between them. They'd had a good laugh about her tipsy night, and he'd started a running joke about hiding alcohol from her.

She'd stayed with him a few times since then, and he'd taken to showing up wherever she and Jillian were hanging out and watching them like hawks, as if that one tipsy night had erased all the years he'd known her to be a minimal drinker and had proven she needed a babysitter.

Seeing him in the clubs had underscored what she'd already known. Nick wasn't *always* a teeth-grinding gentleman. He had a freaking harem in those clubs, and they paid homage to him as if he were a celebrity. He also had dance moves that put every other man to shame, and he knew how to use them. *Just not with me.*

"I still don't know why you bother thinking about him that way when you can have any guy in here." Lindsay eyed the other guys who were watching them. "Braden had his chance. Don't you think it's time you got over him and gave a few other guys a chance? It's not like you're on the hunt for a husband, for Pete's sake, and thank God for that."

While Trixie believed in love and happily ever after, Lindsay, a wedding planner and photographer, only believed in those things for others. She had no interest in long-term relationships and had no problem steering her friends away from them, too. But while Trixie might not be looking for a ring on her finger right now, because she had a business to build, one day she wanted everything her parents had. She wanted the fairy tale—a man who couldn't imagine a life without her, down on one knee, promising her the world she knew he'd stop at nothing to give her, just as she'd stop at nothing to give him everything he wanted. She was pretty sure Nick wouldn't be that man. He'd never hidden the fact that he wasn't the marrying kind, but she felt so connected to him, she'd let herself get wrapped up in the idea of them as a couple.

How ridiculous am I, pining for a man who doesn't want me?

Maybe Lindsay was right, and it was time Trixie stopped waiting for a man she could never have. So what if she was sure Nick's kisses would be as hot as sunshine and as searing as whiskey? Couldn't another man's kisses be just as hot and delicious? She had never been shy about her sexuality, even if she'd kept it reined in most of the time around her gossipy hometown. She had ways of navigating that, like when she was seventeen and had dragged her friend Austin Andrews, a well-thought-out choice, into his barn to finally lose her virginity. Austin was smart, hot, and always prepared. More importantly, he'd never talked about his personal life the way most of the guys she'd grown up with had. She was fairly certain she'd taught Austin a thing or two that night.

And she'd only gotten better in the decade since. Not that she'd been with that many men, but it didn't take many to know she liked intimacy and knew how to gain and give pleasure.

But she wanted more than sex with Nick. She wanted to climb beneath his skin and explore a relationship, to see if they could be as perfect together as she'd imagined. To see if he truly was *The One*.

There I go again.

Just as she rolled her eyes at herself, goose bumps chased up her arms the way they did only when she felt the pull of Nick's stare. She turned and found his dark eyes locked on her from beneath his ever-present black cowboy hat. Her pulse quickened, and her hopeful heart had her thinking that one last flirtation wouldn't hurt. Maybe he'd even realize there was more to her than her ability to run a ranch.

She began rolling her hips and swaying her shoulders, turning on her dirtiest dance moves. Nick's eyes narrowed, shifting to the other men checking her out, his chest expanding with a deep inhalation. *Ever my protector.* She imagined him as a bull, pawing at the floor readying to charge through the crowd, scoop her up with his horns, and ride off into the mountains with her on his back.

If only the clench of his jaw and the restraint in his corded muscles had to do with her effect on *him* instead of his need to protect her from the other men ogling her.

As the song came to an end, Lindsay said, "Are you done eye-fucking him yet?"

"Lotta good it did me. You're right, Linds. He'll be hard to beat, but the man I need will see me as a woman *first*, which means Nick Braden is *not* everything I need."

"Damn right. Come on, the band's taking a break."

"I could use a cold drink." *And a hot cowboy who's actually attracted to me.*

As they made their way toward the bar, her brothers were chatting up a group of girls, but Nick's eyes remained trained on Trixie. He pushed from the bar. At well over six feet tall and as broad as a truck, with serious eyes and a square jaw, Nick always looked like he was ready for a fight. The people standing in front of him instinctively stepped back.

"Trix. Lindsay," Nick said gruffly. He lifted his chin in a familiar greeting as he reached for Trixie's hand and pulled her up to the bar. He guided Lindsay beside her, then stood behind them like their bodyguard. "*JJ*," he called out to her brother behind the bar, and pointed at Trixie and Lindsay.

If she was going to move past the brooding Braden, she had to make it clear that she didn't *need* watching over. "I can get my own drink, thanks."

She hoisted her belly onto the bar, dragged herself across it, and reached for a couple of cold beers from the ice shelf beneath the ledge where JJ kept them for quick service. She quickly opened them, then wiggled back down to her feet as she handed a bottle to Lindsay. Nick looked like he was chewing on glass, eyeing the other men who had probably watched her go ass-up on the bar.

Trixie lifted the bottle to her lips, taking a long pull on her beer. "*Ah*," she said dramatically. "Now, *that* hits the spot." She feigned a sorrowful expression. "That was rude of me. Let me get you one, Nick."

As she turned to climb back onto the bar, Nick clutched her waist with both hands, holding her in place, and practically growled in her ear, "That ass goes up one more time, I'm carrying it right out of this bar."

Lindsay stifled a laugh as Trixie turned around. Nick was *right there*. He smelled musky and rugged, and all her neediest parts threw a little celebration.

Down, girl...

She reminded herself she was supposed to be getting *over* him.

Using her most seductive tone, because it was fun to get him riled up, she said, "Experience tells me that if that were to happen, at the end of the night I'd be *very* disappointed, Mr. Party Pooper."

"Don't play games with me, Trixie," he warned. "You want

every guy in here thinking they can get a piece of you?"

She stepped closer, her body brushing his. "I think you know me better than that, Nick. Nobody's getting anything I don't want them to."

The muscles in his jaw bunched.

"I wish I had my camera to capture *that* look," Lindsay teased.

Nick's eyes remained trained on Trixie as he said, "She earns it often. I'm sure you'll have plenty of other chances."

Sable pushed through the crowd, eyeing them. Trixie's brother Trace was married to one of Sable's younger sisters, Brindle. Sable was as ballsy as any man, and the smirk she wore told Trixie she was in prime form tonight.

Sable crossed her arms, jutting out her hip, and drummed her fingers on her forearm. "What's going on, Braden? You look like you either want to strip Trixie naked and bend her over the bar or take her over your knee and teach her a lesson."

A slow grin curved his lips.

"Does that mean both?" Lindsay asked with a laugh.

"Any man who raises a hand to me won't live to talk about it," Trixie said. "Unless it's a slap on my ass *with* my permission, of course."

"Damn right," Sable said, giving her a high five.

Nick gritted his teeth as Trixie pushed past him, giving Sable room to step up to the bar.

"You keep talking like that, sis, and I'll drag you out of this bar myself," Jeb said.

Trixie rolled her eyes at her oldest brother. Jeb, like Shane, who was giving her a warning look from behind Lindsay, was a pretty private guy when it came to his own dating life, but he had no trouble putting his nose in his siblings' business.

"What is this, the fifties?" Lindsay said. "I'm so glad I don't have brothers."

"Hey, there's nothing wrong with taking care of our own," Jeb said. "Right, Nick?"

"You got that right," Nick said.

Sable turned around with a glass of water in her hand and said, "I'd better get back to the stage." She dragged her eyes lustfully down Nick's body. "If you want to give those hips a workout later, come find me."

Jealousy clawed up Trixie's spine as Sable headed back to the stage. Nick shook his head, his grin forcing those claws in deeper.

Jeb arched a brow. "You and Sable knocking boots?"

Shane stepped between Trixie and Lindsay, putting his arms around them, and said, "Careful, dude. Sable eats men for breakfast."

"Not this man," Nick said. "She's a spitfire, and some man is going to get off on her unique brand of magic, but I'm not that guy."

Trixie wondered if he was being honest. She'd never known Nick to lie, but men did weird things when it came to women. She downed the rest of her drink, trying to shake off the unfamiliar scratch of jealousy.

"Speaking of unique brands of magic, did Trix tell you about her party pony idea?" Shane asked with an amusing lilt to his voice.

Trixie shrugged out from under his arm, scowling as she set her bottle on the bar. "They're not *party ponies*. They're miniature horses."

"Get it right, bro." Amusement glimmered in Jeb's dark eyes. "They're going to be unicorns with pretty colored manes and tails."

Her brothers laughed. The band started playing, and Nick's expression turned even more serious as he listened to her brothers tossing jokes back and forth about her business idea.

"Y'all are asses," Trixie finally snapped. "They're therapy horses."

Nick looked at her and said, "Wait. What exactly is your idea?"

"Why? Do you want to make fun of it, too?" It was a knee-jerk reaction, and she deserved the scowl it earned.

"Aw, come on, Trix," Jeb said. "We're just teasing."

"I think it's a brilliant idea," Lindsay said. "We're going to partner for unicorn photo sessions and birthday parties."

"Thank you, Linds. Brilliant is so much better than *cute*."

"You want to put horns on miniature horses and call them unicorns," Shane pointed out. "You've got to admit, it's a funny premise, and a cute idea."

Trixie glowered at him. "I know you mean well, but if I hear you say my idea is *cute* one more time, I'm going to do some serious damage to that pretty face of yours."

"His *cute* face," Jeb joked, sparking laughter from Shane and a litany of other *cute* jokes, all of which circled back to Trixie's business idea.

Just when she was about to lay into them, Nick put a hand on her back and said, "Let's go," quietly and firmly into her ear.

Even with her brothers' comments grating on her nerves, his touch sent prickles of desire through her traitorous body, and her thoughts stumbled. Shane and Jeb made another joke at her expense, and Lindsay lit into them.

"Dance floor. *Now*," Nick said gruffly, dragging her away from the others.

Trixie cocked her head. "Excuse me? I'm not your property."

"Don't make me take you over my knee."

"You wish."

She turned to walk away, but he tugged her into his arms.

"What the hell, Nick?"

"I didn't like the way your brothers were making fun of you."

His words softened her toward him, and he began moving those dangerous hips to the slow country song. But she didn't *want* to soften toward him. She needed to stop thinking he was so wonderful.

"I don't need protecting. I'm a big girl."

"No shit, Trix. I know you can hold your own. Do you want a miniature horse business or not?"

"Hell *yes*, and nobody's going to stop me from putting my whole heart into it. So if you think you can talk me out of it, don't even try."

"Why would I do that? Am I an asshole?"

"Well, you are a man," she teased.

He held her tighter. Irritation and something deeper that she couldn't read simmered in his eyes. "You're too smart for bullshit, Trixie. You can tell the difference between an asshole and a gentleman in seven seconds flat. Figure that shit out, and don't you dare put me in the wrong category."

Sometimes she wished he didn't know her that well, but that was one of the reasons she'd fallen for him in the first place. He *got* her. He saw in her the potential she felt. She knew her brothers did, too, but Nick had never taken a chance of hurting her feelings by making cutting remarks, even if joking around. When she'd wanted to learn stunt riding, her brothers had tried to dissuade her from the idea. She knew they'd done it out of love, of course, because they hadn't wanted her to get hurt. But when she'd told Nick she wanted to learn, he'd gone over the dangers, and then he'd taught her to ride. As her resolve softened, she became more aware of his strong arms around her and the feel of his body moving deliciously against her.

"You okay?" he asked.

She tried to fortify the walls between them, but it was like lifting liquid bricks that instantly drained from her hands. "What are you doing, Nick? Why do you care about my idea?"

"I'm a businessman, and you're a damn good rancher. You've got a special touch with horses, and if you're putting your huge fucking heart into something, it's not going to fail. I want to hear your business plan."

Through a roaring din of shock, one word slipped out. "Really?"

"Have I ever lied to you?" he said sternly.

As far as she knew, he hadn't, but jealousy slithered in, and there was no holding it back. "Maybe. You and Sable?"

His brows knitted. "You're not serious."

"Dead serious." Her pulse quickened.

"Sable's great. But she's not my type."

"So you just screwed her? I heard her comment about your hips."

"What? *No.* We danced together at my brother's wedding. Christ, she's family."

Now she felt stupid, but she couldn't help needling him. "Then what is your type?"

He laughed softly. "Trix, you want to talk about your business? Want to make it happen? Or do you want to talk about nonsense?"

Her pulse sprinted as she debated keeping the conversation going, chipping away at his likes and dislikes and picking up the pieces in an effort to construct the answers she sought. But what if his answers hurt even more than not knowing? It was one thing to get the vibe that he wasn't attracted to her, but did she really want to hear him say it?

"Trix?" he said, reminding her he was waiting for an answer.

She was being stupid. Nick was a take-charge guy who pursued and conquered the things he wanted, and she was obviously not one of them. She wasn't his type. *Period.* Shoving those hurt feelings down deep, she focused on her business and said, "Let me tell you about my business idea. Remember last year when I delivered a pony and a horse to that family with two little girls, one who had cancer and the other who was in a wheelchair? Elsie and Cara? In Echo Beach?"

"How could I forget? You talked about that family nonstop. They'd adopted the girls, right?"

"Yes. They really had an impact on me. When Elsie saw the pony, she lit up. Just petting him and being near him changed everything about the way she carried herself. I could *see* her happiness in the way she acted and hear it in her voice. And when Cara sat on the horse? Oh, *Nick*." She sighed. "Imagine a little girl who can't walk seeing the world from the saddle, experiencing that type of freedom for the first time."

"It can have a life-changing effect."

"It did. Their mom told me that they both struggled with acceptance from kids their age, but the connection between the girls and the horses was immediate. An hour later, I could still feel their renewed energy, and the light in their eyes was even brighter. The girls talked about the future with such hope. It was obvious *that* was new for them, too. When I finally left later that afternoon—"

"Their mom cried about the differences the pony and the horse had already made."

"You remember," she said softly.

"You had tears in your eyes when you told me. That's kind of hard to forget."

Her hopeful heart wanted to cling to that and pick it apart, but she'd only turn it into something more than it was meant to be, so she continued telling him her story. "I've seen kids and horses millions of times, but something clicked inside me that day. That's when I started reading up on equine therapy."

"You mentioned that to me a while back."

Another nugget she wanted, but refused, to pick apart. The song changed to a faster one, but they continued swaying slowly. "Anyone who has horses knows they make a difference in people's lives. But once I started researching and learned more about the ways in which even groundwork with horses could help people who are suffering from all types of illnesses, I knew I'd found what I was meant to do. That's when I came up with the idea for Rising Hope. I want to work with miniature horses so they can go into hospitals and nursing homes, and I'll dress the horses up as unicorns. I also want to offer kids' parties, because that'll be fun *and* I'll need to keep income coming in while I train the minis as therapy horses. I might work with regular-size horses, too, wherever I set up my business, to offer therapeutic riding in addition to groundwork. Buttercup is ready for that." Buttercup was a six-year-old mare she'd raised from a foal.

"She has the perfect temperament. This sounds right up your alley. You'd be great with kids. Now the unicorn thing makes more sense."

He didn't say it with amusement, and she appreciated that. "What's more magical than a unicorn? I think it'll bring even more joy to kids and maybe even to some adults. We all need a little magic and hope in our lives, right? I have so many ideas, Nick, and I know it'll take about two years to get it off the ground with training the horses and lining up contacts with hospitals, nursing homes, rehab centers, and other organizations."

"Two years sounds about right for the training," he agreed. "The minis will need to learn to adjust to a wide array of environments—stairs, elevators, sights, sounds."

"I know. I plan to continue working on our ranch, and I've got savings. I've got my eye on a farmette in Meadowside that may be going into foreclosure later this year." Meadowside was a neighboring town to Oak Falls. "If that doesn't pan out, I heard that another family I know is thinking about subdividing their farm."

"Really?" Surprise rose in his eyes. "You're going to buy a place?"

"Only if I can get one at a good price. I already talked with Beckett about getting a loan." Trixie had grown up with Beckett Wheeler, who'd made it big in finance and was now a private investor.

"Why not run the business from your parents' ranch and save the money? I'm sure they have the space."

"They do, but you know how my brothers are. If I set up on my parents' property, I'll always be fending off their jokes, trying to prove that what I'm doing is important. I don't want to deal with that even though they're only kidding. I want to be out on my own, Nick, driven by the vision I have for the business, not by a need to prove something to someone else. I'll still help at my family's ranch, but I *need* to do this. I want to bring light and hope into people's lives through the animals that I love. I'm sure bringing minis to birthday parties sounds a little silly to you, but it's a start while I'm training the horses, and I *know* I can make a go of this."

"It doesn't sound silly at all. I believe in equine therapy, and I know your brothers do, too, despite their bullshit comments. But have you looked into the business side of all of this? Can you make a living and pay a mortgage when you're starting out?"

"I believe I can. Insurance is expensive, and I know I won't earn anything like what you're used to. You train horses that are used in movies, and I can't imagine you're earning peanuts for your exhibitions and competitions. But this is a totally different type of business, and I'm a simple girl. I don't need luxuries."

He cocked a brow. "You are *not* a simple girl."

"Okay. I'm a pain in your ass, but I live simply."

"I'll buy that. Have you thought about doing shows to supplement your income? You could earn a pretty penny that way. You're a great trick rider and a fantastic trainer."

Nick didn't lavish people with praise unless he meant it. It was one of the things she liked about him. "I learned from the best."

"That you did," he said arrogantly.

"But I think I want to focus on getting the horses trained and building a therapy business rather than putting my energy anywhere else, except my parents' ranch, of course."

"That makes sense. Have you thought about buying minis that are already trained for therapy?"

He always listened, tried to help, and made her feel smart and validated. She was glad she hadn't tried to pry information out of him about his type of women. His friendship fulfilled her in ways nothing else ever had, and it would have been stupid to push him when nothing would ever come of it anyway.

"Yes, but they're really expensive, and I want to train mine from the start. It'll be a lot of work, but I know it'll be worth it. Do you think that's a mistake?"

"Nope. I'm just making sure you've covered all your bases."

"Thank you for not laughing at me, Nick."

"I'd never laugh at you, only with you." He chuckled. "I've got an idea. My buddy Travis Helms breeds the best stock of minis in the tristate area. If you're serious about this and about not buying trained therapy horses, he's the one to get them from. And you know my cousin Tempest is a music therapist." Tempest was Ty's older sister, one of Nick's six cousins who lived in Peaceful Harbor. "I bet she can give you the rundown on the best approach to take with hospitals, nursing homes, and maybe even places you haven't thought about yet."

"I forgot about Tempe. She's a great resource."

"I have an idea. Why don't you come stay at my place for a few weeks, do some research, set up a real business plan, get your horses. You'll probably want to visit with the horses over multiple days to be sure the temperaments are right for therapy. How many horses are you looking at starting with?"

"Three or four, I think."

"Then you'll want to also make sure they're accepting of each other before you buy them. And you know if you buy young, they're not going to be used to being away from their mamas. You'll need to treat them with kid gloves. I'll help you get them acclimated and help with training if you'd like, and you won't have to dodge any well-intentioned ridiculing from your brothers."

She couldn't believe how much he was offering. When it came to horses, he was the most knowledgeable person she knew. Her family were cattle ranchers. Her brothers might break wild horses, but they weren't *trainers* in the way Nick was. Nick trained horses that were used in movies filmed on the East Coast, and he did it with a velvet touch. He was authoritative in a patient and kind way that demanded and gave respect. He was the same way with people. She'd learned so much from him about working with horses, his offer felt like the best gift she'd ever been given.

"Are you serious, Nick?" Her mind spun with questions and ideas. She'd been putting off taking a leap into starting her business, and now she realized why she'd hesitated. It was because her brothers hadn't taken her seriously, and for all her confidence, *that* had held her back.

"Absolutely."

"Thank you!" Excitement bubbled up inside her, and she threw her arms around him. "I don't know how to pay you back, but I'll pay rent, I'll cook, muck your stalls. I'll do whatever you need!"

He laughed. "I don't need anything, Trix. I just want to see you succeed."

"Oh my gosh. I'm so excited I can barely think straight."

"Yeah, you're shaking." He held her tighter. "When do you want to head up?"

"Um. When do you want me?" As the words left her lips, a little voice in her head said, *He doesn't...*

Would that ever stop?

Would the ache it brought ever subside?

How was it possible to be elated and ache at the same time? She knew the answer. She'd had feelings for Nick for years.

Putting them away for good was going to take some time.

"Tomorrow? Next weekend? Whenever you'd like. You don't have to decide now. Text me and let me know. I'm heading home in a few minutes."

"Okay. Let me get my ducks in a row. Holy cow, Nick! I'm *really* doing this! And you're making it not only possible, but so much better!" She hugged him again, wiggling with excitement, holding him tighter than she ever had. "Thank you so much. I'm going to make you proud for believing in me."

As she stepped back, Nick pulled her close again, gazing into her eyes with a tortured expression.

"What? Do you regret the offer already?" Her heart lodged in her throat. "Do you want to take it back? It's okay if you do. I understand."

"I don't believe in regret."

"Then why are you looking at me like that?" She lowered her voice to tease him and said, "Is it because I got drunk in Colorado? You can hide the alcohol."

He grinned, shaking his head. "You know it's not that."

"Then what's got your britches in a knot? You're making me nervous."

His eyes flamed, stoking the embers that were impossible to extinguish around him, and said, "You looked in a mirror lately? We might be just friends, but I'm still a man."

In her excitement, it took her a minute to understand what all her hugging and wiggling had done to him. But now she felt his enticing arousal. Confused by the new revelation, she could do little more than stare at the flexing muscles in his jaw as he put space between them. There were couples dancing all around them, but she'd been so lost in their conversation, and now *this*, she'd forgotten they were even on the dance floor.

Sometime later, two minutes or ten, she had no idea which, he tipped his hat, flashing a panty-melting smile, and said, "See you soon, darlin'."

Too stunned to move, she watched him stride through the crowd toward the exit, *Don't overthink it* running through her head like a mantra.

Chapter Two

TRIXIE WAS RUNNING on pure adrenaline as she moved cattle from one pasture to the next and worked through the morning's chores. She'd been up all night thinking about Nick's offer and overthinking the effect she'd had on him. She was definitely taking him up on his offer and planned to talk with her family about it over lunch. It was the other part of the equation that she needed distracting from. Had his reaction been a fluke? Or had she simply never noticed the effect she'd had on him? She'd thought hard work would be the perfect distraction, but her thoughts kept cruising back to that moment, and his voice had been crawling through her mind all morning. *Have you looked in a mirror lately? We might be just friends, but I'm still a man.*

Futilely trying to push those thoughts away, she carried a saddle into the tack room and took a moment to look at the pictures on the walls of the ancestors who had worked the ranch before her. The Jericho ranch had been passed down through two generations and was known as Oak Falls's premier cattle ranch. Trixie loved everything about working there, from the grueling chores and scents of livestock, hay, and leather, to working with Shane, Trace, and their father. They all handled chores and worked with the animals, but Trace and Shane also maintained the equipment and structures, oversaw the ranch hands, and handled staff schedules. Trixie was the point of contact for buying and selling livestock, and she handled other administrative duties such as inventory of supplies. Their father's arthritis had gotten the best of him the last couple of years, and he no longer did physical labor. Now he maintained their books and went over them monthly with Trixie and her brothers. She had been raised to understand every aspect of the business, and her frugal parents had taught her well. She felt fully prepared to start her own business. But the thing she loved most about working on the ranch was being part of their family's legacy.

The irony that now she needed something of her own wasn't lost on her. But was it any wonder? Her brothers had earned a reputation as horse whisperers. They'd been training wild horses before the break of dawn for as long as she could remember. Even Jeb and JJ, who no longer worked on the ranch, still took part in their predawn rodeos, aka male-bonding sessions. Even though Trixie had been raised herding cattle, calving, and doing ranch chores before and after school practically since the time she'd learned to walk, her brothers were old-school. Just as they'd tried to talk her out of stunt riding, they'd never allowed her to get on the back of a wild horse. Not that she wanted to, but she didn't like to be told she couldn't.

She walked out of the barn, squinting against the harsh summer sun. Trace came around the side of the building. "Hey," she said, falling into step beside him. "Are you heading up for lunch?" Another perk of working with her family was the great meals their mother made for them.

"Yeah. Shane's already up there. It's hotter than hell today, isn't it?" He took off his hat and dragged his forearm across his forehead. He shared their mother's cleft chin and bright outlook. He had always been the cockiest of her brothers, but ever since he and Brindle had welcomed their baby girl, Emily "Emma" Louise into the world, he'd had a certain peacefulness about him. "Brindle's bringing Emma Lou over."

Everyone else called his daughter Emma, but Trace insisted on calling her Emma Lou, which Brindle thought was too *country*. But like Trixie and their other siblings, Trace was proud of his country roots and would defend them until the end of days.

"Awesome. I can't wait to see her." Trixie adored her niece, and she'd miss her if she went along with her plan to stay at Nick's for a few weeks while she got things under control for her business.

"Me too. She cried again when I left this morning. Man, I hate that. I went back in twice to try to calm her down before finally taking off."

"I wondered why you were late this morning. I thought Brindle told you not to go back in when she cries. You should probably listen to your wife."

He looked at her out of the corner of his eye as they climbed the hill to their parents' house. "Could you leave with that little princess bawling her eyes out?"

"Probably not."

"Exactly. This parenting stuff is rough." His expression turned serious. "Have you got something to tell me about you and Nick?"

"What are you, psychic?"

He scowled. "Are you shitting me? It's true? You're hooking

up with him? He's a great guy, Trix, but he lives in Maryland. Where can that possibly lead?"

"*What?* I am *not* hooking up with Nick." *But thanks to you, now I'm thinking about last night again.* "Who told you that?"

"No one. I heard you two got a little too close on the dance floor last night."

"Shane's got a big mouth. We were *talking*, and if Shane hadn't been so busy checking out Heather Ray, he would have seen Nick leave two hours before me." Heather Ray was a buxom blonde with a reputation for being easy.

"Oh, sorry. It sounded like something was going on between you two."

"Something *is* going on, but not what you think." She stopped walking and put her hand on her hip. "But if I *was* hooking up with him or anyone else, that would be *my* business, not yours or Shane's."

"We're just looking out for you."

"Is that why you tag along with me sometimes when I make runs up that way? To make sure nothing is going on between us?"

"Nope." He cocked a grin. "I go with you because we all know you head to Maryland to cut loose with Jilly at the bars."

"So what? How is that any of your business? Besides, you know I stay at Nick's. Do you really think I'd bring some random guy back there?" She stalked up the hill. "He's as overprotective as you guys are."

"You can't tell me that you don't roll into Nick's place at two in the morning sometimes."

"So?"

"So, everyone knows nothing good happens after midnight."

She laughed. "Are you serious? You sound like Dad. You're the one who used to say that *everything good* happened after midnight."

"It still does," he said arrogantly. "But I don't want to think about *you* doing those things."

"You're an ass," she said as they crested the hill. Brindle's car and Jeb's truck were in their parents' driveway.

"What's Jeb doing here?" Trace asked.

"I don't know. He was talking with Dad in the yard about an hour ago."

They headed into the rambling six-bedroom farmhouse. Trixie took comfort in the plaid living room couch and chair that had survived their childhood and the faded area rugs that she and her brothers used to roll up and push aside so they could slide in their socks across the wood floors. As they passed the stairs, she remembered tiptoeing down them to sneak out and meet her girlfriends in the middle of the night. One of her brothers usually caught her and dragged her back home, lecturing her the whole way. As annoying as that had been, she'd still had a great childhood, and she wouldn't trade it for the world.

They followed the aroma of fresh-baked cookies toward the spacious kitchen. The table was set with a platter of sandwiches, their mother's famous macaroni casserole, a large tossed salad, and their mother's homemade dressing. Their father stood by the refrigerator, cradling Emma in his arms and chatting with Brindle. Jeb was leaning against the counter, eating a slice of watermelon, as their mother cut up the remaining fruit next to him.

Brindle's smoky eyes brightened. "There's my hubby!" She hurried over to Trace, looking cute in a pair of shorts and a flouncy pink top, her blond hair cascading past her shoulders.

"I missed you, babe." Trace smooched his wife, and holding her hand, he made a beeline for his daughter. "Okay, old man, give me my baby girl."

"I hope you're hungry," their mother said cheerily. Nancy Jericho was as sweet and upbeat as their father, Waylon, was tight-lipped and serious. Her chestnut hair was pulled back in a ponytail, and she wore one of the many simple sundresses she lived in all summer.

"I'm starved. Thanks for making my favorite cookies, Mom." Trixie picked up a raspberry chocolate chip cookie from a cooling rack by the stove and took a bite.

"She made *my* favorite cookies." Jeb snagged the cookie from her hand and shoved the whole thing in his mouth.

"*Brat.* I'll just take these." Trixie picked up a cooling rack and carried it to another counter across the room.

Brindle and their mother laughed.

"That's my girl," their father said. He was a big, thick-chested man, with more salt than pepper in his short hair and deep-set serious eyes that could silence all five of his children with a single stare. "How'd it go with Blossom, Trace? She give you any trouble?" Blossom was one of their older horses, and she had seemed out of sorts yesterday.

"She's fine. She was just in a mood." Trace sat at the table cradling Emma and pressed a kiss to her wispy dark hair.

Trixie heard the front door open seconds before JJ's voice rang out. "I smell cookies!" His heavy footsteps closed in on them. "Y'all having a party without me?" He strode into the kitchen, rubbing his hands together as he eyed the food. "Looks like I'm right on time."

"Is your fridge empty again?" Trixie teased. JJ worked long

hours. It wasn't out of the ordinary for him to show up to mooch a meal.

He cracked a grin as he took two cookies from the rack. "Nah. I got groceries the other day. I was on my way home from…uh…" He raised his brows, and their brothers chuckled.

"Seriously? You're on a drive of shame and you came to Mom and Dad's?" Trixie looked at Trace. "And you guys worry about *me?*"

"You're a girl," JJ said, dropping a kiss on Emma's forehead.

"A tough girl who can handle herself and has enough self-respect not to do those things," their mother said, turning her cheek up for JJ to kiss. "Hi, sweetheart. You know I don't like you boys catting around."

"Don't worry, Ma. I wasn't catting around. Y'all raised me right." JJ slid into a chair and said, "Where's Shane?"

"Right here." Shane breezed into the kitchen. He kept his hair shorter than her other brothers, and he was the only one of them with tattoos decorating his arms. "I had to take a call."

"From *Heather?*" Trixie arched a brow.

"Is there a romance brewing that I don't know about?" Brindle asked, sitting down beside Trace.

"Wouldn't you like to know." Shane sat at the table and grabbed a sandwich.

"Yes, I would, actually," Brindle said. "I like to be *in the know.*"

"Not me. Please keep those details to yourself." Trixie sat down and dished macaroni casserole onto her plate and looked at Shane. "But if you don't stop spreading rumors about me, I'll be sure to spread some colorful ones about you."

Shane's irritated gaze shot to Trace.

"Don't look at him. You know I didn't leave with Nick last

night," Trixie snapped.

Their father slid one of his narrow-eyed stares to Shane—
the one that worked like truth serum.

Shane splayed his hands. "What? All I said was that she and
Nick looked cozy on the dance floor, which they did. Right,
Jeb?"

Jeb looked apologetically at Trixie as he sat down and said,
"You were slow dancing to the fast songs, so yeah. Sorry, Trix."

"Sable said the same thing." Brindle glanced at Trixie. "But
I told her that if you and Nick were an item, *I'd* know before
the rest of Oak Falls would. Right?"

"Of course," Trixie said. Brindle and two of her sisters,
Amber and Morgyn, were on Trixie's most-trusted-friends list
with Lindsay. Morgyn was married to Nick's youngest brother,
Graham. Nick's sister, Jillian, was also on that list, although
Trixie didn't confide in Jillian about her feelings for Nick. She
didn't want to make things weird between them.

"Y'all were on the dance floor for a *long* time," JJ said,
reaching for a sandwich.

"Good for you and Nick, honey," their mother said to Trixie. She set the bowl of watermelon on the table and joined
them. "That young man is a true gentleman."

Her brothers exchanged smirks.

"If you have something to say, boys, I suggest you come out
with it." Their mother's knowing gaze drifted to each of them.

Her brothers schooled their expressions and shoveled food
into their mouths.

"Well, *I* have something to say about Nick," Trixie announced. "He offered to help me get my business started. He
knows one of the best miniature horse breeders around, and he
has other connections that would be really helpful for me. He's
even offered to help me train the horses. If we can work out

schedules with our ranch hands, I'd like to go up this weekend, and stay for a few weeks."

"Wow. That's fantastic," Brindle exclaimed.

"Yeah. I'm really excited," Trixie said, though now she was nervous, as tension riddled her brothers' faces.

"I didn't realize you were ready to get started," JJ said.

Shane leaned forward and said, "We've got miniature horse dealers around here, and Dad's offered you space on the ranch. Why do you need to go to Nick's?"

Jeb crossed his arms over his chest and said, "Those are good points."

Her father watched the discussion unfold. Her parents had always let them work things out among themselves before stepping in. Trixie believed it was one of the reasons they all had such strong personalities.

"What's Braden getting out of this deal?" Shane asked.

Anger clawed up Trixie's chest. "He's helping me because he respects my abilities, *not* because he's expecting sexual favors."

"Back off, Shane," Trace said. "Let's hear her out."

"Yeah, it's not like we don't know and trust Nick," JJ pointed out.

Their father nodded approvingly.

Annoyed that this was even a discussion about anything other than schedules, Trixie said, "Nick's offering me space, connections, and his time, and I'm taking him up on it. Can you work out the schedule so I can get a few weeks off or not? I know our new guys want more hours."

"You're right, they have asked for more hours," their father said. "But I would like to know why you have to run off to do this."

A sliver of guilt trampled through her. "I'm not running off, Dad. My business will be located here, like we've been talking about. Meggie Tipster has been looking at foreclosures for me, and I heard rumors that the Kincaids might be subdividing their property. I've already spoken with Beckett about getting a loan." They'd grown up with Meggie, who was now a real estate agent. "I'm not going to Maryland for good. But I can't do what I want and feel good about it here." She looked at her brothers. "I've been talking about doing this for months, and you guys still think my business idea is *cute*. I get that, but it undermines the value of something that's important to me."

"We're only joking around about party ponies, Trix," Jeb said.

"I know, but still. You guys have directed what I can and can't do my whole life. I had to go to Nick's to learn to stunt ride, and I'm a freaking awesome rider. I love you guys, and I know you'll support me, but I can't—*no*, I don't *want* to try to get my arms around my business here, where I'm not taken seriously."

"Whoa, sis," Trace said. "You're a key member of our business. Just because we kid around doesn't mean we don't take you seriously. We know how awesome you are."

"That's true. He raves about how you get things done all the time," Brindle added.

"I'm sure he does. But—"

"That's enough," her father said sternly.

Her nerves flared. "But, Dad—"

Her father held up his hand, silencing her. "You've done enough explaining. We raised four good, loyal men, and we raised you to be a strong woman who speaks her mind. But we've clearly made a mistake somewhere along the way, because no daughter of ours should ever feel like she's not taken seriously. We'll cover your time while you're away, and when you come back, things around here will be different."

Chapter Three

THE REST OF Trixie's week passed in a whirlwind of packing and outlining a more detailed business plan, getting together with her girlfriends, and accepting apologies from her brothers. She appreciated them, but she was certain she'd made the right decision. When she'd texted Nick to say she'd like to come up for a few weeks, he'd suggested they make it an even month so she could come to his next exhibition before going home. She hadn't been to one of his shows since last year, and she was excited to see him perform again. A month would give them time to get her miniature horses fairly well trained for general handling. She couldn't believe she was taking the leap and was finally on her way.

It was late Saturday afternoon, and she was almost done with the two-hour drive to Nick's. She'd made the drive dozens of times, but this time felt different. She wasn't just running livestock from one state to the next or going to hang out with Jillian. She was starting a new chapter in her life, and she was getting more excited by the mile.

And more nervous.

She was still overthinking the last time she'd seen Nick.

She tried to focus on her surroundings instead of the formidable distraction she'd felt behind his zipper. Pleasant Hill was bigger than Oak Falls and just as charming, even if more upscale. The center of town was lined by tall buildings and fancy shops, with brick-paved sidewalks, flowering dogwood trees, and wooden benches on every corner. Nick lived on the outskirts of town, on a rural oasis that felt much more like home.

Trixie's phone rang with a call from Lindsay, and she answered through Bluetooth. "Hi, Linds."

"Hey!" three voices shouted in unison, followed by giggles. "I'm with Amber and Brindle," Lindsay said. "We wanted to wish you luck."

"Thanks, you guys," Trixie said. "What are you doing tonight?"

"We're trying to convince Amber to close her bookstore early and go shopping with us," Lindsay said.

"But she's busy drooling over Dash Pennington," Brindle chimed in.

"I am *not*," Amber insisted. She was a beautiful brunette and the demurest of Brindle's sisters.

"Oh, *please*. You practically pushed Lindsay out of the way to see the screen," Brindle said with a laugh. "A man *finally* caught your attention. You *need* him, Amb. Now all we have to do is get him here."

Amber had epilepsy, and though it was well managed with medication, she lived a quiet, controlled life, and rarely dated. They had been trying to change that by encouraging her to put herself out there a little more.

"Would you *stop*," Amber pleaded, and Trixie knew from her breathy voice that she was blushing. She blushed so easily. "I don't *need* Dash Pennington."

Trixie laughed. "Who is this mystery man? And why haven't I heard his name before?"

"He's just a football player who's publishing a book," Amber said.

"His PR rep got in touch with Amber about setting up a signing," Brindle explained.

"You have to Google this guy, Trix," Lindsay urged. "He's hot as all get out."

"Sure. I'll get right on that. I'm glad you guys called. I could use a little help getting my mind off the hot guy I'm staying with for the next month. I can't stop thinking about what happened at the bar." Trixie had filled her friends in on Nick's erection incident when she'd met them for dinner Thursday evening.

"The pocket rocket?" Brindle teased.

"The *what*?" Amber asked.

"Puff the one-eyed dragon?" Lindsay laughed.

"The Bone Ranger?" Brindle hollered.

Trixie cracked up. "You guys are *not* helping."

"*Oh!* I get it," Amber exclaimed.

"That's right, Amber. Trixie wants to get the *big O*," Lindsay said, causing them all to crack up.

"No I don't!" Trixie laughed. "I mean I *do*, but I can't keep thinking about that. Nick didn't say he was *into* me. He said he was a man, meaning pretty women turn guys on. Period. He's just my hot friend. Haven't you ever had a hot friend that you thought about from time to time in a different way?"

"Yeah. I screwed his brains out and married him," Brindle said with a laugh.

"*Ugh.* Don't make me think about my brother having sex," Trixie said. "Nick is doing me a huge favor. I can't be lusting after him like a ridiculous teenager."

"She's right, you guys," Amber said. "Even if he was turned on, they're going to be working together. She can't cross that line."

"Yes she *can*," Lindsay said.

"You'd never cross that line, Lindsay," Amber said.

"I work with brides and grooms," Lindsay pointed out. "If I crossed that line, it would ruin my Yelp rating."

They all laughed.

"I'm almost there," Trixie said as she turned off the highway. "Why am I having such a hard time regaining perspective on our relationship?"

"Because you had his big cock pressed against you," Lindsay said.

"Lindsay!" Amber chided her, and they all laughed again.

"I'm going to miss you guys. A month is a long time," Trixie said.

"We'll text and call, and keep you in the loop on all the good stuff," Brindle reassured her. "I think I have a solution for your cock trouble."

"Ohmygod," Trixie mumbled. "Can you *not* call it that? It only makes it harder."

"That's what he said," Lindsay said.

"I'm turning onto his street. Talk fast!"

"Okay, this is your future, Trixie," Brindle said in her most serious voice. "You're being given a heck of a chance to get your new business in order without being overshadowed by your brothers, and you can't afford to get sidetracked by that particular hard-bodied cowboy."

"She's been sidetracked by him for *years*," Lindsay said.

"I know. That's why she has to plan a night out with Jilly as soon as she gets there, with the sole purpose of finding a *different* guy to keep her mind occupied," Brindle said.

"You want her to sleep around?" Amber asked. "I don't like this plan."

"Neither do I," Trixie agreed.

"Not to *sleep* with. Just to hang out with," Brindle said. "They say the best way to get over a guy is to get under another one, but Trixie hasn't slept with Nick, so she's not looking to erase that particular memory. Trix, you just need to fill your fantasy bank with new images."

"I'm not sure I'd take relationship advice from a girl who ran away to Paris to try to *forget* the guy she'd loved since she was thirteen," Lindsay said.

"That trip proved Brindle and Trace's love conquers all," Amber said.

"Darn right, sis," Brindle agreed.

"I actually think Brindle's on to something," Trixie said. "I have been pretty much singularly focused in the fantasy department. I look at other guys and dance with them when I'm out, but Nick's the only one I think about when I...*you know.*"

"Hope you brought a boatload of batteries with you," Lindsay teased.

Trixie laughed, though she'd never bring a vibrator to Nick's house. With her luck, one of his dogs would get ahold of it and drop it in the middle of the living room. "I'm going to try Brindle's idea, but I'm about to turn into his driveway, so I'd better go. I love you guys."

"We love you, too!" they said in unison.

"Have fun," Amber said. "And remember, true love trumps everything else. Maybe you'll meet your true love while you're there."

"Or at least get laid," Lindsay added.

"Just find another guy to drool over. Trust me on that," Brindle said.

"Okay. Thanks for all of your advice. I'll let you know how it goes."

After ending the call, Trixie drove down Nick's long driveway, which was lined with gorgeous maple trees and pastures as far as the eye could see. When his stone home came into view, a familiar wave of comfort warmed her. Nick's house was very much like him: sturdy, rugged, and supremely masculine. The interior was all rustic wood and stone, with an open floor plan. There were two master suites, one at either end of the first floor, separated by a great room, dining area, and kitchen. There were two bedrooms and a loft upstairs and a full basement that he used to talk about making into a man cave, complete with a pool table. When he'd realized he'd need to have people over to play pool, he had given up that idea. The back of the house was almost all glass, offering gorgeous views of his property and the mountains beyond. Nick hated to be confined, and because of that, those glass walls had always made sense to Trixie. She'd caught him gazing out them in the middle of many cold winter nights, as if he longed to be outside.

It was nearly seven o'clock, and she knew she'd find Nick with the animals. As she drove toward the barn, Rowdy, Nick's rambunctious one-year-old golden retriever/Australian shepherd pup, barreled toward her truck, his tail wagging. She spotted Nick by the larger of the two cream-colored barns. His black cowboy hat was low on his brow, and he was grooming Snickers, an older miniature chestnut mare he'd rescued several years ago. Rowdy's mom, Goldie, a golden retriever, lay in the shade a few feet away with Nick's precious Pugsly, an eleven-year-old pug. Pugsly was blind in one eye and grunted as much as Nick did. Nick treated all of his animals like they were his children, which Trixie found endearingly funny for a guy who didn't want a family. It was probably a good thing he didn't want kids, given his unoriginal naming themes.

Nick turned around as she parked, a smile curving his lips, and he tipped his hat.

God, she loved his smile. She swore the smile he flashed every time she arrived was unlike any other and different from the smile he gave everyone else when he greeted them. The special smile he showed her changed *all* of his features, softening the hard ridges of his cheeks and jaw and doing something miraculous to his eyes. Those dark eyes took on a look that was rugged but somehow also gentle, and familiar in a way that said, *Hello, darlin'. Good to see you again.* It was even different from the smile he reserved for his family. That one was even more open, while the one he gave her still carried a hint of distance.

His voice whispered through her mind. *I'm still a man.* Was his reaction at the bar the reason he kept that distance?

She cut the engine, taking a moment to admire him walking toward her truck with an air of confidence that commanded attention, his powerful thighs wrapped in worn denim, his muscles rippling beneath his black T-shirt. Pugsly waddled toward him, and he scooped up his buddy with one hand and nuzzled his face, carrying him against his chest. As Nick rounded her truck, his dark eyes locked on her again, causing butterflies to flutter in her belly. His broad shoulders blocked the sun as he opened her door, that pulse-quickening smile on his lips.

"Hey there, darlin'," he said as she climbed out. "I'm glad you're here."

He drew her against him with one strong arm. It wasn't just his house that felt like home. It was *him*. They were like two long-lost friends coming back together, sliding into the place that had been reserved for them the whole time they were apart without fanfare or even conversation.

Forget finding another man to drool over. No one could hold a candle to him.

WHY DID IT always feel so damn good when Trixie showed up? The ever-present knots in his muscles eased at the sight of her. She was the only person who evoked that instant response, but as he embraced her, that calm was obliterated by the other tangled-up feelings she'd been giving him lately.

"Last chance to rescind your offer," she said as he released her.

"Not happening, darlin'."

She leaned in to love up Pugsly, and Pugsly licked her face, wiggling and grunting excitedly.

I know how you feel, buddy.

"Hello, my sweet grunty boy. Come to Trixie." She took Pugsly and covered his furry head with kisses.

Rowdy barked, his tail wagging excitedly as she bent over in her cutoffs and signature short-sleeved button-down shirt tied above her belly button, treating Rowdy to the same loving attention—and giving Nick a glorious view of her ass.

"Don't be jealous, little man," she said to Rowdy. "There's plenty of me to go around."

Nick gritted his teeth. What was he thinking, offering to let her stay for a month? The longest Trixie had ever visited had been a week, and when she'd stayed for that long two months ago, Nick had been fit to be tied by the time she'd left. He wanted to help her, but how the hell would he survive a month of this?

"My parents invited us over for dinner tomorrow night. Jax and Jilly will be there. Sound okay?" Jax and Jillian were his younger twin siblings, both of whom lived in town. Graham and his wife, Morgyn, were traveling on the West Coast. Beau and Charlotte lived in Colorado during the summer and Pleasant Hill over the winter, and Zev was treasure hunting off the coast of Silver Island with his fiancée, Carly.

"Sounds great. You know I love your family. I brought you peach cobbler, your favorite. You can share it with them."

He scoffed. "Like hell I will. They can get their own cobbler." Nobody made peach cobbler like Trixie. She always brought one of his favorite desserts when she stayed with him, and lately that thoughtfulness made her even more irresistible. But he'd bet the taste of *her* would blow that cobbler away.

"I'll carry your bags up so you can get settled while I finish grooming Snickers, then we'll throw some burgers on the grill."

She snuggled Pugsly. Rowdy rubbed against her leg, whimpering, and she reached down to pet him.

Christ, even his dogs couldn't get enough of her.

He tore his eyes away and walked around her horse trailer, putting space between them. He'd probably spend the next month keeping his distance, which was a shame, since he loved hanging out with her. But after the way he'd caught fire the other night, he needed to regain control of his own damn body.

"I'll get my bags," she said, coming around the truck.

"Last time I looked, I was still a gentleman. Pop the lock, cowgirl."

Chapter Four

AS NICK GROOMED Snickers, he imagined Trixie blaring her music and dancing around in her Daisy Dukes as she unpacked. Sometime over the years, the second master suite had become her bedroom. Not that Nick had many visitors. He liked his solitude, and his only other occasional overnight guests were extended family, and they stayed upstairs. He hadn't thought too much about that until Trixie's last visit, when his late-night thoughts had snuck across the house to the woman behind the door that she always left slightly ajar.

Trixie had never been one to hide behind anything. When she felt safe, it was evident in everything she did, like the way she walked around in her sleeping shorts and skimpy tops, stole food off his plate, and challenged him at every turn. When she was scared, nervous, or insecure, flecks of gold shimmered in her eyes and she reared up like a grizzly bear, unwilling to let anyone smell that fear. But Nick could always sense it. He hadn't seen her scared often, but there had been a few times, like a couple of years ago, when she'd been up his way for a river rafting race and Jeb had been thrown from a wild horse and knocked unconscious at four in the morning. When her father had called, she'd stomped around packing her things, seething about how stupid her brothers were for riding before dawn. He knew how close she was with her brothers, despite her annoyance at their teasing, and it had been painful watching her try to hide her fears. He'd finally hauled her into his arms. After she'd struggled to get free and called him every bad name in the book, she'd broken down and sobbed. He'd held her until she'd had no more tears to cry, and then he'd driven her home and stayed with her until Jeb was out of the woods. Her trust in him was one reason his dirty thoughts about her made him a dick—and he hated feeling like a dick.

He finished grooming Snickers, and the miniature mare pressed her muzzle into his stomach. He loved her up. "It's nothing a few cold showers and a couple of shots of whiskey can't cure. Right, girl? I can get this shit under control."

Snickers bobbed her head.

There was no greater sounding board than a horse. Nick had fallen in love with horses as a kid when his family was visiting their father's cousin Hal's ranch in Weston, Colorado, where Hal had raised his six children. Hal had put Nick on the back of his first horse, and Nick could still remember the feeling of having all that power and beauty beneath him. He had always looked up to his older cousins, especially Rex, who now ran the ranch with his father. Nick had spent time there during school breaks and summers, and Hal and Rex had taught him how to run a ranch. They bred Dutch Warmblood show jumpers, and by the time Nick was ten years old, he'd known he wanted to follow in Hal's footsteps...with a twist.

Shortly after that first ride, Nick had started taking riding lessons in Pleasant Hill from Walt Elliott. Walt had worked in Hollywood as a stunt rider before retiring to his ranch in Maryland. Nick had quickly become addicted to riding and caring for horses, and when he was seven, Walt began training him to stunt ride. At eight, Nick was competing—and winning—and at ten, he was helping at the ranch before and after school. By the time Nick was a teenager, if he wasn't at school or helping his family, he was at Walt's ranch. Walt had groomed him to become the sought-after stunt rider and showman he was, though Nick had never wanted the Hollywood lifestyle Walt had loved. Walt had downsized and subdivided his property about seven years ago, keeping a small plot of land and his house and barn. He'd sold the remaining acreage, one barn, and what had been the original farmhouse to Nick. The house and barn had been in sorry shape. But Nick had rallied his family to help renovate. His father was an engineer, and Graham had been studying to become one at the time. They'd convinced Beau to come home long enough to help get the job done, and later, they'd built the second, smaller barn and outbuildings.

Nick was living the life he'd always wanted. He had nine horses, had rescued a small herd of pygmy goats, and had added a flock of chickens to his family.

He made two quick clicking sounds, and Snickers fell into step beside him, heading for the barn entrance. It'd been hot and humid lately, so he'd kept the horses in the barn, but now that the sun was coming down and the temperature was dropping, he'd let them out to pasture for the night.

"Nick! Wait up!"

He turned and saw Trixie running toward him, her dark hair flying over her shoulders, her gorgeous breasts bouncing temptingly, but her killer smile was doing far more damage than all the rest. Where the hell was the whiskey when he needed it?

"Hey, Trix," he said as she caught up and went to pet

Snickers. "You all settled in?"

"Good enough for now. I wanted to help turn out the horses and check on Chewy, Cluck, and everyone else." Chewy was one of his goats, and Cluck was a big old chicken that followed her around like she was the Pied Piper. "Like this old girl. Hi, Snicky." She put her arms around the horse's neck and rested her cheek on her mane. "I've missed you." She lowered her voice conspiratorially. "Has Daddy been good to you? What was that? He spoils you rotten?" She pulled a carrot out of her back pocket and fed it to Snickers, giving Nick a victorious look. "But not as much as I do, right?"

Nick laughed under his breath and headed into the barn, trying to ignore the tug in his chest at the love she showed his animals.

Trixie and Snickers followed him in, and all the horses started bobbing their heads and nickering. Nick wondered if that low, throaty greeting was meant for him or Trixie. He swore his animals missed her as much as he did.

As he put Snickers in her stall, Trixie greeted the other horses, chatting them up as if they were old friends and promising them each something special. "Midnight, we're going to ride down to your favorite spot by the creek and have a picnic, and, Lady, you and I are going to hit the trails. I'm going to ride you *a lot* while I'm here..."

How about giving me the same offer? And just like that, he felt like a dick again. He gritted his teeth, opening another horse's stall as Trixie escorted Lady out of the barn.

Nick had a strong bond with all of his horses, but Lady, a gorgeous black Friesian, was a special girl. He'd first met her as a yearling when he'd halter trained her for her owner, Carol Lancaster. He'd saddle trained her a year later, and less than eight months after that, Carol had been diagnosed with cancer. Carol's health had rapidly declined, and during that time Nick would visit to take care of Lady and ride her so Carol could watch her in action. When Carol passed away, her husband had offered Lady to Nick. Nick began trick training her, and she'd taken to it as if she were born to be his mount. That was five years ago, and she was still his best partner.

Goldie and Rowdy tagged along as they put out the rest of the horses, which took a while because Nick was as bad as Trixie when it came to giving them extra attention. He refilled the dogs' food and water dishes, and when he came out of the barn, Trixie was standing at the fence petting Romeo, a six-year-old brown Morgan.

Trixie headed for Nick and said, "Okay, big guy. I'm ready to go see Chewy and the gang."

Romeo whinnied, and Trixie stopped walking, grinning from ear to ear. "Sorry, Nick. Just give me one more minute. I promise to be quick." She went back to the fence and climbed up, bringing her eye to eye with Romeo. She showered him with attention and promises to spend more time with him over the next few weeks. "Go have fun and play with your friends."

She sauntered over to Nick, leaving poor Romeo staring longingly after her. *Get in line, buddy.* Nick had been watching guys vie for Trixie's attention for so many years, he knew all about the trail of wanting looks she left in her wake.

He arched a brow. "And you think *I* spoil them?"

"Shut up. He misses me. You want to muck the stalls before we do the rest?"

"I'll take care of them after dinner." They headed down to the goat pen. "How'd your brothers take the news of you coming out here?" He'd worried about them giving her crap.

"Like I expected them to. They gave me a hard time at first, wondering why I was coming here to get started. But they apologized the next day. My dad was okay with it, though."

"Yeah, I know about your old man. I called him after I got your message saying you were coming out."

"You called my father?" Her brows slanted in anger. "Why would you do that?"

"Out of respect for him. To let him know I'd make sure you were taken care of."

"I can't *believe* you did that," she said angrily. "You're as bad as my brothers."

"Yeah, I had a feeling you'd be pissed."

"And you *still* did it?"

"Damn right."

She swatted his arm.

He laughed. "Sorry, darlin'. I know you can take care of yourself, and your father does, too, but no matter how old you get, you'll always be his little girl. I don't know much about being a parent, but if Lady went off without me for a month, I'd damn sure want to know she was taken care of."

"That's kind of sweet *and* kind of awful. I'm not a *horse*."

He stole a glance at her, all pissed off and stomping across the grass in her cowgirl boots, sexy as hell. "No, you sure aren't."

"I think I need to start surrounding myself with men who *aren't* cowboys, because y'all drive me nuts."

I could say the same about you. "I'm pretty sure it comes with the genes, so unless you start batting for the other team, you're in for a lifetime of it." The last thing he wanted to think about was Trixie and some other guy, so he changed the subject. "Travis is making time for us tomorrow afternoon. Does that work for you?"

"Absolutely. I'm excited to get started."

She looped her arm into his, leaning against his side as they walked down the hill, reminding him of that night in Colorado. His mind took a dark turn, thinking about how much he'd like to *get started* with her. And man, there he went, being a dick again. He clenched his jaw, pushing those thoughts away.

She turned her beautiful brown eyes on him and said, "Thank you for giving me this chance, Nick."

"You know I'd do anything to help you. That's what friends are for."

"You're a better friend than most."

You wouldn't think that if you knew what was going on in my mind.

BY THE TIME they took care of the animals and Nick washed up, it was after nine. He stood on the patio grilling burgers, corn on the cob, potatoes, and vegetables. Most women would bitch about working all evening and eating so late. Hell, most guys he knew ranked their next meal right up there with sex. But Trixie had never questioned his habits the way others did. He watched her sitting in the grass with Pugsly on her lap by the picnic table, gazing out at the horses. Goldie and Rowdy ran around her playing, stopping for pets and kisses every few minutes. As much as Nick loved his solitude, Trixie made his days better. He couldn't define the reasons, especially since she talked too much, challenged him all the time, and had become a hell of a big distraction, causing him to think about shit he didn't want to think about. But there was no denying that he was happier when she was there.

She set Pugsly down and pushed to her feet, brushing the grass from her shorts. The setting sun cast a glow around her, giving her an angelic appearance. Nick laughed to himself. The saucy temptress was far from angelic.

"That smells incredible," she said, coming over to him with Pugsly waddling behind her. Rowdy and Goldie took off toward the field. "I always forget how good of a cook you are. I am *so* glad you're a Gruff Gus." She plucked a cucumber from the salad they'd made and popped it into her mouth.

"A *what?*"

"Gruff Gus. I think the saying is really Grumpy Gus, but you're gruff and growly, not grumpy." Her smile played mischievously in her eyes. "If you were friendlier, some woman would have probably broken down your walls and changed your mind about marriage by now. Then I'd miss out on all the great meals you make, so thanks for being a growly guy."

"They're just burgers, Trix."

"*Just burgers* are those skinny slabs of something that looks like meat that you get at McDonald's. You make thick, juicy burgers with cheese and onions inside them and special Braden spices." She pointed to the foil packets on the grill. "And you grill tomatoes, peppers, and mushrooms to go on top and all the yummiest sides to go with them."

"If you say so." It never failed to amaze him how appreciative she was of the things he did every day and thought nothing of.

"I do, and I know what I'm talking about. You, Mr. Braden, are a catch."

"And you of all people, Miss Jericho, know that's not true.

I'm an impatient workaholic and a perfectionist who'd rather hang out with my horses than with people."

"Maybe you're right. You're not marriage material," she said snarkily, and snagged his hat off his head, putting it on her own.

She was the only person he'd allow to do that shit. She looked damn cute in his black hat.

She peered into the stone pit as she walked past. "I see you haven't used the firepit since I was here last."

"You do this to me every time you visit."

"What?" she asked with an innocent flutter of her long lashes. "Try to get you to enjoy the things you have?"

He shook his head.

She planted her hand on her hip. "You don't have to invite people over to use it, you know. But inviting friends and family over every once in a while *would* make your house homier."

"My house is homey enough," he said, transferring the food onto platters.

"Let's sit at the picnic table!" She moved the place settings from the patio table to the picnic table, setting their plates side by side, as she always did, and went back for their drinks and the salad.

Nick carried over the rest of the food and condiments and set a plain hamburger on a plate in the grass for Pugsly. He whistled, and Pugsly waddled over as they sat down. Trixie sat so close to him, her arm brushed his. She'd never known the meaning of personal space where he was concerned.

He'd never forget the first time they'd met. It was at Mr. B's, his uncle Ace's restaurant and microbrewery in Peaceful Harbor, where Graham and his cousins were celebrating after a race. He'd dropped by to join them, and Trixie had been there teaching his cousins Sam and Cole to do the two-step. She was all attitude in cutoffs and a plaid shirt tied over her belly button, giving his cousins shit for not following along. She'd set her eyes on Nick with a challenging smirk and said, *You gonna jump in and show 'em how it's done, cowboy? Or are the hat and boots just for decoration?* She'd stuck to him like glue after that, giving him sass about everything, eating fries off his plate, and using him as a human cushion to lean against. The funny thing was, she hadn't been flirtatious. She'd simply acted like she'd known him forever, and it had felt that way to him, too.

As they filled their plates, she said, "Catch me up on things." She plucked a tomato from the salad he was putting on his plate.

"A'right. Did Jillian tell you Zev and Carly got engaged? They're getting married over the holidays."

"*No.* I haven't talked to Jilly in a couple of weeks. I need to call her and let her know I'm here. That's great news! I'm happy for Zev. After what happened when he was young, I thought he was destined to be a bachelor forever, like you." She stacked tomatoes, mushrooms, and peppers on top of her burger and smothered it in ketchup.

"We all did." Zev had fallen in love with his childhood sweetheart, Carly Dylan, when they were kids. Carly was best friends with Beau's first love, Tory Raznick, and the four of them had been inseparable, until Tory was killed in a tragic car accident right after Zev and Carly had finished their first year of college. Tory had been like a sister to Nick and his siblings and like a daughter to his parents. Her death had devastated everyone, but it had broken Beau and Zev. They'd distanced themselves from the family. Beau had buried himself in work outside the area, and Zev had broken up with Carly, quit college, and taken off with nothing more than a backpack over his shoulder, leaving Nick to try to fill the voids his brothers had left behind and hold their grieving family together.

In the ten-plus years since, Beau had built a thriving contractor business and had fallen in love again and married Charlotte Sterling, the owner of the Sterling House. Zev became a successful treasure hunter and reconnected with Carly, and Nick had learned the hard truth about what putting one's heart on the line did to a man.

She put the top of her bun on her burger and said, "I still can't believe Zev and Carly reunited in such a flukish way."

After a decade apart, Zev and Carly had reconnected at Beau and Charlotte's wedding at the Sterling House, the same place the awards banquet for Trixie's race had taken place.

"Jilly says that the inn has magic in it." Trixie nudged his arm. "Considering that's where Char and Beau met and Zev and Carly reconnected, I'd say she's right."

Nick didn't believe in magic, but something had definitely changed him that night he'd watched over her at the inn. "It's bizarre, don't you think? Zev traveled all over the world and met thousands of people, but he told me there hadn't been one woman who made him feel a damn thing. And the second he saw Carly, he felt like he'd been holding his breath for all those years and could finally breathe again."

"That's not bizarre, Nick. It's *fate*." She took a bite of her burger, closed her eyes, and moaned.

Jesus. He looked away, taking a bite of his burger.

Pugsly finished eating and pawed at Nick's leg. Nick picked him up and set him on his lap. "I don't believe in fate. I believe in hard work and reality. Shit happens. Sometimes it's good, and sometimes it sucks."

"Then what do you call you being at JJ's Tuesday night when my brothers were giving me a hard time?" She took another bite, arching a brow.

He couldn't very well tell her that he hadn't been able to stay away. He fucking hated this. If she were any other woman, he'd take his fill and get her out of his system. He stabbed a hunk of potato with his fork and said, "A coincidence."

"You're such a guy."

No shit.

He filled her in on the rest of his family as they finished eating, and then they carried everything inside. Trixie began putting away the leftovers as Nick washed the dishes. When his phone on the counter dinged with a text, he motioned toward it and said, "Would you mind checking that for me in case it's Jax? He was trying to reach me earlier." Jax was a sought-after wedding gown designer. He often catered to celebrities and other wealthy clientele. But he was as down to earth as a guy could get and always made time to work with local folks. He and Nick hung out often.

She put a container of leftovers in the refrigerator. "Let me guess, you still haven't put a password on your phone."

"I got nothing to hide, darlin'. I hate the damn thing anyway."

She picked up the phone, opening the message, and rolled her eyes. "*Shayna.* I see your buckle bunnies are as classy as ever."

He'd met Shayna a couple of years ago at one of his exhibitions. They'd hooked up and had a good time, and when she blew through town, she'd hit him up for a repeat performance, no strings attached. Just the way he liked it. But in the last several months, thoughts of Trixie had left no room for any other woman.

"What're you talkin' about?" He dried his hands and took the phone to read the message. *Busy? Want to take a cowgirl for a ride?* He sure as hell did, but she was the wrong cowgirl. He put the phone on the counter and went back to washing the dishes.

Trixie threw the extra salad into a container. "Don't let me keep you from your hot Saturday night."

She said it teasingly, but the way she was manhandling the plastic container told him otherwise. "You're not."

"Then why aren't you answering her?" She put the container in the fridge, set the remaining dishes by the sink, and leaned against the counter beside him.

"No interest."

She grabbed a dish towel and began drying the dishes as he washed. "Nick, you can go have your booty call. I'm fine by myself."

"You *know* I don't go out when you're here." And lately he hadn't wanted to go anywhere but down to Oak Fucking Falls.

"Well, that's just stupid. If I were one of your harem and you blew me off without answering, I'd be pissed."

"Then it's a good thing you'll never be one of them." He ground his back teeth together.

"Damn right I won't." She grabbed the next dish before he put it in the drainer, and their eyes locked. Her scowl sparked flames in her eyes, and she yanked the plate from his hand. "Why are you like that, anyway?"

"Like what?" He grabbed another dish and scrubbed the hell out of it. "A red-blooded man?" His gaze drifted down her body, bringing a pulse of heat to his cock. "You can't tell me you don't enjoy a good time every now and then, Trix. I've seen the way you dance."

Her eyes narrowed. "A girl can dance seductively without taking home random guys, as you *know* since I stay with you every time I'm here."

"So you prefer men who you know rather than random guys?" *Good to know.*

Her cheeks flushed, but her challenging expression remained. She was fierce, but that blush was a first, and he liked it a hell of a lot more than he probably should.

"I'm not going to discuss my sex life with you," she said sharply, putting down the dish and throwing the towel on the counter.

He leaned closer. "Then don't ask about mine, darlin', because like I said, I got nothing to hide."

"I wasn't asking about your sex life," she snapped. "I was asking why you'd rather go out with groupies who sleep with Lord knows who else instead of having a real relationship with a woman who might actually make you happy."

He scoffed. "Anyone who needs someone else to make them happy is a sorry soul. Besides, I don't need a woman trying to control my every move."

"Not all women try to tell men what to do."

"Bullshit. Look at you right now."

She crossed her arms and lifted her chin, the defiance in her eyes intensifying the heat between them. "Have you ever even *had* a real relationship? I mean one longer than ten minutes in the sack."

"I don't know who you're messing around with, but ten minutes isn't even enough time to whet my appetite."

"Says every man on earth. You think you're different, but you're all the same. Interested in a quick roll in the hay and nothing more."

He stepped closer, and she inhaled so hard, her breasts brushed against him. "I have yet to meet a woman who holds my interest in and out of bed for more than a round or two."

She rolled her eyes.

"You're awful judgy for a girl who hasn't had a long-term boyfriend for as long as I've known her. I've seen you when you're out with Jilly, and I don't think you and I are all that different."

She squared her shoulders. "Prove it."

She was always pushing, *goading* him, until fire roared through his veins, and this time he didn't hold back. "I think you're looking for a guy to take you against the side of the barn one day and bend you over the kitchen table the next. Someone who won't kowtow to your every whim, who'll open the door for you and slap your ass as you walk through it."

Flames ignited in her eyes.

"You just gave away your hand, darlin'." He knew he was playing a dangerous game, but he was in too deep to back off. "Admit it. You don't want a safe guy in your bed every night, taking you for ten minutes, then queueing up a movie. You want a *real* man, who knows how to satisfy those fantasies of yours."

She glared at him, her nostrils flaring. "For your information, I want *love*, and with love comes passion *and* safety. I want the fucking fairy tale, and I'm not ashamed of it."

"You're so damn misguided, you're going to let some asshole hurt you." *And that pisses me off.* "You want to know what love brings, Trix?" He was pissed that Trixie pushed him into saying things he shouldn't, and even angrier at himself for taking it so far, but there was no stopping the truth from coming out. "Love brings *destruction*."

Sadness rose in her eyes, cutting him like a knife.

"That's not true," she insisted. "Love *heals*. It's caring enough about someone that you'd do anything to help them feel better. It's trusting someone enough to be yourself with them in good times *and* bad and accepting *all* of their moods. It's supporting their dreams and knowing they'll support yours. Love is *good*, Nick. It makes everything else worthwhile."

There had been a time when he'd believed that, and he wished to hell it were true, but he knew better. "If you'd watched your brothers' hearts break and your family fall apart at the seams, you'd think otherwise. I'm going to muck out the stalls." He grabbed his phone and stormed out before he said anything else he'd regret.

TRIXIE STARED AFTER him, wondering what the hell had just happened. She sank back against the counter, curling her fingers around the edge to stabilize herself against the emotions whipping through her. She'd seen him go after people when pushed, but he'd never turned all that power on her, much less said such blatantly sexual things *about* her. About others, sure, but never about her. She'd obviously struck a nerve, and she felt bad about that. She hadn't meant to start such a heated debate, but when she'd seen that text, she'd been consumed with jealousy she had no business feeling, which had made her angry, and she'd been unable to hold back. She knew he hooked up with women. He'd never hidden that from her, but seeing that text had made it real, and she'd wanted to know *why* he chose those types of women.

She *still* wanted to know why, but now she *also* wanted to know why he tied love to destruction, and why he'd said those things about his family when he had an incredible family who supported each other through thick and thin.

She hurt for him. But she was too distracted by the other things he'd said and the way he'd said them to think it through. He'd practically read her mind about the kind of man she wanted, and hearing *Nick* say those things had made her want *him* to be that man. She knew that was crazy, especially since he apparently had a warped view of love. But the raw hunger in his eyes, the greed in his voice, and the carnal desire that had pulsed between them, made her think he wanted her with the same bone-deep ache she wanted him. Had she imagined it? Was she misreading his anger for passion?

Her mind sped through the other things he'd said, lingering on his comment about her *never* being one of his women, and she knew she had misread him.

He *didn't* want her.

He was just being Nick, the guy who didn't like to be backed into a corner, who never started a fight but *always* finished it.

She was confused and disappointed and a little heartbroken. She stared at the door, wanting to go after him and knowing it was better to give him space.

A heavy sigh fell from her lips.

She took off his hat, clutching it against her chest as she headed into her bedroom. Despite the hurt and confusion, she was consumed with worry for the man, the friend she cared about so deeply and the pain he was in from whatever secrets he was keeping.

Chapter Five

AFTER SHOWERING, TRIXIE put on a pair of comfortable shorts and a tank top and sat on her bed with her laptop looking over the business plan she'd put together in the days before she'd arrived, trying not to overthink things with Nick. But her gaze kept drifting to his hat on the dresser, making it impossible not to think about every word he'd said. They'd argued and challenged each other before, but he'd never stormed off. This was different, and it felt personal. Not just because of what he'd said about her, but also because of what he'd revealed about himself.

If you'd watched your brothers' hearts break and your family fall apart at the seams, you'd think otherwise.

Pushing to her feet, she paced, trying to puzzle out his past. She knew he'd been talking about when Beau and Zev had left home, but beyond telling her why they'd taken off, he'd never talked about that time in his life. If his family had struggled to hold things together, she'd never seen it or heard about it, though she was sure they'd all been affected by what had happened.

She picked up his hat, holding it against her chest again.

What aren't you telling me?

She shoved her feet into her boots and pulled open the glass doors that led to the patio, stepping into the balmy night. As she closed the doors, she heard the faint sound of Nick's guitar, and her heart constricted. She loved listening to him play and loved listening to him sing even more. But he refused to sing in front of her or anyone else. Usually, she'd let him be and would chill on the patio, secretly enjoying his music. But not after the bomb he'd dropped. She wasn't about to let her friend think love meant *destruction* for the rest of his life. She had no idea what kinds of secrets he was harboring, but it didn't matter. She wasn't going to let the stubborn mule stew in his heartache alone.

She followed the sounds of his guitar toward the pasture. A few minutes later she saw him sitting on the hill in the distance. He was shirtless, one knee bent, gazing out at the horses as he strummed his guitar. Goldie and Rowdy sat by his feet, and she was sure the dark bundle beside him was Pugsly. She approached them slowly, soaking in the rare moment when Nick's every muscle wasn't on full alert. But even before the dogs sensed her, Nick whipped his head in her direction, those dark eyes narrowing as she neared. The dogs barked and dashed toward her.

"Hi, guys." As she knelt to love them up, Nick turned away, the muscles in his jaw bunching. She scooped up Pugsly, letting her grunty boy give her kisses as she made her way to Nick. Goldie and Rowdy took turns nosing and licking her free hand.

"*Here*," Nick barked, and the dogs trotted over to him.

He continued playing the guitar. He must have come in to shower when she was in her room, because his hair was wet, and he smelled like soap, man, and frustration all wrapped up into one incredibly muscular, broody package. She'd always loved his body. He had just the right amount of chest hair, and she'd thought about how it would feel beneath her fingers and brushing over her breasts too many times to count. But she wasn't there to admire his physique. That was just a bonus.

"Hi." She lowered herself to the grass beside him.

He nodded, jaw tight, eyes on the horses as he played the guitar.

Pugsly stood on her lap, noisily breathing and staring at Nick, but Nick didn't even look over. That made her a little nervous. He adored Pugsly.

"Have you cooled down yet, or should I get the hose?"

He slid her an unamused look.

"Why are you so mad?" She petted Pugsly. "If anyone should be pissed, it's *me*."

He continued playing, his brows slanting in confusion.

"You said some serious shit about me, Nick," she reminded him.

"Didn't hear you denying it," he said gruffly.

"You think you know me."

A slow grin climbed across his face, but he continued staring straight ahead.

"What's that shit-eating grin for?"

He didn't respond.

"What*ever*. What was all that stuff you said about your family? Do you really think love equates to destruction?"

His jaw clenched.

"Why? What happened after Tory died and your brothers left?"

His chest expanded, and he looked away.

"I'm not leaving until you talk to me," she said.

Tension billowed off him, and he continued strumming his

guitar.

"I saw a crack in your armor, and you hate that, don't you?"

His eyes narrowed.

"You want everyone to think you're untouchable, but I know you, Nick. I've seen you sleep in the barn with your horses when they were acting out of sorts and pamper Goldie when she was pregnant. I was with you at the county fair when we found that lost little girl, and you were hell on wheels tracking down her parents. You *feel* a heck of a lot, and that's a good thing. But not when you lock it inside and let it eat away at you."

He kept strumming that damn guitar.

"*Talk* to me, Nick. I'm your friend. I care about you."

She put Pugsly on the grass and grabbed the neck of his guitar. He glowered at her, but she didn't care. She tore it from his hands and put it in the grass, scrambling onto his lap. Goldie and Rowdy jumped up on all fours as she wound her arms around Nick's neck, clinging to him.

"*Trixie*," he warned. "Get *up*."

"No. I'm sitting here until you talk to me."

He gritted his teeth. "Get your ass up."

"*Nope.*" She held him tighter. "Tell me what happened all those years ago."

"You don't want to know."

"Yes I do. I know you're hurting, and that hurts me."

"The only thing that's going to be hurting is your ass if you keep sitting there."

Before she could process his threat, he grabbed her by the waist and plopped her down on the grass. He shot to his feet, sending the dogs into an excited flurry of commotion. "Stop bringing up shit I don't want to talk about," he growled as he walked away.

She ran in front of him, blocking his path. "*No.* Like it or not, I care about your feelings."

"Then *stop* pissing me off." He stepped around her.

She followed him. "I just want to help, Nick. Maybe talking about it will help."

"Help *what?*" he shouted, stalking toward her. "What do you want to hear, Trixie? That my brothers left a fucking black hole in everyone's lives? That not only did our family lose Tory, who was at our house every damn day from the time she was a little kid, like a sister to all of us, but then we also lost Beau and Zev? And then Carly when she left for good? That my fucking mother cried at night worrying that she'd lost her sons forever? Or that Jilly cried for weeks because she thought she'd never see them again? That she begged me to go after them? But I couldn't leave because someone had to pick up the fucking pieces they left behind." He loomed over her, hands fisted. "What part of that are you going to *help* with? The past is the past, Trixie. I was fine then, and I'm fine now."

Tears burned her eyes at the pain and anger coming out of him, but the walls he put up, the temporary-at-best women he saw, were all suddenly making sense. "You were there for everyone else, but who was there to pick up your pieces?"

His eyes bored into her. "I didn't have any fucking pieces."

"Bullshit." She lifted her chin, trying to keep her lower lip from quivering. "You suffered the same losses. You're so close to your family, Nick. I've heard stories about how close you and Beau were as teenagers, how competitive and there for each other you were, and how you watched over Zev. You must have been devastated, losing them."

"So what? My parents had enough shit on their plates. They

didn't need to hear that one more person missed the two sons they couldn't bring home. I wasn't a kid when Beau and Zev left. I knew what they were doing and why they were doing it. They loved too much, and it *broke* them. I don't blame *them* for being too weak to stick around."

"That's not weak, Nick; it's brokenhearted."

His jaw clenched. "Same fucking thing."

Her heart was breaking for *him*. He was so angry, so insistent that he was some kind of unfeeling robot, when she knew otherwise. Tears slipped down her cheeks. "No, it's not."

"Aw, come on. Don't fucking cry."

"I can't help it," she said angrily. "You're one of my best friends, and now I think everything your family went through broke you, too."

His expression softened. "I'm not broken, Trix. I like my life just the way it is. I created it the way I wanted it." He gathered her in his arms.

"Yeah, without anyone around you." Her voice cracked. "Alone on your ranch, when you should be surrounded by friends and family."

"Don't be sad, darlin'. I've got friends around me all the time; they're just different from what other people have. I've got Pugs, Goldie, and Rowdy. I've got Lady and Romeo and the rest of my buds." He tipped her chin up, gazing into her eyes with that pleading look he got on the rare occasion when she was sad. "I've got the best female friend a guy could have. Why do I need some other chick eating my burgers and giving me shit?"

"Because you have so much love in you, Nick. You deserve to know what it's like to *be* loved."

"That's what family's for."

"I'm pretty sure your family doesn't want to climb into a hot shower with you at the end of a long day and wash your back or lie naked in your arms beneath the stars after you've made love in the field, dreaming of the future."

He *almost* smiled. "Yeah, that'd be weird."

She stepped out of his arms, a dull ache brewing in the pit of her stomach. "You really don't want to know what it feels like to be loved so deeply that you're *everything* to someone else? The center of their world? Or what it's like to love someone so much that you think about them and want to be with them every second?"

"I've already got that." He picked up Pugsly and kissed his head. "Right, Pugs?"

"That makes me sad. I look at my parents, and Brindle and Trace, and Morgyn and Graham, and I see how happy they are, and I want that. And yes, love hurts sometimes, but Beau found love again, and Zev and Carly never lost their love for each other. Look at your parents, Nick. You describe how broken they were, but their love pulled them through. Doesn't that mean anything to you?"

"Sure. I'm happy for all of them. But you know me, darlin'."

"Yeah, I do." *You love hard and unconditionally. You put your needs last after all creatures—big, small, two legged, and four legged.*

He draped an arm over her shoulder, heading for the fence. "I'm a selfish, arrogant prick, and I sure as hell don't believe in fairy tales." He let out a loud whistle and hollered, "*Yayaya!* Come *on*, guys!"

The horses ran in from the dark corners of the pasture, their gorgeous manes flying in the moonlight. Nick never ended a night—rain, sleet, or snow—without saying good night to them. The horses crowded around him at the fence, tossing their heads and pawing impatiently as he loved them up one by one, speaking in a warmer tone than he did to most humans. The horses in the back of the herd pushed forward, craning their necks, vying for a fair share of his attention. Trixie wanted to be right up there with them.

She was wrong about Nick. He wasn't broken. But he was the one who was misguided. Or maybe he was just fearful of being vulnerable and appearing weak. Either way, she'd never known a stronger man, and if anyone deserved a fairy tale, it was the guy who took on everyone else's burdens as his own and expected nothing in return—and that was Nick Bullheaded Braden to a T.

Chapter Six

NICK GREETED SUNDAY morning the same way he greeted most days, sipping coffee on the veranda between the house and the garage as the sun crept over the mountains, serenaded by birds chirping and the gentle shuffling of leaves rustling in the trees. Ribbons of gold, orange, and yellow bled into the dusky sky, spreading light over the horses grazing in the pasture. Goldie and Rowdy were already hard at work, doing their rounds down by the chickens and goats, and Pugsly lay snoring on Nick's lap.

Nick had always appreciated the beauty of Mother Nature and all the torrents she brought. But there was something about watching the dawn of a new day that centered him, and this morning he needed that more than most. By the time he and Trixie had turned in last night, they had devoured half of the cobbler and were joking around as they normally did. But alone in his room, he'd tossed and turned, unable to get her tears and all the shit she'd said out of his head. When he'd finally fallen asleep, he'd had a scorching dream about taking a shower with her, or rather, *taking* her *in* the shower. He'd woken up hot, hard, and horny as hell. The cold shower that had followed had barely taken the edge off.

He spotted the dogs running toward the front of the house and smiled to himself. They were great watchdogs, keeping predators away from the other animals, but they sucked as guard dogs against humans. They were all kisses and snuggles, which made them great companions. Especially since they didn't challenge every damn thing he said and did.

The dogs barked, and he looked toward the front yard. Trixie was jogging toward the veranda wearing black spandex shorts and a pink sports bra. Heat spread through Nick like wildfire. Her hair was pinned up in a ponytail, and when she flashed that knockout smile, it hit him right in the center of his chest.

"Hey, cowboy," she said, slowing to a walk as she came onto the veranda.

"How's it going?"

She sat beside him, and Rowdy and Goldie flanked her, begging for attention. "Good. I knocked out a couple of miles and saw Walt on my way back."

"Oh yeah? How's he doing?" Nick knew he was okay. He'd just spoken to him two days ago. Walt was seventy-nine years old but swore he felt sixty, and he had a soft spot for Trixie.

"He's as flirty as ever. He looks good, though. I swear he never ages. I wonder why he never got married. He's so charming."

Nick set Pugsly on the ground and pushed to his feet, unwilling to go down that rabbit hole again. "What's with you and all the marriage talk lately?"

"I guess last night's conversation is still on my mind." She loved up Rowdy. "*You* brought it up when you told me about Zev."

He picked up his mug and headed for the door.

She followed him into the kitchen. "What time are we seeing Travis?"

"After lunch." He washed his mug and grabbed his hat from the table. "I've got to take care of the animals, fix the fence on the lower pasture, and run a couple of errands before we go." Nick had cleared his afternoon because he knew that once she saw those miniature horses, she'd want to spend hours with them.

"Great! I'll help. That'll give me time to run a few ideas by you about Rising Hope. Just give me a second to put on my boots."

He eyed her tanned, taut stomach, remembering the feel of her on his lap last night, the warmth of her freshly showered skin, and the floral scent of her bodywash. His mind scooped up the thought of Trixie in the shower and ran with it, imagining stripping off those running clothes and living out last night's fantasy.

Great, now he was getting hard.

He looked away and said, "Don't you want to put on some clothes?" *Please put on some clothes. Otherwise I'm going to need a fucking ice bath.*

"Don't be silly. I'm just going to get dirty again. I'll be right back." She tossed a wink over her shoulder as she headed for her bedroom.

About a dozen scenarios of getting *dirty* with Trixie flooded his mind. He filled a glass with ice water and guzzled it. It was official. Trixie Fucking Jericho was going to kill him one slick-tongued comment at a time.

And now he was thinking about her tongue.

THE BONER GODS must have taken pity on Nick, because when Trixie came out of the house to go see Travis later that afternoon, gone were the skimpy shorts and sports bra. She was looking at her phone, wearing jeans and a blue sleeveless button-down shirt that she usually tied above her belly button, but it was tucked in.

He kind of missed that belly-baring shirt, but he was glad Travis wouldn't see it. She rarely wore shirts that didn't reveal at least a sliver of her taut, tanned stomach, and she never cared when people gave her shit for it. Hell, she'd always climbed onto his lap, flashed the same killer smile, teased and goaded him, too. She hadn't changed a bit the whole time he'd known her, which meant his sudden and insatiable desire for her was all on him.

She shoved her phone into her back pocket and looked up. She'd done her hair and put on makeup. Her gorgeous smoky eyes peered out from beneath her cowgirl hat. Silver earrings dangled from her ears, and a simple gold chain hung around her neck. She never wore jewelry. So why was she now? She looked like a million fucking bucks.

For Travis.

He opened the door of his truck for her and said, "Why'd you get all dolled up to go see horses?" As she climbed in, he got a whiff of that feminine bodywash. How had he ever ignored those things before?

"Because you're doing me a favor by hooking me up with him. I can't have your friends thinking I'm not a serious businesswoman."

He chewed on that all the way to Travis's and realized she was right, and she was smart to take that into consideration. He was proud of her for that and felt like an idiot for being jealous.

When they arrived at Travis's horse farm, he helped her out of the truck, and she said, "I'm excited to start choosing horses. I still can't believe I'm *really* doing this. Did I tell you I talked to Tempest? We're having lunch tomorrow at Emmaline's." Emmaline O'Connor was one of Jillian's best friends, and she owned a café in town.

"No, that's great. She should be a big help."

"I think so, too. Thanks again, Nick, for offering to let me stay with you. I probably would have hemmed and hawed for another few months before taking the plunge. I think I needed someone to say, *Hey, what are you waiting for?*" She stood by the side of the truck, gazing up at him, and said, "Thanks for being that guy."

He felt that unfamiliar tug in his chest again. "You've got killer instincts and more confidence than anyone I know. I can't imagine you hemming or hawing over anything. You always go after what you want."

She shifted her gaze to the barns and paddocks, and when she glanced at him, it was almost bashfully. "Not always."

Their eyes held just long enough for him to twist around that response and her new bashful smile until he was good and confused. He forced himself to break the connection and said, "We should find Travis."

As they crossed the parking lot, he spotted Travis walking out of one of the barns. Travis Helms was a single father in his early thirties, and according to Jillian, he was a *tall, dark glass of champagne*, whatever the hell that was supposed to mean. His adorable three-year-old ringlet-haired daughter, April, toddled beside him in overall shorts and pink rubber boots, holding the lead rope of a palomino miniature horse. She was so damn cute, she almost made Nick want kids.

"Oh my gosh, *Nick*. Look how cute that little girl is!" Trixie exclaimed.

He waved to Travis. The way his buddy's eyes lit up at the sight of Trixie made Nick wish Trixie *wasn't* such a savvy businessperson to have gotten all dolled up. No, that wasn't true. He was glad she had a great mind. Her instincts were easily as good as his, and the kicker was, it didn't matter what Trixie's hair or clothes looked like or if she was wearing makeup. She could be covered in dirt and she'd still shine brighter than any woman he'd ever seen.

Trixie leaned closer, lowering her voice. "Is that Travis? You didn't tell me your friend was *hot*."

Nick gritted his teeth. "That's his *daughter* walking beside him."

"He's married?" she asked.

Christ. Really? "Divorced."

Travis had married his high school sweetheart right after graduating from college, and they'd divorced before finding out she was pregnant. Travis and Jenny shared custody of April. Nick had never known a divorced couple who had gotten along better than the two of them.

"Interesting," she whispered.

He narrowed his eyes.

Trixie giggled and waved to Travis, walking toward him and calling out with all her Southern sweetness, "Hey there!"

"Hi. You must be Trixie. I'm Travis. Nick's told me great things about you." He shook Trixie's hand, lifting his chin in greeting to Nick.

"Has he? That's good to know." Trixie eyed Nick curiously. "He had great things to say about you, too. Thanks for making time to show me around."

April toddled over and exclaimed, "*Nick*, see my hawsey?"

"I sure do, darlin'. That's one fine-looking horse," he said as April walked around him and grabbed at his back pocket.

"Wow, even little girls can't keep their hands off you," Trixie teased.

He gave Trixie a deadpan look and whipped a lollipop out of his pocket.

April's eyes lit up. "Lolli!"

He crouched as he unwrapped the candy for her and tapped his cheek. April pressed her tiny lips there, and he handed her the lollipop.

Travis touched her shoulder and said, "What do you say?"

"Mine!"

Everyone laughed.

"Close enough," Nick said. "Remember to give the stick to me or Daddy when you're done." He caught Trixie watching them with a dreamy expression, and she quickly averted her eyes. "How's it going, Travis?"

"Great. I'm really glad you set this up." Travis's gaze flicked to Trixie.

I bet you are.

Trixie crouched beside April and said, "Hi. I'm Trixie, a friend of Nick's. What's your name?"

"Apwil. This is my hawse, Dolly."

"She's *beautiful*," Trixie said as Dolly lowered her head for April to pet her. "And she sure loves you."

Oh yeah, you'll do great working with kids.

"You could pet her," April said.

Trixie grinned up at Travis as she petted the horse and said, "She's a cutie pie."

"Thanks." Travis looked lovingly at his daughter. "Around here Peaches is the boss."

"*Peaches?* What an adorable nickname," Trixie said, rising to her feet.

"You'll never believe this now with all her curls, but when she was born she had a head full of peach fuzz." Travis shrugged and said, "The nickname stuck."

"I love that." Trixie pushed to her feet and said, "You bring her to work with you?"

"We live in a house on the back of the farm, and my grandmother lives in that house." He pointed to the old farmhouse up the hill. "She watches her for me, but Peaches wanted to show Nick this week's favorite horse."

Nick had known Travis for years, and April since she was born. They didn't see each other all that often, but when Travis was going through his divorce, he and Nick would often grab a beer. Travis watched over Nick's animals when Nick traveled, and Nick helped out when Travis needed backup. And Nick always brought a little something for April when he stopped by.

"Why don't you tell me what you're looking for and we'll get started," Travis suggested.

Trixie bubbled over with enthusiasm as she told Travis all about her plans.

"We can definitely help you get started," Travis said.

"Are any of your younger horses, say six or seven months old, halter trained or comfortable with people?" Trixie asked, stealing a glance at Nick and April.

"Absolutely," Travis said. "We're lucky to have several volunteers, which allows us to be more hands-on with the horses.

We start halter training shortly after birth and lead the foals with their mothers. Do you know what size minis you're looking for?"

"I've been thinking a lot about that. I want to get three horses, two that are thirty-two to thirty-six inches to accommodate the height of a hospital bed, and a smaller one for younger children. Maybe twenty-four inches or so."

"Great." Travis looked at Nick and said, "Why don't we head down to see the horses."

"I go!" April exclaimed.

"We're going, darlin'." Nick walked with April, giving Trixie a chance to talk with Travis about the horses. Trixie was impressive as hell, asking all the right questions about his breeding practices, veterinary care, and other things. She radiated confidence, and Nick could see that Travis was equally impressed.

"Nick said you wouldn't mind if I came by a couple of times this week to get a feel for the horses. Is that still okay?"

Travis nodded. "Of course. We recommend it, actually. We want to make the best matches for you and the horses. I've just turned them out, so you'll have plenty of time to watch them in their natural surroundings and see which ones are naturally curious, get a feel for their sizes, and that sort of thing." Unlike regular-size horses, miniature horses couldn't be left out to pasture for too long or they'd eat themselves into oblivion. "When you're ready, you can choose a few and we'll bring them up to the barn. That can be done today, tomorrow, or whenever your schedule allows, so you can see how you feel about them individually. Once you've narrowed down your selections, then we can see how they do together. For some people, connections are immediate, but we have other people who take weeks to decide. There's never a rush on our end, and since you're looking for therapy horses, it's all about temperament and approachability, which makes taking your time even more important."

"Great, thank you. I think we've covered all the bases."

As they neared the pasture, Travis said, "So, how do you and Nick know each other?"

"We met through his cousins in Peaceful Harbor when I was a teenager. I've competed in some of the same races as Nick's brother Graham and his cousin Ty."

"You're kidding? We've got that in common, too. I grew up at the Harbor with Ty, Sam, and the rest of the Braden gang. I'm a race guy, too. What type of races do you compete in?"

"Running, swimming, biking. Whatever I have time for. I did the Mad Prix last year."

Nick watched April leading her horse, trying to ignore the uncomfortable twinge of jealousy nagging at him.

"That's a tough race," Travis said. "Sam just sent out an email about a river race he's throwing together in September. Did you hear about it?" Sam owned Rough Riders, a rafting and adventure company in Peaceful Harbor.

"No. I haven't checked emails in a couple of days."

"It's up on their website. You should check it out. It'll be fun."

"I definitely will." She looked at Nick. "I wish I could get Nick into rafting, but I can't even get him to go running with me."

Nick flashed a cocky grin and said, "Some people are built for running; others are built to *ride*."

Trixie rolled her eyes, and Travis chuckled.

"When do you run, Trixie? I do a few miles in the mornings

when my ex-wife has Peaches, and I'd love company," Travis said as they came to a pasture where miniature horses were playing and grazing.

That twinge turned to a spear, slicing through Nick, and he *hated* it. He had no business being jealous over a woman who could never be *his*, and Travis was a great guy. But that didn't stop the gnawing in his gut.

April dropped Dolly's lead and toddled over to the fence, her ringlets springing with each step. She stuck her head through the fence and hollered, "Hawsey! C'mere!"

As Nick picked up the lead, Trixie's eyes connected with his, a coy smile sliding into place as she said, "I run around six in the morning. I'd love company, too."

Nick turned away, gritting his teeth as they made plans to run tomorrow morning and exchanged phone numbers.

"They coming!" April announced.

"They're so cute," Trixie exclaimed. "Nick, look at the white one!"

"She's got a gentle temperament. We call her Mama Hen," Travis said, taking Dolly's lead from Nick. "Thanks, man."

"No problem."

April squealed with delight as the horses neared.

"Careful, darlin'." Nick crouched beside April to make sure she didn't get bitten and put an arm around her as the horses put their noses through the fence.

April giggled. "They kiss me!"

"Keep your hand flat, sweetheart," Nick reminded her.

"That one's so pretty, and look at…" Trixie sighed. "That's *so* sweet."

Nick glanced over to see what horse she was talking about, but she was watching him with that tender expression again.

She quickly turned away, as she had earlier, and began raving about the horses. *What the hell was that?* Had he imagined that look? The way his mind worked around Trixie lately, he wouldn't doubt it.

"Why don't I take Peaches up to the house for her nap and give you time to check out the horses." Travis hoisted April onto his hip.

"Dolly," she said sleepily.

"I've got her, Peach." Travis showed her the lead. "Nick, Trixie, I'll come back in a bit, but you've got my number. Shoot me a text if you need anything."

"Sounds great, man. Thanks." Nick winked at April. "Sleep well, darlin'."

April buried her face in her daddy's neck, and Travis headed up to the house.

"Thank you!" Trixie called after him. "Nick, there are *eleven* horses at the fence line. You know what that tells me? Travis's staff is good to these babies." She crouched so she was eye to eye with the smaller horses and tugged Nick's pants leg. "Come here."

He knelt beside her.

"Look at them, Nick. Don't you want to bring them all home?"

"You know I do."

"I realize I have to get to know them to see which ones are best suited for therapy, but I could just sit here and look at them all afternoon."

"We've got all day, darlin'." He sat on the grass and patted the space beside him.

Her eyes widened. "You don't mind?"

"This is your future. We can't put a time limit on that. We

have dinner with my parents and Jax and Jilly tonight, but we can put that off if need be."

"No. I want to see everyone. I miss them."

She sat down and leaned against his side. They didn't talk as they watched the horses. There was no rushing to get to the next thing or needing to fill the silence. Every now and then Trixie would laugh as the horses played, and it made Nick smile. This was how it had always been with them. But like everything else, this time it felt different. Not only was he realizing the ways in which his feelings had changed toward her, but he was also noticing other things about himself, like how often he smiled when she was there and how relaxed he felt with her when she wasn't goading him. He leaned back on his palms, and Trixie moved closer, resting her head on his shoulder. He waited for that fire to burn inside him, but it didn't come. What he felt was even more dangerous. He could sit there all damn day, listening to her sweet sighs and soft laughs as she began this new adventure in her life.

A while later, she said, "There's such a difference between horse farmers and cattle ranchers. My brothers love horses, but not the way you and I do. They love the wild ones, but they'd never want to sit and watch them like this to see how they interact or learn their idiosyncrasies. I think that's the best part of getting to know all kinds of animals. You can learn so much by observing them in their natural surroundings. If you spend enough time with them, you realize that even the most aggressive ones have their tender moments."

Why did he get the feeling she wasn't only talking about horses?

He rested his head against hers, wondering how a woman could torture him one minute and make him feel like he never wanted the moment to end in the next?

TRIXIE COULDN'T HAVE asked for a better day. They'd spent hours observing the horses, and by the end of the afternoon, they'd chosen six clear winners in the temperament department. She'd arranged to come back tomorrow, and she was looking forward to getting to know the horses better. But it wasn't just the horses that had made the day so wonderful. She'd loved spending downtime with Nick just as much as she loved working with him on his ranch. She got to enjoy totally different sides of him. While working on the ranch, Nick was a rugged man on a mission, gruff, demanding, and layered with sarcasm and grit, which left Trixie hyped up and often revved up, too. But afternoons like today left her feeling drunk on him.

As they climbed out of his truck in front of his parents' brick and stone manor-style house, she looked forward to being treated to yet another side of Nick. Around his family, he fell into a place between that gruff rancher and laid-back friend. He was less guarded around them, but not really *open*, and he was a different kind of fun.

Nick helped her out and closed the passenger door, asking, "What's that goofy smile for?"

"I'm just excited to see everyone." *And that other side of you.*

She headed up the walk, and Nick hooked his finger into her belt loop, tugging her toward the side yard. "Sounds like they're out back."

As they neared the backyard, Jillian's voice and Jax's laughter rang out. Jax was playing basketball with their father, and

Jillian was sitting on the patio with Nick's mother. Coco, Jax's dog, was lying on the grass by the basketball court. Coco was one of Goldie's pups from the same litter as Rowdy.

Coco darted toward them, and Jillian popped to her feet, looking cute in tan cinch-waisted shorts that made her petite frame look even tinier and a flowy white top with gold trim—one of her signature pieces. "They're here!" She ran behind Coco in her wedged heels as if she were wearing sneakers, her burgundy hair flying over her shoulders.

Nick and Trixie crouched to love Coco up.

"Hey, sweet girl," Trixie said as Coco licked her cheek, then kissed Nick's, going back and forth as they petted her.

"You watching your daddy lose?" Nick joked.

"Hey, don't talk shit to my dog," Jax hollered, following Jillian across the lawn as their parents joined hands in the middle of the yard. Jax was shirtless, his expensive-looking navy shorts riding low on his hips, leaving all of his lean muscles on display. He carried himself with an air of confidence, but not arrogance, and looked more like a model or an athlete than a wedding gown designer, with short, light-brown hair, a chiseled jaw, and eyes that held a hint of mystery.

"I missed you!" Jillian said, hugging Trixie. "I can't believe I get a whole month with you! We need to plan some get-togethers."

"She *just* got here," Nick said.

"*So?*" Jillian said.

Nick's jaw clenched. "Give her a little breathing space before you start throwing her to the wolves."

Jillian patted his back and said, "She doesn't need a body-guard this month, Nicky. I'll watch out for her." She was the only person Nick allowed to call him that, and Trixie secretly loved that he had a soft spot for his younger sister.

"You need a babysitter more than she does." Nick went back to petting Coco.

"Hey, beautiful." Jax kissed Trixie's cheek, embracing her.

Jax wasn't wild like Zev, serious like Beau or Graham, or gruff like Nick. He had a personality all his own: calm, cool, and collected. But he and Nick *did* have one thing in common. They were both eternal bachelors.

"Be sure to save me a dance when you go out." Jax winked.

"*Christ*," Nick grumbled.

Trixie nudged Nick. He had always hated it when his brothers flirted with her. If it were up to him, she and Jillian would be locked away from all men. "I will definitely save you a dance, Jax, but your gaggle of groupies may not like it."

"That is *if* Trixie can make space on your dance card," their mother said. Lily Braden was a petite blonde with shoulder-length hair and a loving disposition. She drew Trixie into a warm embrace. "We're so glad you're here, honey."

"I've missed you guys," Trixie said. His parents had been married forever, like hers, and they'd always treated her like part of their family.

Nick kissed his mother's cheek. "Hi, Ma."

"Hi, sweetheart." Lily hugged him.

"Get in here, darlin'." Clint embraced Trixie. He was a relatively quiet man, with mostly gray hair and serious eyes.

Nick clapped his father on the back. "Good to see you, Pop."

"You look good, son. You look happy."

"Trixie has that effect on most guys," Jillian said, earning a shake of Nick's head.

Clint hiked a thumb at Nick. "Trixie, do you think you can

survive an entire month with this guy?"

"Well, he *is* easy on the eyes."

Nick flashed an arrogant and devastatingly hot grin.

"But we all know how bullheaded he is, so the jury is still out," Trixie added, earning a glare from Nick and laughs from everyone else. "Would you like help with dinner?"

"No, thank you, honey. It's almost ready," Lily said as they headed to the patio.

"Then we have time for a game of two on two." Jax draped an arm over Trixie's shoulder and said, "What do you say, gorgeous? Want to team up and show these two how it's done?"

"Heck yeah, I'm in. Jilly, do you want to play?" Trixie always asked if Jillian wanted to join them, even though everyone knew that she would sooner shave her head than play sports.

"Sure, right after I go skydiving." Jillian sauntered over to the patio with Coco on her heels and said, "I'll just be over here with Coco checking Tinder and cheering you on."

"Like hell you will," Nick said, and he and Jax stalked toward her.

"Relax. I'm not really going to cheer you on." Jillian laughed.

Trixie knew she wasn't on Tinder, but it was fun watching her tease her brothers.

Nick dove for Jillian's phone. She shrieked and ran across the yard. Jax caught up with her and snagged her phone.

"Give it back!" Jillian yelled through her laughter.

"Right after I delete all the dating apps," Jax said, poking around on her phone.

Jillian might not be on Tinder, but she was on other dating apps. Trixie snuck up behind Jax, and then she ran around him, grabbed the phone, and sprinted across the lawn with Jax and

Nick chasing after her.

"Run, Trixie!" Jillian cheered.

Their mother and father watched with amusement for a minute before Clint hollered, "Boys!" causing Jax and Nick to stop cold. "Jilly's an adult. Leave her alone now."

Jillian stuck out her tongue at them.

"Oh, *Jilly*," Lily said with a shake of her head.

Trixie gave Jillian her phone and said, "What is with you Bradens not locking your screens?"

"I hate having to unlock it," Jillian said. "Thanks for saving my dating apps."

"You owe me one."

Jillian's eyes lit up. "When we go out, I'll let you take your pick of the hottest guys."

"Let's go, Jericho." Nick grabbed Trixie's arm, dragging her toward the basketball court.

Jax caught up with them and said, "Nick, are you going to keep that cowboy hat on?"

"What do you think?"

Jax arched a brow. "Have it your way. I know Trix can play in her boots, but you're not as coordinated as she is. You might want to borrow a pair of sneakers from Dad."

Nick might not have been into mainstream sports, but he was as agile as he was powerful, especially in his boots, and Jax knew it. But like Jillian, he loved to mess with his siblings.

Nick cocked his arm, as if he were going to punch Jax, and Jax shuffled out of reach, laughing. Nick mumbled, "Fool."

Jax was fit, but Nick was massive. Trixie had a feeling if Nick ever wanted to hurt someone, one punch was all it would take to do serious damage.

After a round of witty banter, they started playing. Nick

dribbled the ball, his eyes darting around Trixie as she waved her hands, blocking him. Jax stuck to their father like glue.

"Don't drop it, cowboy," she teased, arms out to the side and leaning in.

He darted right, and she followed, but he turned, doubling back faster than her, and blew right past his father and Jax, dunking the ball. His fist shot up in the air. "Hell yeah!" He smirked at Trixie and said, "That's how it's done, darlin'."

"Nice shot!" his father said, high-fiving him.

"We let you have that one," Jax said.

Nick shook his head. "You're losing your touch, bro. What happened? Did you take a bridesmaid home last night and she wear you out after ten minutes?"

"Two bridesmaids, and it was about three *hours*," Jax countered. "Jealous? We all know the only one keeping you up at night is an old, half-blind dog."

Nick scoffed. Jax took the ball to the head of the court.

"You'd better cover Trixie," Clint said to Nick as he went to cover Jax.

Nick set his dark eyes on Trixie, his lips curving slyly. "Hey, hot stuff."

As Jax began dribbling, she imagined kissing Nick to throw him off his game, but she knew if she ever got enough courage to do that, she wouldn't want to stop. She tucked that delicious thought away and said, "About time you noticed."

She ducked under his arm, and Jax threw her the ball. She sprinted toward the basket, dodging Nick's arms, and threw the ball back to Jax, who made the shot.

"Oh *yeah!*" She planted her hand on her hip. "What was that about how it's done, cowboy?"

Nick chuckled. "Nice play."

"Woo-hoo!" Jillian cheered. "You can't beat the dynamic duo of girl power *and* twin power!"

They played a few rounds, laughing and giving each other a hard time. The score was tied when Lily announced, "Dinner will be ready in five minutes," and she and Jillian headed into the house.

Trixie dribbled the ball, listening for Jax to say he was open. It was a balmy evening, but the summer air had nothing on the scorching heat blazing off Nick's body as he hovered over her back.

"You're gonna lose, hot stuff," he warned.

"I never lose." She shuffled right, then left, trying to look over her shoulder, but Nick was *right there*, his big body blocking her view. "Jax? Where are you?"

"Downtown!" he hollered, which was their code for "by the basket."

Trixie prayed for the best and darted to the right. Nick's arm swept around her, lifting her off her feet and crushing her back against his chest. She shrieked and cursed, clinging to the ball. "Put me down!"

In one swift move, Nick stole the ball with his free hand and heaved it toward the basket.

"No!" Trixie hollered.

Jax jumped up to block it, but it sailed just above his fingertips and into the net. Jax and Trixie yelled, "No!" at the same time Nick and Clint yelled, "Yes!"

Trixie pushed out of Nick's arms and shoved him with both hands. "You're a cheater!"

He scooped her up and tossed her over his shoulder, ignoring her kicking feet and flailing arms. Everyone laughed—including Trixie—as he said, "Looks to me like I'm the only guy on the court willing to do whatever it takes to win."

"Watch your back, Braden!" She smacked his ass. "You're going *down*."

He set her on her feet with a sinful look in his eyes and said, "I've never had any complaints in that department."

She lifted her chin and threw her shoulders back. "Then that makes two of us." She strode off the court with a determined sway in her hips, the heat of Nick's glare chasing her down like a shadow.

Chapter Seven

THERE WERE FEW things finer than enjoying a home-cooked meal with his family, and when Trixie joined them, it usually made those home-cooked meals even better. Nick's mother had made her famous melt-in-your-mouth chuck roast with all the fixings, including corn bread, which he normally devoured. But after the comment Trixie had made before walking off the basketball court, Nick's appetite was shot. He wanted to twist that comment into an invitation, but after watching her and Travis spark a connection that went beyond miniature horses, he couldn't stop the jealousy gnawing at him. She was driving him insane, and at the same time, she was sitting next to him at the table, laughing and joking with his family, nudging him conspiratorially as if she hadn't just sent his frigging mind reeling.

"Nick told me that Zev and Carly are getting married. I'm so happy for them. They give love a whole new meaning, right, Nick?" Trixie glanced at him with a mischievous look in her eyes.

Why did she always fuck with him? "Sure."

"They were fated to be," Trixie added.

"Like Beau and Char and Graham and Morgyn," Jillian said

as she cut a piece of meat. "I just wish old lady Fate would set her sights on me."

"When the time is right, you'll find love, honey." Even after what happened to Beau and Zev after Tory died, their mother still touted love, as if it were a cure-all.

"Did you ever think Beau and Zev would be open to love again after what happened with Tory?" Trixie asked.

His mother's expression turned thoughtful. "When they left all those years ago, I thought they'd be back in a few weeks or months, and when that didn't happen, I wasn't sure what to think. But I'd hoped, of course, that one day they would heal and eventually find love again."

"That was a difficult time for all of us," his father said, placing his hand over their mother's. They always sat near each other, rather than at either end of the table.

It struck Nick that Trixie did the same thing with him.

"It was like we lost four of our children that summer, and it was hard on everyone." Their father squeezed their mother's hand, his emotional gaze moving around the table. "Our kids were all growing up and trying to start their lives. Nick was making a name for himself in the horse industry, Jax and Jilly were getting ready to leave for college, and Graham was in high school, but our family was no longer whole. There's a big difference between sending your kids off to school to start their lives and having them leave home because they're grieving, lost, and heartbroken. I remember feeling like I could help them with trouble at college, but I had no idea how to help them through that type of grief from who knows how many miles away."

Nick's chest constricted.

His father had put up such a brave front that summer. But

like with Trixie's fears, Nick had seen through the smoke and mirrors to his father's devastation. He'd never forget the night he'd stumbled into the house at one o'clock in the morning about a week after his brothers had left. He'd heard a crash in his father's office, and he'd sprinted through the door and had found his father sitting at his desk with his head in his hands. His papers and the things that were normally on his desk were scattered on the floor, including a framed picture of their family and another of Beau, Tory, Zev, and Carly they'd taken at a high school dance. Seeing that mess had rocked Nick to his core. His father was the most even-keeled person Nick had ever known. He *never* lost control. Nick had asked if his father was okay. His father had lifted grief-stricken eyes and had tried so damn hard to school his expression, it had been painful to watch. *Of course. I'm just having a tough time with a project.* Nick had started picking up his father's things from the floor, but his father had put an arm around his shoulder, leading him out of the office—*I'll take care of that later, son. How was your night?*—as if it were just another night. Nick had learned a lot that evening, like the fact that it *was* just another night. A night in the life of their *new* normal.

"I definitely felt like I lost a sister when Tory died. I think we all did." Jillian looked across the table at Nick. "I worried all the time about Beau and Zev, remember, Nick?"

He'd never forget how often he'd find her stewing or crying because she couldn't reach them. He'd hold her while she cried and try to reassure her that they were okay and would be home at some point. He'd never understood how everyone else had sat back and let Beau and Zev drift so far away. That was why he'd tracked them down and had gone head-to-head with them many times over the years, trying to convince them to come home.

"I never understood why you didn't lean on me, Jills," Jax said.

"Because I would have just brought you down, and you were already having a hard time. But Nick was…" Jillian's brow furrowed. "I don't know. *Solid.*"

Jax cracked an amused grin. "Always the unbreakable cowboy."

Nick smirked. *Damn right.*

Trixie put her hand on his arm, giving it a squeeze, and said, "He is solid, isn't he? But even cowboys break sometimes."

Nick scoffed. "Not this one."

"Our Superman," his mother said, but there was something sad in her eyes that made his heart twist. She breathed deeply, and a small smile appeared. "Well, the past is behind us, and I'm thrilled that three of our boys have found love. Hopefully one day you'll all find love as special as ours."

"Some of us are too busy for love, Mom," Jax said.

"I don't mean *now*, sweetheart." Their mother's eyes skirted from Jax to Nick. "But one day a woman is going to knock you off your feet, and then you won't be able to do a darn thing but love her back, just like your brothers."

Nick stabbed a piece of meat with his fork and shoved it in his mouth. "Not me. I like my life just the way it is."

"You never know, Nicholas," his mother said. "Look how fast Graham fell in love with Morgyn. He was our most meticulous thinker, prepared for everything, studying outcomes and ramifications well before ever making a move. And then along came sweet Morgyn Montgomery with her whimsical lifestyle and infectious personality. Your brother was totally unprepared and instantly lovestruck."

"Don't get your hopes up, Mom," Nick said.

"I never do," she said. "In any case, we have a wedding to look forward to. Trixie, watch your mailbox for an invitation to Zev and Carly's wedding."

"I wouldn't miss it for the world, Mrs. B. Thank you."

His mother couldn't look more pleased. "Good. Now, please tell us how your business is coming along."

"Nick said he was going to introduce you to Travis Helms." Jillian's eyes sparked with excitement. "Isn't he tall, dark, and tasty?"

"*Christ*, Jilly," Nick muttered. "She went to see him about horses."

"So? That doesn't change the fact that he's the hottest single dad around." Jillian turned her attention back to Trixie. "All my friends adore him."

"I met him today, so I *totally* get it," Trixie said. "And his little girl, *Peaches*? Oh my gosh. She's the cutest!"

If Nick clenched his teeth any harder, they'd crack.

"Right? She's a doll," Jillian said.

"He was super helpful and really accommodating. I'm going back to assess the horses tomorrow afternoon, and he's letting me come by as many times as I need to until I make my decisions." Trixie took a drink and said, "It turns out he's into races, too. We're going running tomorrow morning together."

"You *are*?" Jillian's eyes widened. "Girl, you are so lucky."

"Why haven't you gone out with him?" Trixie asked.

Jillian shrugged. "Good question."

"Travis is such a nice young man. It sounds like you two have a lot in common, Trixie." His mother looked at Nick and said, "Wouldn't it be nice if Trixie met a wonderful man and fell in love while she was here? Then she'd be around all the time."

Trixie feigned wide-eyed innocence. "Yes, Nick, wouldn't that be great? Then you could see those lovely buckle bunnies every night of the week without me cramping your style."

Jax stifled a laugh.

Nick glowered at him.

"Don't get me started about those types of girls." His mother gave him a disapproving look. "They've been after Nick since he was a teenager."

"It's that Braden charm," Jax said. "It's a curse, really. So many women, so little time."

"It's his cowboy pheromones," Jillian chimed in. "It comes with the territory. Travis sure gives off a delicious scent, right, Trixie?"

Nick stabbed another hunk of meat. "Are you two going to talk about guys all night, or can we get back to Trixie's business?"

"I'm good with guy talk," Jillian teased.

His father chuckled.

"If I didn't know better, I'd say you were jealous," Jax said with an amused smirk.

"I'm not fucking *jealous*. I just don't want to talk about nonsense."

"Watch your language, son," his father said sternly.

"What would Nick have to be jealous about?" Jillian asked. "He and Trixie are just friends, and he has more women after him than he can shake a stick at."

Jax glanced at Nick and said, "If you say so."

"I thought we were talking about Trixie's business," Nick said as calmly as he could, which wasn't very calm at all. "Do you think we can get back to it?"

"I think that's best," his mother said, giving him a curious look. "Trixie, honey, what happens next?"

"I have so much to do between picking out and training the horses, going through the legal steps to create the business, and then actually getting started, my to-do list seems endless. Tempe is going to give me the lowdown on working with hospitals tomorrow, and I'm sure that will lead to a number of other things I haven't even thought about yet." She touched Nick's arm again. "I wasn't exactly standing on the platform ready to jump when Nick suggested I come here to do the legwork. It was just the nudge I needed."

She told them about her business plans, passion flowing in her every word, illuminating her beautiful face. Just hearing her enthusiasm calmed the gnarly, jealous beast inside him. Thankfully, the rest of their evening was far less stressful. They talked about Zev and Carly's wedding. It was going to be at a creek where they used to hang out, and the reception would be at Hilltop Winery, which was owned by their mother's family.

After dinner, Nick, Jax, and their father did the dishes while their mother and the girls sat out on the patio, their laughter floating in through the screen door.

"You did a good thing, son," his father said after they finished cleaning up.

"We always help clean up."

"He's talking about helping Trixie," Jax said, and headed out the patio doors.

"Oh. Thanks, Dad."

His father patted his shoulder. "You seem a bit tense tonight. Are you okay?"

"Fine."

"Then you're okay with Trixie going running with Travis?"

Nick leaned against the counter and crossed his arms. "Why wouldn't I be?"

"I don't know. Maybe because Jillian's right. Travis is as hot a commodity around here as you boys are. He's been divorced for quite some time. Rumor has it, he's looking for a wife, and Trixie is definitely the type of woman you bring home to Mom and Dad."

Tell me something I don't know. "It's her life."

His father nodded. "You're right, Nick. I don't know why I thought your lives were intertwined. I guess she's been staying at your place for so many years, it feels like she's your girl." A laugh tumbled from his lips. "I must be losing it in my old age. Come on. Let's go join the party."

Nick chewed on that for the rest of the night.

After saying goodbye to his parents, they walked out with Jillian and Jax.

"I had so much fun," Trixie said. "I love your parents."

"How about me?" Jax teased.

Trixie nudged him. "That goes without saying. The first thing I said to Nick when I arrived was how much I missed your handsome face. I doodle your name on my notepad with little hearts around it, too."

Nick chuckled.

"Most girls do," Jax said without missing a beat. "We should all go out for drinks sometime."

"That sounds fun," Trixie said.

"I'm loaded down with late meetings, but I could do Friday night at Tully's," Jillian suggested. "Or we could head up to Nova Lounge. There are always tons of great-looking guys there, and Jared gives me free drinks all the time."

Jared was Nick's buddy Jace Stone's younger brother, and

the owner of several restaurants, including Nova Lounge. He was a good guy but was known to be a player. Nick set his eyes on Jillian. "Why is Stone giving you free drinks?"

"Because he's a single guy and I'm a single woman, and it's none of your business," Jillian said snarkily.

Trixie eyed Nick as she said, "There's a better chance of the ladies distracting my bodyguard at Tully's."

"You're right. Tully's it is! We can get their to-die-for chocolate pie that you love." Jillian nudged Trixie. "You know who will probably be there? Fifty Shades of Sweetness. He's always out on Friday nights."

"Jon Butterscotch? He's such a flirt, but I *love* him," Trixie said. "I bet he signed up for Sam's race, too. I'd love to see him."

Jillian whipped out her phone. "I'll send him a text and let him know we'll be there."

"You've got to be shitting me," Nick grumbled.

"You look like you're going to kill someone," Jax said.

If Butterscotch puts a hand on Trixie, I just might. He needed to get a fucking grip, or this month was going to be hell.

ON THE DRIVE back to Nick's house, Trixie texted with Lindsay, telling her about meeting Travis, seeing the horses, and how Travis just might be the right friend to keep her mind off Nick, as Brindle had suggested. Lindsay's response rolled in a minute later. *Do whatever it takes, or it's going to be a hard month. Unfortunately, not the kind of hard you want. Unless...Travis?* Trixie laughed, earning another jaw clench from

Nick. He'd been stewing the whole drive home, though she couldn't imagine why. They'd had a great day, and she thought they'd had a great evening.

She thumbed out a response to Lindsay. *No. First, because he's Nick's friend, and second, because he has a daughter. I have way too much to accomplish to get involved with a guy with a kid. Even a kid as cute as Peaches.* She sent the text, and her phone chimed with another text as Nick turned into the driveway. Travis's name appeared on the screen, and she read the message. *Still on for our run in the morning?*

"*Jesus,* how much can you girls possibly have to say to each other?"

"I could talk to Lindsay all night, but this is from Travis. He's confirming our run for tomorrow morning. We're meeting here at six." She typed a response as Nick parked. *Yes. Looking forward to it!* She added a smiling emoji and sent it off. "I can't believe I have a running buddy. I don't mind running alone, but this will be so much better."

Nick threw open his door and climbed out, heading straight for the barn. Goldie and Rowdy ran up from the lower field to greet them.

Trixie went after him. "What's wrong? You seem mad."

"Nothing," he growled, walking fast. "I just need a minute alone."

"*Oh.* Okay. Give me your keys, and I'll let Pugsly out." He always kept Pugsly inside when he was gone, but the other dogs roamed free on the ranch, and slept in the barn.

He handed her the keys and headed down to the barn without another word.

She was used to his moods, but usually she could figure them out. Tonight she was perplexed. He never got mad when

Jax or Jilly teased him, so she knew it wasn't that.

Pugsly greeted her at the front door with grunty excitement. She picked him up and kissed his head as she carried him through the living room, and out the back door. "Your daddy is grumpy tonight."

Pugsly whimpered.

"Don't worry, he'll get over it." She put him down in the grass, and as he went to do his business, she looked out at the barn lights, wondering if Nick had gone down there to call one of his buckle bunnies. The thought of him touching those women and letting them touch him made her feel a little sick, and that irritated the hell out of her. Why did he scare guys away from her when he played the field? She wasn't *his*.

The more she thought about it, the angrier she got. She didn't know if she was right or not about him making that phone call, but that didn't stop the irritation from clawing up her spine. She had half a mind to walk down there and interrupt whatever he was doing, which would probably piss him off even more.

Good.

Her hands curled into fists, and she debated doing just that. But what if he *was* setting up a booty call? That would piss *her* off even more. She saw him walking to the fence with the dogs and heard him call out to the horses. Pugsly barked and took off running toward Nick as the horses galloped in.

Just like your harem.

She stalked inside in search of the cobbler. Why did she have to crush on *him* of all guys? Why couldn't she like an easy guy? One who might actually like her back? She dished a heaping mound of cobbler into a bowl, and even though it was practically sacrilegious to reheat good cobbler in the microwave, she did, because she was too annoyed to wait for the oven to heat up.

She was standing at the counter, shoveling her second helping into her mouth, when Nick came through the door with Pugsly in his arms.

He set Pugsly down and came into the kitchen. His gaze dropped to the cobbler. Then those brooding eyes hit hers with a flash of heat. "Why are the lights off?"

She shrugged. "I didn't think to turn them on. Are you in a better mood?"

He didn't respond.

She knew she had no business saying what was about to come out of her mouth, but she couldn't hold back. "If you want to call your women, you don't have to hide from me to do it."

His eyes narrowed. "What the hell are you talking about?"

"Something's got you all tied in knots. I figured you wanted to…" She couldn't say it, because the thought was going to bring the cobbler back up.

"*What?* Call some random woman? Set up a quick fuck? Have you ever known me to do that while you're here?"

She pushed from the counter, standing taller. "No, but you're acting weird."

He gritted his teeth.

"Like *that*. What was that for?"

"Maybe I just don't like to watch you flirt with my friends."

"Flirt? With *who*?"

"Your *running buddy*."

"Travis?" Laughter bubbled out. "I didn't *flirt* with him! And you know what? That's bullshit, Nick. You've seen me flirt with guys dozens of times when I go out with Jilly. What's *really* bothering you?"

His eyes narrowed, and in that moment, his eyes changed from brooding to...

Holy. Crap.

A firestorm of desire and restraint stared back at her.

She held her breath, sure she was misinterpreting that look. Could he...? *No.* He was messing with her. Wasn't he? Her heart thundered so hard she couldn't hear past the blood rushing through her ears. There was one way to find out, but could she do it? Could she risk their friendship? Ask the question that could cost her everything?

Every silent second that passed made it harder for her to think, much less speak, so she didn't even try. Instead, she stepped closer, hoping to read his body language.

His jaw tensed, and he breathed harder. "*Trixie.*"

His warning was clear, but how long could she torture herself over him? How much more of this could she take without losing her mind? Mustering all of her courage, she said, "Don't *Trixie* me. Why do you care who I flirt with?"

He gritted his teeth. His eyes were so intense, she was unable to look away. *The heck with it.* This was her chance. She threw caution to the wind, pushing harder, closing the gap between them so their bodies touched from her thighs to her breasts.

Heat flared in his eyes, bolstering her confidence.

"You just gave away your hand, cowboy. But you always go after what you want, so why aren't you?"

He backed her up against the fridge, every inch of his hard body pressed against her.

"Don't fuck with me, Trixie." He sounded angry, but now she knew it was primal desire driving him, not anger. "I don't want to screw up our friendship."

She took his hat off his head and put it on her own. "What's a little nakedness between friends?" *Oh God! Did I really just say that?*

His eyes widened for barely a second before narrowing again, as if she'd shocked her big, bad cowboy. "You're not thinking straight. You have no idea what you're asking for."

"My thoughts are crystal clear. I know *exactly* what I'm asking for."

"This isn't going to end with you and me riding off into the sunset."

"The only thing I want to ride is *you*. But if you're not into me..."

She took a step away, but he grabbed her arm, yanking her back, and crushed his mouth to hers so fiercely and demanding, his hat flew from her head. Years of dreaming, hoping, wishing, *wanting* came rushing forward. For a few unbelievable seconds, she couldn't breathe, think, or move. But then her mind and body caught up, and she kissed him feverishly, touching as much of him as she could, his arms, neck, back, ass. His mouth was hot and possessive, and kissing him was even more incredible than she'd imagined. He tasted of greedy man and insatiable lust and touched her like he couldn't get enough, groping her ass, hips, and breasts. One hand dove into her hair and fisted.

Oh God, yessss.

They ate at each other's mouths. Her entire body was on fire. She needed *more*. She tugged at his shirt, and he broke the kiss long enough to pull it off. He grabbed the two sides of her shirt and ripped it open. Buttons flew in the air as he stripped it from her body. Her nipples ached for his touch, straining against her black lace bra.

His eyes hit her breasts with the heat of a thousand suns. "*Fuuck.*"

He took her in another penetrating kiss, pressing his bare chest to hers, sending lightning scorching through her. He yanked her head back by her hair and sealed his mouth over her neck, sucking and grazing his teeth along her skin. Pinpricks of pleasure skated beneath her skin as his mouth moved lower. He unhooked the front of her bra, freeing her breasts.

"You're so fucking gorgeous," he said hungrily as he lowered his mouth over one breast and sucked *hard.*

She bit her lower lip to keep from crying out and grabbed his head with both hands, arching forward, holding him there. She panted and moaned, unable to keep the noises from streaming from her lips as he sucked, licked, and nipped, sending titillating sensations raining down the length of her. He rocked his hard length between her legs, and *oh*, how she loved the feel of him. He worked her jeans open and shoved his hand into them, his thick fingers sliding through her wetness.

"*Yes,*" she pleaded.

He pushed his fingers into her and took her other breast in his mouth, thrusting deep with every suck. She moved with him, riding his fingers, gasping for breath. Need stacked up inside her, her body igniting anew with every stroke of his fingers, drawing sharp gasps and pleading whimpers. Desire pounded through her. A climax hovered just out of reach. She went up on her toes, chasing it, and he used his thumb on that needy bundle of nerves, catapulting her into oblivion.

"Oh *God! Nick—*"

She was blinded by passion and pleasure, her body bucking and pulsing. She clawed at his head, arms, and shoulders, crying out in long, surrendering sounds. He captured her mouth, kissing her through the peak. Just when she came down from the high, his fingers pushed rougher, deeper. Electricity arced through her, and she bowed off the fridge.

"*Come again,*" he demanded.

She was almost there, but she couldn't help demanding right back, gritting out, "Make me."

A growl rumbled out of his lips as he reclaimed her mouth, *feasting,* as his fingers worked their magic. He grabbed her breast with his other hand and pinched her nipple. Searing pain and pleasure shot between her legs, and her orgasm crashed over her in ravaging waves. Her head fell back as loud, indiscernible sounds broke free. His mouth covered hers, swallowing those sounds as her body shuddered and quaked.

She clung to him, trembling, trying to drag air into her lungs. She'd known they'd be explosive together, but she'd never imagined anything so powerful.

He didn't give her a chance to recover, tearing her jeans and panties down. But they got stuck on her boots. "Get your damn boots off."

She might be okay with taking what she could get, but she was going to be treated like she mattered. She stared into his dark eyes, lifted her chin, and said, "Oh no, cowboy, that's not how it works. *You* take my damn boots off."

His brows slanted in annoyance or confusion, she didn't know or care which. She couldn't stop the smile tugging at her lips as he processed her demand. His jaw clenched, but he dropped to his knees and stripped off her boots and clothes. When he rose to his full height, his stormy eyes drilled into her, studying her face for only a few seconds, which was long enough for her to see his guard slip and something softer and warmer rise to the surface, before it disappeared as fast as it had come.

He grabbed her arm, eyes blazing. "You sure you want this?"

Her heart raced, unable to believe they were really doing this and wanting him so badly, she knew she'd never turn back. "Hell yes."

He spun her around, bending her over the counter, and used his knees to spread her legs. A second later his wallet landed on the counter by her hands. She heard him unzip his jeans and shove them down. The crinkle of a condom wrapper had her closing her eyes. He cursed, and then she felt his cock press against her entrance. He grabbed her shoulder with one hand, pressing the other flat against her back, pushing her chest down and her ass up, and drove into her in one hard thrust. She gasped, her body stretching to accommodate his thickness.

He stilled, gritting out, "Aw, *fuck, Trixie.*"

The desperation in his voice mirrored her own, making it all that much more thrilling. He drew back slowly, then thrust hard and fast, sending pleasure radiating through her. He did it again, cursing under his breath, and with the next thrust *slow* went out the window. She gripped the counter as he pounded into her. There was no finesse, no tender touches or sweet words, and in that moment, the ecstasy was so exquisite, she didn't care. She closed her eyes, pleasure consuming her, stealing her ability to think, speak, or do anything other than *feel.* Scintillating sensations climbed up her limbs and whipped through her core. He moved one hand between her legs, homing in on the bundle of nerves that sent her up on her toes, needful pleas falling from her lips as he took her higher. Her body hit a crescendo, and she shattered, crying out as her body convulsed around him. He grabbed her waist with an iron grip, driving deeper, harder, *faster*, sending her right up to the stars as he gave in to his own powerful release, gritting out her name in gruff, relieved sounds. His hips jerked several times, and just when she thought he was done, they jerked again and he cursed, collapsing over her.

His arms pushed beneath her stomach, and he embraced her, resting his forehead on her back. She felt his heart racing, just like hers. He placed a single kiss to her spine and withdrew from between her legs. She heard him taking off the condom and pull up his jeans. When he stepped away, she pushed from the counter.

He gathered her clothes and handed them to her, his jeans hanging open, his expression one she'd never seen before. A mix of relief, confusion, and something she couldn't define.

"We good?"

Kinda, sorta, not really. "Yeah."

With a nod, he picked up his shirt and strode toward his bedroom with Pugsly trailing after him.

What the hell?

She heard his bedroom door close, driving the hurt deeper.

Now that lack of sweet words and tender touches bothered her. How could he do something so intimate and feel so close and so distant at once? She clutched her clothes against her chest, stunned and a little hurt. But she'd offered herself up on a silver platter. She knew she didn't have the right to expect any other outcome, but that didn't make her feel any better. What had she thought would happen? That he'd carry her off to his bed and suddenly want her to be his everything? That she'd be different from all the others?

Yes, damn it. I am different.

We're different.

She believed that with everything she had. She'd seen it in

his eyes in that split second before he'd turned her around. She'd heard it in his voice when their bodies had first come together, had felt it in his last embrace, and even in that single kiss to her back.

His voice whispered through her mind. *You want to know what love brings? Destruction.* And understanding dawned on her. This was all sex was to him. A release. An act of greed or need. But was that all it had *ever* been? He'd been twenty years old when his brothers had left. Had he felt something more for *anyone* before that?

She stared at his closed bedroom door, her heart aching for both of them. What they had *was* special, and damn it, she was going to prove that to him. But somewhere deep inside her was an even more important need. A yearning to show him how good it felt to be loved. He might like his life the way it was, but she knew that he'd enjoy it even more without the wounds of his past holding him down.

Nick trusted her with his animals and his ranch, but would he ever trust her with his heart?

Buckle up, my broody stallion. I have a feeling we're in for a rough ride.

Chapter Eight

NICK WAS UP at the crack of dawn and was riding Romeo onto the trailhead where his and Walt's properties came together as the sun came up. Walt had long ago worn trails through the mountainous preservation land behind their properties, and Nick's frequent rides had kept them clear. They galloped along the meadows, and he let Romeo set their pace on the uphill climbs. He pulled his hat down low, shading his eyes from the sun as they ascended the last hill. It was going to be another oppressively humid day. He slowed Romeo to a halt at the top of the hill and gazed out at the hills and valleys before him, dotted with trees and snaked with meadows, all beautifully unmarred by civilization. The view had always centered him, but he didn't think anything could fix the shit that had been going on in his head since last night.

Trixie had caught him off guard, and now he was all fucked up.

Had she been into him before last night? Had he missed her cues? He didn't think so. She'd never flirted with him the way she did with other guys. Either way, he'd been stupid, thinking he could take her up on it to get her out of his system. He'd fantasized about kissing her, touching her, *fucking* her for so long, he'd thought he'd known exactly what it would be like. But Lord have mercy, he hadn't even been close. His brazen cowgirl had felt gloriously feminine and so damn right in his arms, she'd blown him away. He shouldn't have taken things so far, but she'd looked at him like he was her earth, moon, and stars and had nearly taken him to his knees. He'd *needed* to be inside her, to feel that connection, and he'd thought just *once* would do the trick, and then he'd be able to let those fantasies go and move on. He'd tried to escape the emotions that had swamped him by taking her from behind. He'd thought not seeing her face would help. But it hadn't worked. The emotions had already seeped in too deep, clinging to him like a second skin. And the vulnerability he'd seen in her eyes afterward had driven those feelings deeper, making them inescapable, as much a part of him as the blood that ran through his veins.

And now here he sat atop his trusty steed, Trixie's sweet taste still lingering in his mouth, her sinful sounds echoing in his head, and those wanting, hopeful eyes etched into his memory. He was drowning in her, and she was miles away, probably regretting what they'd done. Especially after the way he'd left things. A tsunami of guilt consumed him.

Had he—*they*—ruined his most treasured friendship? How could things ever be normal between them again? He sat there for a long time, wishing he felt the need to take off, holler, or do *anything* physical. But all he wanted was to know they hadn't fucked things up beyond repair.

"Let's go, Romeo. It's time to face the music."

As they made their way down the trail, he relived last night all over again, moment by moment. Nothing had ever felt so good, and despite knowing he shouldn't, he wanted to do it again. *Desperately.* He told himself to apologize and back off. To try to fix things and *never* touch her again. Nothing could come of it. He knew that as well as he knew his own name. But he'd never been good at being told what to do. Not even when he was the one doing the telling.

As he came off the trail, he saw Walt in the pasture. Walt waved and headed his way.

Nick stroked Romeo's neck, watching his old friend amble toward the fence in his short-sleeved denim shirt tucked into his jeans, his belt notched tighter than in years past. Even at seventy-nine, Walt had a rugged air about him, with a strong jaw, cheeks mapped with wrinkles, a handlebar mustache, and bushy white brows. His thick white hair poked out from beneath his hat. Nick worried about him living alone and checked on him often. He remembered how Walt had seemed larger than life when they'd first met, a Hollywood transplant who knew everything there was to know about horses and stunt riding. Nick had worshipped him in the same way other boys worshipped their fathers, hanging on to his every word, each one worth its weight in gold. Nick had those feelings for his father, but his relationship with Walt had always been different. Over the years, Walt had become his sounding board, his voice of reason, and the first one to give him hell when he deserved it.

Like someone else I know.

"How's it goin', old man?" Romeo stretched his neck over the fence, pushing his muzzle into Walt's sternum.

"Mighty fine." He scratched Romeo's head. "You must've had a great ride. This old boy's sweating. I saw you riding the fence line this morning like a bat outta hell. You a'right?"

"'Course."

Giving Nick a once-over, he cocked a brow. "You kinda look fit to be tied. I thought it might have something to do with that pretty little filly friend of yours out running with young Helms this morning."

Nick shook his head. "What are you doing, sitting on your porch waiting for her to jog by now that you know she's here?"

"Hell yes." Walt laughed. "Nah. I was hanging an old rug out on the rails when they ran by. So, that look in your eyes has nothing to do with Trixie?"

"I didn't say that." He looked away and said, "She drives me crazy."

"A good woman will do that to a man. Bet you drive her batty, too. You're two of the most stubborn kids I know. But you're a good man, helping her follow her dreams. When she stopped by yesterday, she told me about how you swooped into town and offered her a chance to get away from it all for a while."

"That's what friends do."

"Is it?" Walt looked at him curiously. "How long is she here for?"

"A month. She needs time to buy the horses, and I'm going to help her with some initial training while she gets her legs under her. She's also going to pick Tempe's brain about a few things. It takes time."

"Sure," Walt said, as if he wasn't buying it. He'd always been able to see past Nick's smoke and mirrors. "That all there is to it?"

"I don't like the way her brothers give her shit about the business she's starting."

"I think Jilly might say that's the pot callin' the kettle black."

"Not in this case. I supported Jilly's business efforts one hundred percent." He'd even lent her money at the beginning, when she'd hit a rough patch and hadn't wanted to go to their parents.

"That you did." Walt took off his hat and wiped his brow. "A month is a long stretch. That gonna cramp your style?"

He wondered what Walt would think about *a little nakedness between friends.* "Guess we'll see. You need anything? Help around here? Groceries?"

Walt set his hat on his head. "Not unless you've got a magic wand to turn back time a few decades. This aging shit is for the birds."

"I wish I did just for you. I'll stop by next week."

"Sounds good. Bring my girl with you."

My girl. Walt got along with Trixie as well as Nick did. Hell, who wouldn't? "Will do."

Nick and Romeo headed home. Jealousy prickled the back of his neck at the sight of Trixie and Travis talking in the driveway by Travis's truck. She was wearing another pair of ridiculously small spandex shorts and a bright yellow sports bra. *Bet Travis loves that.* The damn knot in his chest felt like it was made of barbed wire, twisting painfully and tangling with shards of guilt. The reality that he might have screwed up their friendship brought a harsher stab of pain. He stilled, a bead of sweat forming on his brow. He couldn't imagine a life without Trixie in it.

Forcing his legs to move, he led Romeo to the side of the barn to cool off, cursing himself for not being a stronger man and walking away before they'd done anything last night. He wondered if it was possible to regret and *not* regret something at once. He regretted risking their friendship, but he didn't regret being close to Trixie.

He was so fucked up.

How could he be the same guy who had caught Zev stealing Beau's condoms when he was a teenager and had dragged his ass out to a drugstore and made him buy his own? Zev had been seeing Carly back then, and Nick had lectured him about the proper way to treat her. He'd told Zev that if he was old enough to have sex, he was old enough to buy condoms to protect Carly and that having sex came with a shitload of responsibility beyond preventing STDs and unplanned pregnancies. He'd told his younger brother to treat Carly with respect, make sure she felt safe and special, not to be a dick afterward, and that if he ran his mouth about it, he'd have Nick to deal with.

Where the hell was *that* Nick now?

He'd spent the last decade having *only* meaningless sex. He'd done what he'd had to in order to survive with his sanity intact, and he'd always kept the women he was with safe and had let them know where he'd stood *before* he'd even kissed them. But now that he was thinking about it, now that who he was had affected his relationship with Trixie, it pissed him off that he'd acted like that.

That wasn't the young man he'd been before all that shit went down, and it sure as hell wasn't the grown man he wanted to be.

He tried to push those thoughts away as he tugged off his sweaty shirt and tossed it over the fence. He removed Romeo's saddle as Romeo rehydrated. After putting the saddle away, he retrieved the sweat scraper and brush. He had a formal wash area for the horses, but Romeo hated it. Nick got that. He'd shower outdoors with the hose, too, if he could.

When he returned with the supplies, he led Romeo out of the corral and tied his lead to the fence. As he tugged the hose over, Travis honked, waving out the window as he drove away.

Trixie was jogging down the driveway toward him, waving and shouting, "I want to help!"

She didn't sound like she regretted what they'd done, and her infectious smile sure didn't look like she wanted to kick his ass. Damn, that was lucky...and confusing. Why was *his* head messed up if hers wasn't? Did she really want to just be friends with benefits? No strings, no questions, no hurt feelings? That was great, but what the hell was he supposed to do with his own tangled emotions?

"You took Romeo out this morning?" Trixie toed off her sneakers and peeled off her socks, as if it were just another day on the ranch.

"Yeah, on the trails. I'm just going to cool him down." He picked up the hose, and she hurried over in her bare feet. She was too damn cute.

"Good. I could use some cooling down, too." She grabbed the hose and took a long drink from it. "*Ah.* I needed that." She sprayed her arms and bent over to wet her legs.

Flashes of last night flew through his mind at record speed—her face contorted with pleasure as she came against the fridge, the sexy smirk when she'd told him to take off her boots, and her gorgeous naked body bent over the counter, her beautiful bare ass there for the taking. *God* she had a gorgeous ass. He wanted to get up close and even more personal with it.

Cold water hit his stomach, jarring him from his stupor. "Hey!"

Trixie laughed. "You looked like you needed cooling down."

Yeah, no shit. He had to get this off his chest. "Listen, Trix, about last night—"

"Stop," she said sharply. "We're good. We don't need to

talk about it."

Surprised, he said, "You sure?"

"Yes, see?" She sprayed him with the hose again, laughing.

"Give me that damn thing." He yanked the hose from her, still conflicted, but mildly relieved. He sprayed the horse's legs and walked around him as he sprayed the rest of his body. Like with so many other things, he and Trixie had long ago fallen into sync when they bathed horses, each washing one side. Trixie began brushing Romeo's head and face while Nick lifted one of Romeo's legs to spray his hoof.

"How was your run?" he asked begrudgingly, hating that it felt that way.

"Oh my gosh, *so* good. I was a little worried that I might not be able to keep up with Travis, but he went at my pace, which was nice, since I'm sure I'm slower than him. But we had a great time."

Nick used the sweat scraper on Romeo's shoulders and body, mulling over the happiness in her voice.

A few minutes later, she said, "I like him," and handed Nick the brush. "We're running together again tomorrow."

Fucking fantastic. "Great." He bit back his jealousy and gave her the sweat scraper, silently stewing as they washed Romeo.

"He asked me out," she said too damn casually.

Their eyes met over the horse's back. "Good for you." *Goddamn Helms.*

Her brows knitted. "You don't care if I go out with him?"

"Who am I to tell you what to do?"

"You can tell me if you don't want me to go."

He wasn't going down that spike-reinforced rabbit hole. "It's your life. You should do what you want."

"I always do," she challenged.

"Yeah, I found that out last night."

TRIXIE STRUTTED AROUND Romeo and stood face-to-face with Nick. Tension rolled off him. She *wanted* to tell him so many things, like their connection had been deeper than friendship even *before* they'd had sex and that they could be amazing together. She wanted to say, *Let your guard down. I promise I won't hurt you.* But telling him what to do was the equivalent of telling a woman to relax. Plus, he truly believed he didn't want a relationship, so saying those things would only make him feel backed into a corner, and she knew he'd come out fighting whether he cared about winning or not, just like she would. So she went for a softer approach, picking up the hose and spraying him.

He glowered a warning.

"Stop being a Gruff Gus," she said cheerily, spraying his deliciously broad chest again.

"*Trixie*," he growled.

If looks could kill, she'd be flat-out dead. "*Nicholas*," she countered, just as serious.

He stalked toward her, scowling, and she walked backward, laughing. A smile tugged at his lips.

"What's wrong, cowboy?" She lifted the hose and sprayed him in the face.

He sprinted toward her, and she shrieked, spraying him as she ran away. But he was too fast and snagged her around the waist, crushing her back against him with one arm around her stomach as he'd done at his parents' house. They were both cracking up. He ripped the hose from her hands and turned it on her, soaking himself in the process.

She covered her face. "Stop!" she said through her laughter.

He dropped the hose, and she turned in his arm. Laughter tumbled from his lips. She'd never seen his smile so big or his eyes so bright and carefree. But then their eyes connected, and the air sizzled and sparked.

Their laughter quieted, but his grin remained as he said, "Think you're funny?"

"Hilarious, actually." She slid her arms around him and kissed his wet chest.

His muscles tensed, those dark eyes narrowing. Holding his gaze, she traced a path with her fingers from just above the dusting of chest hair all the way up to his shoulder and pressed a kiss there. Heat flared in his eyes *and* everywhere else.

She pressed her hips forward, whispering, "I can *feel* how much you want me."

"You're fucking with my head," he said tightly, his playful smile nowhere in sight.

"Maybe I like fucking with *all* your body parts. Kiss m—"

Her words were lost to the hard press of his lips. He gripped the back of her head and her ass as he intensified the kiss. His tongue thrust deep, penetrating her mouth the same way he'd taken her last night, as if he had so much pent-up passion he couldn't hold back, and she *loved* it. He *possessed* every inch of her mouth, making her entire body smolder. Her knees weakened, and she dug her fingernails into his back, earning the sexiest sound she'd ever heard. She wanted to hear more of it, and kissed him ravenously, grinding against him. She'd never felt like this, had always craved more, but she'd never known exactly what *more* was.

Until now.

More was the visceral, intangible possession of her entire being, mind, body, and soul. He ground his hips, his hungry sounds sending lust spiking through her. His heart thundered against her chest, and she was right there with him, frantic to take them further. She wanted to strip off their clothes and ride him like the stallion he was right there in the grass. But she was greedy for a different type of *more*. A type that *only* Nick could give her. And she knew she'd never get it without slowing him down and making him consider his actions instead of just taking her in the heat of the moment.

It took all of her willpower to break their kiss, instantly mourning the loss of their closeness. He gritted out a curse, his eyes boring into hers, intoxicated and frustrated, which was exactly how she felt. She could tell it wasn't a feeling he was used to either, because beneath those conflicting emotions, she saw more than a hint of confusion.

Don't worry, cowboy. We're going to figure this out together.

Her body trembled with desire as she forced herself to step out of his arms and said, "I should go shower."

"*Right*," he said gruffly.

She felt the heat of his stare as she picked up her sneakers and socks and walked across the grass. She glanced over her shoulder, and her body flamed anew at the desire and restraint staring back at her, like a lion tethered to his cage as the lioness escaped. She flashed a pout and said, "If only I had someone to wash my back."

His eyes smoldered.

With an extra sway in her step and her hopes in the clouds, she headed for the house. Her pulse raced with every step, hoping she'd read their connection right. It felt like she was sneaking between the cracks in his armor. That he was allowing his feelings for her to lead him, not just his hormones. But the farther away she walked, the less hopeful she became. By the time she reached the house, she realized she was wrong, her hopes completely deflated.

Accepting her fate, she pushed open the door. When she turned to close it, Nick barreled in. He lowered his shoulder and tossed her over it. She shrieked with laughter, relief and happiness consuming her as he kicked the door closed and blazed a path toward his bedroom with Pugsly on their heels.

She smacked his ass. "Took you long enough!"

"Shut your piehole, woman. I couldn't leave Romeo tied up."

The fact that he'd thought of the horse when he was riddled with desire made him even more irresistible.

They stripped and stumbled into the shower in a tangle of gropes and kisses. Warm water rained down on them, slipping between their hungry lips and beneath their eager hands. She shook with desire as he groped her breasts and teased between her legs. She explored his hard muscles, loving every manly inch, and finally took what she craved, fisting his cock. A growling moan rumbled up from his chest into their mouths as she stroked him, tight and slow. When she brushed her thumb over the head, he tore his mouth away with another enticingly rough sound. She wanted to *taste* him, to hear more of those sinful noises. She wanted to drive him to the brink of madness.

"Nick," she said nervously.

"Huh?"

"Do you ride bareback?"

He lowered his chin, his face a mask of confusion.

"*Women*, not horses."

"Never," he said almost angrily. His jaw tensed. "*Once,* when I was a teenager."

His honesty meant everything, but something in the way he added that last fact also felt important. She wondered if there was more to that story. But that could wait. She wanted to unearth the feelings he had for her, not get lost in what he might have felt for someone in his past.

She went up on her toes, and he enveloped her in his arms, kissing her so deeply, her thoughts skittered away, and she came away light-headed.

"*God,*" he said in one long breath. "I fucking love kissing you."

She wrapped that little gift in a gold ribbon and tucked it away as he lowered his mouth to her neck. She fisted his hard length, earning another titillating sound. He reached between her legs, but she moved his hand away. His confused expression hit her again.

"I want to make *you* feel good." She kissed his chest, teasing his nipples with her teeth and tongue.

"*Fuck.*"

"*Mm.* I like hearing that."

She put her hand on his chest and pushed him back against the wall. He might be a man of few words, but the burning desire in his eyes told her she was doing all the right things. She tasted and nipped her way down his body, her gaze flicking up to his as her hand circled his cock. His hips thrust, and she slicked her tongue around the broad head. His eyes went dark, and he sucked in air through clenched teeth. His reactions were so raw and real, she craved more of them. His body shuddered as she licked the crown, so she did it again, earning the same reaction along with a guttural moan. She licked and sucked only the head of his shaft, reading his every reaction and doing more of what he liked. He tangled his fingers in her hair, holding so tight, it stung. When she licked him from base to tip, he growled, "Suck it."

Her body torched at the command, and one day she might even follow it, but right now, she was in control, and she liked it. She cradled his balls and licked his length, lavishing the places that made him shudder and shake. His chin hit his chest with a hiss, and his hard length swelled in her hand. She made a show of licking her lips before lowering her mouth and taking him to the back of her throat.

"*Christ*, Trixie."

She sucked and stroked, fast and tight, then slow and light, reveling in his quickening breaths, the tightening of his fingers in her hair, the flexing of his thighs and stomach. She gently squeezed his balls, and a long, low groan fell from his lips, sending rivers of heat coursing through her. She worked him faster, tighter, sucked harder.

"Trix...*darlin'*," he panted out. "*Holy fuck.*"

The need in his voice and unexpected intimacy of *darlin'* spurred her on. She continued teasing, taunting, and *taking*, until he was thrusting into her mouth, moaning, tugging her hair. Every sound, every *tug*, sent lust shooting through her, taking her closer to the edge. Water streamed down their bodies, making every touch feel more erotic. Her eyes were riveted to his face, clenched with restraint. Seeing him like that sent thrills racing through her. She'd never known it could be as exciting for her as it was for him, and she knew in her heart that this was just the tip of the iceberg for them. She was tempted to make him come, but she *needed* him inside her, to feel even closer to him, more than she'd ever needed anything in her life.

As if he'd read her mind, he hauled her up to her feet, taking her in a punishingly fierce kiss, forcing her mouth open as far as it would go, like he couldn't get enough, and *oh*, what that did to her!

"I need you," he said urgently, and spun her around, palms to the wall.

Not this time, big boy. She turned, meeting his confused and ravenous eyes. "I want to see your face." It came out more heartfelt and breathier than demanding.

His jaw clenched, a silent struggle showing in his eyes. She ached for him, hiding behind such thick walls. She had a feeling he'd been living in the confines of that self-induced prison for so long, he probably didn't even realize it anymore.

She caressed his cheek. "Nick, if you want me, you have to look at me."

For a few seconds, she thought he might back away. Then his eyes focused, *really* focused through their lustful haze, and with a single nod, his mouth came down over hers. He lifted her into his arms, and her legs circled his waist as he lowered her onto his shaft. Pleasure radiated through her, mirrored in the appreciative sounds he made.

"*Fuck, Trix,*" he panted out. "You feel incredible."

He reclaimed her mouth, more demanding this time. Their teeth gnashed, tongues battled for dominance, and their bodies thrust and rocked in perfect sync. Their moans echoed off the walls as he pounded into her, but nothing could drown out the happiness in her heart.

Suddenly he stilled, and "*Condom,*" fell from his lips. "*Shit.* I'm sorry."

It took a second for her brain to catch up. "I'm on the pill. It's been forever for me, Nick. I'm clean."

His eyes held a second of contemplation, and then he sealed his mouth over hers, taking her harder, faster, impossibly deeper. She met his every effort with one of her own. Fire and ice seared through her. She dug her fingers into his shoulders, earning more appreciative sounds. He clutched her ass so hard, she was sure she'd bruise, but the decadent pleasures it brought drove her right up to the edge. He tore his mouth away, kissing her jaw, her neck, her shoulder, then sank his teeth into her flesh, sucking so hard she lost control, and cried out, "*Nick!*"

She clung to him, her sex clenching, her hips bucking wildly as he followed her over the edge, and her name flew from his lungs like a prayer. "*Trixie. Fuuuuck, Trix.*"

They rode out their passion, holding each other so tight, they felt like one being. When she finally collapsed, wasted and sated in his arms, he held her until their breathing calmed, and then he kissed her cheek and shoulder, whispering, "*Damn, darlin'.*" She tucked away that rare and tender moment as he set her on her feet and turned his face up to the warm shower spray.

She could feel him putting his walls up again. She was glad for the headway they'd made, but she wanted him to trust her, to *know* her, to let himself breathe for longer than a good time. She poured bodywash into her hands, the woodsy, rugged scent filling the steamy air as she began gently washing his broad back. His muscles tensed, but she didn't let it dissuade her. She rubbed his shoulders, kneading the knots out of them, and worked her way down his torso, touching as much of him as she could. She took her time, washing him slowly, caressing all his taut muscles. She washed his ass and the backs of his legs, all the way down to his ankles, feeling his tension ease as she went. She worked her way back up his body, taking extra care to massage the tightness around his shoulders. He let out a long, surrendering sigh, and his head tipped forward. She stepped around him. The water was running down his face, his dark lashes glistening with droplets. But he didn't wipe them away. He didn't move at all. He watched her as she bathed his shoulders and chest.

She went up on her toes, brushing a feathery kiss to his lips. When he tried to take it rougher, she drew back and said, "This isn't about sex."

"It's always about sex," he said with a cocky grin, one hundred percent testosterone-laden man, ready to service at the blink of an eye.

"Not always."

He may not realize that he needed a different type of release, but she did. She continued washing him, kneading and caressing his muscles. He got aroused when she washed his privates and thighs, and he reached for her. But she smiled sweetly and shook her head. He scowled, and that was so *Nick*, it endeared him to her even more. His scowl eased with her touch. He closed his eyes as she worked her way back up his body. She felt his heart beating sure and steady, no longer frantic with need.

When she was done, she caressed his face and whispered, "Okay."

He opened his eyes, and they were brimming with so many emotions, it overwhelmed her. His hands circled her upper arms, holding tight, and he lowered his forehead to hers, his eyes closing again as he said, "*God*, Trix. What the hell are you doing to me?"

Loving you.

Chapter Nine

TRIXIE HUMMED AS she breezed into Emmaline's Café, greeted by the aroma of fresh-roasted coffee and warm baked goods. Everything at Emmaline's was delicious, from the specialty sandwiches to the freshly made desserts and designer coffees, and the atmosphere couldn't be more upbeat with sunflower-yellow walls boasting gorgeous paintings from local artists and a chalkboard displaying today's specials in bright pink and green, interspersed with sayings like TODAY'S YOUR DAY! and WELCOME TO YOUR HAPPY PLACE! Trixie scanned the room, looking for Tempest. Almost all the tables were taken, but she didn't see her friend anywhere. In the rear of the café, a spiral staircase led to a loft with more seating. She wondered if Tempest was sitting up there.

Emmaline, a vivacious brunette, waved from the far end of the counter, where she was adding a dollop of whipped cream to a piece of pie. Trixie hoisted her messenger bag over her shoulder and went to say hello. Emmaline handed the pie to another employee and asked her to bring it to a customer sitting at a table near the front of the café. Then she came around the counter and hugged Trixie.

"It's so good to see you," Emmaline said.

"It's great to see you, too."

"I heard you were meeting Tempe for lunch. I saw her pop into the ladies' room a minute ago." Emmaline lifted her brows and leaned closer. "Jilly told me you moved in with *Nicky boy* for a month while you start a miniature horse therapy business. That is *so* exciting. A whole month with that hot cowboy *and* starting the business. I swear that man could melt the panties off an iceberg."

"He sure can." *Please don't talk about him and other women.*

"You know, there was a time when Jilly and I thought you and Nick would end up together. We thought, hot cowboy, gorgeous cowgirl making cute cowpokes. But then you guys fell into your awesome friendship. I guess that's better, right? Without the complications of all that other stuff that goes along with sex."

Like the walls Nick has around his heart and the random women he hooks up with to keep those walls in place? She tried to push those thoughts aside, grasping for the elation that had carried her into the café on the tails of the breakthrough she'd felt in the shower and said, "Yeah, I guess so." She spotted Tempest coming out of the bathroom. "There's Tempe."

"Go. I'll come by your table in a few minutes to take your orders so you don't have to wait in line."

"Thanks, Em." Trixie headed over to the table.

Tempest looked beautiful in a short floral dress. She had a gracefulness about her that set her apart from her siblings. "It's so good to see you," she said, embracing Trixie.

"You too. How are Nash and Flip?" Nash, her handsome artist husband, had been a single father to his son, Philip, who everyone called Flip, when Tempest had met him.

"They're both great. Flip is getting so big, and Nash is…"

She sighed as they sat down. "Well, he's just wonderful."

"I love seeing you so happy, and you look *amazing*. Are you using new makeup, or is your happiness making you glow?"

"No new makeup, but there is something new in my life." She put her hand over her belly and grinned. "I'm pregnant."

"Oh my gosh! Congratulations!" Trixie hugged her again. "You must be so happy."

"We are. We just told my parents last night, and I'm sure my cousins' phones will be ringing off the hook with the news by nightfall."

"I'm thrilled for you. Does Flip know?"

"We told him last night, too. He is over the moon, and already talking about teaching his baby brother or sister how to feed the chickens and collect eggs and how he's going to read to it and do just about everything else under the sun."

Trixie laughed. "He's going to be such a great big brother."

"Thank you. And I'm excited for you and your new endeavor. I remember what it was like when I started my business and moved away from Peaceful Harbor. I was as scared as I was excited."

"I'm more excited than scared. But I'm not moving away from home. I'm just here to get started without the distractions of my brothers and working on the ranch."

"Well, you couldn't be staying with a more knowledgeable horse guy. Nick's the greatest. It's kind of funny, isn't it? I started a business to get out of the hospital environment, and you're starting a business that will bring you into it." Tempest had felt confined by her music therapy job at the hospital and had started her own music therapy business. She and Nash had renovated one of their barns, and now she saw clients there.

"It is funny. I hadn't thought about that."

"It's too bad you're not staying in the area because we could work together. I'm working with kids who have emotional challenges and physical limitations. They could definitely benefit from horse therapy."

Emmaline arrived with two glasses of water. She set them on the table and said, "Sorry to interrupt. What can I get for my sexy ladies? One of our famous mile-high sandwiches, perhaps?"

"Not for me, thanks. I'll just have a cobb salad with ranch dressing," Tempest said.

"That sounds great. I'll take the same."

"Okay, two boring salads it is." Emmaline winked and went to fill their orders.

"I love her," Trixie said. "You know, Tempe, maybe we *can* work together. There aren't many hospitals, rehab centers, or nursing homes in and around Oak Falls. I'm going to have to travel outside the area, and you're only about two hours away. There are so many facilities within an hour of here, I could potentially be traveling this way every week."

"If that's the case, we could coordinate visits," Tempe said.

"That's what I'm thinking. I'm sure Nick won't mind if I stay with him more often." As she said it, she had a painful thought. What if Nick's walls never came down? What if he never felt as much for her as she felt for him? Could she handle going back to being just friends?

"That would be fantastic, but that's a lot of travel," Tempest said, jarring Trixie from her thoughts. "Are you sure you want to do that?"

"I won't have much of a choice," she said, answering Tempest's question and her own. She felt a wave of disappointment, but she refused to give in to it or allow *what ifs* to kick her legs out from under her before she and Nick even had a chance to see where their new connection might lead. Determined to succeed with the business *and* breaking down Nick's walls, she said, "Besides, I know it'll be worth it, and I travel a lot now delivering and picking up livestock for our ranch."

"I guess that means there's still no special guy waiting for you back home?"

"Nope, and the guy I'm interested in is definitely not looking to settle down anytime soon."

"I'm sorry to hear that. But it sounds like we should keep the door open for working together," Tempest said. "I'd love to work with you when you're ready. And if you're really going to work here and in the surrounding areas, then I can introduce you to some of the administrators and volunteer coordinators I know. I have contacts with nursing homes, too, and rehab facilities."

"That would be fantastic."

"Hospitals have a pretty rigorous chain of command that can take a while to get through. You'll get quicker responses with the other types of facilities."

"That's fine with me. I want to help as many people as I can." Trixie took a drink and said, "I was going to ask your advice on the best way to start getting my name out there."

"It's all who you know. The medical community is like one big network when it comes to this type of thing. When you meet with the volunteer coordinators, you should ask who else they know that might be interested in using your services. They're always willing to give me names for music therapy referrals. I'm sure they'll do the same for you. Cole gave me a list of contacts when I first started. I'll share that with you, too."

Her oldest brother, Cole, was an orthopedist and had a medical practice in Peaceful Harbor.

"That would be great. Thank you."

"The only thing I'm not sure about are the guidelines about horses entering the facilities. But I know someone who can answer those questions."

"I've done some research on that, but it would help to speak with someone in the industry."

"My friend Jordan Lawler runs the volunteer program at Pleasant Care Assisted Living. I'll give her a call and see if she can fit you in next week. Then you can begin getting answers to your questions and start meeting people to get your name out there."

"That would be great. Thank you. I've looked into insurance, and I know the horses need to have proper vaccinations, of course, and wear shoes to protect the hospital floors from anything they may have picked up in their hooves. Oh, and they have to be reasonably housebroken."

"I didn't even know you could housebreak a horse."

"That's why I said *reasonably*. A big part of it is training the handler to know when to feed, how to make them go on command. That sort of thing. I'll use potty bags, just in case nature calls at the wrong time, but training is vital." A potty bag was a manure catcher that attached to a therapy horse's vest or harness.

"Sounds a lot more complicated than music therapy. You said you were going to continue working at your family's ranch while you're getting started. How will that work if you have to travel?"

"I won't need to travel for the first year or two while I train the horses."

"It takes that long to train miniature horses?"

"Mm-hm. I don't think people realize how much effort goes

into training them for on-site visits. Staff and patients change all the time, so every visit will essentially be a new experience. They need to be ready for anything, comfortable with all different types of flooring—plush and low-pile carpets, patterned flooring, linoleum—and adept at going up and down stairs and in elevators. You know how many smells, sights, and sounds there are in those facilities. Think about it. There's so much stimuli. The horses need to be comfortable with excited and fearful children and adults, the sounds of medical equipment, even the sounds of people walking, talking, coughing, and crying. They have to be unflappable, or it would be unsafe to bring them near patients."

"Wow. I'm guilty of not realizing all of that myself. I never thought about carpet patterns and different types of floors, much less elevators. No wonder it takes so long. So you'll just continue working at your parents' ranch during that time?"

"Yes, but I'll also do kids' birthday parties with the miniature horses, some riding and groundwork therapy at my facility, wherever that is, and I'll work on making connections. All the research I've done has shown that therapy horse businesses can be booked up to a year in advance for many hospitals and larger facilities."

"I believe that. When I was working in hospitals, I was booked well over a year in advance. I'm booked fourteen months out right now for my classes, and I've been turning people away. I never expected my business to take off so much."

"You're lucky," Trixie said. "What are you going to do when the baby is born?"

"I've talked with my clients, and they know I'll be taking time off. But I don't know how much I'll want to work after the baby is born. I'm only three and a half months pregnant, and I already can't imagine leaving our baby for any length of time. But I don't want to stop doing music therapy, either. I think working a few hours one or two days a week will probably be enough for me after the baby's born."

"I can understand that. My brother has a hard time leaving his little girl, too."

"Do you want a family one day?" Tempest asked.

"Yes, one day. But not anytime too soon. Maybe four or five years down the line, when my business is running smoothly, if I'm married by then," she said as Emmaline arrived with their lunches.

"Two salads with a side of cookies, because you're female and you need them." Emmaline set down their salads and placed a plate of cookies in the middle of the table. "You're my official taste testers for my newest recipe. These are chocolate caramel pecan with a dash of cinnamon."

"Forget the salad." Trixie grabbed a cookie and took a bite. The sweetness melted in her mouth. "These are *incredible*. Nick would love them. He has such a sweet tooth. Can I buy a half dozen to bring back to him?"

"Did you hear that, Tempe?" Emmaline said with a curious arc to her voice. "She wants to bring Nick *cookies*. You know what they say about the way to a man's heart."

Trixie rolled her eyes. "They lie. I've been bringing Nick goodies for as many years as I've been staying with him, and that man's heart is still locked down tight." She saw Jillian come through the café doors and plow toward them like a woman on a mission.

"Hey, Jilly." Emmaline looked at Trixie and said, "Try sex. That usually works."

Tempest blushed.

"Sounds like I got here right on time. We're talking about sex?" Jillian snagged a cookie and took a bite.

"Sex with *Nick*," Emmaline said.

Jillian choked on her cookie and coughed. "*No*, we are *not* talking about that. And what is up with you bitches having a girls' lunch without me?"

They all laughed.

"I told you last night that I was getting together with Tempe today," Trixie reminded her.

"Not for lunch at Em's with delicious cookies," Jillian complained.

Trixie pushed a chair out for her. "Sit down, you big baby."

As Jillian sat down, Emmaline said, "I have to go do some real work while you girls chitchat. I'll grab your usual sandwich, Jilly."

"Thanks, babe." Jillian snagged another cookie. "I'm glad I ran into you two. Do you have time to come by my shop after lunch? I got a few new things in. I have a new dress that's super feminine and sexy for you, Tempe, that will drive Nash wild, and, Trixie, the newest outfit in my Multifarious line is perfect for Friday night. Which reminds me, Tempe, do you and Nash want to meet us for drinks Friday? Jax and Nick will be there."

"I wish I could, but we promised Flip we'd have a family movie night. Besides, I can't drink for a while." Tempest's eyes brightened. "I'm *pregnant!*"

"Ohmygod!" Jillian jumped up and hugged her. "Another baby to spoil!"

"Speaking of babies to spoil." Trixie pulled out her phone. "I have to show you the newest pictures of my niece."

"Emma is so freaking cute," Jillian said.

"Jilly is Emma's honorary auntie," Trixie explained.

"I'm everyone's honorary auntie," Jillian said. "It's not like my brothers are giving me any nieces or nephews to spoil. I should call our cousin Josh. He and his wife, Riley, have a new children's clothing line. I need to stock up now that Tempe's having a baby." Josh and Riley were world-renowned designers and split their time between New York City and Weston, Colorado.

"I love their stuff," Tempest said. "I bought Flip the cutest pajamas from their summer collection."

They chatted as they ate, catching up on each other's lives. Jillian was excited about the possibility of Trixie working in or around Pleasant Hill so they could see each other more often. She offered to make wings and unicorn horns for the horses and gave Trixie the name of someone who could help her design a logo and make a website. Tempest talked with her about the differences between working with hospitals and other facilities, and Trixie took a million notes. As they were talking, they came up with other ideas, like making visits to schools with the horses for presentations and taking part in parades to help spread the word about Rising Hope.

After lunch they headed over to Jillian's shop, where Trixie and Tempest tried on every outfit Jillian picked out. They had a blast. By the time Trixie headed over to Travis's to see the horses, she had two shopping bags full of new clothes, including an outfit to wear to Tully's, two dresses appropriate for business meetings, and a few cute things she simply couldn't resist. She hoped Nick wouldn't be able to resist them, either.

Chapter Ten

ROMEO AND LADY charged around the ring, heads held high, manes flying. Nick stood with one foot on the back of each horse, reins in hand, adrenaline pumping through his veins as the horses flew over the meter-high jump. There was no bigger adrenaline rush, or a better way to clear his head, than taking jumps while Roman riding, which took total concentration. He rode the horses over two more jumps before stopping for the day, and it did the trick. His head was finally clear. Trixie had once again knocked him for a loop, and he'd *let* her, which was the most surprising aspect of all the crazy shit going on with him. He never gave up control in any situation, to a man or a woman, but that hot little wild thing did him in. At least now he was back in control of his thoughts and his actions, and he planned to keep it that way.

His muscles burned as he dismounted, and sweat glistened on his skin. He whistled, and the horses followed him out of the arena to the corral for water. He picked Pugsly up in one hand and loved up Goldie and Rowdy on the way. When the horses had enough to drink, he took off their tack and set them free in the pasture. As he closed the gate, Jax's slick black Lexus came down the driveway. Goldie and Rowdy sprinted off to greet him. Nick grabbed his hat from the fence post, where he'd left it earlier, and made his way across the grass.

His brother climbed out of his car in his designer slacks, crisp white button-down, and shiny black shoes, looking about as out of place on the dusty ranch as Nick did in Jax's fancy design studio.

"Hi." Jax crouched to love up the dogs.

"What's up?"

"Mom made us all pot pies." Jax pushed to his feet and gave Pugsly a quick pet. "When I went to pick mine up, she said you weren't answering your phone."

He patted his back pocket out of habit. "Yeah, I have no idea where I put it."

"No surprise there. She was going to bring your pot pie over, but after the sparks that were flying between you and Trixie last night, I didn't want her to catch you two naked, so I told her I'd bring it over."

"What the hell makes you think we'd be naked?"

"Come on, Nick. You and I both know the steam coming off that basketball court wasn't caused by my good looks alone."

Nick gritted his teeth. "Then here's a better question. Why would you come over if you thought we might be *busy?*"

Jax cocked a grin. "Trixie Jericho, *naked.* You figure it out."

"You're an idiot." Nick put Pugsly down and went to take the equipment to the tack room.

Jax followed him into the barn. "Where is she, anyway?"

"No idea. Probably at Travis's checking out the horses." He'd been looking forward to seeing the horses with her and had hoped she'd come back after meeting with Tempest, but she'd been gone all day.

"The horses, *right.*"

Nick threw open the door to the tack room and put away the equipment.

Jax stood in the doorway, watching him. "By the way you're manhandling things, I guess I read the two of you right, and you two hooked up. I'm also guessing you're freaking out about it."

"I'm not freaking out. But she is fucking with my head." He strode out of the tack room and into the office.

"Well, that's a first, and I'd say it's a good sign."

Nick scoffed. He grabbed a bottle of water from the fridge and offered one to Jax.

"No thanks. I knew something was wrong with you these last few months."

"There's nothing wrong with me." Nick guzzled the water.

The truth was, Jax had been giving Nick hell for a long time about acting strange, but Nick had kept his thoughts about Trixie to himself. He trusted Jax. He was a great sounding board, and he always gave it to Nick straight, no matter how pissed off Nick might get. But what could Nick say? *Hey, bro, you know my best female friend? The one who trusts me implicitly? Well, I can't stop thinking about getting her naked.*

"Then you tell me why you've been acting grouchier than usual, why you're going to Virginia a hell of a lot more often, and why I can't remember the last time you went home with a woman when we were out."

Nick headed out of the office. "How about you tell me, *Dr. Jax*, am I totally fucking up here?"

"I don't know. I'm ready to celebrate. I was trying to figure out how to fit Pugsly for a wedding dress."

Nick laughed, but he quickly schooled his expression and slid an annoyed look to Jax.

"What? Think about it, Nick. The only women you allow in your house are family and *Trixie*, and she gets you, man. She puts up with all your moods, laughs at your dry humor, and you're more comfortable around her than you are around anyone else. Including me." Jax held his gaze steady. "But you've been telling me for years it wasn't like that between you two. So what's the real story?"

"It *wasn't* like that. This is new." He leaned against the side of the barn. "She's one of my best friends, Jax. Her life is in Virginia, mine's here, and I respect the hell out of her. I don't want to screw up any of that *or* hurt her."

"Then don't. Is she cool with it? Or did you push a limit you shouldn't have?"

"I'd never do that to anyone, especially Trixie," Nick snapped. "*She's* the one who suggested it *and* went after it. I've been trying to keep my distance, but she started talking about being naked friends and pushing all my buttons. You know how she challenges me. It just happened."

"Yeah, I can see her doing that. But if you don't feel good about it, then stop."

"I don't fucking *want* to stop." He blew out a breath. "I don't know what I want, but I definitely don't want to hurt her." He finished his water and tossed the bottle in the trash barrel. He spotted Trixie's truck coming down the driveway, and his heart thumped a little faster. "It's just...she gets under my skin and I don't know..." *How to handle that.*

"Know what? How to deal with the fact that she's here for a month and fooling around with you but hanging out with Travis? Or the fact that you're watching her truck come down the driveway right now with the same longing and excited look in your eyes Pugsly gets in his good eye when you come home?"

Nick pushed away from the side of the barn. "Forget I said anything."

Jax grabbed his arm as Trixie parked, stopping him in his tracks. "Listen, Nick. You guys are good together. You are the last man on earth I'd tell to let a woman into his life, but Trixie's already in it, man. She has been for years."

"Hi, Jax!" Trixie called out, carrying two enormous shopping bags from Jillian's Boutique. "What a nice surprise."

"I finally secured a passport to enter the premises," Jax teased. "Guess you've been to my sister's shop."

"I had the greatest day. I had lunch with Tempe, and Jillian showed up. We ended up at her shop, and I bought way too much. But she and Tempe got me even more pumped about starting my business. Thanks for suggesting that I get in touch with Tempe, Nick. She was incredibly helpful. She's going to introduce me to some of her contacts. She thinks I'll be able to make a lot of connections in and around the area. She also has a list of contacts that Cole gave her that she's going to share with me. Then I went to Travis's, and I called you, because I really wanted you to come with me, but you didn't answer, so I figured you were busy."

"I lost my phone."

"Oh, that sucks. I'll help you find it. Anyway, I was able to pick three horses out of the ones that we saw yesterday. Do you think you can go with me one day this week to make my final decision? I *really* want your opinion. I know it's all about my connection with them, but you might pick up on something I don't."

Why did he feel like a teenager winning a date to the prom? "Sure."

"Awesome! And I'm rethinking the idea of getting a trained

therapy horse. It might be worth the investment, even though it'll mean I can't get my own property for a while because it'll take a lot of my savings. But what if I meet with Tempe's connections and then I have nothing to show them?" She was talking so fast, he couldn't get a word in. "I won't even be able to say I'll be ready in three or six months because there's no way I can be. I thought having two years to train the horses would give me breathing space and that I would need that time to prepare, but I'm not sure I want breathing space anymore. You gave me a nudge to get started, and now I want it *so* bad, and I don't want to wait two years to start putting the pieces together and making a name for myself. I'm ready to jump in with two feet, even if it means starting at my dad's ranch."

She took a breath, and Jax looked at Nick with his brows lifted.

Yeah, I know. She's a whirlwind.

"So, like I said, I think you might be right, Nick. Maybe I should look at buying a couple of trained horses in addition to buying two that I can train myself. I'm still undecided, but I'm thinking about it."

Nick cocked a grin. "Jax, did you hear what she just said?"

"That you were right?"

"Yup. Write this day down in the history books."

Trixie rolled her eyes. "I didn't say you were *definitely* right. I said I'm leaning that way."

"That's not what I heard. How about you, Jax?"

Jax opened his car door and said, "Don't put me in the middle. I'm just the pot pie delivery boy." He grabbed the pot pie from the car and handed it to Nick. "Here you go, bro. Good luck. See ya, Trix."

"Bye, Jax. See you at Tully's Friday night. That looks delicious." Trixie eyed the pot pie. "I'm starved."

Jax waved as he climbed into his car.

Trixie blinked up at Nick, her eyes dancing with excitement. "What do you think?"

Nick draped an arm over her shoulder, thinking she was the most adorable, sexy whirlwind he'd ever known, and said, "I think you should tell me again how I'm right."

TRIXIE TALKED A mile a minute throughout dinner and while they did the evening chores, debating the pros and cons of buying horses that were already trained. When he said good night to the horses, she climbed up on the fence beside Nick and talked to them about her debate, then proceeded to tell the horses what great listeners they were.

"I just listened to you talk nonstop for two hours," he said as they headed inside. "Where's my praise?"

She laughed and kissed his cheek without missing a step. "Can we watch a movie? My brain is going in circles, and I need to slow it down because I'm going running with Travis tomorrow morning and I'll never sleep if I don't distract myself from my thoughts."

Christ, really? Travis again?

"I know you don't love television, but we can watch a cowboy movie. Clint Eastwood? *The Good, the Bad and the Ugly? The Outlaw Josey Wales?*" She leaned into his side, her long lashes fluttering around her beautiful brown eyes. "*Please?*"

"Fine." When had it become impossible to tell her no?

"Yay!" She hugged him.

He showered and changed into a pair of black sweats, and she put on her sleeping shorts and tank top, with no bra, of course. Lord help him. She ran around turning off all the lights, with Pugsly scampering after her, as he queued up the movie. She always turned the lights off. She said it made her feel more like she was in a theater.

"You ready, Energizer Bunny?" He stretched out on the couch, leaving her the leather recliner, which she claimed was the best seat in the house.

"Just about." She went into the bedroom and returned a few minutes later with a blanket.

"Cold?"

"A little." She plopped down on the couch, stretched out in front of him, and began spreading the blanket over their legs.

"What are you doing?"

"Getting comfy. Turn the movie on."

He started the movie, wondering how in the hell he was supposed to pay attention to a movie when she was snuggling closer and wiggling her ass against his groin. When he put down the remote, she pulled his arm around her, tucking his hand beneath her ribs, and placed her hand over his, sighing content-edly. Pugsly jumped onto the sliver of cushion in front of her and curled up. Trixie pulled Pugsly closer, so he was resting against Nick's hand, and put her hand over his again. It was a strangely wonderful feeling, having his two favorite *friends* so close. He knew he was digging a hole he'd have a hard time finding his way out of if he stayed in that position, but Trixie was soft and warm and fit perfectly against him. He didn't want to move.

Apparently neither did she, because she stayed right there. He was surprised that he didn't spend the whole movie fighting the urge to strip her naked and take her six ways to Sunday. There was no denying that he wanted her, but he liked this, too, just being together, knowing she was safe in his arms. He wished the movie would never end.

But, of course, it eventually did.

Trixie sat up slowly and yawned. "Thanks for watching with me. I'll see you after my run in the morning. G'night." She kissed his cheek and stepped away.

He sat up and grabbed her wrist, jealousy and something much deeper digging its heels in. Her brows knitted, and he said, "I don't like the thought of you going out with Travis."

A sweet smile curved her lips. She tilted her head and shrugged. "Then don't think about it."

As he watched her walk into her bedroom, his chest felt like it was cracking open, and he realized Jax was right. This thing between them wasn't as new as he thought, at least not on his side. She'd been in his life, in his head, and in his heart, for a very long time.

He was completely and utterly screwed.

Chapter Eleven

THERE WAS NOTHING quite like a morning run, and running with Travis made it even more enjoyable. He was funny, smart, and as easy to talk to as he was on the eyes. As they neared the end of their run, he told Trixie about his family.

"It's just me and my two sisters. Tatum, the oldest, is a dive instructor in Florida, and our younger sister, Chelsea, owns two boutiques. One here in town, the other in Peaceful Harbor. Nick's cousin's wife runs Chelsea's boutique in Peaceful Harbor."

"I had no idea you were Chelsea's brother. Nate's wife, Jewel, raves about her. Small world. So you were the only boy in a house full of estrogen. That must have been fun."

"I've got no complaints. My sisters are great, and from what you told me about your brothers, I can safely say that I wasn't nearly as much of a pain to them as your brothers were to you."

"I'm sure your sisters appreciate that. Give me the scoop on the good stuff. Were there any Braden-Helms crushes when y'all were growing up?"

He laughed. "I don't think there was a girl around who didn't have a crush on a Braden. But I knew better than to put my hands on Tempe or Shannon. Those girls were like forbidden fruit. Their brothers watched over them like hawks. I've heard stories about guys who got too close back then."

"I've heard some of those stories. Now that Tempe and Shannon are married, the only Braden forbidden fruit around here is Jilly." Shortly after Ty and Aiyla's wedding, Shannon, the last of Nick's single Peaceful Harbor cousins, had married Steve Johnson in a small, private ceremony.

"I swear Jilly has coffee running through her veins. Nick says she never sleeps, and I believe it. Whenever I see her in town, she's zipping around in heels like she has fifteen places to be. That's a woman who belongs in New York City, not our rinky-dink town."

"That's our Jilly. I love her, but she really doesn't sleep. That's why I stay with Nick. She says she hears her muse best in the wee hours of the morning." As they jogged down Nick's driveway, Trixie said, "Thanks for listening to me rattle on about my horse dilemma."

"No worries. You've got great business sense. You should trust your instincts. If you think you should get trained horses, then do it."

"I still don't know what I'm going to do, but I appreciate you giving me time to figure it out before making a final decision about your minis."

"There's no rush on my end."

She saw Nick walking toward them with a slightly tense expression. She guessed that was to be expected, given how he felt about Travis asking her out. She'd loved lying in Nick's arms last night, and even though he'd been rigid as nails when she'd first laid beside him, it hadn't taken long for the tension to ease from his embrace. She'd wanted to fall asleep cuddled up with her favorite man, but she couldn't be the only one taking steps in that direction, or she'd never know if she was forcing their connection and making it into something it wasn't.

Nick waved, and they waved back. She was glad Travis's asking her out wasn't coming between Nick and Travis's friendship.

As she and Travis slowed to a walk, Nick lifted his chin in that manly greeting she'd come to love and said, "She run you ragged, Travis?"

"Just about. When are you going to throw on some running shoes and pound the pavement with us?"

Nick's gaze slid to Trixie, making her already overheated body sweat even more as he said, "I told you I was built to ride, not run."

Yes, you were. She'd been thinking about doing just that since their shower yesterday. She wanted to be on top, to see every ounce of pleasure glowing in his dark eyes. The way those eyes were raking down her body told her he might be thinking the same thing. Her nerves caught fire. Could Travis see it? Could he feel the electricity zinging between them? In an effort to break the sexual tension, she said the first thing that came to mind. "If Nick ever ran with us, he'd probably blow us away. Have you ever seen him train? The man has legs of steel."

"Yeah, I know it." Travis whipped off his shirt and used it to wipe his face, inciting another teeth-grinding look from Nick. Travis dragged his shirt down his beautifully sculpted chest and abs and said, "See you tomorrow morning? Same time?"

"Definitely."

"Great." Travis pulled open his truck door. "See you around, Nick."

Nick nodded and put a hand on Trixie's lower back as they

walked down the driveway. She liked that new little sign of possessiveness.

"You need to get changed. I'm heading up to Pennsylvania to check out a horse, and I'd like you to come with me. I could use an extra hand."

"Sure." That sounded fun. She loved taking road trips with Nick. "Don't we have to feed the animals first?"

"Already taken care of, darlin'. I'm going to hook up the trailer while you get cleaned up."

"Okay, give me fifteen minutes for a quick shower."

As she headed for the house, he called after her, "Be sure to do your hair and makeup. I don't want my associates thinking you're not a serious businesswoman."

She smiled to herself at the tease and lifted her arm, flipping him the bird as she walked away, which earned her a rumble of laughter.

TRIXIE SANG ALONG to the radio on the way to Pennsylvania, trying to get Nick to do the same, but he just shook his head, drumming his fingers to the beat on the steering wheel. When he turned off the highway, she gazed out the window, thinking about Emmaline's comment about their friendship. They did have an awesome friendship, and wasn't the ability to have amazing sex and still work on the ranch together *and* enjoy a road trip without getting bored or irritated the ultimate test of a relationship? If the look on Nick's face was any indication, she'd say they'd nailed it.

He turned down a rural road lined with fields, which reminded her of Nick's road. "What kind of horse are you looking at?"

"They've got a few I'd like to check out. We're almost there."

They drove by a pasture of miniature horses. "Nick, look at all the minis!"

He turned down the next driveway, passing a sign for the MILLER RANCH AND TRAINING CENTER—THERAPY-TRAINED MINIATURE HORSES.

Trixie's heart stumbled. "*Nick...?* What are we really doing here?"

The edges of his lips tipped up. "You can't make an informed decision about buying trained therapy horses without knowing your options."

"You came all this way for me?" She felt giddy.

He winked, which was so *him*. Most guys would want accolades. Then again, most guys would probably just say how they felt. Nick *showed* her, and even though she knew her big-hearted friend would have done it whether or not they were sleeping together, the fact that they were made it seem even more special.

"I've known Ed and Mary Miller for years. They're good, trustworthy people. They've been breeding minis for twenty years and training them for therapy for a decade." He cocked a grin, stealing a glance at her. "I called them yesterday after you admitted that I was *right*."

"I never said you were *definitely* right," she teased, unable to stop grinning. She knew how hard it was for him to show his true warm and squishy emotions, and his actions spoke louder than words ever could. She unhooked her seat belt and slid across the bench seat as he parked. When he cut the engine, she threw her arms around him and planted a hard kiss on his cheek. "Thank you *so* much."

"No prob, darlin'."

"Why didn't you tell me about this place sooner?"

"You were dead set on training your own horses, and I know you too well to try to change your mind. But I'll warn you, their horses are expensive. They range from fifty-five hundred to eight or nine grand, depending on the level of training and the horse."

"I knew trained minis would be expensive, but since I hadn't wanted to go that route, I hadn't spent much time researching them. I was going to look into my options this afternoon. You beat me to it."

"I poked around last night on the Internet to see what else was out there and made a few calls this morning to people I know. You can probably get an older therapy horse for a good bit less, but you know how that goes. You might not get many years out of them."

"That's true, but if I buy a couple of horses at the prices you mentioned, it will eat away at my savings. I'd have to wait to buy my own place. There's a lot to think about."

"But you'd be turning a profit much quicker and would be able to do this full time much sooner. I'll look at the numbers with you when we get home if you'd like. Why don't we check out the horses and see how you feel about them? You don't have to make any decisions today. We can come out here anytime. I just didn't want you to spend all of your money on untrained horses before you checked out all your options."

Her giddiness turned to deeper appreciation as he climbed out of the truck. He reached for her hand to help her out, and she pulled him closer, so he was standing between her legs. She took his face between her hands and pressed her lips to his. She'd planned on giving him just a quick thank-you kiss, but he clutched her waist and leaned in, taking it deeper.

When their lips parted, he kept her close, searching her eyes, as if he were trying to puzzle her out, and said, "What was that for?"

"For being *you*. For watching out for me and not rushing me through the process. For taking me seriously even though I'm sort of putting the pieces together as I go, and for telling me to do my hair and makeup because you knew that I wanted to be taken seriously." She pushed playfully at his chest. "Now, step out of the way, cowboy, before it goes to that big head of yours. We have horses to see."

As Nick stepped back, an older, portly man wearing a bright red button-down shirt, faded jeans, and a warm smile came into view. He had a trim gray beard, and his friendly eyes shifted between Nick and Trixie.

Nick extended his hand. "Mornin', Ed. It's good to see you."

"You as well, Nick." Ed took Nick's hand and pulled him into a manly embrace. "It was good to hear from you."

Nick put his hand on Trixie's back, as he had that morning, as if to say, *She's mine,* and that made her all kinds of happy. "Trixie Jericho, this is Ed Miller, the finest therapy horse trainer around."

Ed tipped his hat. "It's a pleasure to meet you, Trixie. I hear you're trying to decide if you want to purchase trained horses or train them yourself."

"Yes, that's right. Thank you for letting us visit."

"The way Nick sang your praises, I'd have to be a fool not to make time for you. It sounds like our horses would be lucky to be in your hands."

She stole a glance at Nick, and he winked, stirring butter-flies in her chest. *Could this day get any better?*

"We've just turned out some of the horses. Why don't I show you around and give you the rundown on our training process."

As they made their way down the driveway, a ranch-style house, two large barns, and an enormous warehouse came into view. Trixie took note of the manicured lawns and sturdy fencing around the pastures and corrals. Everything was well cared for, and she liked that. Several horses trotted over to a fence as they walked by, bobbing their heads for attention. They were beautiful bays, black, white, and pinto horses, all bright eyed and curious.

Ed stopped so she could admire them. "These are our mares and geldings."

"They're gorgeous. Look how friendly they are, Nick." She petted them.

"It takes a special horse to be a service animal. We pride ourselves on breeding for temperament and size. All of our minis are between twenty-four and thirty-two inches at their withers. Our foals stay with their moms for the first six months, which allows for gradual, stress-free weaning. We believe that helps with their gentle nature. And they're all up to date with vaccinations." Ed pointed to a corral where a woman was working with a horse and said, "In addition to therapy training, we offer horses with advanced gold-star training, which includes trick training. We're the only facility on the East Coast that offers videos of our horses on the job in hospitals and other facilities, so you know you're getting a horse that is actually trained."

"That's incredible. Are there different levels of training?" Trixie asked as they followed a paved path toward a massive, two-story arena.

"Yes. We classify our levels as basic, intermediate, and advanced. We begin halter training shortly after birth, and once the horse is ready, the timing of which varies, we begin the real training. Gently, of course, with the mothers by their sides. Usually by four to six months, we start bringing the mares and their babies to nursing homes together, to get the foals acclimated to what they'll be doing in the future."

"That's the best way, starting when they're young," she agreed.

"We believe so. There are no hard-and-fast guidelines for the levels of training, because, like people, horses' abilities vary. We consider a horse to be trained on a basic level when they've worked through housebreaking, mock visits, and obstacles and have been exposed to loud noises, floorings, furnishings, and have other unique therapy horse experiences. We do that training here. Basic trained horses are ready to make their first solo soft visits in controlled environments such as Walmart or a home-improvement store. We use those visits to evaluate where the horses need more attention and training."

"Is it difficult to set those visits up with the stores?" Trixie said.

"Most people are eager to help, but, of course, you've got to have insurance in place, and you need to control the number of people approaching the horse, so the horse doesn't get overwhelmed," Ed explained. "All of that is discussed ahead of time. If you decide to train your own minis, we have contacts through our associates in several states. We can help you make those connections, whether you buy a horse from us or not."

"That's so nice of you. Thank you." She looked at Nick, who nodded as if to say, *See? He's a good guy.* "What kind of training does a horse get after basic?"

"After mastering those first visits, they're ready for intermediate training. They progress to soft visits in assisted living facilities, hospice, and rehab centers. We take them to facilities that aren't as busy as hospitals to prepare them. Their first visits are solely to learn the environment and get used to the sights, sounds, and smells, not to visit with patients. Once the handlers feel they're ready, they begin one-on-one visits with patients. And when a horse has completed at least a year of consistent training and patient visits, the horses that we feel can handle more move on to advanced training. That's when they visit with groups, where there's more going on, such as airports, children's events, parades, and the like."

"That's a lot of training. Have you had horses who simply aren't suited for therapy?"

"We've been lucky. We've had only a handful in the last ten years that haven't been right for therapy." He nodded to the arena and said, "Let me show you some of our training facilities."

Inside the arena were three handlers who looked to be around Trixie's age working with mares and their foals. Trixie's heart squeezed at the sight of the babies watching their mamas and following in turn. They were adorable and eager. But the horses weren't the only impressive sight. She'd never seen such an elaborate training area. On one side of the arena, a woman with a long blond braid was walking a foal up a wide set of steps to an elevator. On the other end of the arena, another handler was taking a mare and its foal over various types of flooring, and in the center of the arena was a younger woman working with another mare and her baby on basic commands.

Trixie leaned against Nick and said, "Look at those babies."

He gazed down at her with the softest expression she'd ever seen on him and put an arm around her, keeping her close.

"The foals are hard to resist," Ed said. "The handlers are my daughters, Caroline, Molly, and Heidi. They've been working with horses since they were waist high."

"Me too, although not like this. My family owns a cattle ranch, but we also have horses. We do general training, and Nick taught me freestyle training techniques."

Ed nodded. "He told me you have a way with horses and that you're quite the stunt rider."

"I'm not bad," she said modestly. "I have to ask, is that a *real* elevator?"

"Yes. It goes to the second floor, where there are more training stages. We have rooms set up with hospital beds, wheelchairs, and various types of rehab equipment to help acclimate the horses before they go on their first visits. We play sound clips replicating the sounds in hospitals, too. The earlier and more often they're exposed to those things, the more comfortable they'll be. The horses also frequent our house, so they're used to being indoors and navigating around furniture."

"You've got a great setup, Ed. It's very impressive," she said.

"Thank you. Are you ready to meet a few of our beauties?"

"Yes," she said excitedly.

"After talking with Nick, I took the liberty of picking out a few horses that I thought would fit your needs," Ed said as they left the arena and headed down another path toward a small red barn. "Nick said you would be bringing the horses to children's parties, too, so I've chosen four advanced horses. They're comfortable with groups and screaming children, and they get along well with each other, which is important."

"Perfect." She mouthed *Thank you* to Nick, and he nodded.

Beside the barn was a small fenced area with four beautiful horses. "Here we are," Ed said. "The white filly is Annabelle. She's thirty-two inches and four years old. Annabelle's been doing advanced visits for two years. She's a sweetheart, and she's trick trained."

"How much is she?" Trixie asked.

"She's the most expensive of these four, at sixty-eight hundred dollars."

Trixie tried not to react to the price, and slid her hand into Nick's. He held her hand tighter and stepped closer, making her feel even more connected to—and supported by—him.

"The handsome chestnut is Dreamer. He's a three-year-old gelding, and twenty-eight inches tall. Dreamer has a little more than a year of advanced visits, and he's a real charmer. Dreamer is five thousand dollars."

Nick squeezed her hand again.

"The bay gelding is Alfie, and the pinto filly is Elsa. They're four years old. Alfie is twenty-six inches, and Elsa is twenty-four. They're gentle as can be, and both have two years of advanced visits. They're fifty-eight hundred each. I'm not here to sell you on my horses. They'll do that themselves," Ed said kindly. "But I will say this. A trained horse will help bring other horses up to speed. It takes a lot of patience to train a therapy horse, but minis are smart, and they're eager to learn."

Nick brushed his thumb over the back of Trixie's hand and said, "Trixie is as patient and charming with the horses as she is with people."

His vote of confidence and that intimate touch sent shivers of delight through her. She wondered if he really thought she was charming. She didn't think of herself that way.

"Well, then, why don't you spend some time with them and see if you connect," Ed suggested. "If you don't feel comfortable with any of them, we can choose others. There's no pressure from my end. We're here every day, and you can come back as many times as you'd like. But if you do connect with any of them, you can work with one of my girls to take the horses for a test drive through the arena training areas and watch the videos to see them in action."

"That sounds great. Thank you, Ed." Trixie was worried about the cost of the horses, but as Ed opened the gate and Dreamer came to greet them, the excitement of working with trained horses took over. "Hi, beautiful. How are you today?" She petted him as the other horses approached. Annabelle rubbed her neck against Nick's leg. "I hear you, girlfriend. He just draws you in, doesn't he?"

Nick and Ed chuckled.

Ed stayed with them while they visited for the first half hour, answering their questions and going over the commands the horses were taught. When he left them alone with the horses, Trixie looked up from where she was crouched beside Annabelle and said, "These horses are amazing! They follow every command, and they're so docile. I love that Ed's family works here. It reminds me of home. I feel good about this, Nick."

They spent the next hour getting to know the horses, taking them through more commands and talking about their personalities. She loved them *all*, and her excitement bubbled out. "If I move forward with two trained horses, I could spend a month bonding with them, get them used to my parents' ranch, set up the company and insurance, and start the business in no time. Assuming I can pick up clients, of course."

"You know you will, Trix. You just have to make the connections, and you said Tempe is going to help you get started with that. You'll do great. Who could possibly resist you?"

The way he held her gaze gave her the feeling he was including himself in that comment, and that sent another thrill through her. "You really believe in me, don't you?"

"I always have." He paused just long enough for her to wonder if he meant something more by that. "I wouldn't have offered to help you do this if I didn't believe in you. You know horses and you're great with people, which is why your old man has you working with customers. You're determined to succeed, and your heart is in it. There's no way you'll fail."

"Then you don't think it's a mistake to use some of the money I was going to use toward buying property on these horses instead?"

He crouched beside her. "Without the horses, there is no business for a year or two, and from what I just heard, probably closer to two."

Alfie put his muzzle in her chest. "Hello, beautiful boy." She loved him up. "Do you like helping people?" She looked at Nick, loving that *he* liked helping *her*, and said, "It feels like the right thing to do. I can get two trained horses from Ed and two that aren't trained from Travis. Then I get the best of both worlds, and as Ed said, the trained horses can help lead the way for the others."

His expression turned serious. "Then I guess the big question is, can you handle working on the ranch with your brothers' taunting you without losing your mind?"

She loved that he was always two steps ahead *and* looking out for her. "I've survived it this long. I think I can handle it for a little longer." She nudged him playfully. "I put up with you, don't I?"

He smiled. "That you do."

"Besides, I told you what my father said, and they all apologized. Hopefully, things will be different when I get back. What do you think? Can I steal a few more hours of your time to take them through the arena, watch the videos, and try to make a decision as hard as Sophie's choice?"

He leaned in like he was going to kiss her, but stopped short, as if he'd caught himself, and said, "My day is yours, darlin'."

Chapter Twelve

NICK NEVER IMAGINED he'd be spending a Tuesday night drinking champagne in his barn with Trixie. But there he was heading across the grass with a bottle of his best bubbly and two glasses, after an incredible day of watching her not only chase her dreams but grab hold of them with both hands and make them come true. She'd connected with so many of the horses, she'd had a hell of a time deciding which horses to bring home. In the end, Nick was pretty sure the horses had made the final decision for her. Annabelle and Alfie had taken to Trixie as if she'd raised and trained them herself. Annabelle had also taken a liking to Nick, which Trixie had claimed was a sign that the beautiful white filly was meant to be hers. He'd fucking loved that, almost as much as he'd loved the way she'd leapt into his arms and kissed him after they'd gotten the horses in the trailer. He'd never seen her so happy, and hell if that hadn't elated him, too. But ever the whirlwind, on the way home she'd snapped into business mode and had called Dirk Boyle, her father's business attorney, and Wylie Knoll, his insurance agent. She might have had a loose plan before, but now Trixie Jericho was plowing full speed ahead, and Nick knew she was going to take the horse therapy world by storm.

It'd been hell trying to rein in his emotions all day. But this was *her* big day, and she didn't need him pawing at her. When they got home, she showered Annabelle and Alfie with love and stayed by the corral with them. They'd put the horses into a shared stall for the night to help ease the stress of leaving their friends and everything they knew behind. He and Trixie had sat in the stall with them for a couple of hours to help them settle into their new surroundings. Throughout the day, as Trixie took charge and loved on her new babies, Nick felt himself falling harder for her. He'd seen her with horses for years, and he hadn't expected to feel anything different today. But it was getting harder to fight his feelings, and now that the lines had blurred between them, he was having a difficult time remembering why he should.

Trixie was coming out of Annabelle and Alfie's stall with her phone pressed to her ear when Nick walked into the barn. He held up the champagne bottle, and her eyes widened, along with her smile. And just like that, he had the urge to pick her up and kiss her again. What the hell kind of spell did she have him under?

She held up one finger as she spoke into the phone. "I spent two hours with Ed's daughter, Molly, going through commands and training techniques. I know what they're used to." She paused, listening. "I've got it under control, Dad. I called Dirk and Wylie on the way back from getting the horses. Dirk's setting everything up this week. He'll give Wylie the legal information, and Wylie will use your address to set up the insurance."

They'd ordered pizza for dinner, and Nick had known they'd be out there for a while, so he'd set up camp outside the horses' stall, piling up blankets for them to sit on. He placed the glasses and bottle on the floor beside the blankets and carried the empty pizza box to the trash. He knew her father would be supportive, but he hated the idea of Trixie starting her business on her family's ranch, when she'd been adamant against doing so. He also knew she'd have been miserable waiting a year or two to start doing what she really wanted. She'd made the right decision with the horses. He just hoped her brothers didn't drive her nuts.

"Okay. Thanks again, Dad. I love you, too. I will. Bye." She shoved her phone in her pocket, her eyes glittering in the evening light. "I thought you went inside to charge your phone."

"When's the last time I gave a damn about my phone?"

She eyed the bottle. "Is that *champagne?*"

"Well, it ain't whiskey."

She crossed her arms and jutted out her hip, looking sexy as hell. "When did you become a champagne guy?"

Jesus. Why did her challenges make him want her even more? "When you bought your first therapy horses." He grabbed her wrist and hauled her against him, growling against her lips, "You want to challenge me or celebrate?"

She slid her arms around his waist, rubbing against him, her eyes dark and seductive. "I guess that depends on *how* we're going to celebrate."

Man, she destroyed him. He lowered his mouth to hers, taking her ravenously, as he'd been dying to do all day. She pushed her fingers into his hair, sending his hat to the ground as he deepened the kiss. Every swipe of their tongues sent bolts of lightning to his groin. He'd never known such a passionate woman who gave as much as she took. Then again, he'd never let any woman *take* with him, until *her*. He kissed her harder, trying to outrun the emotions that sparked, but she palmed him through his jeans, and his thoughts fractured, unleashing the beast he'd fought to keep chained down. He tore off her shirt and bra and unzipped her jeans, shoving them down.

"Boots," she panted out, tugging at his shirt. "Take this *off.*"

She was so damn bossy, it made her even *hotter.* He swept her into his arms and laid her on the blankets, taking off her boots and stripping her naked. He made quick work of ridding himself of his boots and clothes and came down over her.

"You drive me crazy." He reclaimed her luscious mouth, his hard length brushing against her wetness. Her legs circled his waist, making him ache to be inside her. But he had plans for her big night, and after a year of *wanting* her, he was going to give her an unforgettable night.

It nearly killed him to delay gratification, but he broke their kiss, meeting her confused, and fucking hot, gaze. "We haven't even begun celebrating yet, darlin'."

He grabbed the open bottle of champagne and tipped it up to his lips, holding the champagne in his mouth as he set the bottle down, then took her in a long, passionate kiss. The sweetness of the champagne mixed with the fierce and delicious taste of *her* sent lust spiking through him. He wanted to kiss her all damn night, but he was too hungry for more of her. He rose onto his knees, and holy hell, she was stunning. Her dark hair fanned out around her face, her glistening lips were pink from the force of their kisses, and the desire in her eyes showed as much greed as he felt.

"Open your mouth," he said roughly.

Her eyes flamed, the trust in them overwhelming, as her lips parted. "*Sweet Jesus.* You're so damn sexy." He lifted the champagne bottle and poured a slow stream into her mouth.

She lapped at it, and he moved the bottle lower, pouring champagne down her chest and over her breasts.

"*Ohmygod*," she panted out as he set the bottle down.

"I have been dying to do body shots off you ever since you mentioned it in Colorado."

As he lowered his lips toward hers, she whispered, "You have?"

"Every damn minute of the day." He slicked his tongue along her lips. "*Delicious.*"

He followed the path of liquid down her chest with his mouth, tasting, sucking, licking. She rocked and writhed, moaning as he sucked her nipple against the roof of his mouth. Her eyes closed, and he lavished her other breast with the same attention. "Open your eyes, darlin'. I want to see how much you enjoy this."

She watched as he poured champagne along the gentle swell of her stomach, in her belly button, and down to the apex of her sex. The cool liquid dripped between her legs, and she sucked in air through clenched teeth, fisting her hands in the blanket. He set the bottle down, his mouth watering for his first real taste of her. He lowered his mouth to her stomach, licking the champagne dripping down her sides, earning needy whimpers. He palmed her breasts, squeezing her nipples as he licked in and around her belly button.

"*Nick, I can't take it.*"

His eyes held hers. "Trust me, darlin', you're going to take it hard and fast, and torturously slow. I'm going to make you feel so good, you won't be able to think of me without needing to come."

Her eyes widened, and just as quickly they narrowed, and she said, "Prove it."

He knew she meant it as a challenge, but it came out breathy and pleading, and so damn needy, it nearly did him in. "Hold on tight, darlin'. I'm in the mood for a feast."

He spread his hands on her thighs, pinning them down as he slicked his tongue along the very heart of her, earning a low, sexy moan. Her essence mixed with the champagne, as sweet as sugar and as rich as honey. He teased her with his tongue, making her squirm and moan, her every sound heightening his arousal. He used his mouth on the bundle of nerves where she needed it most, and she bowed off the blankets, her thighs flexing. He sealed his mouth over her sex, fucking her with his tongue and using his fingers on those sensitive nerves, taking her to the brink of release. Her body trembled and shook.

"Come for me," fell demandingly from his lips as he quickened his efforts.

She spiraled over the edge, arching and writhing, crying out his name. He stayed with her, taking everything she had to give, and when she finally came down from the peak, he sent her soaring again. Her hungry sounds were music to his ears. He gripped the base of his cock to stave off his own release and stayed with her, licking and sucking, until she collapsed to the blanket, panting and limp. Only then did he kiss his way up her body, tasting the lingering sweetness of the champagne. His heart hammered against his ribs as her eyes fluttered open, and he laced their fingers together, pinning them beside her head.

She craned up as he lowered his lips to hers, meeting him in a hungry, passionate kiss as their bodies came together. Like an addict getting his next hit, a sense of euphoria overcame him, chased by a surge of desire that sent his hips pumping. He'd been wrong when he'd thought he'd felt nothing before her. He felt so damn much with Trixie, he realized he *had* felt something before.

He'd felt *empty*.

That realization had him holding her tighter, moving more fervently. She met his urgent, greedy pace. He'd meant what he'd said about satisfying her, and he spent the rest of the night proving it.

Chapter Thirteen

TRIXIE SAT IN the grass in the shade of the barn Wednesday afternoon between the corral where Annabelle and Alfie were playing and the ring where Nick was trick riding, trying to focus on work. She'd been *trying* to focus all day, but every time she thought about Nick, her body vibrated with sexual energy, which had made her run with Travis interesting and helping Nick with the morning chores torturous. She'd spent the last couple of hours making phone calls, going through her budget, and making lists of facilities she wanted to contact once she had her pitch down pat. All of which had taken much longer than it should have because of said *cowboy withdrawals*. Thank goodness she was keeping things low-key with the horses for a few days while they got used to their new temporary surroundings. She and Nick had walked them around the ranch and groomed them. She'd taken a million pictures and had even coaxed Nick into taking a few with her.

Her phone dinged with a text message from Destiny Peters, Jillian's friend who Trixie had spoken to earlier about creating a logo and a website for Rising Hope. They'd come up with a great logo concept—a miniature horse with wings and a unicorn horn set against the backdrop of a rising sun. She thumbed out a response to Destiny's question about color schemes, attached a picture of Annabelle for her to use for the logo mock-up, and sent it off. Then she sent some of the selfies she'd taken with the horses to her family and friends with the caption *Meet my babies, Annabelle and Alfie!* She sent one to Nick, too, although she'd seen his phone on the kitchen counter when she'd gone in to make lunch. At least he'd have it when he retrieved his phone.

She looked at him riding Lady, and her breath caught. He was a sight to be reckoned with, standing atop the gorgeous horse as she sped around the ring. Nick was in full control as he lowered himself to the saddle, then spun around, sitting backward. His biceps flexed as he swung both legs over one side, his feet purposefully hitting the ground, vaulting him up, and he threw his leg over the horse and sat forward. Trixie had no idea how a man of his size could be so agile, but he performed one trick after another, each more beautiful than the last. *Beautiful* might be a funny way to think of stunts others called *cool* or *exciting*. But Nick Braden doing what he loved was the most beautiful sight she'd ever seen. He moved seamlessly into a shoulder stand, hanging off the side of the horse upside down, his legs pointing straight up to the sky. From there he returned to the saddle, intently focused as he slid off the side of the horse again, lying parallel to the ground and holding himself up with one strong arm. Lady never slowed down; their trust in each other was explicit. Lady was his perfect partner.

And she was going to have to share, because Trixie was sure Nick was *her* perfect partner, too. Her mind tiptoed back to last night. When they'd finally gone inside, she'd kissed him good night and went to her bedroom. She'd thought he might tug her back into his arms or come after her, but he hadn't. That had stung, but it had also been okay, because she knew in her heart that even if it took him time to sort out his feelings and let her in, their connection was soul deep. She felt it in his touch, tasted it in his kisses, and he'd shown her as much by giving her so many little treasures of hope throughout their amazing day yesterday, holding her hand and touching her like she was his girlfriend. She'd caught him gazing at her a number of times when she was getting to know the horses and working with Ed's daughter, and she wondered if *he* had an idea that the way he looked at her had changed in the last few days, too.

Annabelle moseyed over to the fence, bobbing her head for attention. Trixie set down her laptop and went to pet her. Alfie trotted over to get in on the lovin', and both of the horses stared out at Nick. Her new little girl sighed as Nick climbed off Lady and headed their way.

I'm right there with you, Annabelle.

Trixie's phone dinged rapidly with texts from her brothers and friends. She read Lindsay's message first. *OMG! I want one! So cute!* Trixie petted Alfie as she read Shane's message. "Uncle Shane says you and Annabelle look just like me. He's such a dork." As she read Jeb's message, *Congrats! I'm happy for you!* a text from Trace rolled in. *Love your party ponies. Congrats!* He'd added a winking emoji.

"Hey." Nick petted Annabelle and Alfie.

"Hi. You were awesome out there."

He cracked a soft smile, another thing she'd been graced with a little more often lately. "Thanks."

"I can't wait to see your show. Are you bringing a crew, or do you need me to help with the horses?" The crew usually consisted of a couple of volunteers who helped take care of the horses, brought them out when he was ready, and took them back to the stalls after the show.

"No. I have a local crew in Heart Valley. I've done that show a number of times."

"Is any of your family going to the show?"

"No. They go when they can, but it's about two hours from here, and everyone's busy. But I'm glad you'll be there."

He held her gaze, and the air sizzled between them. "Me too. What's next after that show?"

He looked away, as if the connection were too strong. They never talked about the sexy things they did or the hard-to-ignore blistering heat between them. Things never got awkward, but they had *these* moments, when Nick needed that little bit of space to find his footing. A little space was okay. She was glad things weren't awkward between them, and she chalked that up to the fact that they were *that* right for each other.

Nick took off his hat and pushed a hand through his thick dark hair. As he put his hat back on, he said, "Roanoke, in October."

"Oh, good. I'll try to go to that one, too, and cheer you on." It was tough to ignore the way her body caught fire every time their eyes met, but there were worse fates than craving a man too much.

"That'd be great." His eyes found hers again. "Do you want to go in and grab something to eat?"

"I made us lunch." She pointed to the cooler by the side of the barn, where she'd been sitting. "Sandwiches, fruit, chips. Nothing special."

A surprised "Huh" tumbled out. "Thanks."

They ate in the shade of the barn, and she caught him up on the things she'd accomplished that morning. "I think I'm going to get two minis from Travis. It's easier to get settled into new places and routines with a friend, and then they'll be fully trained at around the same time."

"That sounds like a good idea. Have you considered working with a partner in the future? When you have four trained horses, another handler to take them out on visits might be helpful."

"I was thinking about that. It's a good idea, but I'd have to really trust the person." Her phone chimed with a text, and she glanced at the screen. "It's Jilly. I sent her a picture of my babies."

"She'll go apeshit over them."

Trixie read the message. *OMG! I can't wait to meet them. Let's have dinner before meeting Jax and Nick at Tully's Friday. I'll pick you up at six. Okay?* "You're right. She's excited, and it looks like she's picking me up for dinner Friday night before meeting you and Jax for drinks." She thumbed out a response. *Okay. See you then!*

He looked at the horses, the muscles in his jaw bunching. Trixie had seen the same look on his face when he'd said he didn't like the idea of her going out with Travis. But saying he didn't like the idea of it was very different from saying he wanted her all to himself. Like that night, she was tempted to try to get a clearer reaction out of him beyond his silent frustration. But whatever came of them, or didn't, had to come from his heart without use of a crowbar.

She tucked away the urge to climb onto his lap and coax him into talking to her and focused on the horses instead. "Is it weird that I feel like Annabelle and Alfie were meant to be mine? Look how easily they're adapting to being here. It reminds me of how comfortable I felt the very first time I stayed here. It's pretty amazing how quickly humans and animals can bond, isn't it?"

Nick's eyes collided with hers with a look so intense, it sent her insides into a wild flurry. She thought he was going to grab her and kiss her. *Yes, please.* But he didn't, and the longer he stared, the heavier that look became, like the darkening sky before a storm. Her pulse quickened. Was he annoyed? Angry? She thought about what she'd said, but she had no idea what could have bothered him. Just when the silence stretched too long and she reached her wit's end, the shadows in his eyes lifted and his lips curved up, bringing a gust of relief.

"Maybe y'all are fated to be."

A nervous laugh tumbled out before she could stop it. "You don't even believe in fate."

"No, but you do." He winked and pushed to his feet. "Thanks for lunch, darlin'."

He picked up the cooler and headed toward the house, leaving her slack-jawed, and utterly confused.

Chapter Fourteen

FRIDAY EVENING, TRIXIE still had no idea what that look Nick had given her by the barn Wednesday afternoon had meant, but she could describe in great detail what it felt like to be hot and bothered for days on end, thanks to the smoldering-eyed cowboy. She was thrilled that he was helping her with the horses, and he seemed as excited about her business as she was. When Tempest had called to let her know that Jordan had set aside time next Tuesday afternoon to meet with her, Nick had said they'd needed to celebrate. They'd taken a long trail ride, and it had been just the break she'd needed. They'd stopped by to see Walt on the way back, and that had been fun, too, except that she and Nick were insatiable for each other. They could barely look at each other without wanting to tear their clothes off, which had made working side by side, seeing Walt, and yesterday morning's visit with Travis to select her horses *interesting*, to say the least. She was sure Travis had noticed, though he hadn't said anything about it then, or when they'd gone running this morning. At least she and Nick had chosen two of the sweetest horses, a twenty-eight-inch white filly with brown spots she'd named Buttons and a thirty-inch black gelding she and Nick had named Prince, because he carried himself so regally. They were picking them up tomorrow afternoon.

She paced as she put on her earrings, wondering how the heck she was going to act normal at Tully's with Jax and Jillian. She was sure they would know what was up the minute they saw her and Nick together. She felt like she had a neon sign on her forehead telling the world she wanted to get him naked, and the worst part was, she wanted so much more with him than *just* getting naked.

A knock sounded on her bedroom door, and before she could answer it, the door flew open and Jillian breezed in, looking gorgeous in a white miniskirt with lace overlay and silk sleeveless top with a plunging neckline, two of her own designs.

"Hi!" Jillian whistled, looking Trixie up and down. "Holy cow, woman. You're going to blow the guys *away* tonight."

There was only one special guy Trixie wanted to blow away with her off-the-shoulder midriff-baring, bell-sleeved black top and fitted peach miniskirt. "Thanks! I have a great designer," she teased, since she was also wearing Jillian's designs. "You look amazing, too."

"Thank you. We're going to be the hottest girls at that bar tonight, and we're celebrating. I just met your new babies. They're *so* stinking cute, and they don't mind the dogs. That little one is hardly bigger than Goldie. Nick said they're housebroken, too."

"They're incredible. I'm so happy Nick suggested looking at trained horses."

"He said you're still getting two more from Travis?"

"I think I am." She slipped her feet into her nude heels, trying to calm her nerves. She needed to tell Jillian about her and Nick. Not just because Jillian would notice the sparks flying between them, but also because she might need backup, in case Nick flirted with his groupies at the bar. That thought made her feel a little queasy. Even though they didn't talk about what was going on between them, and she had no right to be jealous since they weren't exclusive, she'd be devastated if he flirted with other women, and she'd need Jillian to drag her away before she could do anything stupid.

"Before you know it, you'll have a herd, like my brother."

"No, I won't. Nick has his own ranch, and I won't be getting my own place anytime soon. Those two beautiful babies out there were hugely expensive. I have to start the business at my parents' ranch and see how it goes from there."

"That's even better." Jillian waggled her brows. "Then I can see those hot brothers of yours more often when I come visit."

Speaking of hot brothers…

Before Trixie could chicken out, she said, "Jilly, I need to talk to you about something, but you have to promise you won't say a word to *anyone*."

"Okay," she said cheerily.

"I mean it. No one. Not Emmaline, not Morgyn, or anyone else."

"You know I won't, especially now that you've told me not to." Jillian's brow furrowed. "What's going on?"

Trixie took her hand and sat on the bed, bringing Jillian down beside her. "Don't freak out, but Nick and I are kind of hooking up."

"*What?*" Jillian bolted to her feet. "*No.* No, no, *no. Please* tell me you're not. You're one of my last single friends!"

"*Shh.* Keep your voice down!"

Jillian waved toward the patio doors. "He's outside. He can't hear me."

"Please don't be mad, Jilly. I'm sorry, but I'm also not sorry."

Jillian sighed. "I'm not *mad*. I'm just a little shocked. But I guess I shouldn't be. Emmaline and I thought you guys were going to get together years ago." She gasped, wide eyed, and sat beside Trixie. "You'll be my *sister-in-law*! My mom will be so happy!"

"Whoa. *Stop!* It's not like that."

"So, you're just..." Jillian looked over her shoulder at the bed and cringed. "Do I need to bleach my outfit."

"*No.*" Trixie laughed. "We haven't even done it in a bed." In the last two days, they'd gotten down and dirty in the barn, on the patio, and in the kitchen again, but *not* in a bed.

Jillian groaned. "Why does everyone get hot sex except me?" She leveled a serious stare on Trixie. "If you were having sex with *anyone* else, I'd want all the juicy details. But now I think I need to bleach my brain."

"Would you *stop*?" She was glad for Jillian's levity, but she was still nervous. "I need your help."

"Why? Is he being a dick? Because I'll set him straight."

"No, and you can't say a word to him about any of this. You can't let on that I told you. It's just...I'm the one who started this with an offer of being friends with benefits, and I know he doesn't want anything serious, but at the same time, I really think he feels the way I do and he just won't admit it. *God*, Jilly, I want more with Nick *so* badly." She had no idea where all of *that* honesty had come from, but she felt better having said it.

"Whoa, babe. There are *so* many parts of this to weed through. *You* started it?"

Trixie nodded.

"Look at you, taking what you want. You go, girl," she said supportively. Then her nose wrinkled. "Okay, that's a little gross since he's my brother, but you two *are* perfect together."

"I think we are."

"Yes, you're two *stubborn*, boot-wearing peas in a pod."

"But do you think I'm barking up the wrong tree and setting myself up to get hurt?"

Jillian's brow knitted. "It's hard to say. On the one hand, you couldn't have picked a more autonomous guy. But on the other hand, you already have more with him than anyone else ever has."

"I do?"

"Yes. He's almost thirty-one, and I don't think he's ever had a real girlfriend."

"I wondered about that," she said, thinking about what he'd said about having sex once without using a condom and wondered if he'd always been a no-strings-attached guy.

"There were rumors when I was in high school about him seeing a girl who lived someplace else. But if he did, I never met her, and knowing Nick, it wasn't a girl, but a *horse*. I swear, when we were younger, if he wasn't doing something with the family, he was at Walt's. I don't think he's ever brought a girl to meet our parents. I'll have to ask my mom, but I can't remember him going to prom or anything."

"Oh God, don't ask your mother. It's not like we're dating or anything."

"But it sounds like you're serious about him."

"This might sound bad, since I've stayed at his house for so long. But I've crushed on Nick since I was a teenager. I compare *every* guy to him, Jilly, and it's not like I try to compare them. It just happens."

"That's not bad, Trix. You guys clearly have a connection, or he wouldn't let you stay here. I know he's not warm and fuzzy like my other brothers, but he's a great guy, and he's got the biggest heart."

"I know he does. He's also got a great brain, and don't get me started on his body."

"*Ew.*" Jillian shook her head. "Please don't go there."

Trixie winced. "Sorry. Thanks for understanding."

"Thanks for trusting me. I won't tell anyone. I'm getting excited about it. You guys are really good together. But why did you tell me if you're just hooking up?"

"Because we won't be acting like a couple at the bar tonight, and I wanted you to know why I won't be flirting with other guys."

"That makes sense."

"*Aand…*"

"Oh boy, the truth comes out," Jillian teased.

"I don't know how I'll handle seeing him and his harem now that we've crossed that line, so I might need you to keep me from clawing someone's eyes out. Like Nick's."

"You think he'll flirt with those women in front of you? He'd better not."

Trixie shrugged. "I don't know what to expect, but we're not a couple. Travis asked me out, and—"

"Hold on! *Travis* asked you out? Geez, woman. How'd you manage that one?"

"I don't know. But I turned him down."

"Maybe you shouldn't have. Travis would be a much easier mark than Nick."

"But *Nick…*" She placed her hand over her heart.

Jillian's gaze softened. "Oh, Trix. You've got it bad for my bullheaded brother."

"I do. I didn't tell Nick that I turned Travis down. That sounds horrible, but I wanted to see what he'd do, or if he got jealous."

"That's not horrible. It's one of the only strategies we have to get past all the *I don't cares* and the other bullshit guys say. How did Nick respond?"

"He didn't at first. But then said he *didn't like the idea* of me going out with Travis. But he never said not to, or that *he* wanted to go out with me."

"He's a bonehead."

"I don't think he is, Jilly. I think he's afraid of getting hurt."

"Oh please. *Nick?*" Jillian scoffed. "He's ironclad. Nobody can hurt him."

Trixie didn't want to breach Nick's confidence, so she shrugged and said, "Maybe I'm wrong."

"He's the toughest guy in all of Pleasant Hill. When we were all falling apart after Tory died, he was tough as nails. I love my brother, but if he flirts in front of you tonight, then he *is* an ass, and you should give him hell and *never* hook up with him again."

"I know."

"Don't worry, Trix. I'm here for you. But I don't think Nick will do that. He's not good at warm and fuzzy, but he's not a jerk. He'd never hurt you like that. He's always so protective of you, showing up at the bars when we go out, and he worries about your repu—" Jillian's jaw dropped. "Holy shit. What if he's been into you all this time? I know exactly what you and Nick need to get him to open up."

"A crowbar?"

"Nope. You need the magic of Charlotte's inn. It brought

Beau and Char together, and Zev and Carly. We need to get you and Nick to Colorado."

Nick's voice sailed through Trixie's mind. *I have been dying to do body shots off you ever since you mentioned it in Colorado.* Her heart skipped. "I just realized something. I think we might have already been touched by the magic of the inn."

"What? How long has this been going on? Did you guys sleep together after that race last year?"

"*No.* We didn't even kiss. He walked me back to my room after the awards banquet, and I tried to flirt with him, but I was pretty drunk. I didn't think he noticed, but the other night he said something that made me wonder if I was wrong."

"*Trixie.*" Jillian's eyes lit up. "If you've been touched by the magic of the inn, Charlotte says nothing can break that spell." Her shoulders slumped. "I'm happy for you, but *damn it. I* was supposed to be next in line for that magic."

They both laughed.

"You realize believing in magic makes us total weirdos, right?" Trixie said as they pushed to their feet, feeling better.

"We totally rock the weirdo category. Besides, the way my love life is going, I need Houdini himself to cast a spell."

Chapter Fifteen

TULLY'S WAS A family-oriented pub during the day and a hotspot for scantily clad women and lustful men at night. Music and the scents of perfume and lost inhibitions hung in the air. Before the awards banquet in Colorado last year, Nick had frequented places like that with the sole purpose of finding a willing woman for a few hours of fun. But as he stood at the bar waiting for the drinks he'd ordered for him and Jax, who was sitting at the table talking with three women, that felt like a lifetime ago. His gaze cut to the crowded dance floor, where the only woman he wanted to get lost in was dancing with his sister. Trixie was so damn beautiful, dancing with her arms over her head in that curve-hugging outfit, her hips swinging to the beat, he was having a hell of a time keeping his emotions in check. It didn't help that practically every guy in the place was leering at her.

The bartender pushed two glasses across the bar, pulling him from his thoughts. Nick paid for the drinks and made his way toward the table.

"Hey, Nick." Shayna, the voluptuous blonde who had texted him a few days ago, stepped into his path, flanked by two brunettes. "I was hoping to catch you here. It's my last night in town. Want to buy a few lonely girls drinks?" She stepped closer and lowered her voice. "We'll be happy to thank you properly later." Her friends eyed him hopefully.

"Not tonight, ladies." He stepped around them.

"*Aw*, Nick. It's been *forever*," Shayna whined.

How had that ever been enough? And how had he gone from being the guy who only wanted no-strings-attached hookups to the guy who'd caught feelings for a woman who was only looking for a *little nakedness between friends*?

Forcing a smile, he lifted one of the glasses and said, "It was fun while it lasted. You girls have a nice night."

As he walked away, Shayna said, "Let's go. There are plenty of hot cowboys in this bar."

He saw Trixie coming off the dance floor as he made his way to the table. She and Jillian were talking animatedly. When her eyes hit his, he swore he felt a shock of heat. She bit her lower lip, looking sexy as hell. Jillian said something, and Trixie burst into hysterics.

"*Hey*," one of the brunettes Jax was talking to said in a sing-song voice.

"How's it going?" Nick set the drink on the table.

"It's going *good*," she said, wiggling her ass. "We were just asking Jax if he wanted to party with us."

Jax raised his brows and took a drink.

"Have fun with that," Nick said.

"You can come, too," the taller of the girls offered.

"I'm good, thanks."

Trixie and Jillian giggled as they approached. Trixie eyed the girls, and her expression turned fierce with a hint of amusement, and she said, "Oh, good, you have a drink! I'm *so* thirsty."

She took the glass from Nick and downed half of his drink. Pure seduction glittered in her dark eyes as her tongue swept along her lower lip, then slowly glided across her upper lip. His cock twitched behind his zipper. He knew just how talented that beautiful mouth was.

"Thanks, cowboy. I needed that." She looked out at the crowd, nudging Jillian, and eyed Nick as she said, "Hot guy, two o'clock."

Don't fuck with me, darlin'.

"Oh yeah," Jillian said. "That is one fine specimen."

Nick looked over to see who they were talking about, and hell if it wasn't Jon Fucking Butterscotch heading their way. *Fanfuckingtastic.* He finished his drink, needing about twelve more.

"Don't you want to run your fingers through that mop of dirty-blond hair?" Trixie wiggled her fingers. "And look at that chest. *Mm.*"

My chest is twice his size, and you know it.

The other girls who were talking with Jax turned to see who they were checking out, and one of them said, "He's definitely hot, but he's got nothing on Jax."

"Damn right he doesn't." Jax pushed to his feet and pulled out his wallet. He handed a few twenties to the three girls and said, "Why don't you head up to the bar and grab another drink. I'll meet you there in a little while."

The girls gushed over his generosity, and as they walked away, Jillian said, "Three women, Jax. Really?"

"Two's company. Three's a crowd." Jax cocked a grin. "But *four* is a party."

"Did I hear *party?*" Jon said as he swaggered up to them in his dark slacks and dress shirt, unbuttoned three buttons deep.

He looked more like an upscale surfer than a doctor, with an ever-present tan, a dusting of scruff, and longish hair. "Nick, Jax, good to see you." He flashed a smile at the girls. "My two favorite ladies. Trix, it's been too long, baby. Get your beautiful self in here and give me some sugar."

He hugged her for too damn long, and Nick's muscles corded tight.

When Jon finally released Trixie, he said, "When are you going to run away with me?"

Trixie laughed softly. "Trust me, Jon, I'd drive you crazy."

"That's what I'm counting on." Jon waggled his brows.

"I'm serious." She looked at Nick and said, "Just ask this guy."

Nick scoffed. "You can say that again."

"So, are you two…?" Jon asked.

Trixie shook her head. "Not like that, no. I'm only here for a few weeks. Nick's helping me get a horse therapy business started."

Nick's chest constricted with the reminder of his *temporary* role in her life.

"That's right. Congratulations," Jon said. "Jilly filled me in on your new business. I'm so damn proud of you for taking the plunge. Cole and I have contacts up and down the East Coast. We can hook you up with as many medical facilities as you want."

"That would be fantastic, Jon. Thank you. Tempe gave me a list of names that Cole had given her. We'll have to compare notes."

"Yes we do. We also need to celebrate." Jon looked at the rest of them. "What's it going to be, shots or dancing?"

"Dancing!" Jillian and Trixie said in unison as Jax and Nick said, "Shots."

"Dancing it is. We'll come back for shots. Gentlemen, if you'll excuse us." Jon put his arms around the girls, leading them to the dance floor.

Trixie looked over her shoulder and said, "See ya!"

Nick gritted his teeth. Jax put a hand on his shoulder and said, "Breathe, brother. They go way back; you know that. They've been racing together for years, and you know how Jon is. He gets under your skin just enough to make you want to hate him, but he's a tough guy to hate because he's so likable."

Tell me about it.

He watched them dancing like a damn dirty dancing trio. Trixie was a sensual dancer, and it was torture watching her move in sync with another man. He told himself to look away, but he was captivated by her. The music and the other people faded away, until all he saw was Trixie and Jon. Jealousy roared through him. He knew he *shouldn't* be jealous. She and Jon were just having fun. But she'd gotten so deep under Nick's skin, into his thoughts, she'd shattered his ability to think rationally. Images of Trixie and Travis dirty dancing slammed into him, followed by thoughts of Travis's hands on her. Trixie's voice crashed into his mind—*What's a little nakedness between friends?*—and something inside him snapped.

Fuck this.

He plowed through the crowd onto the dance floor and took Trixie by the arm. "I'm cutting in."

Jon gave him a thumbs-up.

Nick pulled her into his arms, speaking directly into her ear. "I drank champagne off your body, and now I've got to watch you with him?"

"We're just *dancing*," she said with a laugh.

"You think I don't get that? I know you're just having fun, but I see you dancing with Jon, and it tears me up inside."

Challenge simmered in her eyes. "You could have asked me to dance."

"No shit. But you fuck with my head so much, I'm not exactly thinking straight. All I know is, I *can't* share you. I *won't* share you. While you're here, you're *mine*. I don't want anyone else's hands on you."

She lifted her chin. "I thought you were into no-strings-attached hookups."

"Not with *you*."

Her eyes narrowed. "That works both ways, cowboy, or not at all."

"Damn right it does." He covered her mouth with his, claiming her with everything he had. She wound her arms around his neck, and he ran his hands down her back and grabbed her ass.

She smiled against his lips. "You know everyone just saw that."

"That's the point."

She giggled, and he kissed her again, longer and slower, until the world felt right again. He brushed his lips over hers and said, "Do you want to break the news to Travis, or should I?"

"I already did. I turned him down the day he asked me out."

He arched a brow. "Think you could have told me that?"

"What fun would that have been?"

"That mouth of yours is going to be the death of me."

"You like my mouth."

"You're damn right I do." As he lowered his mouth to hers, he said, "But I like it best when it's on me."

TRIXIE CLUNG TO Nick to combat her wobbly legs as he kissed her senseless, and she tried to process what had just happened. This was so much more than she'd even hoped for. If she'd known that dancing with Jon could get his attention, she'd have done it every time she'd come to town. She'd thought she'd be lucky if Nick realized his feelings for her by the time she left to go back home to Virginia. His public claiming made her head spin and her heart swell.

When their lips finally parted, she was a little dizzy, and he was looking at her like he wanted to throw her over his shoulder and drag her to his cave. She'd happily climb him like a mountain and drape herself over that shoulder.

Nick's eyes shifted, and his jaw clenched. She followed his gaze and realized Jillian and Jon were staring at them with shocked expressions.

"If that's what *not* being together is like when Trixie's in town"—Jon squared his shoulders—"I want to put my name in the hat."

"Hands off, Butterscotch," Nick growled.

"That kiss was *hot*," Jillian said. "But I think you just impregnated every girl on the dance floor."

Trixie laughed, but Nick's jaw clenched. Did he regret his grand gesture already?

"I need a drink," he said gruffly, and with his arm wrapped possessively around Trixie—*which she loved*—he strode toward the bar.

"Are you okay?"

"Fine." He ordered drinks and pulled her tight against him,

his stormy eyes locked on hers.

Her heart lodged in her throat. "Nick, are you sure you want this?"

"Yes," he said firmly. "I just need a minute before facing the peanut gallery."

"I'll go wait at the table." She tried to step out of his arms, but he tightened his hold, his eyes serious.

"I want a minute with *you*, Trix, not alone."

"You do?" Happiness fluttered inside her.

"Yeah, I do."

He kissed her smiling lips and continued kissing her until the bartender interrupted them. They took their drinks and headed back to the table with Nick's arm securely around her waist, as if he thought she might slip away. Didn't he know there was no place she'd rather be?

Jon had joined Jillian and Jax, and there was a bottle of tequila and five shot glasses in the middle of the table.

"So, we're doing this?" Jax waved a finger at them.

"Are we *Facebook official?*" Jillian teased.

Nick glowered at her, and Trixie just went on grinning as Nick pulled out a chair for her. That was new, too, and she wasn't the only one who noticed. The others shared an impressed glance. When he sat beside her, he moved his chair closer and draped an arm around her.

Jillian said, "Geez, Nick. I'm pretty sure everyone saw you piss on your territory on the dance floor."

Jax and Jon chuckled. Jon filled the shot glasses and said, "I feel sorry for any man who's dumb enough to try to take your girl."

"Me too," Jax said. "But I do need to clarify a few things. Are you two going steady? Does she have your letter jacket?"

Everyone but Nick laughed. He uttered a curse.

"I'm thinking fall wedding, off-the-shoulder dress, with a detachable train," Jax said.

"Oh, yes!" Jillian exclaimed. "I'll make the bridesmaid gowns."

Nick grabbed a shot glass and downed the tequila. "How long are we doing this?"

"I have no idea what you're talking about," Jillian said innocently.

"You guys are going to send him running for the hills," Trixie said.

"How about a toast." Jon refilled Nick's glass, and they all grabbed one and held them up. "To Trixie's new business and to the couple who *isn't like that.*"

Nick cracked a smile at that one, clinked glasses with them, and they drank their shots.

Trixie leaned toward Nick and said, "You know you brought this on yourself by making a big deal on the dance floor."

He pulled her closer, speaking directly into her ear. "That's nothing compared to the big deal I'm going to make in the bedroom."

She closed her eyes as a shiver of heat skated through her and felt Nick kiss her head.

"Best picture ever!" Jillian exclaimed, showing Jax and Jon her phone across the table.

Jax shot a look at Nick, nodding approvingly. "Perfect engagement shot."

"You two look good together," Jon said.

Jillian showed the picture to Trixie and Nick. Their eyes were closed as he kissed her head, his arm was around her, his hand holding her shoulder like he never wanted to let her go. The look on his face was so peaceful and different from the energy he'd been exuding, it tripped Trixie up. She glanced at Nick, and he drew in a deep breath and shook his head, as if he had a hard time processing the image.

"Can you send me that picture?" Trixie asked.

"Already on it." Jillian thumbed out a message on her phone. "I'm sending it to everyone. Mom's going to be so excited."

"Christ, Jilly. Give it a break," Nick said.

"*Oopsie.*" Jillian set her phone down. "Too late."

"It's a good thing we're not in Oak Falls, where gossip spreads faster than STDs in a brothel," Trixie said. "Everyone would have already heard about our kiss on the dance floor by now."

Trixie's and Nick's phones chimed. Trixie pulled hers out of her purse, and Nick snagged it from her hand. "Hey."

He turned it off and did the same with his. "Can we deal with everyone's shit tomorrow?"

"That's a good idea," Jillian agreed. "By then Trixie's brothers will be on your doorstep, and you can do it in person."

Everyone laughed, but Nick cursed under his breath again, sparking another round of jokes. As the night wore on, the jokes about Nick and Trixie became fewer and farther between. She and Jon talked about the race at Rough Riders, Jax told them funny stories about bridezillas, Jillian made everyone laugh with quirky comments and sisterly banter, and Nick finally loosened up, laughing along with everyone else, taking part in their conversations, and driving Trixie out of her mind. He whispered dirty things in her ear and touched her upper thigh under the table. She tried to concentrate on what Jax was saying as the women he'd been talking with earlier returned to the table, but Nick's fingers were so close to her panties, and his hand was so hot, all she could think about was being touched by him. As her hand slid up *his* thigh for the hundredth time that evening, she felt his muscles flex, and she palmed him through his jeans.

Nick pulled her closer, whispering, "You're playing with fire."

"Maybe I want to get burned." Heat flared in his eyes, and she said, "Dance with me."

His brows slanted, but he pushed to his feet, drawing her up beside him.

"Are you leaving?" Jillian asked.

"Dancing," Trixie answered. "I figure I better get one last dance in before our phones are turned on and he freaks out and says it was all some kind of joke."

Jon stood and reached for Jilly's hand. "You and me, girl. Let's get it on."

"*Hey*," Nick warned.

Jillian rolled her eyes. "Keep your man busy, will you, Trix? I want to dance."

Trixie grabbed Nick's shirt, tugging him toward the dance floor. "Come on, handsome. Show me your moves." The dark look he gave her made her wish they *were* leaving.

He swept her into his arms and pressed his hand flat against her lower back, keeping their bodies flush. All around them, people were dancing fast, but Nick moved in a slow, seductive rhythm. She wound her arms around his waist and slipped them under the back of his T-shirt. She brushed her fingers along his back, and his eyes drilled into hers. She still couldn't believe they were together like that in public. She felt high, and a tiny bit worried that he'd wake up tomorrow and take it all back.

She was tempted to say something about that, but before she could, he lowered his lips to hers, kissing her like he'd waited his whole life to do it, and those worries fell away.

His hands traveled up and down her body as they danced to their own private beat. She turned in his arms, swaying her hips. His arms circled her, and she felt every inch of him against her bottom. He kissed her neck and shoulders, his hands sliding over her bare midriff. Every touch of his lips made her crave more. One hand moved up her stomach, stopping short of her breasts, and he tugged her back against him. His teeth grazed the curve of her neck, and she leaned her head to the side, giving him better access.

He kissed a path up to her ear, every touch taking her higher. "You got *deep* under my skin, darlin'."

His husky voice, and the words he said, made her entire body flame. He made her feel sexy, *wanted*, and bolder than ever before. She turned her face so he could hear her above the music and said, "I know you like it *deep*."

"*God*, woman," he said roughly.

She intensified the sway of her hips, and he ground against her ass. She leaned back against his chest, and he sealed his teeth over her neck as they danced, sucking so hard she felt herself go damp. She reached up with one hand and ran her fingers through his hair, then reached her other hand behind her, holding the back of his thigh. He made a greedy sound and turned her in his arms. His eyes were dark as night as he crushed his mouth to hers, taking her in another breath-stealing kiss. Every stroke of his tongue made her ache for him. Her skin prickled with desire. She tore her mouth away and said, "Take me home, cowboy."

Chapter Sixteen

THEY FLEW THROUGH Nick's front door in a tangle of gnashing teeth and groping hands. Pugsly darted outside, and Nick kicked the door closed. He stripped off their clothes on the way to the bedroom. She'd driven him to the brink of madness on the drive home, stroking him through his jeans and kissing his neck. He'd been so revved up from everything that had happened, his emotions were all over the place. He'd been *this close* to pulling the truck over and taking her on the side of the road.

They stumbled into the dark bedroom. He was frantic with desire, needing to get lost in her. He lowered his mouth to her breast, and she demanded, *"Harder."*

He sucked harder, teasing her with his hand between her legs, his thumb zeroing in on the spot he knew would take her over the edge. She panted and whimpered. *"Oh... Nick..."* He backed her up to the dresser and dropped to his knees, devouring her until she came so hard, her entire body shook. He lifted her into his arms, and her eyes fluttered open. She was so damn beautiful, his chest constricted.

"I didn't wear you out, did I, darlin'?"

A challenge shimmered beneath those half-mast lids. "Not

even close."

Everything she did drew him deeper into her. He carried her to the bed, stripped back the blankets, and laid her down. She reached for him as he came down over her. He kissed her ravenously, but she tore her mouth away.

"What's wrong?"

She took his face between her hands, smiling sweetly, and whispered, "Kiss me slower."

Christ, she was killing him. He lowered his lips to hers, taking her in a slow, sensual kiss. His cock pressed against her entrance. Her mouth was hot and sweet and so damn eager, he couldn't hold back. He kissed her harder and thrust his hips, burying himself to the hilt. Sensations exploded inside him, sending his hips pumping as he ravaged her mouth.

She broke the kiss again and grabbed his hips. "Stop."

He stilled. "Too rough?" Pain sliced through him at the thought that he'd hurt her.

"No. I like it when you're rough. I just want to stay still and be in this moment with you. Can you do that for me?"

I'd do anything for you. That truth hit him like a Mack truck. He brushed his lips over hers and said, "I'll try, but you feel so damn good, it's not going to be easy."

That earned another smile. "So do you. I want you to see *me*, Nick."

"Darlin', it's been so long since I've seen anything *but* you, it's a wonder I'm still sane." He didn't recognize himself, spilling his thoughts like that, but the way she was looking at him, so beautiful and trusting, made him want to say more. He brushed his lips over hers and said, "I see you." He ran his hand down her leg and lifted her knee. "I *feel* you." He kissed her neck. "And now I need to kiss you."

"Slow," she said as his lips covered hers.

He kissed her slow and sweet, and as they began moving, he became aware of every little thing about her. How she breathed *with* him, her warm hands moving along his back, her soft thighs against his skin. But she was so hot and tight, and she felt so good, he quickened the pace, needing more of her.

She pressed on the back of his hips, whispering, "Slow," and swiveled her hips slowly, gripping his cock like never before.

"*Fuck*," he gritted out, trying his damnedest to do as she'd asked and keep from driving into her.

She wrapped her arms around him, holding his shoulders. "Go in slow but end hard."

Their eyes collided as he eased in slow and then thrust deep, seeing every bit of pleasure in her gorgeous eyes. Emotions bowled him over, and he stilled. If he felt this much after a few days of being close to her, what would he feel in a week? A month? He closed his eyes, dipping his head beside hers as he withdrew.

"*Yes*, just like that," she whispered.

He had no idea why he let her control their pace, but as he pushed in excruciatingly slowly, ecstasy shot through his core, and his whole body shuddered. "Holy hell, Trix…" He searched her eyes, looking for what? He had no idea.

"Kiss me softly," she whispered.

She said it so sweetly, it had the opposite effect and made him want to consume her. But he fulfilled her wish, kissing her softly. She clung to his shoulders, their bodies moving in perfect harmony as they found a slow, erotic rhythm, as exciting as it was torturous. When the torture became too great, he tore his mouth away, gritting out, "I need more."

Her eyes narrowed. "Then take me like you mean it, *cow-*

boy."

"Woman, you are pure wickedness."

He reclaimed her mouth, ravenous and rough, their bodies slamming together. He lifted one of her knees, and she wound her legs around him. He pushed his hands beneath her ass, lifting and angling her hips, allowing him to take her deeper. She clawed at his arms, and her head fell back with a desperate gasp.

"*Don't stop,*" she pleaded.

He lowered his mouth to her neck, earning one sinful plea after another. She felt so damn good, so fucking *right*, it drove him harder, faster. Her nails cut into him, but he'd proudly wear those marks, because nothing had ever felt so exquisite. She cried out his name, her hips shooting off the mattress, her pleasure slashing the last of his control. Heat seared down his spine as he surrendered to his own magnificent release. They clung to each other, riding out the very last shudder.

He gathered her in his arms, their hearts thundering, bodies shaking, and he kissed her slow and soft, wanting to see that smile again, to know that he made her feel as good as she made him feel. She snuggled into his arms and kissed his chin, gifting him the smile he craved. His chest tightened. He kissed her forehead, holding her as their breathing calmed, and she drifted off to sleep. She looked peaceful and happy, and that did something to him. Hell, the sex had done something to him, too. It wasn't sex as he knew it. He felt transformed, changed from the inside out, and he had no idea what to do with that.

TRIXIE AWOKE TO the feel of something wet on her cheek. She opened her eyes and found Pugsly sitting by the pillow, staring at her. "Hi, sweet boy."

He pushed his nose into her face and licked her. She rolled onto her back and realized Nick was gone. She sat up, looking across the dark bedroom to the open bathroom door. The light was off. "Nick?"

There was no answer.

She climbed from the bed, and Pugsly followed her into the bathroom. After using the toilet, she found their clothes piled on the chair in the corner. She put on her underwear and Nick's T-shirt, which fell to the middle of her thighs, and went in search of him, trying to ignore the pang of disappointment over his leaving her alone in the middle of the night.

The rest of the house was dark. "Nick?"

Answered with silence, she peered out the patio doors, but it was too dark to see. As soon as she opened the door, she heard his guitar, and felt a tug at her heart. As she stepped onto the cold slate patio, she saw him sitting on the hill with his back to her, Goldie and Rowdy by his side. She listened to him playing the guitar, soaking in the sight of him in the moonlight. The way they'd come together had felt too good to be true, and she stood frozen for a moment, wishing, hoping, *praying* this was the beginning of what she knew would be the best coupling, the most supportive and fun friendship, and the deepest, rawest, most fulfilling love known to man, and not the end of every-thing.

Pugsly barked and scampered off the patio. Rowdy and Goldie darted toward them, and Nick looked over. With a gulp of courage and a heavy dose of hope, Trixie went to see where she stood.

Goldie and Rowdy ran off to play, and Pugsly chased them into the darkness.

Nick continued playing the guitar, watching her close the distance between them, which made her nervous. He lifted his chin and said, "Hey."

Hey? No *darlin'* or *Trix?* Her stomach knotted, and she did her best to hide the hurt. "Hi. Are you okay?"

He nodded, but his expression wasn't okay. It was...something else. "I needed some air, so I took care of the animals and thought I'd sit out here. Hope I didn't wake you."

"You didn't." She sat beside him and pulled her knees up to her chest, wrapping her arms around them to feel less vulnerable. It didn't work. Despite how terrified she was of his answers, she had to know where they stood. "I know tonight was a lot, Nick. If you regret it, please tell me. I don't want things to be weird between us."

He set the guitar in his lap. "I don't regret anything I've done with you, Trix, except the way I left you that first time, in the kitchen. I just...It is a lot. You know how I am. I'm not used to having someone in my space."

"I know. I'm not going to lie—that stings a little. But I get it. You've been alone forever."

"Yeah, that's part of it." His jaw tensed.

"Part of it? Talk to me, Nick. *Please.*"

He held her gaze, his jaw clenching. "You make me feel all this shit that I have no idea what to do with. I've never been jealous a day in my life, and suddenly I'm jealous of Travis and Jon? They're good guys. They're my friends, even if Jon grates on my nerves when he hits on you. That jealousy makes me feel like a dick, and I hate that feeling."

She couldn't suppress her smile.

"Why are you smiling when I just told you I feel like a dick?"

"Because I've liked you *forever*, and now my hot cowboy is jealous over me. Just let me bask in that for a minute. But for the record, you'll need to get over your jealousy where Travis is concerned because I like having a running partner, and I'm not giving that up."

"That's cool. He can run with you, as long as I'm the only one sharing a bed with you." He smiled, but then his face turned serious again. "Wait. You've liked me forever?"

"It feels like forever. The day you strolled into Mr. B's with your cocky attitude and badass dance moves, I didn't just feel sparks. I felt like the sun came down and inhabited my body, lighting me up from the inside out and brightening everything around me. You're confident and aggressive and funny. Not *Sam* or *Zev* funny, but *Nick* funny, which for me is so much better. And you were—are—so bullheaded and arrogant, you kind of reminded me of myself. I'd never met anyone like you. And every time I thought about you or saw you, I got so happy, and frustrated, of course, because my crush wasn't reciprocated."

He looked stunned. "How could I not pick up on that? I thought you seriously wanted to be friends with benefits. Why the hell didn't you tell me?"

"Tell you? Oh boy, *that* wouldn't have been embarrassing at all." She laughed. "Have you ever had a crush on someone?"

He set his guitar in the grass and pulled one knee up, leaning his arm on it. He looked out at the pastures and said, "Once. I was nineteen. She was twenty-two and lived in Nashville."

"The *bareback* girl?"

"Yeah." He met her gaze. "Sharon. We met at an exhibition. She was competing, too. We went back and forth when we could, but she wanted me to move to Nashville, and I wasn't going to leave my family."

"Was that when Tory died and your brothers left?"

"No. I ended it about six months before that. There was no endgame. You know my roots are deep. Born here, buried here."

"Were you in love with her?"

He shook his head and shrugged. "Who knows. I was a kid. I liked her enough to travel to see her but not enough to leave home for good."

"And there's been no one special since?"

He held her gaze for a long moment. "One girl, and I'm looking at her." He leaned in and lowered his voice. "A bullheaded, arrogant girl with a phenomenal smile." He kissed her. "Now, what's the real reason you never told me you liked me in that way."

"Give a girl a minute to savor the moment of being special. I'm busy melting over here."

He pressed his lips to hers again.

"The real reason is that you were my friend's cousin, and you were four years older than me, which as a teenager was a lot. Then we became such fast friends, I thought I'd get over my feelings for you, but they just grew deeper. And the one time I tried to flirt with you, after the awards banquet in Colorado, you didn't even notice."

He scrubbed a hand down his face. "Jesus, Trix. I noticed you in Colorado, but I didn't think you were intentionally flirting, because you're always in my space."

She climbed onto his lap. "I like being in your space."

"Really? I couldn't tell." He tucked her hair behind her ear and kissed her. "I not only noticed you in Colorado, darlin', but I stayed with you that night and left just before you woke up. I was worried you'd try to go back to the bar."

"You *stayed?*" More happiness bubbled up inside her. "You took care of me. You *liked* me."

"Ya think?" He laughed softly. "That night changed everything. I've thought about you every day since then. That's why I've been going to Oak Falls so often."

"Seriously? You never acted like it."

"I'm pretty sure my hard-on gave me away."

"I thought that was just a regular guy-girl reaction. And to think I came up here with every intention of getting over you."

He kissed her neck. "I think you mean *under* me."

"I do like being under you."

He kissed her again, lighter this time, and then he framed her face with his hands and gazed into her eyes. His hands were rough and warm, and his eyes brimmed with emotions and an undeniable struggle as he said, "You are special, Trixie. You're the only woman I've ever let touch me the way you did in the shower and talk to me the way you do, telling me what to do and how to do it. And you're the only woman who's ever been in my bed."

"That's…" *Surprising?* Not really. She knew his home was his sanctuary. "I like knowing that."

He pressed his lips to hers and caressed her cheek. It was such an intimate gesture, it warmed her as much as his confession had. "You are a beautiful woman, Trixie, and I want you. I want *us*. I just have to figure some things out."

"So you can stop feeling like a dick?"

His lips curved up, and he nodded. "Something like that."

She was relieved and also a little sad that he'd locked his heart away for so long, he was having this much trouble finding the key. "Take your time, cowboy. My heart has been yours forever. I'm not going anywhere."

She kissed him softly and headed up to the house to give him time and space to figure things out. She went into his bedroom to get her clothes, and the sight of the rumpled blankets on the bed sent a pang of sadness through her. She carried her clothes into her bedroom and climbed into bed, thinking about how much had changed and how he'd opened up to her tonight. Not just at the bar, or outside, but when they'd made love. No wonder he was a little freaked out by it all. So was she, but in a good way.

She must have dozed off, because she woke to the dip of the mattress as Nick climbed into the bed behind her and gathered her in his arms. Pugsly jumped onto the foot of the bed. Happiness seeped into all her empty spots as she snuggled into Nick. His warm breath slid over her skin, his leg hair tickled, and his heart beat sure and steady against her back as she whispered, "I thought you wanted space."

"I do. But I want you in it."

Chapter Seventeen

NICK WATCHED THE sun creep in through the curtains and spill over the bed where Trixie was sleeping, soft and warm, in his arms, with Pugsly tucked against her belly. Nick lay still, waiting for tension to grip him, for the fight or flight instinct to strike. Trixie made a sleepy sound, cuddling in deeper. She smelled sweet and sexy, and last night came back in vivid detail, from her wanting eyes to her sensual requests—*I just want to stay still and be in this moment with you...I want you to see me.* Hearing that had magnified all his senses. He'd wanted to stay buried deep inside her forever.

And now he ached to be inside her again, but it was the tug of his heart that had his rapt attention. When he'd come back into the house last night, he'd thought she'd gone back to his room, and the sight of his empty bed had torn him up. He'd vowed to do everything within his power to let her in, no matter how scary or difficult it might be. He'd thought a year was a long time to try to keep his feelings to himself, but she'd been crushing on him for her entire adult life. He must have been blind to have missed it. She was so patient with him, giving and tender and still so strong. He was in awe of her.

She stirred and turned in his arms, bringing her sweet face

into focus, and he realized fight or flight was nowhere in sight. He felt *less* stressed than he had in months, like he was exactly where he was supposed to be, and so damn lucky that she was *his*.

Pugsly gave an annoyed grunt and jumped off the bed.

"You're still here," she said sleepily.

"That's not exactly the reaction I was hoping for, darlin'."

She smiled and kissed his chin. He loved when she kissed him there, and on his chest, and everywhere else. But it was those unexpected chin kisses that sparked the emotions that were burning through his well-constructed walls.

"I wasn't sure you'd be here when I woke up," she confessed. "I'm glad you stayed."

He felt a pang of guilt, hating that she felt she couldn't count on him in that way. But how could she, when he'd left her alone after they'd been more intimate than ever before? He was bound and determined to fix that. "I'm sorry about leaving you alone last night."

"Don't be. You explained why you went outside. I get it."

He nuzzled against her neck. "But you shouldn't have to."

"Well, you're here now, and you could have gotten up. I'll take that as a win."

"Trust me, no part of me wanted to leave you this morning." He put his hand on her ass, pressing her against him so she could feel what she did to him. Her eyes brightened, and he said, "Do you have to get ready to run with Travis?"

"Nope. He picked up April last night for the weekend, so he can't run for a few days."

"*Mm.*" He kissed along her cheek to her ear. "Does that mean I get you all to myself this morning?"

"Yes. I was thinking that after you're done working with

your horses, and I'm done working with Alfie and Annabelle, and we pick up Buttons and Prince and get them situated, I could practice my pitch for my meeting with Jordan on you."

He rolled her onto her back and moved over her. "I see how this is gonna go." He kissed her neck. "I thought you said all women didn't want to tell men what to do."

"I'm not telling you what to do. I'm…" She bit her lower lip, grinning like a fiend.

He arched a brow. "You're…?"

"*Suggesting.*"

"Nice try, darlin, but I'm onto you." He tugged up her shirt and moved down her body. "First you reel me in and get me to claim you in public." He dragged his tongue over her nipple, earning a sexy moan. "Then you start making my schedules." He moved lower, showering her stomach with openmouthed kisses, and more sinful sounds fell from her lips. "And then you start telling me what to do." He tickled her ribs.

She shrieked, trying to roll out of his reach. "I am *not!*"

"Sounded to me like you were." He tickled her again.

"*No! Stop!*" she said through her laughter. "I'm *not!*"

He nipped at her belly and tore off her panties. Their eyes connected, and the air caught fire. He kissed his way up her legs, lingering on her inner thighs, making her squirm and moan as he pushed off his briefs.

"*Yes.* Don't stop," she panted out.

He kissed and sucked, and then he tickled her again just to hear her incredible laughter, and she shrieked, thrashing from side to side, trying to escape his tickles. "Don't try to control me, baby," he warned.

"*Iwon'tIwon'tIwon't!*"

He crawled up her body, soaking up every melodic sound,

and lowered his mouth over her nipple. She arched off the bed, moaning and panting, little bursts of laughter bursting out like aftershocks.

"*Lord...*"

He shifted higher, grinning down at her. "You can call me *Nick*, darlin'."

"You're a fool." She laughed.

"I'm about to be a very lucky fool."

As he lowered his lips to hers, she said, "Paybacks are hell, cowboy."

He was counting on it.

LATER THAT MORNING, Trixie dried the dishes as he washed. She was gorgeous in cutoffs, one of her million belly-baring shirts, and boots. He'd never been one to value leisure time. He was the guy who got up with the sun and got shit done, but he could get used to mornings like this. He hadn't been completely sure how he'd feel having Trixie by his side every minute, but she made his morning better. He liked waking up with her in his arms, getting lost in each other, playing around in the shower, and having breakfast on the veranda. It had been a damn good morning.

She dried the last dish and said, "Where are our phones?"

"In the jeans I wore last night." He wasn't looking forward to fielding a million messages after Jillian's couple-alert text she'd probably sent to everyone in her contact list.

"Be right back." She left the kitchen and returned a few minutes later with both phones, holding his out for him. "Are you ready for this?"

"Do I have a choice?" He took his phone.

"We could turn them on later, but if Jilly really sent everyone the picture of us, I'm sure they want to know what's going on."

He drew her into his arms. "And what *is* going on, Trix?"

"Well, I guess we're two friends who have taken things further." She wound her arms around his waist and slipped her hands up the back of his shirt, as she'd done last night.

That light touch woke his body up again. He knew she was being careful not to put a label on them, but label or not, she fucking owned him. As nerve-racking as that was, her hold over him worked like truth serum. "I don't want people wondering what we are."

"*Oh.* Do you want to play off the picture Jilly took as nothing more than two friends having a moment?"

The disappointment in her voice made his gut clench. "No, darlin'. I want them to *know* we're a couple."

"You do?" Her smile lit up her eyes.

"What do you think?" He pressed his lips to hers. "By now the whole damn town knows we made out on the dance floor, which means Morgyn and Graham know. If Morgyn knows, Brindle knows, and—"

"Trace knows."

"Exactly. The last thing I want is for your family to think I'm disrespecting you."

"So...you *want* them thinking we're a couple?"

He swallowed hard at the label. "Yeah."

"Like, *Nick and Trixie sitting in a tree K-I-S-S-I-N-G?*"

He laughed and lifted her onto the counter, wedging himself between her legs. "More like Nick and Trixie fucking in the hay, but sure."

She whispered, "I don't think I should sing that to them."

"You're right. I can make much better use of your mouth." He lowered his lips to hers, devouring her sweetness. She came away dreamy eyed, and he liked that look a hell of a lot.

"Well, now I can't sing anything."

He chuckled and gave her a quick kiss. "Let's get this message crap over with so we can take care of the animals."

As they turned them on, their phones chimed like bells on a holiday parade. "Christ, darlin', I don't even want to look."

"Then I'll look for both of us. Yours or mine first?"

He handed her his phone.

She poked at the screen, grinning. "Beau and Graham said it's about damn time."

Nick scoffed.

"Zev sent a picture of him and Carly and said they'll race us to the altar." She giggled.

"Don't go riding off into the sunset just yet, darlin'. One day at a time."

"I know. I'm perfectly happy as we are." She kissed his chin, then read the next message. Her brow wrinkled. "Your dad said he's glad he wasn't losing his mind. What does that mean?"

"It means he's a smart-ass. Are we done?"

"No, there's one from your mom, too. She said she couldn't be happier for us, and that she has to thank Marilynn for the bodywash." Her eyes flicked up to his. "Marilynn Montgomery? Brindle's mom? What does that mean?"

"Hell if I know. She gave me a case of bodywash from Marilynn's sister for Christmas."

"Ohmygod, *Nick*! Brindle's aunt Roxie makes bodywashes, shampoos, and lotions. She swears they're infused with love potions."

"Has everyone gone crazy? That's horseshit."

Trixie giggled. "Or *is* it? Maybe the bodywash and the magic of the inn were just enough to push us over the edge and bring us together."

"Or maybe you just figured out how to get under my skin like no one else ever has."

"I like that reason." She grabbed his shirt and tugged him into a kiss.

"*Mm.* That mouth of yours needs no extra magic." He kissed her again, slower and deeper, and just like that, his body caught fire. He touched his cheek to hers, breathing her in. "How did I resist you for so long?"

"I've asked myself that for the past several years."

He laughed. "Is that all my messages?"

"No. Jeb and Shane texted."

"I figured as much. What'd they say?"

"Jeb said to call him. Shane said if you hurt me, you'll have him to deal with."

"That's hardly a threat, but don't worry, darlin'. I don't have any intention of hurting you."

"Most people don't. It just happens." She slipped his phone into his back pocket and started going through her own messages. "Uh-oh. Shane's called a few times." She navigated through her messages and giggled.

"What's funny?"

"Morgyn said nobody can resist an Oak Falls girl, and Lindsay, Amber, and Brindle are just being goofy and dirty. I love them so much." Her phone rang. "It's Shane and he's FaceTiming." As she answered the call, Nick stepped away to get his hat.

"Hey. Good to see you're alive," Shane said dryly. "We've

been trying to reach you."

Nick knew he should probably leave the kitchen and give her privacy, but he wanted to make sure her brother didn't give her shit about him. He leaned against the island across from her and folded his arms over his chest.

"Sorry. We turned our phones off after Jilly sent that picture. We knew we'd be barraged with messages. Oh, hey, Trace."

"Hi. You two were the talk of the jam session last night." Nick recognized Trace's voice. Every few weeks the Jerichos opened one of their barns for a community jam session, where anyone who played an instrument could get onstage and play. People of all ages came to enjoy the music, dance, and play various games like potato sack races, ring toss, and touch football.

"Great," she said sarcastically.

"You'll be glad to know that you and Nick now have a Team *Nixie* hashtag on our community social pages," Trace said.

"What the hell is a *Team Nixie?*" Nick walked over so her brothers could see him. "Hi, Shane. Trace."

"When Trace and Brindle got together, Lindsay started a Team Trindle hashtag," Trixie explained. "She even had T-shirts made for the Thanksgiving Turkey Trot 5K race. Nixie is our names put together, Trixie and Nick. *Nixie.*"

Nick shook his head. "Fucking small towns."

"I guess you didn't realize that dating someone from Oak Falls is like dating the whole community," Trace said.

"Is that why you're calling?" Trixie asked. "To tell me we have a hashtag?"

"I wanted to say if you're happy, I'm happy for you," Trace

said.

"Thanks, Trace."

"Now I get why Nick's been coming to town more often," Shane said. "Hey, Braden, you've got a sister, so you'll understand where I'm coming from with this. Tell me you're not just dicking around with Trixie."

"You're unbelievable. How do you know I'm not dicking around with him?" Trixie countered.

That's my girl.

"I get where you're coming from, Shane," Nick said evenly. "If Jillian were in this situation, I'd be on the dude's doorstep, but that doesn't mean I'd be right. Our sisters are grown women. They can make their own decisions."

"I'm telling Jilly you said that," Trixie teased.

Nick shook his head. "Shane, I think you know me well enough that I don't need to justify that question with an answer."

"That's fair," Shane agreed. "Now I can feel good about this, too. Trix, Dad said you're starting your business on the ranch. Is that still the plan?"

"*Yes.* We're going to pick up two more horses this afternoon." She told them about Buttons and Prince, then went on to tell them how well she was bonding with Annabelle and Alfie. Nick was glad to see that her brothers were excited for her and interested in what she was doing, asking questions about their training and her upcoming meeting with Jordan.

"You'll nail the meeting," Shane said.

"Yeah, you're great with people, Trix," Trace agreed.

"Thanks, I hope so. I'm going to practice my pitch on Nick later."

Shane said, "Nick, thanks for hooking her up with Travis

and the people in Pennsylvania. I'm glad you're looking out for her."

"Trixie can look out for herself." Nick winked at Trixie. "But I'm glad to help when she lets me."

Trixie jumped off the counter and said, "We have to get going. We got a late start this morning."

Shane held up his hand. "Please don't tell us why."

"I guess we'll be seeing more of you around here, huh, Nick?" Trace asked.

Nick put his arm around Trixie and kissed her temple. "You can count on it."

She turned her radiant smile on her brothers and said, "Hey, do me a favor. Pass this conversation on to JJ and Jeb so they know Nick has been properly interrogated, and give my niece a smooch for me."

After they ended the call, they headed outside to take care of the animals. "Thanks for defending my honor."

Nick slung an arm over her shoulder and said, "Just how thankful are you?"

"You had enough of me this morning."

He nipped at her neck. "There is no such thing as having *enough* of *you*."

Chapter Eighteen

TRIXIE KEPT WAITING for Nick to realize how much he was opening up to her and take it all back. But as the day wore on, he became *more* comfortable, not less, and she decided to go with it and hope for the best. They were working with Alfie and Annabelle and were meeting Travis in forty-five minutes to pick up Buttons and Prince.

"Let's take them inside," Nick said, holding Annabelle's lead and heading for the gate.

"But I wanted to work with them a little longer."

"In the house, darlin', not the barn."

Confused, she said, "The house?"

"You need to keep them comfortable navigating around furniture, right? We might not have fake hospital rooms, but we have bedrooms. They can't take a full flight of stairs, but they should do fine on the porch steps."

"Oh, Nick!" Her heart soared. "You really don't mind if we take them inside?"

"I'd rather have horses in my house than people." He held the gate open. "Let's go, cowgirl. Let's see what these babies can do."

She was beyond excited. They took them to the spot where

they'd been training them to go to the bathroom on command, so they would poop before going in the house.

As they headed inside, the dogs ran over. "*Settle*," Nick commanded, and the dogs stopped in their tracks and kept their distance.

Nick stopped a few feet away from the porch with Annabelle, allowing Trixie to take Alfie up the steps first. His legs were so little, but he ascended the stairs like a champ.

"Good job, Alfie! That's my boy." She loved him up and waited while Nick led Annabelle up the steps. Annabelle took the stairs as well as Alfie did, and they praised her, too.

They took them inside, walked around the furniture in the living and dining rooms, the bedrooms and bathrooms, and the kitchen. Nick lay down on one of the beds so Trixie could practice as if the horses were seeing a patient, and it made it all feel even more real. It was an incredible experience, and she was thrilled that Nick was by her side.

Afterward, they put the horses into the corral next to the pen where they planned to put Buttons and Prince so the four horses could get acclimated to each other while safely separated. They hooked up the trailer and headed over to Travis's.

"Nervous?" Nick asked as he helped Trixie out of the truck. He opened the glove box, took a lollipop from a secret stash, and slipped it into his back pocket.

"A little. I hope they like Annabelle and Alfie and adjust to being at your place okay." Travis had been keeping Buttons and Prince together since she'd made her decision, which would hopefully make their transition easier.

"They will. We'll make sure they're comfortable, just like we did with Anna and Alf."

We felt like a whole different word than it had last week. It felt special and coupleish, and Trixie loved it.

Travis came out of the barn carrying April. April wriggled to be set free, and as he set her down, she yelled, "*Nick!*" She ran toward him in a cute pink sundress, her ringlets bouncing around her pretty face.

Nick crouched, arms open, and April dove into them. Trixie's ovaries nearly exploded.

"Ready to take your new minis home?" Travis asked.

"*Yes.* I can't wait to get Buttons and Prince settled in and introduce them to Annabelle and Alfie. I hope they get along well. But before we get them, I want to tell you something. Remember when I said I couldn't go out with you because I was interested in someone else? Well, that someone was Nick, and it turns out he's interested in me, too."

A soft laugh fell from Travis's lips. "I kind of figured he was the guy you were into."

"You did?"

"Every time you talked about him, which was often, you seemed happier."

"I did? I'm sorry if I talked about him too much. I've liked him for so long, I don't think I know how to like anyone else. But you're a great guy, Travis, and I know you'll find an amazing woman."

"Nick's a great guy, too." He looked at Nick, and Nick lifted his chin in question. "I'm happy for you guys."

"Thanks, man." Nick gave April the lollipop and set her down.

"I'm not going to lose my running partner, am I?" Travis asked.

"No way," Trixie reassured him. "But I promise to try not to talk about Nick so much."

Nick slid his arm around her waist. "She talks about me?"

"Incessantly," Travis teased. "Come on, let's get your horses."

NICK AND TRIXIE spent the rest of the afternoon with the horses. They sat outside in the pen with Buttons and Prince as they got used to their new surroundings. Trixie was glad to see her new babies approach the fence that separated them from Annabelle and Alfie. After a few hours she and Nick walked Buttons and Prince around the property, and at nightfall, they put them into a stall together, near Alfie and Annabelle. They ate dinner in the barn, as they had when Annabelle and Alfie had first come home, only this time they kept their clothes on while Trixie perfected her pitch, and Nick stole kisses and gave her pointers. They laughed and kissed, and she had never seen Nick so carefree.

After putting the other horses out to pasture, they went back to the barn and sat by the minis' stalls. Pugsly curled up beside them.

"How does it feel having all four of your kids in one barn?"

"Surreal, and a little scary. It's up to me to keep them safe and fed, and to train Buttons and Prince. I want to be the best handler I can for them. Do you feel that pressure with your horses?"

"Every day with every animal. You're a natural with them, Trix. You'll be great at all of it. And I'm right here if you need help."

"You've been amazing. I had the greatest day working with

you and Annabelle and Alfie. Bringing them into the house made it feel so real. Thank you for that."

"I had a great time, and I like seeing you do your thing." He kissed her temple. "I like *doing* your *thing*, too."

Her body heated up. "*Mm.* You're very good at doing my thing."

"Ride with me tomorrow, darlin'." He nipped at her ear. "We'll hit the trails early so you can still go running."

This was a huge, unexpected leap. They'd gone trail riding together during the day and in early evenings, but the mornings had always been Nick's coveted private time. "Did I hear you right? Are you asking me to join you on your sacred morning ride?"

"You're going to make a big deal out of this, aren't you?"

"Who, *me*? Not at all. I would be *honored* to join you during your cherished *me time*, when you ponder life-altering things like what to have for breakfast and how growly to be that day." She giggled.

He grinned but shook his head. "Why do I bother?"

"Because you *like* me," she said in a singsong voice, turning toward him. "I would love to go with you for a trail ride, but first I need some answers."

"Here we go." His jaw tightened.

"What changed for you? You seem more relaxed about us."

He leaned his head back against the wall. "It's a hell of a lot easier to just go with it than to fight it."

"Why *did* you fight it? I mean beyond not wanting to ruin our friendship."

"Because your life is in Virginia and my life is here. I wasn't sure where that could go, and I didn't want to complicate things or hurt you."

"But none of that has changed," she pushed.

"No, but other things have, like the fact that I had no clue you were into me. You opened that door and uncapped a damn volcano I'd been trying to keep from erupting. You know I was never looking for this, Trix. A relationship wasn't even on my radar. But it's *you*."

That made her feel good all over.

"And as far as where we live goes, my thoughts on that have changed, too. I like my space, and you're starting a business back home. You're going to need time to get it off the ground. Long distance doesn't sound so bad anymore. I think it'll work for both of us. Beyond all of that, one of the things I was most worried about was that I *liked* who we were together as friends, and I was worried that would change. But nothing has changed, beyond your inquisitions." He pressed his lips to hers. "We're still the same stubborn mules we've always been, and I like that about us. We're not pretending to be something else the way so many couples do. Nothing had to change for us to be together...except what obviously has."

"You mean naked and exclusive?"

"Hell yes." He drew her into his arms and kissed her passionately. Then he rose to his feet, pulling her up with him. "The horses are settled. What do you say we go explore those changes?"

"I'd love that. Just let me say good night to my babies one more time." She gave him a quick kiss and went into the stall. She crouched down, and Buttons walked over. "Hi, sweet girl. Mama's going inside for the night, but I love you, and I will be out bright and early tomorrow. I promise." She put out her hand, and Prince came to her. As she petted him, she said, "I think you're going to need a crown instead of a unicorn horn, my little Princey. I love you, and I hope you and Buttons have a great night."

She gave Prince a kiss on the head, and as she left their stall to say good night to Annabelle and Alfie, Nick was coming out of Annabelle and Alfie's stall.

"Did you say good night to my babies?"

"'Course. They're in my barn. That makes them my babies, too." He held the stall open and waved her in.

"I love that you feel that way." She went up on her toes and kissed his chin.

He winked and headed for Buttons and Prince's stall.

After they'd loved up the horses, they headed up to the house with Pugsly. Nick draped an arm over Trixie's shoulder and kissed her on the way inside. "God, I love kissing you," he said huskily as they stumbled through the back door. He took her in a rougher, deeper kiss, and she went up on her toes, needing more. He lifted her into his arms, guiding her legs around his waist, and carried her into his bedroom.

When he set her down and began stripping off her clothes, she said, "Am I going to wake up to an empty bed?"

"*No*," he said firmly. "But there's a good chance you'll wake to a hard cock."

Oh, how she loved his raunchiness! She reached for the button on his jeans. "I can't think of a better way to greet the day!"

Chapter Nineteen

SUNDAY BROUGHT LESS humidity and a stunning sunrise as the horses carried them up the trail. Nick didn't know exactly what was going on with him, but the more he allowed himself to openly explore his feelings for Trixie, the bigger those emotions became. She didn't say much as they rode, but just having her with him made it better. They took in the view from the top of the trail, and when they made their way back down, she rode beside him in the meadow.

A hint of mischief rose in her eyes. "This is where Romeo and I leave you in the dust."

"What—"

"*Hiya!*" They took off at full speed.

Nick gritted out a curse and kicked his heels, and he and Lady chased after them. Trixie was laughing and waving her cowgirl hat, holding on to the reins with one hand. When they reached the other end of the meadow, she put on her hat and leaned forward, loving up and praising Romeo.

"That was a cheap start," Nick joked.

She looked him up and down, her hair wild and tangled, her cheeks pink, a sheen of sweat on her brow. "Want to go again, cowboy? Romeo and I are a great team. We'll blow you away."

She was so damn beautiful and arrogant, she already blew him away.

"I wouldn't want to wear you out like last night." They'd been wild between the sheets, and she'd been as limp as a rag doll after. She'd fallen asleep with a sated smile on her lips, and with her in his arms, so had he.

She lifted her chin. "Chicken?"

He scoffed. "Let's do this."

Off they went, racing across the meadow. They tied, and she insisted they go again. After they tied a second time, she said it just showed they were a perfect match. As much as defining them as a couple was changing his mindset, he noticed changes in her, too, like the way she openly talked about them as a couple now. As new as it was, she said things that made it feel like they'd always been a couple.

They made their way back down the trail, and Trixie stopped at a fork in the path. "What's that way?" She pointed in the opposite direction from the way they'd come.

"Just another trail down. It lets us off at the other end of Walt's property."

"Let's take it!"

Her enthusiasm was contagious. "Okay, but I haven't been down that trail in a while. Take it slow in case there are trees in the path."

"Sure thing, cowboy."

They followed the trail, and it was nice going in a different direction. He hadn't realized just how long it had been since he'd varied his morning trail ride. They came out at the far end of Walt's property and rode side by side along the fence line toward Nick's property.

"Can we stop to see Walt?" she asked.

"Sure. He's usually outside by now."

A few minutes later they saw him leaning against the side of the barn. He waved, and they tied their horses to the fence and hopped over, heading up the pasture.

"Taking a break, old man?" Nick called out as they approached, eyeing his friend. His right knee was slightly bent, his foot dangling, like he had a bum ankle.

Walt scoffed. "Thought I'd work on my tan. Hey there, darlin'."

"Hi. I got my new horses," Trixie exclaimed.

"That's great. I can't wait to meet them." Walt lowered his boot to the ground and winced.

"What happened?" Trixie asked, her eyes filling with worry.

Walt waved dismissively. "*Nothing.*"

"Yeah?" Nick wasn't buying it. "Let's see you put your weight on that foot."

"I'm busy holding up the barn. Trixie, tell me about your horses."

Nick stepped forward and crossed his arms. "Not until you tell me what happened."

"I twisted my ankle. I'll be fine in a minute," Walt insisted.

Trixie arched a brow. "How many minutes has it already been?"

"Let me take a look." Nick crouched to take off Walt's boot.

"He's always trying to get me out of my clothes," Walt joked.

"Join the club," Trixie said softly.

Walt raised his brows, and then his face contorted in pain as Nick pulled off his boot. "Son of a…"

"That doesn't sound like *nothing.*" Nick felt his ankle. "It's not swollen." He tried to move Walt's foot, and Walt winced again. "We should probably get this looked at. Why didn't you call me?"

"My phone is inside," Walt grumbled. "Why didn't you tell me you're trying to get my girl out of her clothes?"

Nick gave him a deadpan look.

"It was more like me trying to get him out of his clothes at first," Trixie said. "But now it's a joint thing."

Nick gave her the same look he'd given Walt.

"It's about time one of you came to your senses," Walt said.

"Enough." Nick glowered at him.

Trixie planted a hand on her hip and said, "That's it, Walt. I'm buying you a Life Alert necklace."

"Get outta town, will ya? I'm *fine*."

"I'm carrying you up to the house." Nick put his arm around Walt.

"I'm not a woman," Walt griped. "I don't need to be carried."

"You're worse than a woman. You're a stubborn old man. You think you can hop all the way up there without popping a hip?"

Walt glowered at him.

"You're not hopping," Trixie said. "Pick him up, Nick. And for the record, you're as stubborn as Walt is."

As Nick hoisted Walt into his arms, Walt mumbled a string of curse words and continued complaining the whole way up to his house.

"What if you'd had a heart attack? Or broke a leg? You could throw a clot. This is why you shouldn't live alone. You're not a young man anymore," Trixie lectured him. "Maybe it's time we find you a live-in helper, or a wife."

"Christ Almighty, I don't need a wife or a helper," he said as

Nick carried him through the front door of his rustic two-bedroom house. "I've got Nick." He waved his finger at the couch. "Just put me there."

"Then you need to carry your phone. What if we hadn't come by?" Trixie went to the freezer and took out the ice tray. "You could have been out there all day."

She pulled open the drawers, found a ziplock bag, and dumped the ice into it as Nick propped Walt's foot up on a pillow on the coffee table and sat beside him. "I'd like to run you over to urgent care to get it looked at."

"I'm not a pansy, Nick. Give it a day. I'll be fine."

Trixie placed the ice on his ankle. "Keep this on it for twenty minutes."

"Did you get the horses taken care of?" Nick asked.

Walt shook his head. "No."

"We'll take care of them," Nick said.

Trixie sat on the coffee table, holding the ice on his ankle. "Did you eat breakfast?"

"I'm fine."

"And I'm making you breakfast." She headed back into the kitchen.

"I'm going to take care of the horses." Nick pushed to his feet. "If your ankle swells, or it gets worse, I'm taking you in for an X-ray. No arguments."

Nick took care of the horses and mucked out the stalls. When he came back inside, Walt's breakfast dishes were on the coffee table beside a pitcher of iced tea and his elevated foot, which was now expertly wrapped. Trixie was sitting beside him on the couch, captivated by a story he was telling her. Nick picked up the dishes and took them into the kitchen to wash.

"We were high school sweethearts," Walt said with an unusually thoughtful tone. "But she wanted a small-town life, and after high-school graduation, I took off for the glamour and glitz of Hollywood. When I finally came back a few years later, she was married to my childhood best friend."

"Oh, Walt. That's so sad."

"That's just it, Trixie. It wasn't sad. I was happy for them. She got everything she dreamed of, and so did I. But you asked if I was ever in love, and the answer is yes. I loved her dearly. But I loved stunt riding more."

"Do you regret leaving?" she asked.

"I didn't when I left, although I did regret hurting her. She was heartbroken. It wasn't until I retired and came back for good that I slowed down enough to think about things. I'd see them in town, and I realized what I'd missed out on."

Nick had known Walt practically all his life, and he'd never heard that story before. He looked at Trixie's beautiful face, her hand over Walt's, her warm eyes watching him, and he felt a tug in his chest again. When she cared about someone, she got right to the heart of them.

Just like you did with me.

Nick dried his hands and went to join them.

"Nick and I know all about not wanting to move away from our hometowns. But I also understand wanting bigger, better things, like my therapy business." Trixie looked over as Nick walked into the room. "Did you know about Walt's first love?"

"No, I didn't, actually. Is she still around the area? Who is she?"

Walt nodded. "Yes, sir. I knew her as Reeny Hennington. You know her as Irene Helms, Travis's grandmother."

"*Walt*," Trixie said conspiratorially. "Travis told me that his grandfather passed away five years ago. Have you been in touch with her lately?"

"Darlin', that ship sailed a long time ago. I'm an old man, and I've got nothing to offer her or anyone else." He patted Trixie's leg and said, "Now, how about y'all get out of my hair and go get naked or something."

She laughed.

"Stop thinking about my girl naked," Nick warned. "I'll take care of the horses for a few days so you can stay off that ankle."

"And I'll pop over with lunch in a few hours and bring dinner around seven. Remember, your phone is on the table beside you, plugged into the charger. Call if you need anything at all. You have Nick's number, and I put my number in it, too, because Nick is as bad at carrying his phone as you are." Trixie leaned in and kissed Walt's cheek. "I'll grab your walking stick from the front porch so you can lean on it in case you need to go to the bathroom."

The second she was out the front door, Walt said, "You'd better marry that girl, or I will. I haven't serenaded a woman in fifty years, but I'm sure I still have it in me."

Walt had once told Nick there were few firsts a man could give a woman that meant something and to save serenading for the one he couldn't live without.

Trixie breezed back in before Nick could give him shit about his comment. She put the walking stick by the couch. "Here you go." She took Nick's hand as if she'd been doing it her whole life and said, "We should go take care of our menagerie, collect the chickens' eggs, let the goats into the play area, and I want to get some training in before lunch."

"I liked Walt's idea of getting naked." Nick winked at Walt, and they headed outside.

Trixie huddled closer as they walked across the pasture. "I need to call Jilly."

"Why?"

"Because we have matchmaking to do!"

"Trixie, don't mess with his life."

"I messed with yours, and look how happy you are!" She gave him a peck on his cheek, said, "Race you to the horses!" and took off running.

He had a feeling Walt didn't stand a chance.

NICK WENT INSIDE to shower before dinner and followed the heavenly aroma of chili into the kitchen. Trixie stood barefoot in her Daisy Dukes and belly-baring shirt, stirring the chili on the stove and bobbing her head to whatever she was listening to through her earbuds. A freshly baked pie was cooling on the counter beside a dish covered with tinfoil. On the island were two vases overflowing with wildflowers. *When did you pick those?* He leaned over the island and peeled back the tinfoil, revealing Trixie's homemade jalapeño corn bread, one of Nick's favorites. Her voice whispered through his mind. *Inviting friends and family over every once in a while would make your house homier.* They didn't need anyone else in the house to make it homier. She did it all by herself.

When they'd gone to have lunch with Walt, she'd weaseled more stories out of him about his time in Hollywood and the famous women he'd had affairs with. She'd called him *brave* for starting a new life so far away and shared a story about when she was younger and had gone to her first sleepover. She'd called her mother and had gone home in the middle of the night because she'd been homesick. Nick had thought he'd known everything there was to know about his bold girl, but he was learning there was a lot more to her than he'd ever imagined.

He put his arms around her from behind and kissed her cheek, wondering if he could overdose on a woman so sweet and sexy. She pulled out her earbuds and turned in his arms.

"My girl can cook. You've been holding out on me."

"You never asked if I could cook." She kissed his chin. "And you've always known I could bake. I made your favorite jalapeño corn bread."

"I saw, but I'm a little jealous that you went all out for Walt."

"It's not all for Walt. We're having dinner with him, re-member?"

He nipped at her neck. "That's why I came in early. I thought we could have an appetizer."

"This *does* need to simmer for twenty minutes."

"Perfect."

As he lowered his lips to hers, she put her hand flat on his chest, keeping him at bay. "But we'll need to shower before dinner, too, and I seem to remember you saying ten minutes wasn't enough to whet your appetite."

"Is that a challenge?"

She brushed her hips against him. "More like a *dare*."

"You should know by now that I never back down."

"I banked on it."

He hauled her over his shoulder and smacked her ass, earn-ing a shriek and a giggle as he carried her into the bedroom. Between making the first move, revealing her romantic underbelly, and challenging him at every turn, she was going to drive him mad—and he looked forward to every single second of it.

Chapter Twenty

TRIXIE PUT ON the chic navy-blue sleeveless dress she'd bought at Jillian's shop and slipped on her heels. It was Tuesday afternoon, and the conservative dress was perfect for her meeting with Jordan Lawler, the director of the volunteer program at Pleasant Care Assisted Living. She admired herself in the mirror, taking in the rounded neckline and the pretty knotted detail at her hip. The skirt stopped just above her knee, and the diagonal pockets gave it a hint of casual without losing its professional edge. Trixie felt sharp and confident, even if a little out of her element, in the fancy duds. But she couldn't be better prepared. She'd practiced her pitch on Nick so many times, she could recite it in her sleep. He'd been patient and helpful, asking questions and giving her pointers.

Now, if only she could calm her nerves.

Her phone rang, startling her. She grabbed it from the dresser and answered the FaceTime call from Lindsay. Lindsay's and Amber's faces appeared on the screen, and they said, "Hi! Good luck today!"

"Thank you. How are you guys? I'm so happy to see your faces."

"We're great," Lindsay said. "Brindle wanted to join us, but she had a teacher meeting." Brindle taught high school English and ran the drama club at the elementary school. "She sends you loads of love and good luck."

"Be sure to thank her for me. I need all the luck I can get."

"You look beautiful," Amber said. "That's a great color on you."

"Thanks." She held the phone away from her body, so they could see the whole dress. "It's one of Jilly's designs. Isn't it gorgeous?"

"It's perfect," Amber said.

Lindsay gave her a thumbs-up. "You're going to do great today."

"I hope so. It's been a crazy few days. Do you remember Nick's neighbor, Walt?"

"How could we forget Walt the ex-Hollywood flirt?" Lindsay said. "Jilly said you were concocting some sort of matchmaking plan for him."

"I am. I'm just not sure how yet. But Walt hurt his ankle over the weekend, and Nick and I have been taking care of his animals and looking after him, so things have been extra busy around here the last few days."

"Oh no. I hope he's okay," Amber said.

"He is. We had lunch with him today and he said his ankle doesn't hurt anymore, but we're going to help out for a little longer, so he doesn't overdo it. Did I tell you that I got the final logo for Rising Hope yesterday?"

"No," they said in unison.

"I'll text it to you. It turned out even better than I'd hoped, and the website will be ready next week. I can't believe it's all happening so fast. Can you believe I have *four* miniature horses? They all get along, and Nick and I have been working with them a few times a day. Wait until you meet them in person. They're the sweetest, smartest babies."

"You brag like a true mother," Lindsay teased. "Should I be planning your baby shower?"

"Shut up. I just love them so much," Trixie said.

"I like the baby shower idea," Amber chimed in. "That's a great reason to have cupcakes or a big chocolate cake with a horse on it."

"Now I want cake." Trixie laughed.

Lindsay waggled her brows. "You have beefcake somewhere on that ranch. I'm sure he'd love for you to gobble him up."

"I don't have time for that right now, although...*yum*."

"Gosh, you two." Amber giggled. "But speaking of your beefcake, I loved the videos of the horses you sent us yesterday. They're adorable, and it was cool to see you and Nick training them together. It must be nice to have so much in common with your boyfriend."

"What did you just say?" Trixie wanted to bask in the word *boyfriend*.

"About having so much in common with your boyfriend?" Amber asked.

"Yeah," Trixie said a little breathily. "That's the first time anyone has used the *B* word and I kinda love it!"

"Me too," Amber exclaimed.

"I guess that means things are good on the new couple front," Lindsay said.

Trixie sat on the bed. "Better than I could have ever imagined."

"What's he like with you?" Amber asked.

"Well, he's Nick, so he's rough and gruff, but tender in his own way." She lowered her voice and said, "I have never been with a guy that I could be myself with in *and* out of the bedroom. You know how we always wish guys could read our minds, sexually speaking?"

"Not really," Amber said.

"I totally do," Lindsay said.

"Well, he and I are on the same wavelength *all* the time. I can't get enough of him, and luckily, he can't get enough of me, either. Thank goodness he has no neighbors, because we're not exactly quiet. But it's not just sex, you know? It's *everything*. We laugh at the same things and give each other crap just for fun, and we can go without talking for long stretches and it's comfortable and nice."

"You two have always been like that," Lindsay reminded her.

"I know, and I'm glad that didn't change. But I think my favorite thing is falling asleep in his arms." She sighed. "It's the happiest, *best* feeling I've ever had. He's amazing, and we're amazing together, and now I sound like one of those gushing girls we make fun of."

"I don't make fun of them. I want to be one of them," Amber said.

"You will be, Amber." Lindsay raised her brows. "I guess that means Nick doesn't suck in bed after all."

"Oh *yes* he does, thank you very much. He also bites, nips, and does all the other delicious things you can think of."

Amber blushed a red streak.

"Damn, girl. That's awesome," Lindsay said.

"You guys are too wild for me," Amber said sweetly. "Jilly told us how he stole you away on the dance floor and staked his claim on you right in front of everyone. That's *so* romantic. I want my own cowboy to fall in love with. Or maybe not a cowboy, because if they do all that stuff in bed, they might be too much for me."

Lindsay rolled her eyes. "Amber, the right man is going to bring out the secret seductress in you, and you'll love every minute of being out of control and wild with him."

"I second that," Trixie said.

Amber shook her head. "I don't think so. Out of control for me is not a good thing."

There was a knock at Trixie's bedroom door. "Come in."

"Hey, babe." Nick walked in and stopped cold, raking his eyes down the length of her. "*Wow.* You look incredible."

"Thank you. I bought this at Jilly's the other day."

"Don't tear that dress off her while we're on the phone!" Lindsay said loudly.

Nick's brow furrowed.

Trixie laughed and lifted the phone so he could see the girls. "Sorry. I was talking with Lindsay and Amber."

"Hi, ladies. Sorry to interrupt," Nick said. "How's it going?"

"Not as good as it is for *you*," Lindsay teased.

Nick gave Trixie a *what the hell did you tell them* look.

"I swear I didn't tell them about the body shots of champagne and—"

"You just did, darlin'." He put his arm around her. "Let's just say I'm a hell of a lucky guy, but I like to keep that stuff private."

"Trixie's lucky, too," Amber said. "We should let you go. Good luck, Trixie. I'm sending all my good vibes your way."

"Let us know how the meeting goes," Lindsay added. "And I want details on the champagne tryst."

Trixie laughed. "Thanks for calling. Love you guys." She ended the call and slipped her phone into her pocket. "Do you really think I look okay for the meeting?"

"You could walk into a boardroom and command it." He gathered her in his arms and said, "I'm so proud of you for going after what you want."

"I'm getting good at that." She went up on her toes and kissed him.

"Yes, you are. I got you a little something."

Her pulse quickened. "You didn't have to do that."

"I wanted to. It's nothing big, but it's a special day, and I thought you might want these."

He reached into his pocket and withdrew a gold business card holder with the Rising Hope logo inscribed on the top. "Nick, this is gorgeous."

"Open it."

She did, and a lump formed in her throat at the sight of business cards with the logo to the left and TRIXIE JERICHO printed above RISING HOPE in the center, and below that, MINIATURE THERAPY HORSES followed by her contact information and website address. She threw her arms around him, feeling like she might cry. "Thank you so much! I love them. I ordered vests and other things for the horses, and a couple of T-shirts for when we eventually do visits, but I totally forgot about business cards."

"That's because you're all about the horses. Someone's got to be all about you."

She pressed her lips to his, and when salty tears slipped between them, she laughed. "I'm sorry. It's just…The way you support me…It's so unexpected."

He brushed away her tears with the backs of his fingers. "So are we, darlin'." He kissed her again. "I only ordered fifty in case you didn't like them, but we can order more."

"I love them. They're perfect. But how did you get my logo?"

"I called Jilly, and she hooked me up with Destiny, who got me a rush order with someone she knows. Now, go knock this woman's socks off and call me the second you get out."

"I have to put on makeup first." She was on cloud nine as she headed for her bathroom.

"Didn't I see your makeup bag in my bathroom this morning?"

"*Ugh.* Yes. Sorry. I forgot I left it there."

He stepped in front of her, his arms circling her again, his eyes as warm as his embrace. "I like it there."

She was so happy she could do little more than smile.

"Fair warning, darlin'." He ran his hands up her outer thighs, beneath her dress. "When you get back, we might have to pretend my dining room table is a boardroom table, so I can bend you over it."

Heat seared through her core. "*Nick!*" She laughed and stepped out of his arms. "How am I supposed to go into a serious meeting with *that* on my mind?"

"Maybe this will help." He pulled her back into his arms. "If you don't nail it, I won't nail you."

"*Ohmygod.* Why do you do this to me?"

"Because paybacks are hell, darlin'."

AN HOUR LATER, armed with her special new business cards, pictures of her horses, and a heart full of hope, Trixie sat across from Jordan Lawler, a Kate Bosworth lookalike with high cheekbones, blond hair that fell to the middle of her back, and a rock on her finger the size of Mount Everest.

"I've been reading up on miniature therapy horses since speaking with Tempest, and I assume you'll have the proper vaccination reports, insurance, and hoof coverings."

"Absolutely."

Jordan sat back and crossed her legs, tapping her fingers on the arm of her chair with a curious expression. "The idea is intriguing."

"There's definitely a unique *wow* factor to using miniature horses. Service dogs are common, but far fewer people have gotten up close and personal with miniature service horses. Beyond their cuteness, they're intelligent, social creatures, and they have a tremendous amount of love and comfort to give. That's what Rising Hope is all about, bringing happiness, comfort, and joy to those who need it. Working with therapy horses has been shown to help with physical and cognitive skills, to decrease depression and reduce anxiety and blood pressure, build confidence, and increase socialization. The horses are small enough to be present in therapy gyms to help inspire patients who are learning to use adaptive equipment, like wheelchairs and walkers. For patients who are allowed to do more, such as brush the horse's mane or put in hair clips, it can also help with fine motor skills while providing a sense of achievement." As Trixie spoke, she decided she definitely wanted to offer more than facility visits. "I'll also be working with patients outside of facilities, offering groundwork and grooming with my minis and therapeutic riding with my regular-size horse, Buttercup. For a person who is disabled, riding can help with balance, posture, muscle tone, and of course, confidence."

"Tempest said you were just starting your business and would have questions, but I'm impressed. You seem to have a solid handle on it."

"Thank you. I've been around horses all my life. I grew up on a cattle and horse ranch, and I still help my family run it. But therapy horses have become my passion." She told Jordan the story that she'd told Nick about Elsie and Cara. "I hope to bring that kind of hope to others."

"How many miniature horses do you have?"

Trixie took out her iPad and showed her pictures of the horses. "I have four. Two are four years old with two years of therapy experience. Annabelle is the white filly. She's thirty-two inches at her withers, which is the ridge between her shoulder blades, and Alfie, the reddish-brown one, is my littlest. He's twenty-six inches. They're two of the sweetest horses you'll ever meet." She flipped to another picture. "These are my babies who I've just begun training. Buttons is the white one with brown spots. She's a doll. And Prince is the black one. But they won't be ready for therapy visits for quite a while."

"They're all adorable. I feel happier just looking at the pictures."

"I know." Trixie laughed softly. "They're hard to resist, which is part of what makes them such special service animals. And to make the experience even more magical, sometimes I'll dress the horses up with wings and unicorn horns, and when Prince is ready, he might show up with a crown."

"The residents would get a kick out of that. Heck, I'd get a kick out of that."

They both laughed.

"I'm up for anything that lightens people's spirits. Where exactly is Rising Hope located?"

"The headquarters is in Oak Falls, Virginia, which is about two hours from here. But I've been traveling from Virginia to Maryland for years, and I plan to continue. My colleague has a ranch on the outskirts of town with plenty of room for my horses. That's where I stay when I'm here. But if you don't mind, I do have a few questions regarding rules and regulations for your facility."

Jordan answered her questions, and then she said, "It sounds like you have your bases covered as far as regulations go. I would love to have you bring Annabelle or Alfie in for a soft visit. We can see how they do in the facility, and if that goes well, we can talk about scheduling patient visits."

Trixie wanted to climb across the desk to hug her, but she forced herself to hold it together. "I would love to schedule a soft visit."

"Great. It will take me about a week or so to get it approved." She pulled up a calendar on her computer and said, "I can do a week from Monday at two or four."

"Either works for me."

"Great, let's say two o'clock. That way we won't be rushed."

"Thank you for taking the time to talk with me and for offering me my very first soft visit. To be honest, I was nervous about how today would go."

"I know how terrifying and exhilarating starting a new endeavor can be."

"You do?"

Jordan held up her left hand and wiggled her fingers. Her engagement ring glittered beneath the lights. "You're braver than me. I've already rescheduled my wedding three times."

"Oh my goodness. Well, that's a gorgeous ring. I'm sure you'll know when the time is right."

"Thank you. It's a bit much for me, kind of like my fiancé. He works on Wall Street, and once we're married, that's where I'm supposed to move."

"Wow. New York. That sounds exciting."

"It is, but I love Maryland and my job." She shrugged. "Needless to say, I understand why this new turn in your life is scary and exciting, and I'm happy to help."

Trixie saw an opening and went for it. "In that case, I wonder if you have any contacts with other facilities in Maryland, DC, or Virginia that might be interested in using my services."

Jordan opened her desk drawer and pulled out a document. "Actually, Tempest and I talked about that, too. I took the liberty of putting together a list." She slid it across the desk. "We girls need to stick together."

"We sure do, so if you need help choosing a wedding date or anything, let me know. My friend is a wedding gown designer. Maybe you've heard of him. Jax Braden?"

"Are you kidding? He's a legend in this town, and he's on top of my list. By the way, I love your dress—the lines and the detail are exquisite."

"Thank you. Jax's twin, Jillian, designed it. She has a boutique here in town."

"I don't live here in town, but on my way to work I pass by Jillian's Boutique. Is that hers?"

"Yes, that's it."

"The designs in the windows are always gorgeous."

"Sounds like you have an eye for fashion."

Jordan shrugged, smiling. "Old loves die hard, I guess. Why don't I take you on a tour of the facility and we can chat while we walk?"

"I'd love that. Before we go, here's my business card." As she handed Jordan the card, her heart swelled anew at Nick's thoughtfulness. She didn't know what was up between Jordan and her fiancé, but if Nick were in New York, Trixie would be on the next train out of town.

Chapter Twenty-One

NICK HAD BEEN more focused on waiting for his phone to ring than working for the past two hours. As much as he usually resented being tied to the damn thing, he didn't feel that way at all. He was anxious to hear about how Trixie's meeting had gone. He'd managed to keep himself busy doing menial work around the ranch, but it hadn't distracted him from thoughts of her. He leaned on the fence around the corral where the minis were hanging out. They were cute little buggers. He'd put Snickers in with them, and all five got along beautifully. Annabelle and Buttons meandered over, and Nick petted them.

"Hi, guys. Missing your mama? Me too." Nick knew he'd have to get used to that in a few weeks. Alfie brushed against his leg, and he reached down to love him up, too. "She's out paving the way to make you guys into stars. If anyone can do it, she can. You're lucky to have her, you know." He looked at Prince standing in the shade of a tree and whistled, patting his leg, remembering too late that Prince, like the others, hadn't been with them long enough to know his signals yet.

Since when did I *become a* them?

He headed over to Prince and crouched beside the gorgeous black gelding. "What's happening, buddy? Just need a little space? I get that way, too. Well, not so much anymore. Your mama's kinda turning my world upside down."

Prince sighed.

*You got that right. Women...*Nick scratched behind Prince's ears. "She's not like anyone else. She's the best there is."

His phone rang, and his heart freaking skipped. She was turning him upside down all right. He whipped his phone from his pocket, and Beau's name flashed on the screen. Nick tried to mask his disappointment as he answered the call. "Hi, Beau."

"Hi. What're you up to?"

Nick pushed to his feet. "I was just having a conversation with one of Trixie's miniature horses."

Beau laughed. "I guess I can't make fun of you anymore since my wife talks to blow-up dolls and chickens." Charlotte was an erotic romance writer, and she used blow-up dolls to work out the mechanics for some of her scenes.

Nick thought about how Trixie talked with the chickens when they collected eggs in the mornings and felt himself smiling.

"Jilly called, trying to wrangle Char into a matchmaking scheme for Walt," Beau said, drawing Nick from his thoughts.

"I swear those girls work faster than the speed of light. How's married life?"

"Five stars. Highly recommended."

Nick chuckled. "Then you owe me one, since I had to just about kick your ass to get your head out of it."

"Like hell you did."

"Seriously, bro?" He petted Prince's head and made his way to the gate.

"That's my story, and I'm sticking to it."

"Idiot."

Beau laughed. "It's good to see Trixie hasn't made you soft."

"*Shit.* That woman makes every man in a ten-mile radius hard."

"Dude, you're talking about your girlfriend."

"Damn right I am." He rolled *girlfriend* over in his mind. "That's a first."

"What's that?"

"*Girlfriend.*"

"Bullshit. How about Tennessee?"

"You knew about her?"

"You went out there twice when I came home to visit from college. Did you really think I wouldn't notice?"

Nick took off his hat and wiped his brow. "I guess I never thought about it."

"I noticed, Nick. The same way I noticed that when I left for college, you kept your promise to look after Tory."

Nick's muscles tensed. He'd stopped by Tory's house several times during the first few weeks after Beau had left for college, when she'd been so sad, he knew she'd need a shoulder to lean on. After she got over the worst of it, when he'd heard she was going to parties, he'd always stopped by in case she needed a ride home. She was Beau's love, which had made her important to Nick, too.

"That was ages ago, Beau. No sweat."

"I know, but I never said thank you, and it meant a lot to me. You gave me peace of mind so I could focus on school. And after the accident, you tried your damnedest to take care of me, too. You never gave up on me even though I was a broken jerk."

"You weren't a jerk."

Beau scoffed. "Like hell I wasn't. I gave you so much shit, but you never relented. You sought me out and tried to get me to let go of the guilt and come home so many times. I know I never showed it, but that meant the world to me. I needed that connection to our family even if I couldn't grab hold of it. Thanks, man. I want you to know I appreciate you."

Nick got choked up. "What's going on that's got you taking a stroll down memory lane? You're not sick, are you?"

"No. It's you, man. You gave up your life to take care of everyone else, and now you're finally doing something for yourself. You've got a girlfriend, and that's big news in this family. It's hard to believe someone finally roped you in."

"I have a feeling she roped me in long before I had any idea what she was up to."

"That's a good thing, right? You're not going to break Trixie's heart, are you? As close as all our girls are, you're liable to start a riot."

"I'm the guy who wouldn't let you break Char's heart and wouldn't let Zev disrespect Carly when they were young. Why the hell would you even ask me that?"

"Because you've got an attitude bigger than your ranch, and it worries me. Relationships change things."

"Nothing's changed, man. I don't know what you're worried about. Trixie and I are the same people we were, but now we're sleeping together."

"If you believe that, then you're the idiot."

"I'm not an idiot, Beau. I've got feelings for her, but I'm pretty sure they've been around for a hell of a long time."

"But now you're acknowledging them. That's big. That's a *change*. Let me give you one piece of advice. Don't make Trixie live within your fucked-up boundaries."

"That was the advice I gave you about Char."

"And you were right. But, Nick, you've got fucked-up

boundaries, too. You make my old walls look like they were made out of paper."

"Did you call to give me hell?"

"No, but it's kind of fun." Beau chuckled. "I wanted you to know that I'm happy for you. Trixie's great, and you've always been good together. Whatever you two need, I'm here. I can build another barn for her horses, a wedding arch, a bassinet…"

"You're an asshole."

"An asshole who loves you, man."

Another call rang through, and Trixie's name flashed on the screen. "Sorry to do this to you, but that's Trixie calling. I've gotta take it. She had a big meeting today."

"Nick Braden is officially whipped."

"Fuck off, and give my love to Char. Hope to see you before Zev and Carly's wedding."

"We can make it a double wedding."

"Bye, Beau." Nick switched over to Trixie's call. "Hey, darlin'. How'd it go?"

"I have a soft visit! She loved me! She gave me referrals! And I was so proud to give her my business card!"

Nick held the phone away from his ear as she shouted. "That's fantastic, Trix. When's the visit?"

"A week from Monday. I'm so glad I ordered the vests and shoes for the horses. I need to practice with them. Annabelle especially. I want to bring her first. She feels like the big sister. Will you practice with me? I'm not taking her to see patients. We're just walking through the facility. I wish I had a place with people where I could take them to practice when they're all suited up."

"I can ask Cole if we can take them into his office. Would that help?"

"Do you think he'd mind? That's a lot to ask. But it would make me feel more confident if I could do a trial run before the real thing. They'd be around people and noises, and we can take them in the elevator. *Wait.* The building owners might not let us do it."

"Then I can ask my buddy Jace Stone. He owns Silver-Stone Cycles, and they have a new manufacturing plant and headquarters in Peaceful Harbor. It's not a medical facility, but it's got noises, machines, people, and elevators."

"That sounds perfect. But I don't want to put you in an uncomfortable position if it's too much to ask."

"Darlin', I'd be more uncomfortable knowing you didn't have what you needed than asking a buddy for a favor. Besides, you'll dig Jace. He's a great guy, and he's married to a cool chick, Dixie Whiskey. She models for his company, but she's not really a model. She's a tough biker. You'd love her."

"Dixie and Jace? Jilly's mentioned them to me before. She said Jace is bigger than you, which is hard to believe, and a great dancer, and that Dixie's family owns that biker bar Sam likes to go to, Whiskey Bro's. We should go there sometime."

He scoffed. "I'm *not* taking you to a biker bar."

"Party pooper. Look up the driveway, cowboy. I'm home!"

He saw her truck coming down the driveway, and his pulse thumped faster. He shoved his phone in his pocket as she parked. She ran to him, dropped her messenger bag, and launched herself into his arms with a squeal. He spun her around and kissed her. "I'm so damn proud of you." He kissed her again, long and hard.

When he set her on her feet, she clung to his T-shirt, snagging a few chest hairs. The excitement bubbling out of her was worth the sting.

"We did it, Nick! I wouldn't have gotten Annabelle and Alfie if you hadn't suggested it and taken me to meet Ed. We make a great team. I made some big decisions while I was there. Once I get settled at my dad's, I want to offer groundwork with the minis and come up with a schedule where I do site visits a few days a week and work with the animals on the ranch the other days. That way the horses aren't traveling so much. I'm so excited I can barely see straight. I need to go change my clothes. I want to spend time with my babies."

She barely took a breath as she grabbed her bag and his hand and headed for the house. "I felt so confident talking with Jordan, who was awesome, by the way, and I know I felt good because Alfie and Annabelle are so well trained. I want to be sure to train Buttons and Prince just as thoroughly. I'm going to look over all my notes from our visit with Ed and try to emulate his training the best I can. I think I'm going to save up and find a way to make fake patient rooms, like Ed had. I can't buy an elevator, but I can buy an old bed and I'm sure my brothers can help me make fake medical equipment out of wood or something."

"Your brothers? How about me? I'm a pretty handy guy," he said as they went through the kitchen door.

She wrinkled her brow. "But you'll be here. I'm talking about after I go back home."

"Right." What the hell was he thinking? *That I want to be the guy you turn to for help, no matter where you are.* "It's only a two-hour drive, Trixie. I'll do that stuff for you."

She put her bag on the counter and wound her arms around his neck. "If we weren't sleeping together, I'd say I love you! But I know sleeping together brings new meaning to those words, and that would freak you out. So...I love that you'll do that for me!"

When she went up on her toes and pressed her lips to his, he held her tighter, deepening the kiss, trying to escape the bevy of questions pecking at him. Why did it bother him that she dismissed those words so quickly? She wasn't wrong. Hearing them that way probably would have freaked him out. They were heavy words, and they triggered questions he didn't have the answers to, like exactly what he felt for Trixie. His feelings for her didn't feel different than they always had. They just felt a hell of a lot bigger. Was that love? How the hell should he know? It had been easy for him to see a difference in his brothers when they'd fallen in love. Beau had physically changed, from the light in his eyes to the way he carried himself. He'd become less protected, more open. Graham had always been open with his emotions but had never seemed content. Morgyn had given him that, and he'd changed his whole life to include her. And Zev? Hell, he'd gone from a wild child, running from his past, to a man, accepting and becoming one with it. He no longer gave off a perched-to-leave vibe. He had become settled and at peace. But Nick looked at himself in the mirror every morning, and he didn't see any difference. He felt happier and his thoughts were consumed by Trixie, but they had been for the last year. That wasn't new.

As their lips parted, he pushed that can of worms closed before it could fuck with his head any more than it already had.

"I've been thinking," Trixie said.

"Should I be worried?"

She giggled. "No. I want to thank Tempe for helping me, and Jilly for guiding me with this outfit, and Travis for being patient while I looked at the horses. And I want to thank you for everything you've done for me."

"The dining room table is right there." He grabbed her ass. "Ready and waiting for you to thank me properly."

Her eyes darkened. "I, um…I love that idea, but first let me tell you about this other idea I had."

"Does it involve you and me getting naked?" He kissed her neck.

"Afterward, yes."

"Okay, go ahead." He squeezed her butt. "But this ass is mine, and I'm not letting go."

"I'd be disappointed if you did." She smirked and ran her fingers down his chest. "What do you think about having your family, Tempe and her family, and Travis and April over for a bonfire and barbecue? You've got that gorgeous firepit. Sharing it for a few hours would be fun, and I'll do everything. I'll cook, clean up, and make sure nobody's wandering around inside your house."

He opened his mouth to respond, but she put her finger over his lips and said, "Before you answer, I was thinking we could also invite Walt, because we know he's lonely and he'd enjoy it."

"Trix, you know how I feel about having people over."

"I know. Just hear me out. I talked to Travis about his grandmother, and he said she's lonely, too. So I was thinking that since we'd invite your parents and Walt, we could also invite his grandmother."

"So you want to play matchmaker?"

"I…*well*…not *matchmaker*, but maybe open a door between Walt and Travis's grandmother that could lead to more fulfilling days for both of them. He might not have that many years left, and he loved her once. What if that special spark comes back? Love is good, Nick. I know you think it equals destruction, but it's not like that for everyone, and beneath Walt's rugged exterior, I think he's a lonely man who has love to give. You love Walt like family. Don't you want him to be happier?"

How the hell could he argue with that?

"But that's not the biggest reason I want to have people over, and neither is thanking everyone. Although, that was what made me think of the idea." She traced the ridge of his pecs with her fingers, her eyes soft and a little tentative, which was new, and chipped away at his resolve. "I know we're early in our relationship, but having people over is a *couple thing* to do, and I kind of love the idea of doing a couple thing with you."

Fuck. That look in her eyes, and the hope in her voice, tugged at him.

"You can say no to this, Nick. I don't want to push you. That's not who I am."

He scoffed. "That's *exactly* who you are." *And I wouldn't want you any other way.*

"You're right. I'm sorry. I shouldn't have suggested it. I'll set up a time with everyone, and we can all go out for pizza instead. It'll be fun." She kissed his chin, smiling like she wasn't disappointed.

But he knew better.

"I'm going to change my clothes. I'll meet you outside to work with the horses?"

She stepped out of his arms and he pulled her back to him. "You really want to do this *couple thing*, don't you?"

Hope rose in her eyes as she nodded. "But we've come so far so fast, the last thing I want to do is make you uncomfortable. I don't mind going out for pizza instead."

The honesty in her voice made his insides go soft. His eyes

swept over the vase on the counter, filled with fresh wildflowers. When had she refilled it? He gazed into her eyes, and not only couldn't he tell her no, but he no longer wanted to.

"Okay, we'll do it. But I don't want everyone going through my shit."

She squealed and kissed him hard. "Thank you! This is going to be so fun, and we'll keep everyone outside. I promise! Except if they have to use the bathroom."

Her giddiness made him smile. "I think I can handle that. Just tell me what I need to do."

"Nothing. I'll do it all."

"No, darlin'. I'm pretty sure that's not how couple things work. If we're doing this, we're doing it together."

"*Really?*" she said dreamily. "Thank you! I'll go change, and we can talk about it while we work with the horses."

He pulled her close again. "I believe I'm owed a proper thank-you." He glanced at the dining room table and raised his brows. Her eyes flamed as he ran his hands up her thighs and pulled down her panties.

"I think I'm going to have to start requesting more get-togethers."

She stepped out of her panties, stroking him through his jeans. She was just as sexually driven as he was. His mouth came ravenously down over hers as they stumbled toward the table. He tore his mouth away and spun her around. She pressed her palms flat on the hard surface as he hiked up her dress.

"You're so damn gorgeous." He caressed her ass and kissed each rounded cheek. "So soft and perfect. I'm so fucking hard for you, darlin'." He teased her with his fingers, earning those sweet and sinful sounds as he kissed and nipped her cheeks. She writhed, her sex clenching around his fingers. Desire seared through his veins, and he lowered his mouth, taking one glorious lick of her essence. She moaned, long and loud, and so hungrily, he had to do it again.

"*Nick*, I need you," she pleaded.

He dropped his drawers and clutched her hips, pulling her back as he thrust into her tight heat. Pleasure consumed him, and they both moaned. He pounded into her, driven by lust, greed, and something so much more powerful, it took over the rest.

"*Don't stop*," she begged. "*So good.*"

Consumed by pure animalistic need, there was no chance of him stopping, and she was right there with him. Every pump of his hips brought a moan or a plea for more. He couldn't get enough, deepening every pump, grinding into her.

"*Nick...oh God...*"

He wrapped one arm around her, zeroing in on the spot that made her detonate with his fingers. His name flew loud and hungry from her lips. "*Nick!*"

He stayed with her. Her body clenched tight and hot around him, fueling his need. But he couldn't get close enough. He needed more of her. He needed to *see* her.

"I need to see your beautiful face, darlin'," he gritted out as she came down from the peak.

His request whirled in his head as he turned her around, but he didn't fight it. He needed to see her even more than he needed to be inside her. He lifted her onto the edge of the table. The emotions in her eyes drilled into him, seeping into his bones, as their mouths and their bodies crashed together. He lifted her legs higher, taking her deeper, and quickly lost himself in their connection, in the feel of her fingernails carving into his arms and her needy moans climbing from her lungs into his. He clutched her ass with one hand, his other buried in her hair as they pounded out a frantic rhythm. But still she felt too far away. What the hell? Whatever it was, she must have felt it, too, because she lifted off the table, clinging to him. Her legs tightened around his waist like a vise, taking him right up to the edge of ecstasy. But this was *better*. Their bodies were flush, and her every breath became his. Holy hell, this was *heaven*. Her head fell back, and she sucked in quick gasps. She was so damn sexy as she gave in to her release, it slayed him, and he followed her over the edge, their bodies shaking and thrusting through the very last pulse.

When she rested her cheek on his shoulder, breathing hard, he closed his eyes, wrestling with the emotions coursing through him. He clenched his jaw to trap them in, but they tumbled out anyway. "You don't just fuck with my head, Trix. You fuck with every part of me."

She lifted her face with a sweet smile on her lips and kissed his cheek. Then she rested her head on his shoulder again and closed her eyes. He felt her inhale deeply and let it out slowly. She was so trusting, so loving, he was overwhelmed with the urge to do more for her. He didn't know exactly what *more* was, but he sure as hell would figure it out.

"Thank you for saying yes," she whispered.

"You know I can't say no to you." He pressed a kiss to her lips.

As he carried her into the bedroom, she whispered, "But it's fun watching you try."

Chapter Twenty-Two

TRIXIE LAY IN Nick's arms Saturday morning, enjoying their closeness and wondering how she'd ever go back to sleeping alone after having all of this with Nick. She glanced at Pugsly snoring softly beside him, and a pang of sadness moved through her. How could two weeks feel like two months? Her time there was only half over, and they'd already become so much more than she thought possible in an entire month. Her eyes swept over her hairbrush and hat on the dresser and the chair in the corner where their freshly washed clothes were neatly stacked together. Her toothbrush and makeup were on the sink in the bathroom, her bodywash and shampoo were in the shower, and there she was, draped over him like he was hers. The craziest part was that he *was* hers.

She pressed a kiss to his chest. His hand moved down her back, squeezing her bottom as he kissed her head.

"I have to get up soon to run with Travis."

"A few more minutes, darlin'." His deep voice was rough from sleep and incredibly sexy. "What are you overthinking?"

He knew her so well, but she wasn't about to go there. "How much I like your voice in the morning."

"If you weren't going running, I'd remind you how much

you like other parts of me."

"Trust me, you reminded me well last night." They'd gone into town for ice cream and had ended up teasing and taunting each other so much on the way home, they hadn't even made it indoors. They'd eaten their ice cream off each other and had sex in the truck. "We should win a medal for our acrobatic talents."

He chuckled and patted her ass. "That was fun, chickadee."

"You were very *giving*."

Nick's generosity went well beyond his sexual prowess. He gave often and in so many ways, it was no wonder she was crazy about him. He'd not only arranged for her to meet with Jace on Monday at his office so she could practice with Annabelle, but he was going with her so she could practice with both horses. Another woman might not think that was romantic, but Trixie knew that although Nick's walls were coming down, they still existed. All the little things he did for her told her how deeply he cared about her, and that was incredibly romantic. She wished she had more to give to him than only her love. But every time she tried to come up with a material gift, her mind returned to the thing that mattered most: showing him how good it felt to be loved. It was all she'd wanted to do for so many years, she almost felt selfish because loving him came so easily.

"As I recall, you were just as giving," he said, bringing her back to the moment.

"Nick à la mode is my new favorite dessert." She scooted down and kissed his stomach and couldn't resist sliding her hand even lower. He swelled in her hand, and her entire body awoke.

She glanced at the clock, her mind racing through dirty scenarios. She had a few minutes before she had to get up. He reached down and covered her hand with his, tightening her grip and stroking with her. *God*, what he did to her. If she didn't take what she wanted, she'd be uncomfortable the whole time she was out running. The trouble was, she didn't know which she wanted more—to take him in her mouth or to ride her cowboy. The sight of his big hand wrapped around his cock won out.

"Keep stroking yourself." She lowered her mouth over his shaft, following his hand up and down the length of it.

"*Jesus*. Turn around, baby. I need my mouth on you."

She turned on the bed, and Pugsly scampered to the floor with a grunt. Nick shifted over her and lowered his mouth between her legs, sending rivers of heat rushing through her. She fisted his cock, taking him in her mouth. It wasn't long before they both lost their minds *and* their control.

He turned around, kissing her passionately. "Let's hit the shower. We'll be fast."

"I can't," she said groggily. "I'm in a post-orgasmic coma."

He laughed and rolled her onto her side, smacking her ass.

"*Hey!*"

"Come on, darlin'. You've got a running date, and I've got a hundred errands to run. I won't be back until midafternoon."

He dragged her out of bed and into the shower. She stood beneath the warm water, eyes closed, as she wet her hair. She heard Nick open the bodywash, and then his hands moved along her shoulders and down her back. He gathered her hair over one shoulder and kissed the one he'd bared. Her heart bubbled over with happiness. He'd never bathed her before. She had a feeling if he ever untethered all the love he had to give, it would take over everything around him.

They made it outside just in time to meet Travis as he

walked up to the front door. Pugsly ran out to the grass making grunting noises, and Rowdy and Goldie barreled across the yard from the barn.

"The dynamic duo. How's it goin', Nick?" Travis reached down to pet Rowdy.

Nick loved up Goldie. "Great, thanks. Sorry to be short, but my day is going to be crazy, and I've got to take care of our beasts before I leave. Have a good run. See you later, darlin'." He kissed Trixie, whistled and patted his leg, and headed down to the barn with the three dogs.

Trixie and Travis jogged up the driveway. "Sorry I was a few minutes late."

"No worries." Travis cleared his throat. "I miss those mornings when I had to shower *before* running."

She laughed. "Are you trying to make me blush?"

"Nah, just jealous of my two friends. You guys make coupledom look pretty great. I never thought I'd see that stone exterior crack, but the way Nick looks at you...That's something special, Trixie."

"I like knowing you see it, too."

"Trust me when I say that everyone around you two can see it. I'm just glad he didn't rip my head off for asking you out."

"I kind of loved seeing him jealous." They jogged up to the end of the driveway and turned down the main road toward Walt's.

"Women love that shit."

"Oh, *please.* So do guys when women get jealous. Y'all just don't admit it."

"That's true." He cocked a grin. "But if you tell anyone I said that, I'll have to kill you."

"Okay, well, have fun dealing with Nick if you kill me."

He laughed. "So much for that plan."

As they ran past Walt's, they saw him on the front porch and waved. "Did you have a chance to ask your grandmother about joining us next weekend for the barbecue?"

"I did, and she's coming. She acted a little nervous when I told her Walt would be there. She was with my grandfather for so long, she said she wouldn't know how to act around him."

It dawned on Trixie that even before she and Nick had gotten together, she'd been so taken with him, she hadn't really seen anyone else. She couldn't imagine what it would be like to lose the man she loved, much less the man she was married to forever, like Travis's grandmother had been to his grandfather, and then to try to fit someone else into her heart.

"I hope she knows we're opening a door for them but not pushing them through it. I thought it would be nice to get them together and see if they wanted to strike up a friendship again."

"I think she'd like that. I heard her making a hair appointment for the afternoon of the barbecue."

"*Interesting.* Well, if sparks fly, who are we to stand in their way? You never know who will find love at a Braden-Jericho barbecue."

NICK PULLED DOWN the visor in his truck to block the late-afternoon sun as he drove into Pleasant Hill. He'd been gone all day, hitting three counties and making six stops, on the hopes of seeing that brilliant light in Trixie's eyes. *You've got one hell of a hold over me, darlin'.* There wasn't another woman alive he'd give up a day of working with his horses for, much less agree to host a barbecue with. When he'd called his buddy Jace to ask about bringing Trixie's horses over, Jace had noticed that hold first thing. He'd said Nick sounded different when he talked about Trixie. Nick had called *bullshit*, but if anyone could spot a change like that, it would be Jace. Jace was several years older than Nick, closer to forty than thirty-five, and he hadn't been looking for a relationship when he and Dixie had gotten together.

Nick drove through town chewing on the idea that Jace could spot a difference in him over the phone and telling himself it didn't mean he'd been hit by Cupid's arrow. He turned onto his driveway, and as usual, the stress of the day fell away. He drove down to the barns, and as he was parking, he spotted Trixie in a corral working with Buttons. The other minis were hanging out nearby. Goldie and Pugsly were lying in the shade outside the corral, and Rowdy was standing at the fence watching the horses. The sight brought that tug to his chest. That sensation had intensified lately, and it was there damn near every second he and Trixie were together.

Trixie was so focused on her adorable spotted friend, she hadn't noticed his truck yet. He took a moment to watch her walking Buttons through a few commands. He loved watching her working with the horses. She was so full of hope and patience, it made her even more alluring. She'd been working diligently with them, and it was paying off. She praised Buttons, and Nick felt her enthusiasm as if it were his own. It was that energy that lured him out of the truck.

Trixie looked over, and the joy she seemed to always carry widened her beautiful smile. "Nick, watch this. Buttons is doing *so* well."

Rowdy sprinted toward him. "Hey, buddy." He petted him

as they walked over to the corral.

Trixie gave the command for Buttons to walk with her, and the little horse kept pace by her side. She stopped to praise her charge, and then she told Buttons to stay and she walked a few feet away. When she gave the command for Buttons to come, the little horse went to her.

Attagirl.

Trixie lavished her with praise. She guided Buttons in a circle around her, and Nick held his breath. She had been working hard on that command, trying to teach Buttons to keep proper distance between them. Buttons got a little too close, and Trixie tapped her gently with the training stick, guiding her farther away. She stopped, and then they tried again. This time Buttons gave her ample space as she walked in a circle around Trixie.

Yes!

"That's my brilliant girl!" Trixie lavished her with praise as Nick hopped over the fence.

"That was awesome." He kissed Trixie and loved up Buttons.

"Isn't she incredible? She's *so* smart."

"Almost as smart as her mama."

She smiled up at him. "Flattery will get you everywhere. Prince did almost as well today. He also needs a little help with keeping his distance, but he's getting there."

Nick slung an arm over her shoulder and brushed his lips over her cheek. "Look who you're asking him to keep away from. He might be a gelding, but he's still male." He kissed her lips. "Can I steal you away for a minute?"

"Sure. Just give me one second." She took the lead off Buttons and loved her up one last time. "I'll be back in a little bit, sweets." As they left the corral, she said, "Did you get all your errands done?"

"I sure did." He headed for his truck, the back of which was covered by a tarp.

"What'd you get?"

He began unlatching the tarp. "You'll see."

"Mysterious," she said as he made his way around the truck bed.

When he whipped the tarp off, her eyes widened. "Is that…?"

"Used medical equipment. It's not in great shape, but I think it'll do for practice purposes."

Her jaw dropped. "You *bought* all of that?"

"Sure did, darlin'. You wanted to practice, and I figured we could set it up in my basement until you go back to Virginia. Then I'll haul it down there for you. I didn't want you to have to make do with fake equipment for something this important. I got two hospital beds, a wheelchair, an IV pole, a standing heart-rate monitor and a blood pressure monitor, a supply cart, a recliner and one of those regular chairs they have in patient rooms, and a few other things. I also picked up a curtain and a U-shaped rod to go around the bed that we can put up when you get back home."

"Ohmygod, *Nick*." Her eyes dampened. "I can't even…" Tears slipped down her cheeks, and she buried her face in his chest. "I *never* cry. Why do you keep making me cry?"

"Please tell me those are happy tears."

She tilted her face up, grinning as she wiped her eyes. "They're shocked and happy tears, and embarrassing as all get out, because I'm not one of those teary-eyed girls. I'm just overwhelmed. You're only supposed to be helping me train the horses. and look at everything you've done for me. Thank you doesn't seem big enough." She threw her arms around him. "Thank you a million times over. You're incredible."

"About time you noticed." He pressed his lips to hers.

"I noticed a *long* time ago, you big dork." She planted a hand on her hip. "Way before you noticed *me*. But that's okay. You were worth the wait."

He tugged her into his arms and kissed her. "So were you."

"I know," she teased. "But seriously, Nick, how will I ever pay you back for all of this?"

"By being the best damn therapy horse handler there is and enjoying the hell out of it. That's how."

She crooked her finger, beckoning him closer. When he dipped his head beside hers, she whispered, "I've got your number, cowboy. You're just as crazy about me as I am about you." She kissed his cheek. "But you don't have to buy me things. I love who you are in here." She patted his chest over his heart.

Could she feel the way his pulse kicked up at those words? He lifted her hand to his lips and kissed the back of it. "I'll buy what I want to buy, and I'm glad you like who I am in there." He flashed a cocky grin. "Because I really like who you are in *here*." He grabbed her ass, and she laughed as honks rang out behind them.

Jax's car and Travis's truck barreled down the driveway. "What are they doing here?"

He hugged her against his side. "Someone's got to help me set this stuff up."

"I can't believe you did all of this."

"Start believin', darlin', because we're about to transform the basement into a mock hospital room. It's perfect. It's got a concrete floor, which is easy to clean in case they have accidents, and a walkout with oversized doors." He waved to Jax and Travis as they climbed out of their vehicles.

"For that pool table you never bought," she said as Jax and Travis joined them. "Most people would set up the horses' training area in the barn, but not the man who would rather have horses in his house than people."

"Congratulations on your new practice grounds," Jax said, patting her on the back.

Trixie put a hand over her heart. "I'm seriously still in shock."

"I always thought women wanted to be wined and dined," Travis said. "Who knew the way to a woman's heart was through old medical equipment?"

Jax laughed. "Nick knows how to charm his lady."

"Wait a second. Travis, did you know about this when we went running this morning?" Trixie asked.

"I plead the Fifth." Travis bumped fists with Nick.

"Trix, why don't you finish up with Buttons and we'll get this set up."

"I feel like I should help. I can sweep out the basement, help figure out where to put everything, and make sure it's set up like—"

Nick silenced her with a kiss. "I appreciate the offer, darlin', but we've got this."

AFTER THEY FINISHED setting up the mock hospital room, Nick stood in the yard drinking a beer with Jax and Travis as

Trixie showed her parents the setup via FaceTime.

"Isn't it amazing?" she gushed as she walked outside. "I can't wait to take my little guys through it. Dad, do you think you'll be able to make room in the barn for my horses and this setup?"

"We'll make it work, Trix," her father reassured her.

"Thank you." She did the cutest damn happy dance, making all of Nick's running around worth it. "I'm so excited. Monday we're going to see one of Nick's friends who owns an office building with an elevator to practice with the horses. That reminds me. I need to call Sin and ask him if I can use the elevator in the community center."

"I'm sure he'll let you. Marilynn takes her dogs there," her mother reminded her.

"Oh, right. I meant to call Mrs. M. I'll do that tomorrow or Monday when I call the referrals Jordan gave me. I'm hoping to schedule meetings with a few of the ones located within an hour of home the week I get back. Want to say hi to Nick and Jax, and meet Travis?"

"You bet," her father said.

She stood with her back to the guys and held the phone out in front of her so her parents could see all of them. "Say hi to my parents."

"Hi, Waylon. Nancy." Nick tipped his hat. "It's nice to see you."

Jax waved. "Trixie sure is shaking things up around here."

"She has a way about her," her mother said, and looked at Nick like he'd hung the moon.

"We sure didn't raise a pushover." Her father set his serious eyes on Nick. "Son, I'd ask if Trixie is giving you too much trouble, but seeing as you just made her year with that setup, I think I've got my answer. Thank you."

Nick felt a grin sliding into place. "Don't be fooled, sir. She's stirred up a fair amount of trouble."

Trixie looked over her shoulder at him and smirked.

"Mom, Dad, this is Travis Helms." She moved the phone toward Travis. "He's the one I bought Buttons and Prince from."

"Hi. It's nice to meet you." Travis waved.

"You as well," her mother said.

"Thank you for helping Trixie with the horses. We hear you have a real fine setup," her father said.

Travis nodded. "Thank you, sir. It was my pleasure."

"We're running partners, too. He's a little slow, but a lot of fun." Trixie earned a laugh from all of them. "Do you have time for me to show you your new grandbabies?"

"Sure, darlin'. We'd like that," her father said.

"Yay! How's Buttercup? Does she miss me?" she asked as she jogged toward the horses.

Jax nudged Nick. "And here I thought she was moving in."

"Nah, man." Nick tried to ignore the painful twinge in his chest. "She's a daddy's girl, and as married to Oak Falls as I am to Pleasant Hill."

Chapter Twenty-Three

MONDAY AFTERNOON THEY helped Annabelle and Alfie out of the trailer at Silver-Stone headquarters and manufacturing plant. They'd worked with Annabelle and Alfie all weekend, taking them through the basement, and she swore they knew their way around by heart. They'd even taken Buttons and Prince through a few times.

Nick got down on one knee in front of them and stroked their jaws. "You guys ready for this? We know you're going to do great, and your mama and I will be right here by your sides the whole time." He winked at Trixie.

Holy cow.

She thought she'd seen it all and was ready for anything, but nothing could have prepared her for all that was Nick Braden. She swore her babies got melty, too. He went above and beyond for all of them. She loved training with him, but she also feared how attached the horses were getting to him. It was going to be hard enough for her to leave in less than two weeks. But at least she knew she'd still see Nick. The horses wouldn't understand. They'd only know what was happening when they got out of the trailer at her parents' ranch and she tried to settle them into their new surroundings without him. Would they long for him as she knew she would? Would they miss his voice? His smell? His touch?

"You going to make out with those horses or come inside?"

The deep voice boomed across the parking lot, snapping Trixie from her thoughts. She worked hard to push those thoughts down deep. She was Trixie Jericho, and there was *nothing* she couldn't handle. She would love up her babies extra hard, so they didn't have any empty spots in between visits with Nick, and hopefully that would help her fill her empty spots, too.

Nick pushed to his feet. "Jace, Dixie. Good to see you."

Jace had an imposing presence, with thick dark hair that brushed the collar of his gray T-shirt, deep-set brooding eyes, and thick scruff covering his chiseled jaw. He was heavily muscled, with tattooed forearms, but he wasn't as muscular as Nick.

"It's been too long," Jace said as he and Nick shared a manly embrace. Nick was six three, and Jace had a few inches on him.

"Oh my God, look how *cute* these horses are!" Dixie was a tall, slim, strikingly beautiful and tough-looking redhead. She wore skintight jeans and high-heeled black boots that rivaled the height of Jillian's heels. Her black Whiskey Bro's tank top revealed colorful tattoos decorating her arms.

"They're pretty stinking cute," Jace said.

"Thanks. The white one is Annabelle, and the brown one is Alfie. He's my littlest." Trixie loved seeing the horses so well behaved, and seemingly happy, with other people.

"Do you bring them to birthday parties?" Dixie pushed to her feet. "My niece's and nephew's birthdays are next month. They would go nuts over them."

"I'd love to bring them to a party. No charge, of course,

because you're Nick's friends and it'll be my first birthday party with them."

"Thank you. That would be great. I'm Dixie, by the way." She pulled Trixie into a hug, as if they'd been friends forever. "Seems like our badass men have something in common besides riding motorcycles. *Dixie and Trixie?* We could start our own strip club."

The guys laughed, and then they scowled, which made the girls laugh.

Trixie liked her already. "Is Dixie your real name?"

"Dixie Lee Whiskey-Stone, the one and only. How about you?"

"My parents aren't quite as cool as yours." Trixie snuck a peek at Nick and Jace, talking about the horses, and lowered her voice. "Patricia Ann Jericho, aka Trixie."

Nick cocked his head, his brow wrinkled. "Is that true, darlin'? I gotta start calling you Patty. Or do you prefer Patty Ann?"

She planted a hand on her hip and narrowed her eyes. "You call me either one and you'll be sleeping alone."

"That's right, girlfriend." Dixie slung an arm over Trixie's shoulder. "I like this woman, Nick. You'd better do right by her."

"Get in here, you pain in my ass." Nick pulled Dixie into a hug. "How are you doing?"

"Fanfuckingtastic."

As Dixie stepped out of his arms, Nick reached for Trixie's hand. "Jace, this is my girl, Trixie. Trix, my buddy Jace."

Trixie's heart turned over at *my girl.*

Jace's dark eyes moved between the two of them, and a slow smile appeared, softening his rough edges. His eyes glittered like he knew something the rest of them didn't. "It's nice to meet you, Trixie. Bring it on in." He opened his arms and drew her into a warm embrace.

"Thanks for letting us come by," Trixie said, and Nick put his hand on her lower back, holding the horses' leads in his other hand. He always had things under control.

"I have to admit, when Nick asked if he could come by with his girlfriend and her miniature horses to ride the elevator, I don't know which part of that piqued my curiosity more—miniature horses riding an elevator, or the fact that Nick Braden had a girlfriend."

"Oh, please." Dixie rolled her eyes. "That's what people said about you, too. I was right there, but you took forever to notice me."

"We have something else in common. I had a crush on Nick forever, but I didn't think he noticed," Trixie said.

"Seriously?" Dixie said incredulously, eyeing Nick. "This woman could make millions on OnlyFans." OnlyFans was a subscription site that allowed content creators to monetize their pages and charge subscription and/or one-time fees for access to mainly X-rated content.

"*Christ.*" Nick pulled his hat lower on his head. "Why did I think this was a good idea?"

Jace laughed a deep, rumbling laugh. "Because you missed us. Come on, let's get this show on the road. We took the afternoon off to go riding. You and Trixie should join us. We haven't gone riding together in a long time."

"You ride horses?" Trixie asked.

Jace scoffed and Dixie laughed. Jace pulled his shoulders back, which made him appear even bigger, and said, "Motorcycles."

"Oh, of course. Sorry." Trixie shifted her attention to Nick. "I just realized you haven't gone out on your bike since I got here."

Nick glanced at the horses, then dragged his eyes down her body and cocked a grin. "We've been a little busy."

"I bet you have," Dixie said with a wink. "You should come riding with us. We're going to Capshaw Island. It's your kind of place. We can see the wild horses."

Nick pulled Trixie closer. "You want to go on a ride when we're done?"

Trixie's heart nearly leaped out of her chest. "Are you seriously *asking* if I want to go on a motorcycle ride with you? That's as big of a deal—an honor, really—as going on the morning trail ride with you. Heck *yes*, I want to. But do you need to practice for your show?"

"Let's see. You, on the back of my bike, or me on the back of a horse? Darlin', there's no question in that equation." He leaned in and kissed her.

Dixie looked confused. "You haven't ridden with him before?"

"No. But I've wanted to." Even Trixie could hear the lustful way she said it.

Dixie leaned closer. "*Girl*, I totally hear ya on that one. There's no bigger aphrodisiac than Jace on a motorcycle."

"Have you seen Nick on his?" Trixie laughed.

Jace and Nick exchanged a head shake.

Jace slung an arm around Dixie and said, "Let's head inside and Trixie can tell us about her business and how long this thing between her and Nick has been going on."

"I have to admit, I'm a bit nervous about taking the horses inside." Trixie had been trying to ignore the butterflies in her stomach, but she had to get them out. "There are so many cars in the parking lot. You must have a huge staff."

"We do, but I held a staff meeting this morning and told everyone that you'd be coming through," Jace reassured her. "They've been told not to approach the horses. I also asked if anyone might be anxious or afraid around them, just in case, but nobody was."

Trixie exhaled with relief. "Thank you. That's perfect. I'm sure Annabelle and Alfie will be fine. As you can see, they're calm. It's just me that's nervous."

They spent the next hour and a half walking the horses through the building, riding the elevators, meeting staff, and maneuvering around equipment and furniture. Jace and Dixie were more than accommodating. They introduced Trixie to employees, turned on different machines in the workshop and office to see how the horses would react, and when Trixie asked them to, they walked into the horses' paths to see if the horses would stop on command. They also loved up Trixie's babies just as she and Nick did. She was so proud of Annabelle and Alfie. They didn't startle or balk as they made their way through different floors, and Trixie's nervousness subsided. Dixie and Jace asked dozens of questions about her business, and Trixie enjoyed responding to them. When she told them about how Nick had surprised her with the hospital equipment, she felt a different sense of pride. One of being as special to him as he was to her.

"Most guys would go with diamonds or flowers," Dixie teased.

"I don't need diamonds, and I can pick flowers anytime." Trixie looked at Nick, looking handsome holding Annabelle's lead, and thought, *You're all I need. The equipment and everything else are just icing on the cake.*

She was delighted that Annabelle and Alfie did so well and knew either one would do great at the soft visit. But this afternoon had done more for Trixie than just reassure her about the horses. She didn't often see Nick with friends other than his or her family, and the better she got to know Dixie and Jace, the more she liked them. Nick laughed a lot around them, and even though they were primarily focused on the horses, he touched her when he walked by, whispered sweet and sexy things in her ear, and even stole several kisses. She loved how they were becoming a real couple a little more each day. She even let herself fantasize, briefly, about what it would be like to spend more than a month in Nick's world.

Maybe one day...

TRIXIE RAVED ABOUT Jace and Dixie as they brought the horses home and got them settled. Before they climbed onto his motorcycle, he started to give Trixie a safety lesson about riding on the back of it. In true Trixie fashion, she rolled her eyes, planted a hand on her hip, and said, "I've ridden on a motorcycle before."

"Oh. Okay, cool." He handed her a helmet, trying to ignore the pang of jealousy that knowledge brought.

She cocked her head, and her hair tumbled sexily over her shoulder. "I'm curious. Why haven't you taken me out on your bike before?"

"Because riding on the back of a man's bike signifies to other bikers that you're that guy's woman, and you weren't mine."

She wound her arms around his neck and said, "You have no idea how long I've wanted to straddle your hog."

"You keep talking like that, and we're not going anywhere." He lowered his lips to hers, taking her in a lustful kiss, but it still didn't untangle the knot of jealousy in his chest. "Whose bike did you ride on?"

"You're cute when you're jealous. You get all tense and try to hold it back."

He tightened his hold on her. "I hate feeling jealous, but apparently I have no choice in the matter with you, because I can't stand the thought of you on the back of some other guy's bike."

She giggled softly and kissed his chin. "I've ridden on two guys' bikes. Dusty Kincaid's and Austin Andrews's."

"Kincaid? Have I met him?"

"I doubt it. He's a model and spends a lot of time in New York and LA these days."

Nick scoffed. "Pansy ass."

"Hey, that's mean. He's *not* a pansy. Want to see him on Instagram?" She whipped her phone out of her back pocket.

"*No*, I don't want to see him. I can't see *you* going out with a fucking model."

"We didn't go out. He's not a *real* biker, and neither is Austin Andrews. Maybe they don't know what it means to bikers. Either way, they didn't mind having me on the back of their bikes. And I didn't date Austin, either, although I did give him my virginity."

"*Christ*, Trixie. Are you trying to kill me?" He kissed her hard. "As far as I'm concerned, nobody's touched you before me."

"Seriously? Girls have touched you, and I'm not getting upset about it."

"Don't fool yourself. You got plenty pissed when Shayna texted me."

"*Ugh.* That's right. One of your buckle bitches."

"Can we not torture each other and get on the bike?"

"Yeah, that sounds good."

He helped her onto the motorcycle and climbed on in front of her. Before putting on her helmet, she wrapped her arms around him and said, "For the record, you're the only man I want touching me."

"For the record, darlin', you're the only woman who's ever been on the back of my bike. That should tell you everything you want to know."

They put on their helmets and headed out to meet Jace and Dixie. The bullshit of who had come before they became a couple fell away with the rumble of the engine, the warm wind kissing his skin, and the heat and softness of his girl wrapped around him.

A long while later they pulled off the highway and drove over the causeway toward Capshaw Island. Long grasses sprouted up through the water below, *whoosh*ing in the wind. Paddleboarders made their way across the water in the distance, and kites flapped high in the sky.

They drove through the small, rustic fishing town, passing painted brick and wood-sided storefronts with faded scalloped awnings shading wooden benches and planters overflowing with colorful flowers. Nick had gone to the island every few weeks after Beau and Zev had taken off all those years ago, when he'd needed to escape the realities of home, but he hadn't been there in years.

As they made their way toward the main parking lot by the beach, he thought about the simplicity of the island. With only two blocks of storefronts and a bigger farmers market than grocery store, it had always appealed to him. It kind of bugged him that he hadn't thought to bring Trixie there before Jace had suggested it. But then again, when Trixie was with him, leaving home was the last thing on his mind.

They parked the bikes and locked up their helmets. The scents of the sea hung in the air, and as Jace and Dixie climbed off his bike, Nick reached for Trixie. "What do you think?"

"That I loved that motorcycle ride as much as I love riding horses with you." She rose onto her toes, and he lowered his lips to hers. "And I like knowing I'm the only woman who has been on the back of your bike."

He'd meant about the town, but he liked her answer even better. "At my age, I didn't think I had many firsts left, but you, darlin', are showing me how wrong I was."

"You want to whisper sweet nothings to each other, or head over the dunes?" Dixie called over to them with a big-ass smile.

"I want to carry her off and rent a room," Nick retorted. "But that'd be rude, so the beach it is."

They made their way to the edge of the dunes, stopping to take off their boots and socks. They left them tucked beside the dune grass and followed the sandy trail up the dune. The sand was warm beneath Nick's feet. A gust of sea air and the sounds of waves breaking and seagulls screeching greeted them as they crested the dune. The beaches weren't frequented or pristine because of the wild horses. They were rough, a bit rocky, strewn with seaweed, and for the most part, untouched by anything but the creatures that inhabited them.

Trixie shaded her eyes, looking out at the water. "It's so

pretty here."

"Yeah. I used to come here a lot after my brothers took off. There's an overlook a mile down the beach. That's where most people go." He drew her closer and kissed her temple.

"Should we go there?"

"Nope. We're not most people."

They went down to the beach, and Trixie sat between Nick's legs in the sand with her back against his chest, while Dixie and Jace sat side by side. They talked, joked around, and sat in silence, listening to the peaceful sounds of the sea. The girls talked about Jillian and Whiskey Bro's, where Trixie said they should go on a double date one night.

Challenge, challenge, challenge.

Trixie invited them to the barbecue, but Jace and Dixie were going to New York that weekend to see Jace's family. Dixie and Jace told Trixie about how they'd met years earlier and had come together when Jace had won Dixie in a charity bachelor auction at Whiskey Bro's. "Nick was on the auction block that night," Jace said.

Trixie looked over her shoulder at him. "No way. You actually got onstage and were auctioned off?"

Man, he'd hated that shit. "Yeah." He hiked a thumb at Dixie. "This one harassed me every day until I finally agreed to do it. But it was for charity, so I couldn't exactly turn her down and feel good about it."

"And we were very appreciative of him for his service," Dixie said. "He earned several thousand dollars for the Parkvale Women's Shelter."

"I'm not sure I want to know what you did for the winner." Trixie settled against his chest again.

Nick leaned his chin on her shoulder and said, "She was a

hyped-up banker who packed on makeup and talked about herself all night. We went to dinner at one of those places where the meal is overpriced and undersized. I drove her home, gave her a kiss on the cheek, and went back to my place to make a burger."

Trixie went up on her knees and turned around, taking his face between her hands. "Nick Braden, I don't care if that's the truth or a lie. Either way, it was the perfect answer." She pressed her lips to his.

Jace and Dixie laughed, and Nick fell a little harder for his girl.

As she settled back down between his legs, he said, "It's the truth, darlin'. But a better story is that when Dixie put herself up on the auction block, Jace and her brother Bullet nearly came to blows over her."

"Bullet?" Trixie asked.

"His real name is Brandon. Bullet is his biker name—or road name," Dixie clarified. "He's ex–Special Forces."

Trixie nodded. "Oh, wow. I could see my brothers doing something like that if I were auctioned off. Guys are so weird. What did you do, Jace?"

"I told Bullet to back the hell off, and I won my girl." Jace pulled Dixie closer.

"Damn right you did." Dixie kissed him. "He proposed a few weeks later."

"*After* she clocked me in the jaw," Jace added.

Trixie's eyes widened. "She *hit* you? Why?"

"Let's just say I'd been alone for so long, I didn't realize how important it was to answer texts and phone calls." Jace looked at Nick and said, "You should learn from my mistakes."

If the other day was any indication, they'd have no issues in that department.

"What's the plan with you two?" Dixie asked. "Trixie's going back to Virginia and you're going to do the long-distance thing?"

"That's right," Nick said.

"Good luck with that. It was hell for me," Jace said.

"We'll be fine," Trixie said. "We've been long-distance friends forever. Nick will be busy with his ranch, and I'll be too busy with the business to pine away for him. Just today I set up three appointments with facilities near Oak Falls for the week after I get home, and I have more referrals to call." She looked over her shoulder at Nick. "But I'll miss you like crazy."

"I'll miss you, too."

"You can always get down on one knee, Nick," Dixie suggested.

"*Dixie.*" Trixie laughed. "I *just* got him to acknowledge he has feelings for me. We're good for now. Right, Nick?"

"That's right, darlin'." He was so damn glad she got him. "Why fix it if it ain't broken?"

Dixie and Jace exchanged a glance Nick couldn't read, and the moment was interrupted by the familiar sounds of horses galloping.

"Look!" Dixie pointed down the beach to a herd of horses headed their way.

Nick dragged Trixie up to her feet as Dixie and Jace pushed to theirs, and they all jogged back to the base of the dunes, giving the horses space. Nick put his arms around Trixie from behind, and they watched the horses gallop past. They were a majestic sight, their manes and tales flying, powerful bodies untethered by reins.

"They're beautiful," Trixie said with awe.

He kissed her cheek. "Not nearly as beautiful as you."

After the horses passed, they talked on the beach for a long while, tossed rocks into the water, and walked along the shore. Then they headed into town and ate dinner at an outdoor café and ended their evening with a walk down Main Street. It was a low-key, lazy, and incredibly enjoyable few hours. Nick had never been a traveler, but this short trip opened another door inside him he hadn't known existed. He wanted more of this with Trixie—more time away from work, time to sit and watch other parts of the world go by, time to do *couple things*.

When they hit the open road on the way home, with Trixie's warm body against his back and a wealth of new memories he knew he'd treasure, he thought about all the other places he'd like to take her—because after such an incredible day, this trip would definitely not be their last.

Chapter Twenty-Four

TRIXIE SAT IN the stands at the Heart Valley Rodeo Saturday evening, waiting for Nick's exhibition. They'd had a busy, wonderful week. Her business was really coming together with the launch of her website and the arrival of her Rising Hope shirts and the horses' vests and shoes. She'd booked eleven more visits with facilities between Maryland and Virginia starting the week after she returned home, and even though she had a handle on training, Nick was still helping her. She looked forward to it every day, just as the horses did. She'd gotten to watch him practice for his show a few more times, which she'd never tire of. They'd also gone on trail rides together, visited Walt, and had even gone on a dinner date to Whiskey Bro's, because Trixie had dared Nick to take her there.

Maybe she'd pushed him because she didn't like being told anyplace was off-limits, or because she kind of loved seeing him get jealous. But even if those were some of the reasons, they weren't the biggest reasons she'd dared him to take her to the biker bar. She'd wanted to show him that it didn't matter where they were, no other man could threaten their relationship. It had worked a little *too* well. They'd had a great time hanging out with the people they'd met at the bar, playing darts and pool, but they'd stayed until closing and had paid the price of exhaustion the next day.

But the best parts of the week were the evenings they'd spent talking under the stars while Nick played his guitar, or just hanging out, and tumbling into each other's arms whenever the urge hit. Trixie was falling so deeply in love with him, she wished their time together would never end. But the end of her visit was only a week away, looming like a graying cloud ready to open up. She wanted to slow the clock to spend more time with him, and at the same time she wanted to speed it up to get her business started.

Applause rang out, jarring her from her thoughts as the horses that had been in the last event before Nick's show were led out of the arena. Trixie's cell phone chimed. She pulled it from her pocket and filled with happiness seeing Nick's name in the bubble. *This one's for you, darlin'. Meet me at the gate afterward.* They were taking off right after his event. She didn't respond because they were already announcing Nick's show, and she didn't want to sidetrack him.

The crowd went wild, screaming and whistling as Nick rode Lady into the arena. Trixie's heart sprang to life like a fangirl as he rode around the ring waving, bringing rise to louder applause and cheers. He looked so handsome in his black hat and black button-down shirt with gold embroidery on the yoke and around the cuffs. Trixie knew that over the years people had tried to get him to dress more like a showman, with everything from black pants with rivets or fringe down the legs, to colorful shirts and matching pants. But Nick was a simple guy, and he'd no sooner give up his blue jeans than leave Pleasant Hill.

Lady looked gorgeous. They'd groomed her and Romeo together, and Trixie had braided black and gold ribbons into their manes to go with their matching black tack with gold fringe along their saddles and breast collars. Romeo would come out for Nick's finale.

Nick took her breath away as Lady raced around the arena with Nick hanging off one side, lying parallel to her body, holding on with one arm, the other stretched out as if presenting himself to the crowd. He was such a daredevil, he made every move look effortless. He righted himself on the horse and pushed up to a hippodrome, standing on Lady with his arms out to the sides. The crowd went wild, and Trixie was right there with them, clapping and cheering him on. He deserved every one of the awed looks he garnered as he shifted into a death drag, hanging off the side of the horse by one leg. Trixie held her breath. She knew he could do it with his eyes closed, but still it was as exhilarating as it was terrifying to watch.

He moved swiftly up to his feet, standing on Lady again as she charged around the ring, and then he shifted to a shoulder stand, hanging upside down off the side of the horse, his legs pointing straight up toward the ceiling. The crowd never stopped cheering as he got back in the saddle and spun around, riding backward, then turned again, sitting for only seconds before swinging off the side of the horse with one foot in the stirrup, the other against the saddle horn, and riding with his body at a ninety-degree angle to Lady's, his body parallel to the ground, his arms outstretched. The crowd exploded, and Trixie jumped to her feet, cheering louder than all of them. She stood for the rest of the show, all the way through his grand finale, when the lights dimmed, and Nick stood on the backs of Romeo and Lady, Roman riding as they raced around the ring and jumped over a wall of fire. Cheers erupted, and as the lights came on and Nick took his final lap around the arena, she swore his eyes blazed a heart-melting path to hers.

After his show, while the rest of the rodeo continued, she tried to ignore the hammering in her chest as she made her way down from her seat and through the crowds to meet Nick at the gate. Before she even got close, she heard his name called out in multiple female voices. The hairs on the back of her neck prickled, and jealousy seared through her.

When she neared the gate, there was a crowd of perfectly coiffed buckle bunnies blocking it. Damn groupies. Everyone loved a hot cowboy. The girls were dressed in tiny shorts, tied shirts, and sparkly cowgirl boots they'd probably bought on the way over. Their makeup was packed on thicker than their fake country accents. Trixie had an urge to rip off the nonfunctional low-slung designer belts they wore around their hips and whip those damn buckle bunnies with the stupid things.

"Nick! Over here! You sure know how to ride! Want to give me a lesson?" a skinny brunette with big boobs asked with a sway of her hips.

Trixie's hands fisted as she tried to see Nick through the crowd. She'd known what to expect. She'd seen girls throwing themselves at Nick before. She was all about a woman owning her own body, but to actually *see* it in action now that he was *her* man was a heck of a lot different.

"*Nick!* Let's get a drink!" a blonde yelled.

Shut up, bitch. You don't know him.

A redhead went up on tiptoes, waving her hat and a pen. "How about an autograph?"

Nick's deep voice rang out, "Sure thing," and his rugged face came into view between bobbing heads. His jaw was tight, but he snagged the redhead's hat and pen.

The redhead squealed, and the other girls went wild,

screaming his name and calling out things like "Sign my shirt?" "Me next!" "Over here!" Two girls hollered, "We'll keep you company. Think you're cowboy enough to Roman ride the real thing?"

Are you fucking kidding me?

Trixie was fueled with rage, but rooted in place, nauseous, nervous, and too damn jealous, which made her feel strangely vulnerable. They might be overly made-up buckle bunnies, but they were really pretty, and she couldn't help but wonder if he had ever hooked up with any of them. Her stomach lurched, and she reminded herself that if he had, it was before they'd gotten together and it didn't matter. But her heart was beating so fast, it made her even more nervous. *Why is this so intimidating?*

"A'right, ladies," Nick said, trying to push through, but the girls crowded in tighter.

He was trying to get to her, and something inside her snapped. *Back off, buckle bitches. I'm Trixie Fucking Jericho, and you are not getting my man.* She pushed through the harem of wannabees, and the second Nick spotted her, he pulled her through the last of them and against his side, earning curious murmurs and disappointed snark.

Trixie squared her shoulders, meeting their hungry eyes, and said, "Autographs only, girls. I *don't* share."

"But Nick does!" someone yelled from the back of the group.

Trixie fisted her hands, fighting the urge to lunge at whoever had said it and tear them apart.

"THAT'S WHERE YOU'RE wrong," Nick seethed, and grabbed Trixie's arm. "Let's get the hell out of here."

He plowed through the pack of women and stormed out of the arena, dragging Trixie with him, a stream of curses falling from her lips. What the hell was he thinking, meeting her by the gate? He was so used to that shit, it hadn't even occurred to him that it might piss her off. *Fuck.* He was an idiot.

"I'm sorry about that shit," he gritted out.

"Oh my freaking God!" Trixie yanked her arm free and stalked farther into the parking lot. She spun around, breathing fire. "I *knew* about you and your buckle bunnies, but *that...?*" She paced, her body shaking, words falling fast and venomous from her lips. "I wanted to claw their eyes out! I've never felt this way, *ever*, and I *hate* it!" She pounded her chest with her fist. "I'm *Trixie Jericho*, not some pansy-ass jealous girl. What the *hell?*"

"Trix—"

"*Don't!*" she warned, eyes blazing. "You have no idea what it's like to see that shit. To feel like I have to compete with *those* types of women!"

"Don't I?" he fumed, closing the distance between them. "How the hell do you think I felt at Tully's?" His voice escalated. "How about when you dragged my ass to Whiskey Bro's? You think I didn't feel that way with all those guys checking you out?"

"I haven't slept with them!" she shouted, wearing a path before him. "For all I know, you've been with half those girls."

"If I have, that's my fucking *past*," he said through clenched teeth. "This is why I don't do relationships. I'm *not* going to apologize for who I was. Did you see me taking numbers? Signing their tits? Taking them up on their offers?"

She glowered. "What the hell am I doing? I thought I could handle this, but the thought of those girls going after you…I *hate* this feeling, and I'm leaving next weekend. Then what? I can't be at all your shows."

She paced, hurt and anger twisting her beautiful mouth, and it fucking killed him, turning his anger into heartache. He didn't want to hurt her, and he sure as hell didn't want to argue with her. He scrubbed a hand down his face, taking a second to regain control.

"You have to trust *me*, Trixie, the same way I have to trust you."

"I *do* trust *you*! You're the most loyal man I know. I just don't want any of them touching you and pawing after you."

"It comes with the territory, and you *know* that," he said as calmly as he could, which wasn't very calm at all. "You're letting people who don't matter make you crazy."

"Am I?" she hollered, hands fisted. In the next breath, her brow furrowed, and her hands unfurled. "Ohmygod, Nick. You're *right*," she said softly. "What am I doing? This isn't me." She stopped pacing, anger and sadness billowing off her as she looked down at her clothes and tugged at the knot in her shirt. "*Ugh.* I'm *done* dressing like this."

He grabbed her wrists, his heart breaking. "Don't you dare change a thing about yourself. You hear me? You're *nothing* like those girls. You've got dirt on your boots, country in your roots, and more brains than all of them put together."

"I don't want people saying shit about me or mistaking me for one of *them*."

"If anyone has something to say about you, they'll have to deal with *me*. You're *my* girl, and I fucking *love* who you are."

Confusion rose in her eyes. "You *do*?"

"Don't you know that by now?"

"How am I supposed to know that? You never tell me."

His chest constricted, and he realized she was right. He did things for her, showed her how he felt, but he didn't *tell* her. "Then I'm an asshole."

"No, you're not. I'm a jerk for saying that. I *know* you like me, Nick. Everything you do shows me. I just…"

"Hate feeling like someone else could take me away? Join the club, darlin'. Now you understand where I'm coming from when that green-eyed monster sucks me into his clutches." He pulled her into his arms. "Let me spell this out for you. I'm crazy about *you*, Patricia Ann Jericho. *All* of you, from your tied shirts, tight jeans, and skimpy shorts—which make me *crazy*—to your stubborn-ass attitude and the way you challenge every damn thing I say. I'll never lie to you, and I'll never cheat on you." Her lower lip trembled, and he held her tighter. "I was *that* guy before we got together, but not anymore, and I haven't been for a long damn time. You've seeped into every part of me. You could be on the other side of the world, and you'd still be with me. I want *you*, darlin', not *anyone* else. And if you don't believe me, then lock me in a room with gorgeous willing women, and I will prove it to you. Because the only woman I want my hands and mouth on is you, and I sure as hell don't want anyone else touching me."

She banged her forehead to his chest and looked up sadly. "I'm sorry I got so jealous, and I'm sorry I pushed you to take me to Whiskey Bro's. I didn't want there to be anyplace we couldn't go together, but obviously I need to get a grip before you decide your life's a hell of a lot easier without me in it."

"You could say the same about me." He held her tighter. "But you're not getting away that easily. Not after twisting me into knots for a year." He kissed her softly. "But if we're going to do this long-distance thing, we have to trust each other. We're both hotheads. We react before we think, and that's going to pull us apart unless we find a way to handle it."

"When did you get to be so good at relationships?"

He shook his head, wondering that himself. "I guess right now. When a relationship finally mattered enough to try to figure it out."

"Maybe we need a safe word or phrase. Something to tip each other off that we're about to get crazy and need some help."

He chuckled. "A safe word, huh? Like *Umbrella* because shit's about to rain down on us?"

"Yes. That's perfect." Her gaze moved over his shoulder, and she said, "You might want to keep that umbrella handy, just in case."

He followed her gaze to a group of buckle bunnies. "I've got a better idea." He lowered his lips to hers, kissing her until she went soft in his arms, and then he deepened the kiss, earning those sexy little noises he loved.

She came away breathless and whispered, "*Umbrella, umbrella, umbrella.*"

"That mouth of yours is going to be the death of me."

A playful light shone in her eyes. "I feel a storm coming on."

"My beautiful little hurricane." He lowered his lips to hers, kissing her until the rest of the world fell away.

Chapter Twenty-Five

TRIXIE COULDN'T HAVE hoped for a better first visit for Annabelle at the assisted living facility. They spent an hour walking around the facility with Jordan. Annabelle was a hit with residents and staff, even though the point of the visit wasn't to interact with them. Everyone's mood brightened the minute they saw Trixie's little horse decked out in her pink Rising Hope vest and shoes. Trixie wore her Rising Hope T-shirt proudly, and she was glad she'd brought extra business cards, as several people who were visiting residents had asked about her services.

"I think it's safe to say that our residents would benefit greatly from visits with Annabelle or your little one, Alfie," Jordan said as they made their way to the lobby. "She is a gracious guest. Once you're settled in back home in Virginia and have a handle on your schedule, I'd like to arrange a visit with patients. We can hold it in the community room and bring in just a few residents at a time if you'd like."

"That sounds wonderful. Thank you." Trixie petted Annabelle, trying to keep her excitement under wraps.

"Nana, look! A baby horse!" A little girl who must have been there visiting someone ran down the hall toward them, pigtails flying.

"*Susie*, slow down, sweetheart," her grandmother said, hurrying after her.

Trixie stepped between the little girl and Annabelle, just to be on the safe side, but Annabelle was unfazed by the fast-approaching child.

"Hi!" Susie stopped in front of Trixie, big brown eyes smiling up at her as her grandmother, who looked friendly and to be in her fifties, joined them.

"Hello. You must be Susie," Trixie said to the little girl.

Susie nodded, twisting from side to side, her pretty yellow sundress swinging around her knees. "Can I pet your baby horse?"

Trixie glanced at Jordan, who nodded her approval. Trixie crouched beside Susie. "My name's Trixie, and this is Annabelle. She's a full-grown miniature horse. She's not going to get any bigger. But I think we'd better ask your grandmother if it's okay for you to pet her."

"Can I, Nana?" Susie asked, bouncing on her toes.

Trixie rose to her feet and said, "Hi, I'm Trixie Jericho from Rising Hope. Annabelle is a therapy horse and she's used to children."

"Oh, how lovely. I'm Meredith Enders. It looks like we picked the perfect day to visit my mother."

"Can I pet her, Nana?" Susie pleaded.

"Sure, honey, but be gentle."

"I will." Susie petted Annabelle's neck. "She's soft, Nana. Pet her."

Meredith petted Annabelle. "She is soft and sweet. How old is she?"

"She's four," Trixie answered as Annabelle turned her head

to look at the little girl.

"Look, Nana, she likes me! I want a little horse."

"So do I," Jordan said with a soft laugh.

Meredith lowered her voice and said, "Susie's birthday is next month. Does Annabelle do parties?"

"She sure does." Trixie gave her a business card. "Here you go. My contact information and website address are on the card."

"Thank you. We'll be in touch." Meredith took Susie's hand. "Come on, sweetheart. Grandpa is waiting for us. Say goodbye to Annabelle and thank Miss Trixie."

"Goodbye, Annabelle." Susie gave Annabelle one final pet. "Thank you, Miss Trixie."

As they headed for the door, Jordan said, "I have a feeling you won't have to do any marketing for your business. Annabelle will do it all for you."

"Alfie, too. He's a doll." As they walked out to the parking lot, she said, "I really enjoyed our visit. Thank you for giving me a chance to show you how great Annabelle is."

Jordan petted Annabelle. "She's a sweetie. I look forward to setting up another visit and seeing more of both of you. If our next visit goes well, maybe we can set up monthly visits and give our residents something to look forward to."

"We'd love that. I also wanted to thank you for the referrals you gave me. I've been working through the list, and I've already set up quite a few appointments over the next few weeks."

"That's wonderful. It sounds like Rising Hope is on its way to finding its niche. Oh, and I meant to tell you that I met with Jax." Jordan lowered her voice. "You didn't mention how charming he was."

Trixie laughed. "He's a great guy. I hope he was able to help you."

"Are you kidding? He's *Jax Braden*." She said his name the way other people said Henry Cavill or Jason Momoa. "Everything he designs is absolutely gorgeous, but I put off my wedding again."

"You did?"

"*I did*," she whispered conspiratorially. "I think my feet are moving toward the frozen aisle."

"Oh, Jordan. I'm sorry."

Jordan waved her hand dismissively. "If it's meant to be, it'll be. I'd better get back inside. I appreciate your coming out. It was nice spending time with you. Be sure to let me know when we can schedule our next appointment."

"I will. Thanks again." As soon as Jordan was inside, Trixie hugged Annabelle. "We did it, baby! Everyone loved you. You were amazing. Let's go home and tell your daddy!" As soon as she said it, a pang of discomfort and longing hit her, remaining as she loaded Annabelle into the trailer.

Nick's house wasn't *home*, even if it felt like it was, and she didn't want to think about how easily *daddy* had slid off her tongue. He sure felt like he was her horses' *daddy*.

And my other half.

He cared about them just as much as she did. She didn't think that would change in the weeks between seeing each other after she went home, but there was one part of their lives that would. The next time she had a client visit, Nick wouldn't be waiting to hear about it when she got home. Would her brothers or parents be excited to hear about it?

She tried to push those thoughts away as she climbed into the truck, and her phone dinged with a group text from Lindsay to Trixie, Amber, and Brindle. *Amber Alert! Trixie, I hope your meeting went well and you're having fun with Nick the Sex God, but Amber's agreed to host a signing for Dash Pennington at her bookstore! We need to take her shopping and teach her to flirt. Stat! Does next weekend work?*

Before Trixie could respond, her phone chimed with a text from Brindle. *How was the visit with Annabelle?*

A text from Amber rolled in next. *I'm hosting a book signing, not the Dating Show! I'm a professional. There will be no flirting. Trix? How was it?*

Trixie had to get in on this and thumbed out *The meeting was amazing! I'll give you all details later. But don't worry, Amber. We'll find you something that makes you look like a lady in the bookstore and a vixen in the bedroom.* She added a winking emoji.

Another text from Lindsay popped up. *Amber, you can practice flirting at JJ's next week at ladies' night with me and Trixie.*

That pang of longing returned. She couldn't believe that soon she'd be there with them and not with Nick, but she couldn't think about it too long, because Amber texted an angry emoji and *No thank you. You know I hate those weeniefests,* which made Trixie laugh. Trixie thumbed out, *I can't text right now, about to drive to Nick's. YES to shopping next weekend. Amber, you can practice flirting on us peen free. Love you all!* She added a kissing emoji, sent the text, and put her phone down.

On the way home, thoughts of Nick crept back in. They'd gotten so much closer and more aware of each other's feelings in the days since their argument, she couldn't imagine anything coming between them. Last night, after grooming the horses, they'd grilled steaks and eaten them in the moonlight with Pugsly on Nick's lap and Goldie and Rowdy lying in the grass.

Nick had surprised her with a trip to Tully's after dinner for the chocolate pie she loved and had missed out on the last time they were there. The bar had been crowded for a Sunday, but even with women eyeing Nick and one who had been brazen enough to send a drink to their table, Trixie had been more annoyed than jealous. Things had changed when Nick had told her how he'd felt about her, and she'd realized that women would vie for his attention forever. He was a handsome, virile man, and his brooding nature made him even more attractive to women who wanted what they couldn't have. Trixie wasn't about to waste any more time worrying about women she didn't know when she had a man she *did* know and trusted to do the right thing. They'd ended up dancing the night away, and she'd been so swept up in them, she savored every moment, tucking the memories away for the lonely nights they'd have apart in the future.

Now she turned onto Nick's driveway and headed for the barns. She unloaded Annabelle, and they found him coming out of the barn, shirtless, wearing low-slung jeans and his black hat and carrying Pugsly. *Lord have mercy.* It was easy to imagine him twenty years from now with graying hair and a boy of his own to teach about ranching.

Their eyes met and his lips curved up, bringing her back to reality. "I didn't miss your call, did I?" He patted his back pocket, as if looking for his phone.

"No. Were you waiting for me to call?"

"I might have had my ringer turned up."

"I'm sorry. I saw it on the counter when I left and figured it'd be there all day." Pugsly snorted and grunted, wriggling and whining to get to her. She reached for him, and Nick took Annabelle's lead.

"Today was your big day. My mind's been on you, darlin'."

Oh, how she loved him! She went up on her toes and kissed him. "I love that. I promise to call next time."

"How'd it go?"

She nuzzled Pugsly against her chin and said, "It was fantastic."

Nick got down on one knee to love up Annabelle and said, "You did *fantastic*, little lady? That's our girl." He petted her with both hands on either side of her neck. "With a handler like your mama, you can't go wrong." He pushed to his feet, unaware that he'd once again melted Trixie into a puddle of goo, and said, "I want to hear all about it."

She told him about the meeting as they took care of Annabelle and set her free in the dry lot with the other minis, taking a few minutes to give them all a little attention. As Trixie gave Snickers some love, she watched Nick with her minis, and she knew it wouldn't matter how interested or supportive her family was in her business; it wouldn't be the same as coming home to the man who had been there with her, and for her and the horses, since day one.

When they left the horses, Nick scooped up Pugsly and slung his other arm around Trixie. "It sounds like it went great, but how did you feel about it besides that? Was it everything you'd hoped it would be?"

"It was everything I'd hoped and so much more." *Like us.* "It felt natural to handle her and to talk with people about Rising Hope. I don't think it could have gone any better."

"That's fantastic. Would you mind holding Pugsly for a minute? I need to grab something from the barn."

"Sure." She took Pugsly and sat in the grass. He looked up at her, and she said, "I'm going to miss you guys when I leave. I need you to do me a favor, Pugs. I know your big, bad daddy doesn't want anyone thinking he's anything less than superhuman, but I think he's going to miss me, too. I need you to take care of him for me."

Pugsly put his front paws on her chest and licked her chin.

She stroked his back. "I'm taking that to mean that you'll do it for me. I love you, Pugsly." She lowered her voice to a whisper. "And I love your daddy, too, but don't tell him that. We just got past the girlfriend-boyfriend thing."

A few minutes later, Nick walked out of the barn wearing his shirt with his guitar strapped to his back, leading Ghost, a white mare, and Midnight, a black gelding, saddled up and ready to ride. Midnight had insulated bags hanging from the horn on the saddle, and Ghost had rear saddlebags.

Trixie pushed to her feet with Pugsly. "Are you going somewhere?"

"*We* are, darlin'. I haven't done a great job of showing you how special you are to me, so we're going down to the creek for a picnic."

"We *are*? I love that!" She nuzzled Pugsly and said, "Did you know your daddy was so romantic?"

Nick shook his head. "It's just a picnic."

"There's no *just*, my humble cowboy. It's a romantic picnic with my boyfriend, who planned it and packed up the horses. Those are the things dreams are made of."

"Don't get all weird on me."

Too late.

AN HOUR LATER they came to the end of the trail, where it met the creek. The scent of damp earth and romance filled the air as they dismounted and walked the horses to the water's grassy edge for a drink. The creek was wide and deep, surrounded by tall oaks and prickly pine trees. The sun slid out from between the clouds, spreading light over the slow-running water.

"This is one of my favorite spots," Trixie said as Nick pulled a blanket out of a saddlebag and spread it out in the grass.

"Why is that? Because it feels a million miles away from the rest of the world?" He set his guitar on the blanket and headed back to the horses for more picnic supplies.

"I do love that it feels far from reality, but it's one of my favorite spots because it was the first private place you shared with me."

His brow furrowed as he handed her a plastic bag filled with food. "How do you figure?" He went around Ghost and pulled a plastic bag from the other insulated pouch. "I think my house is pretty damn private."

"That's true. I meant outside of your house." He'd brought her to the creek about three years ago, when they'd been out trail riding. She followed him back to the blanket. "Why did you share this place with me? Actually, why did you let me stay at your house when you don't let anyone other than family stay there?"

He took the bag from her and began setting out their picnic. "You were cool, and you needed a place to stay, and I knew if you were with me, you'd be safe. Sit down and relax."

He went back to get something else from the saddlebag without meeting her eyes, and she felt like there was more to that story, but she sat down, taking in the thick sandwiches bundled in clear plastic wrap and the ziplock bags full of chips and grapes. There were also two oranges and two bottles of iced tea.

"You thought of everything," she said as he sat beside her.

He handed her a small package wrapped in tinfoil. "Including your favorite raspberry chocolate chip cookies. But from now on, I'm leaving the baking to you."

"You *made* me cookies?" She unwrapped the tinfoil, her heart exploding.

"I got the recipe from your mom. Sorry they got a little broken."

You called my mom? She picked up a piece of cookie, falling harder for him by the second, and said, "Broken makes them easier to share." She put the cookie in his mouth, and then she kissed him. "I don't care what you say. You're the most romantic man on this planet, and this is the best date I've ever been on."

He laughed. "We just got here."

"So? Look at all of this. You made us lunch, you baked me cookies, and you took me to my favorite spot. It couldn't be more perfect." She ate a piece of the cookie. "This is even better than my mom's. I guess since you can bake, you don't need me to bring you goodies anymore."

He hooked an arm around her neck, hauling her in for another kiss. "Darlin', you stop bringing me goodies, and we're gonna have problems."

He kissed her again, tasting of sweet happiness.

They talked as they ate, tossed grapes into each other's mouths, cracking up when one went down her shirt and another bounced off his nose, and after they finished eating, Nick played the guitar.

Trixie swayed to the music. "Sing something for me."

"You know I don't sing, darlin'."

"You *do* sing, and you have a great voice. You just won't sing in front of people."

He winked and started playing "Beer Never Broke My Heart," and Trixie sang. He laughed when she forgot the words and made up her own. She sang loud, pretending to have a microphone, and got up and danced around as he played song after song.

She plopped down beside him and said, "We make a great team. We should go out on the road, touring. I can see it now. Our names in lights." She looked up at the sky and held up her hand, moving it to the right as if she were reading a sign. "The Cowboy and His Girl."

"I don't need my name in lights." He set down his guitar and lay down on his back with his head in her lap, putting his hat over his face. "Siesta time."

She snagged his hat and set it beside her, running her fingers through his hair. "Tell me the truth, Nick. Why did you let me stay at your house the first time?"

"Because you were hot."

"Well, *duh*." She giggled.

He looked up at her, and his expression turned serious.

"What's that look for?"

He slid his hand beneath her hair to the base of her neck. "I'm just realizing that you've always been special."

"*Ha!* I could have told you that."

He pulled her down and kissed her. "Smart-ass."

They both laughed.

He closed his eyes, and she played with his hair, listening to the sounds of the creek, her cheeks warmed by the sun. She gazed out at the water, wishing he'd want her to stay, or that he'd come to Oak Falls. But even though their friendship had turned into so much more, while she loved him wholly and completely, she knew he was still catching up, trying to get over the last of his walls, and that was okay. They had plenty of time. But she wanted to know all the little things about him she hadn't yet learned. Things she could hold on to while they were apart. "Tell me something I don't know about you."

He squinted up at her. "I'm kinda diggin' this couple stuff."

That made her feel good all over. "Me too. I'm going to miss you when I leave."

He looked at her for a long moment before saying, "Yeah. I'll miss you, too. Your turn. Tell me something I don't know about you."

I love you was on the tip of her tongue. "I'm thinking about stealing Pugsly."

He smiled. "That's one way to break us up."

"I'm kidding. Well, I'm not *really* kidding. If I take Pugsly, you'll definitely come see me."

"You know I'll come see you, darlin'. I promised to come down the weekend after you get there and set up your mock hospital room. We're going to be fine."

"I know." But that didn't mean it wouldn't be hard to be apart.

"Don't overthink it."

Easier said than done. She tried to think of more things she didn't know about him. "I just realized that I have no idea what your favorite song is."

"I know what yours is."

"You do?"

He flashed a cocky grin. "Save a Horse, Ride a Cowboy."

"Now who's the smart-ass?"

"I just tell it like it is."

"Okay, cowboy, cough it up. What's yours?"

"I have two. 'Hurricane' by Luke Combs because it reminds me of you—"

"*Really?* Or are you just saying that?"

"What's our safe word?" They said, "Umbrella" in unison. "Do you have any doubt?"

She ran her fingers along his jaw and pressed her hand to his cheek. His scruff was rough, but his skin was soft and warm. "I love that you think of me when you hear it."

"Want to know my other favorite song that makes me think of you?" When she nodded, he said, "'Black' by Dierks Bentley."

She looked at him curiously. "Why?"

"It's about a blow job."

"*Ohmygod!*" She laughed. "I need to listen to that one more carefully."

"We'll play it tonight, and you can act it out."

She wiggled out from beneath his head and crawled on top of him, gazing into his smiling eyes. "You're such a guy."

"Damn right." He grabbed her ass and kissed her. "Your turn. Favorite song?"

"Don't let this go to your head, but 'Sunshine and Whiskey' because that's what I always thought your kisses would be like."

A sea of emotions stared back at her. "And are they?"

She wrinkled her nose, opened her hand, and wiggled it in a so-so fashion. He smacked her ass, and she laughed. "They're about a million times better."

He rolled them onto their sides, kissing her slow and deep and oh so deliciously, and she said, "I take it back. A million and ten." She sat up and took off her boots and socks.

"I like where this is heading." He pulled off his boots.

As he took off his socks, Trixie rolled up her jeans and pushed to her feet. "Come on, cowboy, you need to cool off."

She went into the creek and splashed him. He stood up, shooting her a warning glare. She kicked more water at him, and he sprinted toward her. She squealed and ran through the shallow water, but he was too fast. He swept her into his arms, soaking her in the process, which made her laugh even harder. He captured her laughter with a kiss as she wound her arms and legs around him, and they both came away laughing.

"You, darlin', are a thief."

"I am not!"

He arched a brow. "You steal all the covers at night."

She grinned. "Okay, maybe that's true."

"You want to steal my *dog*."

"Guilty," she whispered.

"And you've obviously stolen a big damn piece of my heart, because I'm so crazy about you, I can barely see straight."

She threw her arms up toward the sky and said, "Praise the Lord. Miracles do happen!" winning more delectable kisses on the most wonderful afternoon of her life.

Chapter Twenty-Six

"DID I TELL you that Jilly is bringing the unicorn horn and the wings for Alfie and Annabelle? I can't wait to see them." Trixie leaned closer to the bathroom mirror late Saturday afternoon, putting on makeup for the barbecue. "I can't wait to see how Walt and Irene react to each other. I'm glad we didn't tell him she was coming…"

Nick sat on the bed listening to her rattle on about everything under the sun as he pulled on his socks and boots. She was leaving tomorrow at noon, so she'd have time to get the horses settled in at her parents' ranch before nightfall. Where had the month gone? Had it really been five days since their picnic at the creek? Man, he was going to miss her, and *this*—all of it. He'd miss her feminine scent surrounding him, her voice, her snark, the sight of her wiggling into her tight jeans, and the feel of her when he stripped them off. He'd miss the way she played with the dogs and loved the horses and goats. He'd even miss collecting eggs with her in the mornings, when she ran around the chicken coop just to see Cluck follow her. His gaze swept over his shirts she'd claimed as her nightshirts, lying in a clean stack on the chair. Hell, he'd even miss the way she stole the damn blankets. Last night they'd watched a movie, and she'd fallen asleep in his arms on the couch. They'd stayed there all night, with Pugsly curled up at their feet.

He looked at Pugsly now, standing outside the bathroom door watching Trixie. He'd been following her around all day, as if he knew this was her last night there, too. She'd been going a million miles an hour since she got out of bed. First with chores, then working with the horses, and then she'd baked and cooked all afternoon while he'd hung strings of lights all over the damn place because she wanted tonight to be *festive*. She was so excited to thank everyone and to host his family and their friends, she bubbled over with it.

The house smelled as welcoming as his parents' house had when he was growing up. Trixie's voice whispered through his mind. *Inviting friends and family over every once in a while would make your house homier.* She sure had that Southern comfort down pat. But she'd been starry-eyed all day, and he wondered if she was trying not to think about the fact that she was leaving tomorrow, too. He'd finally slowed her down in the shower, and he'd almost asked her if that was what she was doing, but he'd needed to be closer to her more than he'd needed to know. Showering with her, and when they washed each other, had become one of his favorite parts of the day. No matter what else was going on, that time together centered him, and he knew it did the same for her, because when he bathed her, she softened in ways that were different from any other time. He wasn't looking forward to going back to his three-minute solo showers. And tonight he was as selfish as could be, because he wished he didn't have to share her with everyone else.

Jesus Christ. Stop being a pansy.

"Are you even listening to me?" Trixie turned toward him with her hand on her hip.

"*Huh?* Sorry. I was just thinking about Pugsly." He cocked a grin. "Wondering if I should leash him to my wrist to make sure you don't steal him."

"That's probably a good idea," she teased, and closed the distance between them.

She was gorgeous in an off-white dressy tank top with gold trim and a yellow floral miniskirt that hugged her waist and flounced around her thighs. He reached for her, drawing her onto his lap, her knees straddling his waist.

She pressed her lips to his and said, "We have so much to do before everyone gets here."

"*Shh*, beautiful." He brushed her hair over her shoulder and ran the backs of his fingers down her cheek. "I just want a second alone with you." He gazed into her eyes, and that familiar zing of electricity sparked between them, but the hunger in her eyes was shadowed by sadness, landing like lead in his gut. "I want to make sure you're okay."

"Why wouldn't I be? We've had an amazing month, and we're going to have a great time tonight."

She tried to get up, but he held tight, keeping her on his lap. "So you're not trying to avoid thinking about leaving tomorrow?"

"Of *course* I am, but if I talk about it, I'll cry. So we're *not* talking about it."

He hugged her. "We're going to be fine, darlin'. I promise."

"I *know*. I'm just going to miss you. I got used to seeing your stubborn face every day. But we are *not* going to talk about it. I just did my makeup, and I don't need to fall apart. I'll have two hours in the truck to do that tomorrow."

Hell if that image didn't slay him.

She climbed off his lap. "Come on, we have a lot to do

before everyone gets here."

He stood and pulled her into his arms. "Slow down a second. I don't want you to fall apart tomorrow. I want you to know, to believe with everything you have, that we'll be okay. We spent a whole month together breaking down walls, overcoming jealousy, and figuring each other out."

"Becoming a couple," she said softly.

"Exactly, and you're well on your way to making your dreams a reality. You need to be focused on that and trust in us, because there's nothing we can't do, darlin'."

She kissed his chin. "I know, cowboy."

"And you want this, right? Starting your business? A long-distance relationship?"

"Yes! More than anything."

"All right, then. No falling apart. Now, what are you waiting for? Get your pretty little ass out there, before I strip off that sexy outfit and cancel the barbecue."

Her eyes narrowed. "You wouldn't dare after all the work we've done."

"Wouldn't I?" He touched the zipper on the back of her skirt.

She wiggled out of his arms, walking backward toward the door, a big-ass smile lighting up her eyes. "Oh no you don't, Nick Braden!"

He took a step toward her, and she squealed and ran out of the room, taking a big ol' piece of him with her.

NICK STARTED UP the grill as Trixie came out the back door

carrying a stack of plates with all three dogs on her heels. They'd set up two tables, which he'd borrowed from his parents, and Trixie had bought navy-blue tablecloths and votive candles, which made the tables look elegant. She'd picked massive amounts of wildflowers, filling three vases for the outside tables and one for the kitchen. It looked more like they were having a party than a barbecue, but she was so happy, he'd gladly suffer through one night of guests. Only he didn't feel like he was suffering at all. Her homey touches made the patio and the kitchen feel so warm and inviting, it made him want to spend time in both places. But he had a feeling it had more to do with the woman flitting around his house and patio than the material touches she brought.

She dodged the dogs to set the plates on the table and then loved up the pups. "My entourage is very needy today." She smiled at Nick. "I hope we have enough silverware."

"Should I call my mom and ask her to bring some?"

She moved half of the plates to the other table. "I don't know. Maybe?"

He pulled out his phone, and the dogs went racing toward the front of the house. "I thought we still had half an hour before anyone got here."

"Maybe your family came early."

"I'll go see," he said as Beau, Char, Zev, and Carly came around the side of the house, followed by his parents, Morgyn, and Graham, stopping Nick in his tracks.

"Is this where the party is?" Zev hollered.

"Holy shit." Nick shook his head to make sure he wasn't seeing things. "What are you all doing here?"

"Mom said you were having a barbecue. We had to see it with our own eyes." Graham threw his arms around him.

His brothers all shared the Braden dark eyes and athletic build, but while Graham could have been Beau's younger twin, with the same short brown hair, Zev's hair was longer and always looked a little wild.

"You didn't think we'd miss this momentous occasion, did you?" Zev gave him a manly embrace. "I missed you, bro."

"You too," Nick said, as Morgyn, Charlotte, and Trixie ran into each other's arms and tugged Carly into their group hug. Morgyn and Carly were as blond as Char and Trixie were dark.

"I'm so happy for you!" Morgyn exclaimed. "I want *all* the details that Jilly didn't give us yet."

"I can't believe you're all here for a freaking barbecue," Nick said, as Beau embraced him.

"We're here for you, bro, not the barbecue," Beau said. "It's not every day you have a special woman in your life. We wouldn't miss it for the world."

"I talked to Jax as we were pulling in," Graham said. "He and Jilly are on their way over."

"That's great." Nick got a little choked up and tried to regain control as he hugged Carly. "About time you're officially becoming a Braden."

"From what I hear, it's about time you let someone near that ironclad heart of yours." Carly had a bronze tan and a shimmer of love in her eyes as Zev put an arm around her and kissed her cheek.

"I heard it was the magic of the inn that brought you two together," Charlotte said, hugging Nick. She looked pretty in tan shorts and a breezy blue top, her long dark hair falling in natural waves down her back. "Beau said you two are going to do the long-distance thing. Lucky for you, the magic of the inn never wears off."

"I can vouch for that," Carly said as Trixie was passed from one brother's arms to the next.

"They don't need magic. Their auras are red hot," Morgyn said. "I'm talking, back up, people, because you're about to get burned."

"Passion does kind of radiate off them, doesn't it?" Charlotte said.

"So, you're responsible for this intrusion?" Nick teased, embracing his mother.

Her brow wrinkled, but she was smiling from ear to ear. "I'm afraid so."

His father clapped a hand on his back and said, "Son, the second she hung up the phone with you about the barbecue, the Braden hotline was buzzing."

"I bet it was," Nick said, reaching for Trixie. "Thanks for calling everyone, Mom. It's a nice surprise, seeing their ugly mugs all in one place."

"I don't know who you're calling ugly, but I'm the *hot* brother," Zev said. "Just ask my girl."

"I think it's fair to say all of you are good-looking," Charlotte said. "But Beau definitely has an extra something special about him. Not that I'm biased or anything."

"You clearly haven't spent time with Zevy," Carly said.

"Zev?" Morgyn, looking earthy and pretty in a purple tie-dyed sundress, motioned to Graham. "My husband is smart, sexy, and *talented*, if you get my drift."

"You don't know *talent* until you've been with a treasure hunter. He finds all the best hidden spots," Carly chimed in.

"Yeah, well, builders are never without wood," Charlotte said. "Just sayin'."

"Excuse me, but have you met my cowboy?" Trixie chimed

in. "No offense or anything, but the size of the stallion *does* matter. Look at him. Big, buff, and bullheaded, and he knows how to use it in *all* the right ways."

Everyone laughed.

"Oh my goodness." Their mother laughed. "You girls are a hoot."

"Hey, Nick, I see you picked a girlfriend who would inflate your ego," Zev teased, earning a high five from Graham.

Nick reached for his belt. "You want proof?"

His father threw up his hands. "Whoa. Stop right there. We don't need to see proof of anything."

"Says the man who gave each of you those attributes," their mother chimed in.

"*Ew, Mom! Stop!*" all four brothers said in unison, sparking a slew of comments and jokes that had everyone laughing.

"We're here!" Jillian hollered as she and Jax came into the backyard. She held up two bags. "I brought unicorn wings and horns!"

Trixie cheered and ran to Jillian.

"I didn't know we were getting kinky!" Zev shouted. "Let's get this party started!"

Nick had missed being with his whole family like this, and it was a billion times better with his snarky, sexy girl right there in the middle of it.

MUSIC FROM THE stereo streamed out the open windows later that evening to the patio where the get-together was in full swing. Walt and Irene sat by the firepit talking with Nick's parents, and hell if Trixie hadn't been right. Walt looked happier than Nick had ever seen him. Travis was talking with Nash and Beau on the lawn, where Flip and April were playing with the dogs. Graham and Morgyn were smooching by the table, and Zev and Carly hadn't let go of each other all night as they mingled with everyone. It was great to see everyone so happy. His eyes found Trixie, laughing with Jillian, Tempest, and Charlotte at the edge of the patio.

Trixie was the perfect hostess, flitting from one group to the next, making sure everyone had enough to eat and drink. She stole glances at Nick, blew him kisses, and of course he had to collect on the real thing in between hostess stops. She stepped away from the girls and pointed up at the twinkling lights, wiggling her shoulders in a little happy dance and mouthing, *Thank you!* She was right about the lights, too. They made the evening feel more festive. She motioned to Walt and Irene and gave Nick a thumbs-up, then blew him a kiss and went to sit with them, immediately joining their conversation.

Jax came out of the house with a fresh beer in his hand. He'd been quiet tonight and seemed distracted. "Hey, Jax. You okay?"

"Yeah." Jax took a drink.

"That's your third beer."

"I didn't know I had a babysitter."

"Just making sure you're cool."

"Thanks. I rode over with Jilly so I wouldn't have to drive home." Jax took another drink, watching Nick intently. "You really like Trixie, don't you?"

"That yard full of people is your answer. Do you blame me? Look at her. She's comfortable in her own skin, and she cares so damn much about everyone else's happiness. And that smile."

He shook his head. "I swear her smile does me in, Jax."

"I saw that when she gushed over the unicorn wings and horns Jilly made for her horses. I swear you had the goofiest look on your face."

"I bet I did."

Trixie had taken everyone through the mock hospital room in the basement and down to the barn to meet her horses. She was bursting with joy as she told them about the business cards Nick had given her, and her website, and all the appointments she had scheduled for the coming weeks. While they were in the barn, his bright-eyed girl had suggested they all take a trail ride tomorrow before she had to leave. Everyone except Jillian and Jax were game. As much as Nick loved the idea of spending more time with his family, he had so little left with Trixie, he felt it slipping away.

"She makes me think about weird shit, Jax. She was playing with Flip and April earlier. She's a natural with kids. For the first time in my life, I thought about how great it might be to have a family one day. I've never wanted that before."

"What'd you do, trade in your balls for ovaries?"

Nick glowered at him. "What's going on with you? You're never like this."

"Shit. Sorry, Nick. That was a dick comment. I'm happy for you. I, on the other hand, am a bit messed up at the moment."

"From two and a half beers? That's not like you."

"Not fucked up. *Messed* up. I met someone. She's smart, interesting, and she's got the most beautiful laugh I've ever heard."

"That's great. If you've got a date and need to leave, it's no sweat off my back. I appreciate you coming by."

Jax scoffed. "I wish. She's not exactly available."

"She's not married, is she?"

"Not yet." Jax guzzled his beer.

"Aw, hell, Jax. Are you kidding? A bride? You know better than that."

"Yeah, well. I can't help it if sparks fly with the wrong person. But don't worry. She's not hiring me to do her wedding gown, so it's not like I'll ever see her again." He held up his beer. "Now I'm just trying to forget her."

"That sounds like the best plan."

"Except it didn't work too well for you and Trixie."

"We had a decade of friendship. You've only seen this woman once, right?"

"That's right."

"You've got this, Jax. Come on, I hear we're supposed to mingle at these things."

"Do you even know what that word means?"

Nick mumbled, "Jackass," and Jax chuckled.

They joined Beau and the others, and Nick made his way to his beautiful girl as quickly as he could without being rude. As the night wore on, Tempest, Nash, and Flip left and Travis took April home, but Irene stayed to continue talking with Walt, who offered to drive her home.

A while later, Nick carried dishes into the kitchen, and when he came out, he spotted Trixie talking with Morgyn and the girls. Their eyes met, and his body burned to be with her. She met him on the grass, and he pulled her in close. "Are you having a good time?"

"Yes, aren't you? I'm so glad I got to thank everyone and to see your family and meet Carly. Guess what? She and Zev invited us to Colorado over the winter. Carly wants to introduce us to the people who run Redemption Ranch. I had no idea her best friends were horse people. Did you?"

"I'd heard about them. Zev invited us to stay on his boat off Silver Island this fall, too."

"Sounds like we're going to be busy, and it looks like Walt might be, too." She nodded to Walt and Irene heading their way and whispered, "They're so cute together."

They sure were.

"Nick, Trixie," Walt said, with one hand on Irene's back. "Thank you for an enjoyable evening. I think we're going to head out."

"Thank you both for coming," Nick said.

"We hope you had a good time," Trixie said.

We. Damn, he liked that, too. This couple stuff was pretty cool.

"I had a marvelous time. Thank you for inviting me." Irene looked at Walt, and her cheeks pinked up. "It's been wonderful catching up with my old friend and getting to know you, Trixie, and the rest of your family, Nick."

"I'm glad to hear that. You be careful driving her home tonight, old man."

"I've been driving since before you were born." Walt looked at Trixie and said, "I'm going to miss you, darlin'. Don't be a stranger."

"I won't. I promise." She hugged him and then she hugged Irene. "Maybe we can all get together the next time I'm in town."

Walt and Irene exchanged a glance, and Walt said, "We'd like that."

After they left, Trixie smiled cheekily and said, "I told you so."

He gathered her into his arms and kissed her. "Now can we

kick everyone out and enjoy the rest of our night together?"

"*No*, you cannot kick everyone out. Your brothers flew in to see you. Go get your guitar; we'll hang out around the firepit."

"*Fine.* The things I do for you."

"Are only half as good as the things I'll do for *you* later."

Chapter Twenty-Seven

THEY SAT AROUND the bonfire telling funny stories and singing as Nick played the guitar.

Nick's parents sat side by side, holding hands, and next to them, Charlotte sat on Beau's lap. Zev was relaxing on a lounge chair with Carly nestled between his legs, and on the other side of the firepit, Graham and Morgyn were in the same position. Jax was giving Jillian grief as she checked her social media pages, and Trixie sat in a chair beside Nick as he strummed the guitar. She'd never seen him so relaxed.

"In all the excitement, I forgot to tell Nick and Trixie that LWW is going to start filming my movie in LA in October. Beau and I are flying out to watch, and Grace and Reed will be there, too," Charlotte announced. She had published a book called *Anything for Love*, and it was being made into a movie by LWW Enterprises for their Me Time channel. Morgyn's oldest sister, Grace, had written the screenplay. Grace had been an off-Broadway producer before moving back to Oak Falls, where she and her husband, Reed, now ran the Majestic Theater.

"That's fantastic!" Trixie said. "Last I heard, they'd cast Duncan Raz for the male lead. He's a great actor, so believable. But I don't remember hearing who they cast for the female lead."

Nick stopped strumming the guitar and said, "It's still weird to hear people make a big deal over Duncan."

"What do you mean?" Trixie asked.

"We grew up together," Beau explained. "Duncan was Tory's brother. His last name is Raznick, but his professional name is Duncan Raz. He's perfect for the part."

"We're lucky he agreed to do it, since it's not being made for theaters," Charlotte added. "They just cast Harlow Bad for the female lead, and when I saw the video of them reading together, their chemistry was off the charts." Harlow was an up-and-coming actress.

"I *love* her," Trixie exclaimed.

"Good luck, Char. She's Johnny Bad's sister," Jillian said. Johnny Bad was a famous musician with a reputation for being difficult. "I was so excited when I was hired to design his wardrobe for his next tour, and then the *day* I signed the contract, which meant putting off my next clothing line, he delayed the tour. I hope Harlow is not as much of a pain as he is."

"I'm sure the LWW crew can keep her in line if she is," Charlotte said.

"I can't wait to see the movie, Char." Trixie patted Nick's leg and said, "We'll have to watch it together."

"Sure, darlin'."

"Nick Braden watching a romance movie? This ought to be good," Graham teased.

Zev coughed to mask saying, "*Whipped.*"

Nick glowered at him, and everyone laughed.

"Am I the only one feeling nostalgic?" Carly looked over her shoulder at Zev and said, "This reminds me of when we used to have bonfires in your backyard when we were younger."

Zev kissed her. "Yeah, me too."

"You kids had a lot of good years together." Their father squeezed their mother's hand and said, "And we've got many more ahead of us."

"Hear, hear." Beau lifted his beer.

Everyone toasted, and Trixie noticed the Bradens' and Carly's expressions dimming briefly. She couldn't help but wonder if they were thinking about Tory. As if Charlotte had read Trixie's mind, she said, "I think we should toast the friend who's missing."

"Thank you, babe." Beau kissed her cheek. He held up his beer and said, "To Tory."

Nick stopped playing to join them in the toast. "To Tory."

When he began playing the guitar again, Trixie said, "I'll give a dollar to anyone who can tell me why Nick won't sing."

They all looked at each other, shrugging.

"He never has," his mother said. "Nick, why is that?"

He cocked a grin but didn't answer.

"Guys are so weird," Jillian said. "Speaking of guys, Trix, what kind of running shoes do you wear?"

Nick gave her a deadpan look. "You're not going to start running to try to get Travis's attention, are you?"

Jillian sat up straighter. "I already have his attention, thank you very much. And no, I don't run. But I could power walk for a man like that."

Everyone laughed, except Nick, who shook his head.

"I think this has been the best night we've had in a long time," his mother said. "All our kids in one place, four of you paired off and living your happily ever afters." She covered her heart with her hand. "I couldn't be happier. Unless, of course, one of you young couples decided to give us grandchildren."

There was a rumble of comments and coughs.

"Okay, okay," his mother said. "No pressure from me. Morgyn, honey, does your aunt Roxie make fertility bodywash?"

Nick and his brothers all complained at once. "No!" "Mom!" "Come on!"

Lily giggled, and the girls laughed.

"Who's hosting brunch tomorrow? Mom's stove is on the fritz." Jillian looked around. "Beau?"

"Our fridge is empty," Beau said.

"Ours too," Graham said.

"Don't look at us," Zev said. "We're staying at Beau's."

"We'll host," Nick said, his eyes flicking up to Trixie's.

Everyone looked around like they'd misheard him.

Trixie's heart skipped. "We will? You know that means everyone comes here to eat, right? Inside the house?"

"'Course, darlin'. I figured you'd want to, and almost everyone will be here for the trail ride anyway."

"Yay! We're hosting brunch!" She got up and threw her arms around him. "Who are you, and what have you done with my broody cowboy?"

Everyone had a good laugh over that.

They had a wonderful evening hanging out with his family. Everyone helped clean up, and they made plans to meet for the trail ride at seven thirty the next morning and for brunch at ten o'clock. After everyone left, Trixie and Nick took care of the animals, and while he closed up the barn, she waited by the fence, gazing out at the horses in the pasture, thinking about how much she was going to miss being there and how far they'd come. It seemed like a year since she'd arrived.

She heard Nick approaching, and her stomach fluttered. He pressed his body to her back and held on to the fence on either side of her, trapping her against his enticingly hard frame. She felt his warm breath on her shoulder as he lowered his lips and kissed her there, bringing rise to goose bumps.

"Hey, cowgirl. Come here often?"

"Actually, I haven't ever *come* here."

"You're a dirty girl. Just the way I like you." He kissed her neck again, moving her hair so he could seal his mouth over her skin. One hand moved down her belly as he kissed and sucked, driving her up on her toes. He rocked his hard length against her ass, his hand slipping beneath her skirt and crawling over her thigh. "I've been dying to touch you all night, darlin'." He teased between her legs, over her panties, and her head fell back.

"Me too," she said breathily.

She reached behind her with both hands, pulling him tighter against her bottom as he pushed his fingers into her panties. His fingers slid through her wetness, and he moaned.

"I love when you're wet for me."

"I'm always wet for you," she panted out, his fingers dipped inside her. "My *neck*. Suck my neck."

He sucked and licked, grazing his teeth over her sensitive skin as he drove her wild with his fingers, taking her right up to the edge. She rocked in time with his efforts, chasing her release, and there was no stopping the sinful sounds from slipping through her lips.

"That's it, baby," he said in a low, gravelly voice. "I want to feel you come for me."

He pushed his other hand beneath her top, palming her breast, and squeezed her nipple. His teeth sank into her neck, as his thumb hit her clit with laser precision, sending her careening into her climax. She cried out his name, pleasure scorching through her. Just when she hit the peak, his thumb pressed harder, moving in circles, sending flames from her head all the way to the tips of her toes. She clung to his arms, her body quivering, as he showered her cheek and neck with tender kisses, and she tried to remember how to breathe.

He turned her in his arms, his eyes glowing with desire as his mouth covered hers, hard and demanding, kissing her so exquisitely, she nearly lost her mind. She tugged at his shirt, but he took her hand, leading her to a blanket in the grass she hadn't known he'd put there. He guided her arms to his shoulders, as he bent to take off her boots and socks. He ran his hands up her legs and pressed kisses just above her knees. Then he took off his own boots and socks and rose to his feet, taking her in a long, sensual kiss. His hands moved lovingly down her body, over her hips, and up her back. He was so tender, so different from the frantic and urgent man who had first taken her in the kitchen. He kissed her neck and shoulders, slowly and meticulously, like he was savoring every touch as he peeled off her shirt and put it on the blanket. Her bra went next, and his eyes moved slowly over her breasts.

"You're beautiful, Trix."

He brushed a kiss over her heart as he unzipped her skirt, and it puddled at her feet. He drew down her panties and ran his hands up her legs, kissing as he went. God, she loved that. He slowed at her thighs, lingering there, touching and kissing until her legs trembled. Then he kissed his way higher. She closed her eyes as he whispered against her belly, "I love your body." He kissed her ribs, his rough hands moving over her bottom and up her back. He slicked his tongue over one nipple, then the other, bringing them to throbbing peaks as the balmy night air swept over them, making her entire body shudder.

"Gorgeous," he whispered, and sucked one nipple into his mouth, caressing the other, and then his hand slipped between her legs again. "I can't help myself. I love the way you feel."

The emotion in his voice made her knees weak, and his touch made her quiver and quake. He kissed her rough and deep and helped her down to sit on the blanket. She watched as he stripped off his clothes, revealing his hard muscles, his thick cock bobbing eagerly. She went up on her knees, her hand circling his length, and she teased the head the way she knew drove him mad. He groaned and buried his hands in her hair, letting her set the pace as she took him in her mouth. She loved the way his muscles flexed with restraint as she pleasured him with her mouth, but she wanted to feel his power, his desire. She grabbed his ass, urging him to move with her, thrust faster. He didn't hesitate, giving her exactly what she wanted, fucking her mouth as passionately as he took her body. They were so in sync, so perfect together. But then he withdrew, and when she looked up in confusion, his eyes drilled into her as he dropped to his knees.

"I want to make love to you," he said, gruff and urgent.

She lay back, and as he came down over her, his words sank in. He hadn't ever referred to sex as making love. Did he even realize he'd said it?

She wound her arms around him as their mouths came together. He kissed her slowly and passionately, cradling her in his arms as their bodies came together at the same slow, sensual pace, until they were as close as two people could be. Warm air swept over their bodies as they found their rhythm. In his arms, she felt protected from the rest of the world. Their impassioned kisses, the way he held her, as if she were his most cherished treasure, and the way he loved her, was so different from any other time they'd been together, she wanted to hold on to all of it—from the first frantic, unsure-what-it-meant time, to the last urgent and greedy coupling—because they were *all* part of who they were as a couple. Even though every time they'd been together since the first had felt special and meaningful, this time was even more intense, as if all the pieces of herself came together in this one magical moment. But they—*this*—felt even bigger than that, as if she and Nick had truly become *one* body, mind, and soul.

When their mouths parted on a series of feathery kisses and he gazed into her eyes, she saw, she *knew*, he felt it too.

"Trix…?" he whispered roughly.

"I know. Kiss me."

He reclaimed her mouth, kissing her firmly but tenderly as he withdrew slowly, stroking over all her sensitive nerve endings while sinking deeper into their kisses, loving her so completely, she was swept away, floating on a cloud of pleasure. Just when she caught her breath, he began thrusting faster, harder, sending her right up to the cusp of another orgasm. Her body trembled, every inch of her reaching for more of him. But he held her there, wanting, craving, standing on the edge of a cliff. His dark eyes hit hers, fierce and all-consuming, and he didn't say a word. He didn't have to. She felt his love for her in his every touch, stroke, and kiss. As his mouth came down over hers and they tumbled into ecstasy, she felt their two hearts become one, and she knew without a shadow of a doubt, he felt it, too.

They rolled onto their sides, their bodies intertwined, stealing kisses between gasps for air. He rested his forehead against hers, holding her tight, like he never wanted to let her go. When their breathing finally calmed and their bodies slipped apart, he rolled onto his back, gathering her close. She rested her head on his chest, pressing a kiss there. They lay like that for a long time, staring up at the starry sky, and she thought about making a wish, which led to thoughts of how much her hopes and dreams had changed over the past month. She'd come to Maryland trying to let go of her feelings for Nick and dreaming of starting her own business. Now all of her dreams included him, this, *them.*

She wondered if he had the same hopes for the future she did. Butterflies swarmed in her belly as she mustered her courage and said, "What are you thinking about?"

"You, darlin'. Always you."

Chapter Twenty-Eight

SUNDAY BROUGHT SUNSHINE, cooler weather, and bittersweet emotions. Trixie and Nick hadn't said much since they'd woken up and reached for each other, but their emotions *roared* between them. There had been a moment in the shower when Trixie had thought she might cry, but Nick had pulled her into his arms and held her, and she'd soaked in his strength with every reassuring word. *We've got this, darlin'. Don't be sad. I'll come down next weekend and the weekend after that. I'm just a phone call away.*

The trail ride with his family had been wonderful. She'd loved seeing everyone enjoying the outdoors together, and experiencing Nick as their trusted guide, leading them down the trails and sharing random facts about the land and his rides with Walt. The fresh air and company had taken Trixie's weepiness away. She'd worried about becoming sad again over brunch because it was harder not to feel her impending departure when she and Nick were at his house. She saw memories of them everywhere. In the kitchen where they'd first come together, on the couch where they'd made love and slept in each other's arms, in the bedroom where they'd taken their relationship deeper, in the barn where they'd laughed and devoured each other, and in the yard where their love had bloomed into something so beautiful, it could bring tears. But Jax and Jillian had been there when they'd come back from their ride, waiting with fresh pastries from Emmaline's and a big platter of fruit, lifting Trixie's spirits. She and Nick had cooked bacon, eggs, and pancakes, and she'd been nicely distracted by his family's banter.

They'd all eaten too much, and helped clean up as they had last night. She loved that about his family. They were always there for each other, and as Nick had proven, when one of them couldn't be, the others would fill that spot. She knew he'd miss her, but he had his family to fill the gap she left behind.

"Since you're going for simple, and your ceremony is going to be at the creek in winter, we need to be careful about length to avoid it dragging on the ground," Jax said.

He was sitting at the table, sketching Carly's wedding dress, with Jillian hanging over one shoulder, telling him everything he was doing wrong, and his mother over the other, admiring his drawings. Zev sat beside him with Carly on his lap, while everyone else milled about.

"Come here, darlin'." Nick leaned against the island and pulled Trixie into his arms, holding her from behind, and kissed her cheek.

She put her hands over his and leaned back against his chest, soaking in the feel of him and his family's laughter and chatter while pretending the clock didn't feel like a ticking time bomb.

"Can you make the dress look magical? Like a snow princess?" Charlotte asked Jax.

Beau slipped an arm around her and said, "You and your magic." He nuzzled against her neck.

"I like the idea of it looking magical, too," Morgyn said.

"Like the universe made it for me, right, Morgyn?" Carly teased, because Morgyn was all about universal signs. "And, Char, you're the princess in this family. I'm more of a forest fairy. I don't want anything too fancy or overdone."

"You had me at forest fairy. I've got an idea." Jax hunkered down and sketched.

"I *love* where this is heading." Jillian pointed to his drawing. "Use a color for that."

Jax gave her a deadpan look, and Jillian held up her hands in surrender.

Clint sidled up to Nick and Trixie and said, "How are you two holding up?"

"We're fine, Dad." Nick tightened his hold on her.

"I've got to tell you, son, I'm surprised you're not having a panic attack with all these people in your house." Clint glanced at Trixie. "But I guess you're a little preoccupied."

"If it were up to me, I'd have canceled the brunch and kicked everyone out after the trail ride. But Trixie said that would be rude."

Clint laughed softly. "Look at your mother, Nick. She'll be riding the high of this weekend for months. You did a good deed."

"And it won't be the last one he does." Trixie turned in his arms and kissed his chin. "Right, party boy? Maybe we can do it again next time I'm here."

"Whatever you want, darlin'."

His father whistled. "Now I'm riding a high. My boy has finally opened his eyes and found his match."

"Here you go." Jax moved the paper in front of Carly and Zev, and everyone *ooh*ed and *aah*ed. Jax began sketching again. "I'll show you the coat and cape ideas I have for you to wear over it."

Trixie imagined her and Nick in Carly and Zev's place, designing her wedding gown with both of their families around them. She tried to fight that urge because she knew Nick wasn't ready for such a big step, but it felt too good thinking about it, so she allowed herself just a few minutes of dreaming before letting it go.

Jillian patted Jax's shoulder and said, "Jax, that's a gorgeous mermaid gown. It's sleek and elegant. I love the sweetheart neckline."

"Carly, you have a perfect figure for a mermaid gown," Morgyn said.

"She does." Jax pointed to the drawing and said, "Imagine this is a detachable high-low tulle skirt with a horsehair hem and a single strand of gold around the waistline. I can sew small lace flowers into the tulle. Assuming the weather cooperates, if you wear your hair down and weave baby's breath down the sides, you and the gown will give the illusion of snow falling."

"I love that," Carly gushed. "Zevy, do you like it?"

"I'll love you in anything." Zev cocked a grin. "Jax, just make sure it's got a zipper and not those tiny buttons down the back, because I can guarantee you I'll rip that sucker to shreds to get it off if I have to."

They all laughed.

Trixie's phone rang. She pulled it out of her back pocket and said, "It's my dad. I'll be right back." She headed out the patio doors as she answered. "Hi, Dad."

"Hey, doll. Are you on the road yet?"

"No, but I will be soon. Nick's family is here, and I'm just enjoying the last few minutes with them."

"Tell them I said hello. It's good of them to come see you

off. I wanted to give you a heads-up. Your mother and I ran into Lyle and Millie Rucket this morning. Millie's mother has taken a fall and broken her hip."

"Oh no. Didn't her father just have pneumonia a few weeks ago?"

"That's right. They're fixin' to sell their property and move to North Carolina to be with her family. Lyle's got only six acres, and a log cabin that could use some work, but the barn's in good shape."

"That should sell quickly."

"Well, it'll sell today, if you give me the okay."

She looked out at the pasture. "What do you mean?"

"Your mother and I are real proud of you, Trix. You've busted your butt for us your whole life, and you've already turned the key on your business. We know you spent more than you planned on those minis, and your mother and I would like to put a down payment on this little farmette so you can start out right. I've already spoken to our ranch hands, and they're fine taking over your hours here on our ranch, or whatever number of hours you'd like them to."

Trixie's jaw dropped. "Dad, you don't have to do that."

"We want to, sugar. I've spoken with Beckett about a loan for the remainder, and your payments would be about fifteen hundred a month, which you should be able to swing."

"Ohmygod, *Dad*. I can definitely afford that." She thought of Nick and wondered if she should hold off on buying a place until she saw where their relationship went. But in the next breath, she realized she would be letting the chance of a lifetime slip through her fingers for something that might take years.

"When I mentioned it to Trace and Shane this morning, they offered to fix up the property for you. I told you things would be different around here, and I meant it."

Tears brimmed in her eyes. "Really?"

"That's right. But Lyle's fixin' to list his property fast so he can get down to North Carolina. He's got an appointment tonight at six with Jacob Mason, that fancy Realtor from Meadowside. I told Lyle we'd come by after you got home so you could check out the place. That should give us plenty of time to walk the property and strike a deal."

Nervous laughter bubbled out. "I don't know what to say."

"Say you'll be on the road in the next half hour."

"Yes, of course. Thank you, Dad! I love you!" Her thoughts spun as she pocketed her phone and ran inside, yelling, "Nick!"

He turned with worry in his eyes, and she ran to him in the living room where he was talking with his brothers and his father.

"My dad's friend is moving and he's got a place for Rising Hope! Six acres, a barn, and a log cabin. It's *perfect*. My parents will help me with the down payment, and my brothers will help me fix up the cabin." As his family gathered around, she said, "I can't believe it."

"Wow!" Jillian exclaimed.

"That's awesome," Charlotte said. "Beau, maybe you can make time to help with the renovations."

Beau and the rest of Nick's brothers all glanced at Nick. He wore a serious expression, but before Trixie could say anything, everyone spoke at once.

"That's generous of your parents," Morgyn said.

"Congratulations, honey," Lily said.

"You've worked hard, and they see that," Clint added.

"I know. I can't believe it. My babies will have a real barn!" She looked at Nick's expression, which hadn't changed, and said, "I know it's a lot, and it's fast. I'm still in shock, too."

"Babe, are you sure this is what you want?" Nick asked.

"A home for Rising Hope? Are you kidding? You have a ranch. You know how it feels to put your horses in their own stalls, to have your own tack room, your own pasture. Of course I want that. I'd give anything to see Rising Hope in big letters on the front of a barn and go to bed at night knowing that my horses weren't five miles away."

"I thought you were okay starting at your parents' place," Nick said. "I mean, Trix, are you biting off more than you can chew?"

His words hit her like a punch to the gut. She squared her shoulders and lifted her chin. "What are you saying? All of a sudden you don't think I can handle it?"

"Aw, hell," Beau said.

"Let's go outside," his father said, ushering everyone out of the room. "Give them some privacy."

Nick's eyes never left hers. "*Trixie...*"

"*What?*" she snapped, but then a hopeful thought dawned on her. Maybe he wanted more than long distance but didn't know how to tell her. She stepped closer and lowered her voice. "Just tell me what you're thinking, Nick. Yesterday you asked me if I wanted Rising Hope and a long-distance relationship. Did you change your mind about us?"

"*Hell no,*" he said vehemently.

She struggled against the rush of disappointment consuming her, reminding herself that despite how deeply she loved him, it only *felt* like they'd been a couple forever. She should know better than to hope he'd want more than a long-distance relationship so fast.

"I'm sorry, Trix." He drew her into his arms, speaking

soothingly. "You took me by surprise, that's all. You know how I am. I need time to process things."

"I know you do."

"It's a big change from starting on your family's ranch. But if it's what you want, I'm behind you one hundred percent."

"Are you *sure*?"

He cradled her face between his hands, his expression softening. "Yes, darlin'. I'm sure and I'm sorry." He pressed his lips to hers and put his arms around her. "I didn't mean that I didn't think you could make a go of your business. There's *nothing* you can't do. You prove that every damn day. What I meant was that buying a place that needs work and taking on a mortgage is a lot to handle when you're starting a business. But I believe in you, and if I had stopped to think before speaking, I wouldn't have said that. I would've said, let's check it out when I'm down next weekend, and I'll help fix up whatever you need if you end up buying it."

"The Ruckets have an appointment with a real estate agent to list their property tonight, so I'm going to see it with my dad when I get home. I think we might make an offer before he lists it."

"Great." Nick's jaw tightened, but there was a curve to his lips. "Then you can show it to me next weekend, and we'll make plans to fix it up."

"Okay." He was giving her everything he could, and she had everything she wanted, Nick, the business, and soon she'd even have her own place. So why was sadness stacking up inside her? She needed to get out of there before she broke down in tears, and there was only one way to do that. *Fake it until I make it.*

She put on the brightest smile she could muster and said, "I have to get going. If I load up my horses, can you grab my bags?"

"You've got it, babe."

She stepped away, and he pulled her back into his arms, his piercing dark eyes holding her captive.

"I believe in you, Trixie, and I want *everything* that you want." He pressed his lips to hers, kissing her hard, and then he swatted her butt and smiled. "Go get those babies. I'll get your bags and bring my family around to say goodbye."

She kept that fake smile in place as she loaded up her horses and said goodbye to Nick's animals. Pugsly's snorty grunts nearly did her in, but she managed to hold it together, and when Nick's family passed her from one warm embrace to the next, wishing her luck and saying they'd miss her, she struggled again. When Carly and Zev reminded them they wanted to make plans to get together in Colorado after the New Year, Charlotte and Beau offered Nick and Trixie a room at the inn. Jillian and Morgyn jumped on that bandwagon, and before Trixie knew it, everyone was making plans for a family vacation in Colorado.

"I'm going to miss having you here," Jillian said, squeezing her tight.

"Not half as much as I'll miss being here."

Clint put his arms around Trixie, hugging her as long and as tight as her own father would, and said, "Thanks for not giving up on my boy."

"Never," she whispered.

"I haven't seen that spark in his eyes since the first time he rode a horse."

Trixie smiled. "Are you comparing me to a horse?"

"I'm comparing you to a first love."

Oh boy. Tears threatened again. She hugged Lily and whispered, "Take care of Nick for me?"

"You know I will, sweetheart," Lily said. "But I'm no match for the empty spot you'll leave behind."

And just like that, Trixie's tears broke free. She quickly wiped them away, but not before Nick noticed. He glowered at his mother, hauling Trixie into his arms, and ran his hand soothingly down her back and said, "It's okay, darlin'."

"I'm fine." She pushed back, fake-smiling up at him. "But I have to get on the road."

He pressed his lips to hers and said, "Drive safely, darlin'. I'll call you tonight." He hugged her again, tighter, kissing the top of her head, then helped her into her truck. He kissed her through the open window and held her gaze for so long, his brothers cleared their throats. He gave her another kiss and said, "I'll miss you."

I love you. "I'll miss you, too."

He winked and stepped back from the truck, standing with his family. Trixie put on her seat belt and waved. "Bye. Thank you again. I love you all!"

As she drove away from the barns, she watched Nick staring after her in the side-view mirror until she turned up the long driveway and could no longer see him, and the tears she'd been holding back broke free.

NICK FELT LIKE his heart was tethered to the bumper of Trixie's truck and wrenched from his chest as his world, his life, his *love* drove out of sight.

"I can't believe you let her go," Jax said.

"What'd you want me to do? Her life is *there*, Jax. Everything she wants is waiting for her in Oak Falls." *Except me.*

"Are you okay?" Beau asked.

"No, I'm not fucking okay." Nick looked at his family staring at him with the same expression he was sure he'd worn all those years ago when they'd been the broken ones, and he'd wondered how he'd save them all. They were fine now. They'd survived and found their way to happier lives. They didn't need him watching over them anymore. So what the hell was he doing there, while his heart was being dragged on the pavement, shredding to smithereens with every mile Trixie drove?

His father stepped beside him. "What can we do?"

"Not a damn thing." Nick headed for the corral, and they all followed.

"What are you doing?" Beau asked.

"Breaking down those fucked-up boundaries you said I have." He threw open the gate and climbed onto Romeo's bare back. He kicked his heels, and the horse bolted through the gate.

"Where are you going?" Beau hollered.

"To get my girl! *Hiya!*" Nick leaned forward as Romeo cut across the yard at breakneck speed, heading toward the road.

Nick balanced with his knees, moving as one with the horse as Romeo jumped over the fence at the edge of the property. They flew along the shoulder of the road, Nick's eyes trained on the land ahead, searching for Trixie's trailer. His chest was so tight, it was hard to breathe. He was a fucking idiot. *Boundaries.* He didn't even think he had boundaries where Trixie was concerned. He was so fucking wrong. He had harsher boundaries than Alcatraz.

The trailer came into view, and he tightened his knees and

leaned forward, calling out, "*Hiya!*" Romeo did the impossible, cranking up his speed until they caught up with Trixie's truck.

Come on, baby, look over!

They kept pace with her. Nick had never been so thankful for slow speed limits. Trixie finally glanced over and did a double take, her eyes wide. She shouted something, shaking her head. *Always fucking challenging me.* He motioned for her to pull over. Her truck slowed, and Nick sat back, signaling Romeo to slow down, too. It took Trixie and Romeo about the same amount of time to come to a stop.

Nick jumped off the horse as Trixie flew out of her truck. Her nose was pink, her eyes swollen and red, tears streaming down her face as she hollered, "Are you crazy? What are you—"

He plastered his mouth to hers, silencing and loving her. Her salty tears slipped between their lips, and he didn't care. She was in his arms, and he was never going to let her go.

As their lips parted, she said, "Nick, what was—"

He kissed her again. Not to shut her up, but because he needed that damn kiss more than he needed to explain himself. He deepened the kiss until the fight went out of her. She clutched his shirt with both hands and came away breathless.

"Please don't say a word. Let me get this out," he said. "I love you, Trixie Jericho. God, I fucking love you so much it hurts, and I'm a fool for not saying it sooner. You want to be in Oak Falls. I get that. Give me a few hours to pack my shit, load my horses, and take care of my other animals, because I'm coming with you, darlin'. I want to be by your side every day of our lives. I'll fix that cabin up for you, make you a sign for the barn. Hell, I'll do whatever you need, give you whatever you *want*, but I'm coming with you, baby."

Sobs bubbled out, and she gulped a breath. "But you need

your space."

"Not from you, I don't. I want *you* in my space. I want your damn hair in my shower drain, your sweet smell on my sheets, your challenging snark coming at me at the most frustrating times. I want *you*, baby, and I hope to hell you want me, too."

She laughed and cried. "Want you? I *love* you with everything I am. Of course I want you. But you can't leave Pleasant Hill. Your whole life is here."

"You're wrong, darlin'. Without you, I've got no life."

"But your family—"

"Doesn't need me as much as I need you."

More sobs shook her, tears raining down her cheeks. "But Walt needs you. You can't leave him."

"Walt'll be just fine. I'll have Jax and Travis check on him. I need *you*, Trix, and for once in my fucking life, I'm doing what *I* need. What *we* need."

"But I don't want you to move to Oak Falls," she said through her tears.

The air rushed from his lungs, painful and sharp, and his world tilted off its axis. He stumbled backward, trying to process what she'd said. "*Fuck…*"

She grabbed his shirt, pulling him forward. "This is your home, Nick, and it's always felt like mine, too. This is where our life is meant to be, not in Oak Falls. *Here*, where we found each other. Where we came together and fell in love. Where we brought our babies home and gave them their start. Where we gave *us* our start."

"But your family," he said, shaking his head.

"Drives me batty. I adore them and their protective nature, but we're two hours away, Nick. We can visit as often as we'd like. Lord knows I'll always be my daddy's little girl and my brothers' baby sister, but I'm not a little girl anymore."

"What about all your friends?"

"I love my friends, but I don't want to hang out at ladies' night dancing with guys I don't care about, with my brothers hovering around me, when the only man I want, and the only man I need watching out for me, is *you*." A spark of mischief rose in her eyes. "And even that gets to be a bit much sometimes."

He cocked a brow.

She whispered, "*Kidding*," went up on her toes, and kissed his chin.

"God, I love when you kiss me there. I love *you*, darlin', everything about you, and I'm pretty sure I've loved you for years."

"You have," she said cheekily, smiling past her tears. "Just ask me. I'll tell you."

"Always challenging me."

"Always *loving* you."

As he lowered his lips to hers, Romeo pushed his muzzle between them. They laughed and both reached up to pet him.

"Christ, Romeo, you too? Everyone wants my girl."

Trixie flashed her knockout smile. "Then it's a darn good thing she only wants you."

Chapter Twenty-Nine

NICK AND TRIXIE waved as his family pulled out of the driveway later that crazy afternoon. His family was as shocked as she had been to hear Nick had offered to move to Oak Falls. They would have supported his decision, just as her parents had supported hers when she told them she was going to stay and build her life, and business, with Nick in Pleasant Hill. With her babies playing in the corral with Snickers and Nick's strong arms around her, Trixie knew she'd made the right decision.

Nick gazed into her eyes with an all-new open-hearted smile. "I love you, Trix."

"I don't think I'll ever get tired of hearing that. I love you, too."

He lowered his mouth to hers, kissing her slow and sweet. Her phone rang, and he groaned, holding her tighter. She smiled against his lips. "Sorry." She pulled her phone from her pocket and saw Trace's name on the FaceTime call.

"Take it, darlin'. I'm surprised it took him this long to call."

He gave her a quick kiss, and when she answered, Trace connected the rest of her brothers to the group video call. "Before you say a word, let me make the inquisition easy for y'all. Yes, it's true, I'm staying in Pleasant Hill with Nick. We'll be coming back for a day or two here and there while I meet with potential clients over the next month, and we'll definitely be back for the next jam session."

"And next weekend," Nick added.

She looked over her shoulder at Nick. "We will?"

"You promised to take Amber shopping, darlin', and we've got to bring Buttercup home."

"Oh my gosh, *Buttercup*. I feel horrible for not thinking of her right away."

"You've been a bit preoccupied." Nick kissed her.

Shane cleared his throat, bringing her attention back to the call.

"Sorry," Trixie said. "Before I forget, when we come for the jam session in a few weeks, I'd really appreciate it if you could help us load up the stuff from my apartment so we can move it here when we come."

"We'll block off our calendars," Jeb said.

"Absolutely," Trace said. "Trix, I didn't want to give you an inquisition. I wanted to say, it's about time you two figured out what we already knew."

"You did not *know*," Trixie said with a laugh.

"Come on, sis, look at the way Nick's got his hand on your shoulder." Trace nodded toward the screen. "That's not the hold of a man who just tipped the scales from *she's hot* to *she's mine*."

Nick was standing behind her, one hand around her middle, which her brothers couldn't see, the other on her shoulder. He pressed a kiss to her head and said, "They're not wrong."

"We're all happy for you," JJ said. "But I hope you have extra bedrooms at your place, Braden, because we're not going to let our sister just disappear. We've gotta swing by and make sure you're treating her right."

Nick scoffed. "You know your sister will kick my ass if I do her wrong."

"You won't, Nick. You love me too much. And you, JJ, are a dork."

"That's not what the girls say." JJ smiled arrogantly.

"Let me make sure I've got this straight," Shane said in a serious tone. "You're going to be living in sin with Nick, and we're supposed to be okay with that?"

"I didn't think about it that way. Maybe we ought to come there and take that man down," Trace teased.

"You can try, but I don't recommend it," Nick warned.

Trixie smirked and said, "Y'all don't want to hear this, but your baby sister likes sinning. I like living in it, toying with it, and most of all—"

"Stop!" "Man, Trix." "I don't want to know this about you," her brothers yelled over each other, making grossed-out faces and sounds.

"Love you bunches. *Toodles.*" She ended the call, laughing with Nick. As she pocketed her phone, she said, "Well, my big, buff cowboy, where do we go from here?"

His eyes darkened, and he swept her into his arms. "Now we go into *our* house and celebrate, cowboy style."

As he strode toward the house, she said, "No, cowboy."

"No?"

"We're going into our *home*, not our house, and we're going to celebrate *cowgirl* style."

"Are you ever going to stop challenging me?"

"Not in this lifetime."

As he lowered his lips to hers, he said, "I wouldn't want it any other way."

Chapter Thirty

NICK SPUN TRIXIE around and pulled her into his arms as they danced in the barn at the Jerichos' jam session. A handful of people were playing instruments on the stage, and practically the whole town had turned out for the event. Trixie couldn't remember the last time a jam session had drawn such a large crowd. But she was glad to see everyone. It had been six weeks since she'd decided to stay in Maryland, and it was the best decision she'd ever made. Her business had flourished, and true to his promise, Nick had made a gorgeous RISING HOPE sign, and he'd hung it on the front of the barn. She'd signed several monthly clients within an hour of Pleasant Hill, and a handful near Oak Falls, which allowed her and Nick to plan on spending a few days in her hometown every month. Her brothers had appeared on Nick's doorstep with Buttercup and all of Trixie's belongings a few days after she'd made her decision, and they'd stayed overnight. They'd ridden horses, barbecued, and welcomed Nick into the family with open arms. Trixie couldn't have asked for more support or love. Her parents had visited a week later, and Trixie, her mother, and Lily had cooked a feast and invited Walt and Irene to join them. They'd had a wonderful evening, and her parents had stayed over in Trixie's old room, now that she'd moved into Nick's—*their*—bedroom.

She gazed up at her cowboy's hungry eyes as they danced, and her pulse quickened. They'd made love that morning, and she knew he was ready to go again. She had a feeling they'd be insatiable for each other forever, and she looked forward to being that in-love couple who snuck off behind the barn to make out, like Mr. and Mrs. Montgomery did at most of these events. It was no wonder they had seven children.

As the song came to an end, Nick dipped her over his arm, said, "Love you, darlin'," and kissed her. He told her every day how much he loved her, and it brought a thrill each and every time.

"I love you, too, cowboy." She went up on her toes, and he pressed his lips to hers again.

"Come on, lovebirds. You can't kiss all night. You have friends to see." Lindsay took Trixie's hand, pulling her toward a group of friends and family. Trixie's mother was holding baby Emma and chatting with Mrs. Montgomery. Jeb and Graham were talking with Amber, Brindle, and Morgyn. Morgyn and Graham had come back last week and were staying in town until Zev and Carly's wedding.

"There's the big man," Graham said, clapping a hand on Nick's shoulder.

"The big man who stole my bestie away," Lindsay teased.

Nick slung an arm around Trixie and said, "She's here now, and you're welcome to come visit anytime."

"I appreciate that, but it doesn't help me on ladies' nights." Lindsay looked at Amber and said, "I'm working on getting this gorgeous girl out and about more often. We've been practicing her flirting, but she says she's not up for it every week."

Amber rolled her eyes, reaching down to pet Reno, her seizure service dog. "She dragged me out to a bar where I didn't know anyone two weeks ago, and it was a total meat market. *Not* my scene."

"Would you rather practice flirting with Trixie's brothers?"

"I'd be up for that," Jeb offered.

"See what I'm up against, Trix?" Lindsay joked. "I have to go to ladies' night alone, and I'm always left dancing with this one." She motioned to Jeb.

"I didn't hear you complaining Tuesday night." Jeb lifted the front of his baseball cap and waggled his brows.

"Are you whittling Jeb's wood?" Brindle asked. "Why haven't I heard this rumor?"

"Because I'm *not* whittling his wood," Lindsay snapped.

Jeb winked at Brindle and put an arm around Lindsay. "Nothing to be embarrassed about, sweetheart. All the ladies want to get their hands on my wood."

Trixie and Nick chuckled as Lindsay moved out from beneath Jeb's arm.

"This is far more information than a mother needs to hear about her son." Trixie's mother brushed a kiss to Emma's forehead and said, "Although...it might lead to more grandchildren for me and cousins for this pretty little lady."

"Don't count on it," Lindsay said.

Trixie's mother eyed Mrs. Montgomery and said, "Since the bodywash worked wonders for you-know-who, maybe we should ask Roxie about her fertility potions."

"How did you know about the bodywash?" Trixie asked her mother, looking curiously at Nick.

Nick shrugged. "Don't look at me."

Trixie put a hand on her hip, staring at her mother and

Mrs. Montgomery. "Okay, you two. What's going on?"

The two moms exchanged a knowing smile, and Mrs. Montgomery said, "Do you hear that?" She tilted her head up, as if she were listening for something. "I think I hear someone calling our names. Come on, Nancy, let's go check it out." The two of them disappeared into the crowd.

"They're total matchmakers," Amber said. "My mom has been slipping our aunt Roxie's fertility-potion lotion into Grace's bottles for weeks."

Nick pulled Trixie closer and kissed her temple. "I'm cool with the matchmaking, but we're not ready for babies yet. From now on, *nobody* goes near our toiletries."

They all laughed.

"We already have babies," Trixie reminded him. "They just live in the barn."

"Sounds like you need a lesson in sex education," Brindle teased.

"All right, you guys, listen up," Sable said as she and her brother, Axsel, joined them. "Who's got the scoop on the pretty boy with Sin?"

Everyone turned to see who Sable was talking about. Sinclair "Sin" Vernon had run the athletic program at Virginia State before becoming the athletic director for No Limitz, the Oak Falls youth center. He was a large, strappingly handsome guy in his early thirties. Trixie recognized the man he was with as the football-player-turned-author her friends had told her about. He was just as big as Sin, and even better looking than in his photos.

"*Damn,*" Brindle said quietly. "Google didn't do him justice. He looks like a movie star."

"Uh-huh," Amber said a little breathlessly, her mouth hanging open.

"Then again, so does Sin," Brindle added. "How that man has remained single all this time is beyond me."

Trixie's and Nick's eyes met, and he smiled, pulling her closer to kiss her temple.

Several weeks ago, he'd have been gritting his teeth, eyeing the good-looking guy to make sure he wasn't checking out Trixie. But they were well past that jealousy. They'd made it through Nick's Roanoke show without any issues. They'd both been prepared for the onslaught of buckle bunnies, and they'd proudly claimed each other. Nick had signed autographs, and Trixie had taken the time to chat with a few of the girls. After speaking with them, she'd realized they were just regular girls looking for the men of their dreams. Who could blame them? As long as they kept their paws off her man, they'd be just fine.

"The best thing about these jam sessions is seeing all the hottest ladies in Oak Falls in one place," Sin said as they joined the group.

"*Ahem.*" Axsel arched a brow.

Sin laughed. "And the hottest guys—sorry, Axsel."

"No worries. With a body like that, you're always forgiven." Axsel dragged his eyes down Dash's body. "And *hello*, gorgeous friend of Sin's." Axsel was the youngest of the Montgomery siblings and the lead guitarist in the infamous band Inferno. Much to the dismay of all the single women he encountered, he was gay.

Dash smiled, and Trixie swore his teeth were so white, they sparkled. "Hi, I'm Dash. Where do I know you from? Wait, you're that rock star, right?"

"In *and* out of the bedroom," Axsel said flirtatiously. "And you have a great name. Short for *Dashing*, I assume?"

Dash laughed and shook his head.

"Keep your trousers on, Axsel," Sin said. "Dash is straight, and I brought him along tonight to meet Amber. Dash wrote a book and he's doing a signing with her in a couple of weeks."

Amber was still staring at Dash, starry-eyed. Trixie had never seen her like that before, but Dash appeared to be just as taken with her.

Sin motioned to Amber and said, "Dash, this is Amber Montgomery."

"It's a pleasure to finally meet you in person, Amber." Dash held out his hand. "My publicist, Shea Steele, had wonderful things to say about you."

Morgyn bumped Amber with her elbow, startling her out of her trance. Amber blinked repeatedly and shook his hand. "Hi. It's nice to meet you."

"I hear you own a great shop in town," Dash said.

Amber continued shaking his hand. "I...yeah. Books...in the shop."

Sable stifled a laugh. Morgyn nudged Amber again.

"*Bookstore*, sorry," Amber said quickly, her cheeks pinking up as she dropped his hand. "I own a bookstore. But you already know that. Oh my gosh. I better..." She touched Reno's head. "Nice to meet you. I have to...do that thing. Over there." She pointed into the crowd. "Sorry. See you in the bookstore. Come, Reno."

As Amber hurried away, Lindsay lowered her voice and said, "So much for flirting lessons."

"You'll have to excuse my sister. She's had a long day," Morgyn said.

Dash was watching Amber move through the crowd, and he said, "No excuse necessary. She makes *quite* the first impression."

As they talked, Nick leaned closer to Trixie and whispered, "I think she made as big an impression on him as I made on you the first time we met."

Trixie turned in his arms and tapped his chest. "You mean how big an impression *I* made on *you*."

Nick pressed his lips to hers, his gaze sliding to her father, headed over to them.

"Excuse me for interrupting," her father said.

Nick slipped his arm around Trixie. "Hi, Waylon."

"Nick." Her father nodded. "You don't mind if I steal my daughter away for a dance, do you?"

"Not at all."

Trixie whispered, "Try not to get your dance card filled up before I get back." She went up on her toes and kissed his chin. "See you later, cowboy." She giggled as he gave her that look that said she was a pain in his butt. She loved that look as much as she loved all his others.

She took her father's arm and followed him onto the dance floor, passing Trace, who was talking with Beckett. They both looked over and smiled. As she began dancing with her father, she noticed Shane and JJ onstage setting up Shane's drums, with a gaggle of girls waiting nearby.

"It's good to see you so happy, sweetheart," her father said as they slow danced.

"Thanks, Dad."

"Your brothers miss you."

"They do, do they?" She knew her father missed her, too. He called her every other day with excuses about needing to know this or that about their customers. But she knew better. Her father could run the administrative end of their ranch in his sleep. But like with Nick, emotions didn't come easily to him, and she doubted he'd tell her how he felt.

He nodded. "Your mother, too."

"Mm-hm. I know she does. I miss everyone, too."

"I want you to know that I'm sorry if I ever made you feel like you weren't taken seriously. You're my one and only daughter, Trixie, my little girl, and I guess it was hard for me to let that go and see you grow up."

A lump lodged in her throat. "You've done a good job of supporting me, Dad. You never held me back."

"Well, that's good to know, but you've done an even better job of showing us all how strong, smart, and brave you are. Your mama and I couldn't be prouder of you."

"Thanks, Dad," she said.

As the song came to an end, her father embraced her and said, "Everyone's heart has a home, and you've known where yours has belonged for years. You made the right choice, sweetheart, no matter how much I miss you."

"I love you, Dad," she said as tears welled in her eyes.

The lights in the barn dimmed as they drew apart, and Trixie wiped her tears. A spotlight hit the stage. Nick stood centerstage, breathtakingly handsome in his black button-down shirt, jeans, and cowboy hat. Trace and JJ stood to his left, holding their guitars. Shane sat behind his drums, and Jeb was at the piano.

"What's going on?" Trixie whispered.

Her father smiled and shrugged.

Nick's eyes found hers as he lifted a microphone and said, "A wise old cowboy once told me not to sing unless it was to the woman I couldn't live without. This one's for you, Patricia Ann Jericho." He winked, setting Trixie's heart aflutter.

Her brothers began playing "Die a Happy Man" by Thomas Rhett, and with his eyes locked on Trixie, Nick sang about last night being one of their best nights and how her love was all he needed. Tears welled in her eyes. She couldn't believe he was singing in front of everyone. His deep, raspy voice boomed through the barn, so damn sexy, she was mesmerized. When he reached the chorus, he changed the words and sang, "Baby, those Daisy Dukes bring me to my knees, but those tied shirts make it hard to breathe."

Everyone laughed, and Trixie did, too, despite the tears tumbling down her cheeks.

Nick sang about dancing around the firepit and how spending time with her was all he needed to be happy. He sang as he came down off the stage, and the crowd parted for him. He blazed a path straight to her. His eyes remained trained on Trixie's as he sang softer, handing her father the microphone, and took her hands in his. The last of the lyrics rolled off his tongue, but the music continued, and everyone applauded and cheered.

"You sang to me," Trixie said incredulously, her face wet with tears.

"I love you, darlin'."

He dropped to one knee, and Trixie gasped, more tears springing from her eyes. She couldn't breathe, could barely see through the blur of tears as the music stopped and the crowd hushed, and Nick held up a gorgeous rose-gold, emerald-cut diamond ring with a halo of diamonds around it.

"Ohmygod" fell from her lips.

He gazed into her eyes and said, "Darlin', you came into my life acting like you'd always been right there by my side, encroaching on my space, touching my things, and giving me hell."

She laughed nervously.

"I think maybe my space has always been yours, too, Trix. It just took me a long time to figure that out. I have no idea what I did to deserve you, but, darlin', whatever it is, I promise to keep doing it and *more*, because I don't want to live a single day without you by my side."

A sob tumbled out, and she covered her mouth with her trembling hand.

"You taught me what it means to love and be loved, and now I want more. I want to wake up to your beautiful face every morning and fall asleep with you in my arms every night. I want to raise our four-legged babies together, spend nights under the stars doing dirty things, and in the barn, drinking champagne and talking to our animals."

Laughter rumbled through the crowd.

"And someday I hope we have two-legged babies who we'll teach to love the way we do, to ride horses, and to crave the outdoors. I want to help make all your dreams come true, baby, and I will stop at *nothing* to make sure they do, because you are the *only* woman I have ever loved, and I will love you long past my dying days."

More sobs broke free.

"Trixie Jericho, will you marry me, darlin'?"

She nodded, and as he slipped the ring on her finger and rose to his feet, "Yes!" burst out. She threw her arms around him, their mouths colliding as cheers rang out and her brothers began playing "Hurricane" by Luke Combs.

"I love you, darlin'."

"I love you more, cowboy."

He laughed, kissing her again as their family and friends

clapped and whistled.

When their lips parted, the lights went on, and red and white balloons rose all around them, filling the ceiling and bouncing in the air. More cheers exploded as a CONGRATULATIONS, NICK AND TRIXIE banner came down from above the stage, and Nick, and every guy around them, ripped open their shirts, revealing black T-shirts that had #TEAMNIXIE printed across their chests in white and #SHESAIDYES in red beneath it.

"Ohmygod, *Nick*! You got us T-shirts!" Through the blur of tears, Trixie saw Lindsay grinning behind him and knew she'd had a hand in the planning. She mouthed, *Thank you*, and more tears fell down her cheeks.

Trixie laughed and cried as she and Nick were hugged and congratulated by everyone in the place. Graham had Nick's family, Walt, and Irene, on FaceTime during the whole event, and Morgyn had captured it all on video, including Nick singing. Sable's band and Axsel took over the stage, and when Trixie finally landed back in Nick's arms, she was so happy, she could barely speak. She looked at all the people she'd grown up with, at the balloons, T-shirts, and the banner, and felt full to near bursting.

"You're such a private guy. I can't believe you did all this for me."

"You wanted the fairy tale, darlin', and I don't know much about fairy tales, but I know this. There's no greater love than the one we're building, and nobody deserves to have their dreams come true more than you."

As he lowered his lips toward hers, she said, "You're wrong, cowboy."

His brows slanted. "Seriously? You're challenging me on this?"

"You deserve for your dreams to come true, too, and I'm going to make sure they do."

He chuckled. "I dream of the day I can kiss you without a challenge."

As his lips came closer to hers, she whispered, "No you don't."

"Shut up and kiss me."

"Make—" He silenced her with a hard press of his lips, sealing their vows with another breath-stealing kiss.

Ready for more Bradens & Montgomerys?

I hope you have enjoyed getting to know the Bradens and Montgomerys. If you haven't yet read the previous books in this series, you can start with EMBRACING HER HEART, the first book in the Bradens & Montgomerys series. If you've already read the previous books in the series, grab SWEET, SEXY HEART, Amber Montgomery's love story, and then continue reading for more information about my fun, sexy family series—including the Bradens at Weston, where you'll meet Nick's uncle Hal and the cousins Nick adores.

Amber Montgomery is perfectly happy with her quiet life. She loves running her bookstore, taking long walks with Reno, her Labrador retriever seizure dog, and spending time with her close-knit family. She's never needed thrills the way some of her sisters have. In an effort to control her epilepsy, she tries to avoid anything that creates too much excitement or stress—

including relationships. When Amber hosts a book signing for famed-athlete-turned-author Dash Pennington, he's everything she's spent her life avoiding: loud, aggressive, and far too handsome—just ask the hordes of women who surround him everywhere he goes. Sparks fly, but it's a no-brainer for Amber to ignore the chemistry and hold her breath until he leaves town. There's only one problem. Charming Dash has other ideas.

Fall in love with the Steeles on Silver Island!

Get sexy with Grant Silver and Jules Steele on the sandy shores of Silver Island, home to coffee shops, boat races, and midnight rendezvous.

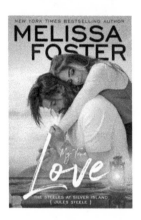

Even war heroes need a little help sometimes...

After spending years fighting for his country and too damn long learning to navigate life with a prosthetic leg, Grant Silver returns to Silver Island to figure out a future he couldn't fathom without fatigues and a gun in his hand. He'd almost forgotten how a man could suffocate from the warmth and caring community in which he'd grown up, and if that weren't bad enough, his buddies' beautiful and far-too-chipper younger sister won't stop flitting into his life, trying to sprinkle happy dust everywhere she goes.

As a cancer survivor, Jules Steele knows better than to count on seeing tomorrow. She doesn't take a single moment for granted, and she isn't about to let a man who used to be charming and full of life waste the future he's been blessed with. She's determined to get through to him, even if it takes a few steamy kisses…

Love the Bradens? Meet Hal and their Colorado cousins!

Fall in love with Treat and Max in the very first Braden book, LOVERS AT HEART, REIMAGINED, free at the time of this printing (price subject to change without notice).

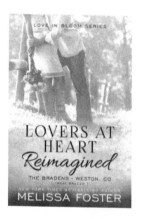

Treat Braden wasn't looking for love when Max Armstrong walked into his Nassau resort, but he saw right through the efficient and capable facade she wore like a shield to the sweet, sensual woman beneath. One magnificent evening together sparked an intense connection, and for the first time in his life Treat wanted more than a casual affair. But something caused Max to turn away, and now, after weeks of unanswered phone calls and longing for the one woman he cannot have, Treat is going back to his family's ranch to try to finally move on.

A chance encounter brings Treat and Max together again, and it turns into a night of intense passion and honesty. When Max reveals her secret, painful past, Treat vows to do everything within his power to win Max's heart forever—including helping her finally face her demons head-on.

Have you met The Whiskeys: Dark Knights at Peaceful Harbor?

If you're a fan of sexy, alpha heroes, babies, and strong family ties even to those who are not blood related, you'll love Truman Gritt and the Whiskeys.

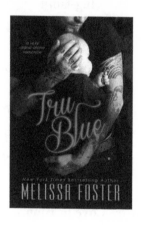

There's nothing Truman Gritt won't do to protect his family—including spending years in jail for a crime he didn't commit. When he's finally released, the life he knew is turned upside down by his mother's overdose, and Truman steps in to raise the children she's left behind. Truman's hard, he's secretive, and he's trying to save a brother who's even more broken than he is. He's never needed help in his life, and when beautiful Gemma Wright tries to step in, he's less than accepting. But Gemma has a way of slithering into people's lives, and eventually she pierces through his ironclad heart. When Truman's dark past collides with his future, his loyalties will be tested, and he'll be faced with his toughest decision yet.

New to the Love in Bloom series?

If this is your first Love in Bloom book, there are many more love stories featuring loyal, sassy, and sexy heroes and heroines waiting for you. The Bradens & Montgomerys is just one of the series in the Love in Bloom big-family romance collection. Each Love in Bloom book is written to be enjoyed as a stand-alone novel or as part of the larger series. There are no cliffhangers and no unresolved issues. Characters from each series make appearances in future books, so you never miss an engagement, wedding, or birth. You might enjoy my other series within the Love in Bloom big-family romance collection, starting with the very first book in the entire Love in Bloom series, SISTERS IN LOVE.

See the Entire Love in Bloom Collection
www.MelissaFoster.com/love-bloom-series

Download Free First-in-Series eBooks
www.MelissaFoster.com/free-ebooks

Download Series Checklists, Family Trees, and Publication Schedules
www.MelissaFoster.com/reader-goodies

More Books By Melissa Foster

LOVE IN BLOOM SERIES

SNOW SISTERS
Sisters in Love
Sisters in Bloom
Sisters in White

THE BRADENS at Weston
Lovers at Heart, Reimagined
Destined for Love
Friendship on Fire
Sea of Love
Bursting with Love
Hearts at Play

THE BRADENS at Trusty
Taken by Love
Fated for Love
Romancing My Love
Flirting with Love
Dreaming of Love
Crashing into Love

THE BRADENS at Peaceful Harbor
Healed by Love
Surrender My Love
River of Love
Crushing on Love
Whisper of Love
Thrill of Love

THE BRADENS & MONTGOMERYS at Pleasant Hill – Oak Falls
Embracing Her Heart
Anything for Love

Trails of Love
Wild, Crazy Hearts
Making You Mine
Searching for Love
Hot for Love
Sweet, Sexy Heart

THE BRADEN NOVELLAS

Promise My Love
Our New Love
Daring Her Love
Story of Love
Love at Last
A Very Braden Christmas

THE REMINGTONS

Game of Love
Stroke of Love
Flames of Love
Slope of Love
Read, Write, Love
Touched by Love

SEASIDE SUMMERS

Seaside Dreams
Seaside Hearts
Seaside Sunsets
Seaside Secrets
Seaside Nights
Seaside Embrace
Seaside Lovers
Seaside Whispers
Seaside Serenade

BAYSIDE SUMMERS

Bayside Desires
Bayside Passions

HARMONY POINTE
Call Her Mine
This is Love
She Loves Me

THE WICKEDS: DARK KNIGHTS AT BAYSIDE
A Little Bit Wicked
The Wicked Aftermath

SILVER HARBOR
Maybe We Will

WILD BOYS AFTER DARK
Logan
Heath
Jackson
Cooper

BAD BOYS AFTER DARK
Mick
Dylan
Carson
Brett

HARBORSIDE NIGHTS SERIES
Includes characters from the Love in Bloom series
Catching Cassidy
Discovering Delilah
Tempting Tristan

More Books by Melissa
Chasing Amanda (mystery/suspense)
Come Back to Me (mystery/suspense)
Have No Shame (historical fiction/romance)
Love, Lies & Mystery (3-book bundle)
Megan's Way (literary fiction)
Traces of Kara (psychological thriller)
Where Petals Fall (suspense)

Acknowledgments

I absolutely loved writing Nick and Trixie's story, and I am forever grateful to my behind-the-scenes team, who keep me afloat and grounded at the same time. Extra gratitude goes out to Lisa Filipe, who coaxed me into taming Nick in a crucial scene and fell as hard for him and Trixie as I did along the way. And I am inspired on a daily basis by my fans, many of whom are in my fan club on Facebook. If you haven't yet joined my fan club on Facebook, please do. We have a great time chatting about our hunky heroes and sassy heroines. You never know when you'll inspire a story or a character and end up in one of my books, as several fan club members have already discovered. www.facebook.com/groups/MelissaFosterFans

While researching this story, I relied upon a number of friends and sources. Special thanks go out to J. D. Harrison, the author of the Gallant Hearts series, for her patience with my never-ending questions about all things horse related. If you enjoy horsemanship, I hope you'll check out her work. I'm also grateful to Rachel Neff, the Executive Director of Promise Landing Farm, and Lisa Moad, the founder of Seven Oaks Farm. I have taken fictional liberties within this story, and as such, any and all factual errors are not reflective of these patient ladies.

Remember to like and follow my Facebook fan page to stay

abreast of what's going on in our fictional boyfriends' worlds.
www.facebook.com/MelissaFosterAuthor

Sign up for my newsletter to keep up to date with new releases and special promotions and events and to receive an exclusive short story featuring Jack Remington and Savannah Braden.
www.MelissaFoster.com/Newsletter

And don't forget to download your free reader goodies! For free ebooks, family trees, publication schedules, series checklists, and more, please visit the special Reader Goodies page that I've set up for you!
www.MelissaFoster.com/Reader-Goodies

As always, loads of gratitude to my amazing team of editors and proofreaders: Kristen Weber, Penina Lopez, Elaini Caruso, Juliette Hill, Marlene Engel, Lynn Mullan, and Justinn Harrison. And, of course, I am forever grateful to my family, who allow me to talk about my fictional worlds as if we live in them.

Meet Melissa

www.MelissaFoster.com

Melissa Foster is a *New York Times* and *USA Today* bestselling and award-winning author. Her books have been recommended by *USA Today's* book blog, *Hagerstown* magazine, *The Patriot*, and several other print venues. Melissa has painted and donated several murals to the Hospital for Sick Children in Washington, DC.

Visit Melissa on her website or chat with her on social media. Melissa enjoys discussing her books with book clubs and reader groups and welcomes an invitation to your event. Melissa's books are available through most online retailers in paperback, digital, and audio formats.

CPSIA information can be obtained
at www.ICGtesting.com
Printed in the USA
LVHW031950080321
680887LV00007B/1569